Praise for
PRINCE OMBRA

"Roderick MacLeish has woven pre-Christian legend, a fairy tale by the Brothers Grimm, and a James Bond thriller into a single haunting book. I read it in one sitting."
—Robert K. Massie, author of *Peter the Great*

"With finesse worthy of Stephen King, MacLeish combines the supernatural and the mundane to fine effect."
—*Publishers Weekly*

"MacLeish combines legend with the chaos of modern life in fascinating juxtaposition, and the believability of the characters enhances the terror of the battles. Highly recommended."
—*Library Journal*

"MacLeish has made the abstract symbols of good and evil so humanly real that the reader . . . is caught up wholeheartedly in the struggle."
—*Los Angeles Times*

(Continued overleaf)

RODERICK MacLEISH

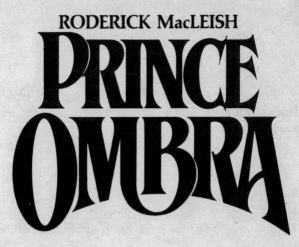

PRINCE OMBRA

A TOM DOHERTY ASSOCIATES BOOK

Copyright©1982 by Roderick MacLeish

A Tor Book

Published by Tom Doherty Associates, 8-10 W. 36th St., New York, New York 10018

ISBN: 0-812-54550-8
CAN. ED.: 0-812-54551-6

Printed in the United States of America

Distributed by Pinnacle Books, 1430 Broadway, New York, New York 10018

For

BRAD MORSE

who has come to the sensible conclusion
that the world can be saved and goes on
trying, with love and admiration these
thirty years later . . .

. . . and with gratitude to:

Beverley Cohen, Fernand Auberjonois, Ben Barber, Simon Barber, Patricia Cheney, Joanna Cohen, Lucy Cohen, Louis and Jacqueline Claiborne, Peter and Maureen Colasante, Sylvia Farnham-Diggory, Candida Donadio, George Gale, Ronald Goldfarb, Charlie Goodyear, Doris Grumbach, Ward Just, Charles McCarry, Cynthia Sumner MacLeish, Eric MacLeish, Michael Michaelis, John and Symmie Newhouse, Patti O'Dwyer, Colin and Julia Sherborne, Carol Thayer, William and Evelyn Watts, Geneva Williams and Leon Yochelson—who listened, encouraged, and suggested as the memory of Prince Ombra came clear.

Then, since the soul is immortal and often born, having seen what is on earth and what is in the house of Hades and everything, there is nothing it has not learned . . . for seeing and learning are all remembrance.

THE DIALOGUES OF PLATO

Prologue

It gets cold on this coast in September. This morning the sea is prickled with raindrops.

Yesterday Miss Gardner and I packed the last carton of my notes. It had taken her six years, working four days a week, to arrange everything alphabetically—from Aah, the Egyptian moon deity, to Zoroastrianism—and type it all.

Last spring Miss Gardner's cousin came on from the Middle West and she introduced me to him. She told him I was a scholar of mythology. That was kind of her, but beside the point. I'm not primarily a scholar. I'm a rememberer.

Nobody alive today knows what that means. It may sound strange to you—rememberer. But there's nothing in the least strange about me.

I'm a seventy-four-year-old woman with most of my original teeth, a driver's license, and two doctorates—one of them in mathematics, the other in comparative religion. There *are* people in the village who think I'm different. But not strange. Joe Persis and the other simpletons who hang around the Stonehaven drugstore look upon me as a *grande dame*. I suppose that's all right with me. But I do wish I could get Joe to stop calling me "ma'am." I keep reminding him that we played together when we were children. He smiles all over that sweet, simple face of his and says, "We sure did, ma'am."

There are seasons vaster and subtler than the cycles of the year. After a time of harmony the world begins to darken. The human race is possessed by fevers, plagues, and madness, as it was toward the end of the twentieth century. In such afflicted epochs a mortal being is born with an odd marking on his face. He carries a secret in his heart. He lives out a timeless destiny. If he is victorious in his life's battle, the world will brighten. If this mortal hero perishes, the darkness on our lives deepens. This has happened a thousand and one times.

The stories of these enigmatic struggles are told in the symbols and wonders of legends. They are the true history of the world.

The great legends were left by people who knew these thousand and one men and went with them to their destinies. I knew Bentley Ellicott. I am the thousand and first rememberer.

This afternoon a nice girl who works at the university library is coming down to collect the carton that Miss Gardner and I packed and sealed yesterday. The preliminary work of my life is over. I have spent fifty-three years studying and analyzing the world's mythology so that I could understand what the rememberers who preceded me were trying to say. I hope my notes will be of some use to someone.

I met Bentley Ellicott when I was seven years old. He told me all about himself. I accompanied him on his strange journey, and I was present when he fulfilled the destiny for which he had been born. It was given to me to know about events beyond the perimeters of his life and mine. The old man who was our teacher thought that all the rememberers had this extra gift of knowing.

I may live to see another summer. I may not. As I have told you, it gets cold in this coast in September. This morning, fog hangs on the southeastern horizon. I have lit a fire in the living room.

And now, at last, I set down the tale that I was born to leave in the world's memory. I will tell you the story of Bentley and the borrowed heart. It begins in an afflicted time of history. Listen.

And remember.

Chapter One

It is said—and it is true—that just before we are born, a cavern angel holds his finger to our mouths and whispers, "Hush! Don't tell what you know."

This is why we have a cleft on our upper lips and remember nothing of where we came from.

Toward the end of the last century—in 1978, to be precise—a smooth-lipped boy appeared in the world.

He grew up in an ominous time. People had lost the power of belief. Plagues of the spirit swept the world; shapeless anxieties spread like fever, self-hatred was rampant, love was bitterly denounced because it wasn't perfect. Evidence of madness glittered everywhere. The workshops of great nations forged weapons that would destroy the societies that used them. Acid rained from the skies.

Rivers putrified. In some places the air was unbreathable. Hucksters sold God on television, and religions were made out of economic theories that didn't work. Tyrants brutalized the people in the name of the people. The new prophets of freedom preached doctrines of selfishness. Knowledge raced far ahead of wisdom. Mankind worshipped facts, but facts couldn't explain the misfortunes that counterweight the blessings of human life. There were machines that could think, and people numbed their minds to keep themselves from thinking. In their deepest dreams men stood within stone circles and saw a darkness darker than dark.

Such epochs of desolation had cursed human history a thousand times before. And, each time, a smooth-lipped mortal was born. These men lived strange, obsessed lives. Some of them lie buried in great mausoleums. Others rotted on the hangman's tree. Some will be remembered forever. Others disappeared into dust and oblivion.

When the time of dementia and sorrow came to the late twentieth century, Bentley Ellicott was born with a twisted leg in Stonehaven on the northern coast. Why he was created as a cripple, why he appeared in a peaceful place far from the world's worst torments, will remain mysteries forever. Bentley Ellicott himself was the only person in the world who knew the purpose of his life. It was a secret. He didn't tell anybody until he was eight years old.

Stonehaven lies on a sheltered curve of the northern coast, between islands dense with pine trees and a distant river spanned by a bridge shaped like a humpbacked monster's bones. The

weather on this coast can be dramatic. Storms
burst from turrets of clouds on the uplands and
send volleys of thunder rolling across the wind-
lashed sea. In winter Stonehaven is entombed in
ice, bitter cold, and silence. The fogs of spring ad
autumn blur the shapes of the village, the forests,
.the coast.

In the time of Bentley Ellicott's childhood, Main
Street was a potholed, two-lane way that passed
the drugstore, the police station, and the bank.
The masts of sailboats swayed with the harbor's
lazy swell, and sea gulls wheeled and cried above
lobster boats and draggers unloading at the town
wharf. There were a freezing plant, a boathouse,
and a sardine cannery.

The Stonehaven House Hotel stood at the end
of Main Street. Years before, when the village
shipped granite in waterline schooners to hot cities
down the coast, the Stonehaven House Hotel had
been fashionable. But the granite quarries had
been closed for years by the time Bentley Ellicott
was born. The hotel was a white, peeling ruin with
broken windows. Tall grass grew all around it. Nobody lived there except Charlie Feavey. He had inherited the hotel from his father. Charlie was a
scrawny man with dirty fingernails who was
always desperate for money.

Potato fields lay north of the village. Along a
wooded strip of shoreline—which everybody called the point—Victorian summer houses overlook-
ed the sea and the seaward islands. After the middle of the last century, young couples like Richard
and Dorothy Ellicott winterized the old houses
and lived in them all year round. Richard was a

mathematics professor at the university sixteen miles inland. Bentley Ellicott was born on the point.

Odd circumstances surrounded his birth.

His beautiful young mother died that night—for no reason the doctors could discover. A jade-eyed stranger named Willybill appeared in Stonehaven as the cold November light was going down. Toward midnight a choppy wind came up out of nowhere and changed directions four times, as if the power behind it were searching for something. McGraw, the Stonehaven police chief, said later that on the night of Bentley's birth he felt as if he and the village were under a glass bell and that a terrible pressure was trying to break through.

Bentley's father retreated into a deep depression after his wife died. Richard Ellicott drove to and from the university every day. But he aged faster than his life proceeded. He slept and read too much. He took long, solitary walks along the shore north of the village. He felt abandoned. He loved Bentley, but, as the boy was growing up, Richard couldn't emerge from his grief and pay attention to him.

So, Stonehaven's Congregationalist minister, the Reverend Homer Tally, became Bentley's substitute father. He was a gentle man of fifty who rarely spoke above a murmur except when he preached. Everybody regarded Mr. Tally as a saint. He had no children of his own, and he adored Bentley. Reverend Tally taught the boy how to ride a bicycle and plant gardens.

Mrs. Tally was not regarded as a saint. Her tart manner, closed mind, and barbed commentaries on the lives of everyone in the village made people tense. As the years progressed she sensed a mystery within Bentley—she was decidedly not stupid—and told everyone the boy was peculiar. He was always wandering off alone in the woods when he was little and search parties had to be organized. That proved his oddity so far as Mrs. Tally was concerned.

In the midmorning of his life, when he was eight, Bentley Ellicott's wiry body could scarcely contain his spirit, which was iridescent as summer light on the water. He was as busy as the foragings of a million bees and as curious as the eternal demand to know the meaning of God's wink.

He was short for his age and had large, dark eyes. His brown hair hung over those eyes until a German graduate student named Helga became Richard Ellicott's housekeeper. Even Helga had a hard time getting Bentley to sit still long enough for an attack on his hair with scissors. Helga was a slender, pretty girl of nineteen. She teased Bentley to make him screech, wrestled his blue jeans and sneakers off of him so she could wash them, and tried to make him stop gobbling his breakfast.

Bentley was irrepressible. He had the energy of a chipmunk, and his face was as changeable as the weather on the northern coast. He bulged out his eyes as he exaggerated his triumphs and failures. He did a terrific imitation of a chimpanzee, bouncing around in circles and scratching his ribs. Other children liked him because he was exuberant and made up interesting games and adventures. In school he fidgeted and shot up his hand and often had the right answers because he loved to learn. He could run in a hopping stumble, but because of his deformed right leg he couldn't run fast enough to play baseball. Baseball was Bentley's favorite thing. He practiced throwing until he was better at it than any kid in Stonehaven. He could knock a tin can off a stump from thirty feet away.

Joe Persis, who was Bentley's best friend, was a year older and a lot bigger. He had a dim mind—which is often the mind that sees the obvious truth everyone else misses. He, too, thought that Bentley was different. Bentley was the leader, but he never made Joe feel dumb.

They were beach and forest prowlers. They dug clams with their bare hands. Joe climbed trees and pulled Bentley up after him. They made a catapult by laying a board across a log, putting rocks on one end, and jumping on the other. They hauled a U.S. Navy ammunition crate out of the water, quarreled about who owned it, and made up.

In his room Bentley had posters depicting birds, fishes, and dinosaurs. He had a toy box half filled with treasures he found along the shore. Sometimes in the evenings he watched television with Helga and her boyfriend. Bentley would pull his sweater up over his eyes when there were scary parts of horror movies. On other evenings he had supper at the Tally's house and rode home on his bicycle. Reverend Tally took him exploring on the uplands of bare meadows, granite outcroppings, forests, and crater lakes that rise behind Stonehaven and the coast. Bentley became a substitute for the son Reverend Tally never had. Mrs. Tally endured him.

McGraw, the Stonehaven police chief, didn't like Bentley. He was the one who'd had to lead all the search parties when Bentley had gotten himself lost. He told the other loungers in the Stonehaven drugstore that the kid was a fool. Willybill, the jade-eyed stranger who had appeared in the village on the night Bentley was born, was still there, still a stranger. He watched the boy.

Bentley Ellicott kept his secret. He tore around the village and the countryside on his bicycle, yelled his head off at schoolyard baseball games, and reveled in his childhood despite the fact that his mother was dead, his father was unreachable, and he himself was handicapped.

Our fortunes and lives seem chaotic when they are looked at as facts. There is order and meaning only in the great truths believed by everybody in that older, wiser time of the world when things were less known but better understood. That ancient wisdom lived secretly within Bentley Ellicott alongside the rackety personality of an eight-year-old boy. He assumed that the great purpose for which he had been born would not summon him for years and years.

No sound ever disappears. Every wind rush stays, every rattle of wave-washed gravel remains in the world, hovering above the gray boulders and rock ledges, dripping with the mists of spring in the pine forests. All of Stonehaven's history murmurs and speaks in the second air—the shouts of Vikings sailing down the cold sea, the rigging creaks of the ships that brought the first French settlers, the rifle cracks of hunting and war, the sounds of adze and mallet as neat white houses and the Cutter mansion were built on the slope above the cove. In the second air, people born with the gift of magic can hear the gossip of Stonehaven's early generations, the grumbles of nineteenth-century fishermen casting off for George's Bank, the gnash of iron machines cutting granite, the scrape of shovels in the graveyard.

Sounds of eternal conditions are all around us—night cries of ecstasy, the whispers of the dying, promises being made, and soft, disappointed weeping.

The echoes of Stonehaven's decline are also in the second air—the clink of beer bottles against the pilings of the town wharf, the roaring endeavor of tractors pushing mobile homes into place, hammers nailing sheet metal onto the sides of shacks to protect against the winter wind, the minuscule scuttle and twirl of spiders busy at their webs in the trash-littered hallways of Charlie Feavey's Stonehaven House Hotel. The world's noise outlives all the generations that made it. In this vast and imperishable archive of every sound ever made, from the beginning of time until the present moment, the voices of animals are understood by those mortals endowed with the gift of listening.

Bentley Ellicott could hear the second air. That was that reason he started wandering off into the woods when he was three, exasperating McGraw, the police chief. McGraw was a tall, bulky man with a weather-burned face and gray eyes. He spoke with the reserve common to people on the northern coast. He was sensible—whether he and his two deputies were called to rescue a dog in a culvert or to disarm a deranged man with a gun. People in Stonehaven relied on McGraw. He was as predictably steady as the rising of the sun. His wife was a heavy, tired woman who worked at the sardine cannery.

McGraw never talked about the dark disenchantment that had possessed his heart since he was thirteen years old. It wasn't anybody's business.

He had had a happy childhood. His parents were religious, and McGraw grew up nestled in their faith. He believed no harm could come to him if he was good, because God loved him. He memorized long passages from the Bible and behaved himself. Then, when he was thirteen, his father abruptly left home and moved into the house trailer of a slatternly woman named Grace Woodhouse. They had a child. McGraw's mother went mad. She prattled incessantly about the enigma of God's ways and hanged herself in the garage.

McGraw's world blew apart. He never spoke to his father again. He finished his adolescence knowing that faith was a lie. There was no God. The world was chaos and people's lives were haphazard. Everything McGraw had experienced as a policeman confirmed his agnostic view of reality. As others saw him, he was a quiet, strong man. As he saw himself, he had been a gullible boy who had had to retrain himself in skepticism in order to survive as an adult.

Bentley Ellicott reminded the police chief of how *he* had been when he was eight. There was, to McGraw, a childish arrogance in Bentley's whooping confidence, in his stubborn refusal to be cowed by his handicap, or by the tragedy of his mother's death and his father's withdrawal. The kid acted as if he believed that some benevolence were watching over him. McGraw disliked Bentley with all the power of self-contempt. He yearned for a cataclysm that would shock the boy out of his confidence. The police chief wanted to see Bentley get his comeuppance.

Bentley tried to avoid him. He knew that McGraw was not his friend.

Neither McGraw nor anybody else could have possibly known the truth about Bentley. Nobody would have believed it anyway.

If Bentley had lived in that older, wiser time of the world, people in Stonehaven would have assumed that he could ravel up the pain of childbirth if he wanted to, and could tell which heron standing on the mud flats was a transfigured king. He would have been instructed by old, one-eyed men who had survived many battles. They would have blessed him with handfuls of dust and given him an amulet. Wonder-workers would have clearly seen the darkening of the world in smoke and water. Everybody would have understood what was happening. They would have known what Bentley was.

Bentley Ellicott was a child born with the memory of another, perfect childhood. In his daydreams he remembered as an old traveler remembers a land beyond the mists of the sea where he had known untroubled love and perfect happiness. He remembered a perpetual noon that needed no sun for its shining. He had played then with countless children from ages gone, never wearying, never bored, never reproached. He had danced in a grove with the robed masters of all knowledge. He had spoken in poems, and he had a golden apple.

He hadn't been sad when they had called him away and loaned him the heart that had been borne in the world by a thousand mortals before him. He knew that the heart had returned a thousand times. All souls always came back when their moments of mortal life were done.

Bentley remembered being born. He remembered floating up from the depths of a grotto toward the rose-colored light of future existence. The hovering cavern angel stopped him but laid no finger on Bentley's lips. Instead, he was told about his great and ominous destiny and given a final instruction: *Don't tell your secret unless you are offered love sealed in silence, or unless someone recognizes what you really are.*

The instant he was born, the imperfection of the mortal condition seized him. His life was flawed now; he was afraid of death.

Bentley also was given powers, ones that no ordinary mortal possessed. The horseshoe crabs, who are the armorers of the shallow sea, taught him an incantation. Ospreys could be summoned to fly in protective circles above him. When he was chanting the spell and standing within his circles, no enemy—mortal or from the distant darkness—could harm Bentley or make him do anything he didn't want to do. He had been endowed with the gift of hearing all the sounds of the past and understanding the speech of animals in the second air. Nobody knew about Bentley's magic.

The borrowed heart sometimes whispered indistinctly to him. But, most of the time, it surrendered to the unquenchable enthusiasm of the boyhood Bentley was living in the old village above the harbor, on the shores and windy uplands and in the forests of the northern coast. Bentley dreamed of the man he would someday be —and in those fantasies the mortal terror he had been born to endure and the glory of his destiny became a supreme adventure.

But then, late in his ninth autumn, Bentley's life suddenly darkened. His heart cried warning to him. *Now!* proclaimed the voice of his unworldly intuition. *It is beginning—now!*

One November night Bentley and Joe were unchaining their bicycles on Main Street after going to the movies. They heard tires screeching. A four-door sedan tore down Cutter Street, skidded as it swung into Main, and roared past them through the spaced pools of lamplight. As the two boys watched, open-mouthed, the car hit a patch where mist had frozen on the road, spun around twice, and slammed sideways into the wall of the freezing plant. Glass blasted outward from the back windows with the impact.

People came running out of a bar across the street. A figure was climbing from the car. Bentley was astounded as Mr. Tally stumbled into the light. The clergyman was bleeding from a cut on his forehead. He began to shout and curse as people surrounded him. Bentley saw a skirmish, and a woman fell to the ground. Mr. Tally had punched her. Four men were holding him back as he tried to kick her. A police car came down the street

from the opposite direction. It stopped, and
McGraw and his first deputy, Mike, jumped out.
Reverend Tally was shouting drunken obscenities
as he was dragged across the street to the police
station.

Bentley was numb with bewilderment. He rode
home trying to reconcile the wild man on Main
Street with the gentle Reverend Tally he had
known all of his life. He didn't tell his father and
Helga what he'd seen. He was afraid they would
explain how such things happened—and that the
explanation would confuse what he already in-
stinctively knew. He put on his pajamas, climbed
into bed, and turned off the light.

He listened to his agitated heart. It cried to him
that Reverend Tally had been assaulted by sorcery
because he was a part of Bentley's life. *You are being attacked. It is beginning! Now!*

The next day Bentley rode his bicycle over to the
Tallys' house after school. Mrs. Tally told him to
go away.

On Thursday everybody in Stonehaven was talking about Reverend Tally's dismissal by his congregation. The episode at the freezing plant had
been the fourth drunken scene since September.

On Saturday Bentley and Joe were in the drugstore buying candy bars when they heard McGraw
telling Polly Woodhouse, the soda fountain girl,
how Reverend Tally's battered car had been found
in the parking lot of an airport miles away down
the coast. The clergyman had disappeared from
Stonehaven, leaving his wife behind.

Bentley told Joe he didn't feel so hot. He rode
home on his bicycle and walked up the dirt road to

the end of the point. He climbed a broken stone wall and limped up a steep meadow that ended at a cliff over the sea.

He put his hands in the pockets of his anorak. The wind blew his hair back from his face. Reverend Tally's disappearance was like a death. Bentley looked out at the horizon and the low, gray sky. Winter was coming. Bentley's heart whispered to him that something else, remembered in legends and glimpsed in the profoundest depths of dreams, was rising with the chilling of the world.

Bentley was suddenly terrified. It had never occurred to him that he'd have to fulfill his destiny before he grew up.

Two weeks later, Joe Persis abruptly changed. It was as if the first winds of winter had brought the world's contamination to the northern coast and Bentley's best friend had become infected.

One December afternoon Bentley and Joe were throwing a baseball on the playground. They did that a lot, and Joe always tried to throw straight so that Bentley wouldn't have to run. That day he was throwing deliberately wide. Bentley had to make limping dashes for the ball. Joe thought it was funny.

Bentley let the ball roll into the wire mesh along the side of the playground. He stood in the twilight listening to Joe's forced, phony laughter. Bentley's heart whispered a warning to him.

"Let's quit," Bentley said. "I'm cold."

Joe was wearing a heavy jacket. His wool hat was pulled down almost over his eyes. "Maybe you *oughta* go home," he said. "Maybe your *mother's* waiting for you! I'm gonna hit!"

He picked up a baseball bat and smacked the ball in a hard drive at three first-graders who were crossing the other side of the playground. The ball hit one of them, who started to cry.

Another little kid threw the ball over some bushes.

"You go get that!" Joe screamed to the child, his amiable, stupid face getting red. He picked up a rock and batted it across the playground. The first-graders screamed and dodged. Joe had become somebody else.

Bentley knew what was happening. He squelched his fear and jumped on Joe's back. Joe yelled in rage and tossed him off. Bentley landed hard on his rear end.

"Crippled crud!" Joe shouted.

Bentley blinked. He was stunned. "You'd better quit hitting things at people," he managed to say.

Joe swung the bat over his shoulder. "Make me! Go on, crippled crud, make me!"

"Chowderhead," Bentley muttered. Swift as a lizard he spun around on his rear end, grabbed Joe's ankles, and yanked him off his feet. The bat skidded ten feet away. Bentley lunged for it. But Joe jumped up, sprinted, and stomped hard, squashing Bentley's fingers beneath the hard ash wood. Bentley screeched.

Cries of "Fight! Fight!" rang across the cold schoolyard. Kids came running from every direction to watch.

Bentley was standing up, two fingers in his mouth, glaring at Joe.

"I'll knock your block off!" Joe yelled.

Bentley took his fingers out of his mouth and grinned. "Your block's so fat they couldn't knock it off with a bulldozer."

Joe spat. "Are you looking for trouble?"

Bentley nodded.

"Crippled crud!" Joe screamed again.

"Lard head!"

"My father says you're nuts! McGraw told him!"

Bentley put on his solemn, chimpanzee face and pranced about, scratching himself under the arms.

The kids standing in a wide circle around them began to laugh.

What happened next was something that Stonehaven children and parents argued about for weeks.

Joe took a sudden, vicious chop with the baseball bat.

Bentley ducked, but he didn't step back. A strange look came into his eyes. He began to make a soft, senseless chanting noise, staring into Joe's face. Joe went berserk and swung the bat again— hard—straight at Bentley's head. But it didn't hit Bentley. He kept on chanting and staring into Joe's eyes. Joe yowled in fury and frustration. He swung the bat again and again. Joe got so mad that he cracked himself on the shin with the bat. He limped off the playground, crying and yelling. He and Bentley weren't best friends anymore.

That evening the children who had seen the fight told their parents about it at supper tables all over Stonehaven. They thought that Bentley was magic and a hero. They were told to stop being silly and eat their carrots. Joe swore that Bentley was the

one who had been swatting rocks at the first-
graders. He also said that Bentley had hit him on
the leg with the bat.

Bentley was scared again. He sat in the woods
listening to the second air. The two beings that lived within him argued as he crouched on his bed at
night, watching the stars. Bentley, the frightened
eight-year-old, tried to persuade himself that Reverend Tally's disgrace and disappearance had no
significance larger than sadness, that the fight
with Joe Persis had just been a dumb thing that
happened. The warnings of his heart grew more
insistent. Bentley waited for a sign that his worst
fears were going to come true.

Willybill was the one who brought the sign.

Strange, inexplicable Willybill. He had lived in
Stonehaven for eight years, but nobody knew him.
People stayed away from him.

Remembering Willybill, it is impossible to know
whether he was thirty or fifty. He was a lean,
scruffy man with long, reddish hair and a beard.
When he didn't have a cowboy hat on, he wore a
rolled bandanna around his head. He never dressed in anything but blue jeans, cracked leather
boots, and faded shirts. He had the sullen expression of a man who has been defeated by the world.
The stains of the wanderer were on him. The only
things he seemed to own were his clothes, his battered pickup truck, and a guitar.

He lived in a rented room above the hardware
store on Main Street and sang songs in a roadhouse on the highway outside town. He had an oddly powerful voice but rarely spoke to anybody.
He had no friends.

Willybill's eyes were alarming. They were the color of pale jade and burned in both sunlight and shadow. He watched Bentley Ellicott a lot. McGraw and his two deputies thought the stranger was sinister, but they could never get anything on him.

A few days after the fight, Bentley was riding home across the potato fields at dusk. McGraw's cruiser came out of the woods along the point and crossed the highway. The siren whirred briefly, and Bentley stopped his bicycle. McGraw pulled off the road and rolled down the windows of his police car. "Joe Persis's father spoke to me this morning," he said.

Bentley's nose was cold. His stomach got tight.

"Having a fight with a boy's one thing," McGraw said. "Hitting him with a baseball bat's something else."

"I didn't hit him," Bentley said. "He hit himself."

"You're a weird kid, Bentley," McGraw answered. "What's wrong with you isn't any of my business. But I get any more reports of you making trouble, I'm going to take it up with your father."

"I didn't do anything!" Bentley said loudly. "You can ask the other kids! They saw it!"

McGraw studied him for a moment. "You just remember what I said." He rolled up the window and drove away.

Bentley pedaled toward the forest and the dirt road that ran the length of the point. He felt angry, humiliated, and helpless. He desperately wanted to believe that it could have happened to anybody, that a power beyond his imagination wasn't attacking him, trying to weaken him and fill him with despair. But the other part of him, his heart that had come to the world a thousand times before in a cause as old as the world itself, told him the truth.

Bentley's mind was still churning around in a muddle between two perspectives as he rode across the highway and into the forest on the dirt road. The dusk was deepening. The air was sharp.

He skidded his bicycle to a stop. A figure was emerging from the shrubbery ten feet in front of him.

Bentley put his foot on the road. He gripped the handlebars tightly and stared at Willybill.

Willybill stared back at him. His jade eyes burned in the gloom.

Then Bentley's conflict stopped. He knew.

Christmas passed. January and February hardened their grip on the northern coast. Bentley Ellicott was alone.

He and Joe weren't speaking anymore, and he'd stopped hanging around the playground because he didn't feel like having fun. Reverend Tally was gone. Bentley became quiet. Helga took him to the doctor, but they didn't find anything wrong. He couldn't tell Helga and his father what he was brooding about because it was part of his secret.

Bentley's heart delivered memories of his other life to him. As he lay awake at night, as he sat on his log in the hushed, gray afternoons, recollection rose in him. He saw, as through a mist, the grotto in which souls about to be born float up toward the glow of mortal existence. Bentley heard again the voice of the cavern angel giving him instructions for his life. Echoing like cherubim song, as clear as the command of God, the angel's voice described the destiny of the smooth-lipped ones born as mortals. They must oppose an enemy that mankind had willed itself to forget; they must confront terrors calculated to turn hearts to stone; the warriors of god must find such courage that they could perform deeds beyond the exertion of ordinary men.

Bentley lay awake at night, wondering if he was brave enough. Up until his ninth year he had assumed that heroic courage would come to him with manhood. But now that he knew his destiny was going to call him before he was a man, he wasn't sure of himself.

He rode to and from school on his bicycle, thinking about being afraid. He lay awake at night, making lists of all the things he feared. He began to work out a plan to prepare himself.

March came. In Stonehaven, Mrs. Tally fixed her critical eye on Polly Woodhouse, the soda fountain girl in the drugstore; she did not approve of that overripe child. Chief McGraw drove around the village in his cruiser; he felt an inexplicable anxiety as spring approached. Willybill spoke to no one. But several people noticed that he stood all day at the window of his rented room. He scanned the village, the harbor, and the thawing islands in the sea as if he were waiting for something.

The more Bentley thought about what frightened him, the longer his lists grew. He was afraid of wasps and the dark. He was frightened that he might see a face on the window glass at night. He was squeamish about wading barefoot because some sea creature might pinch his toes. When somebody in a TV movie was about to open a mysterious door, Bentley hid his eyes.

If he had to, Bentley figured, he could face any of these things. He turned on his imagination and tried to think of what he was more scared of than anything else.

He sat in the forest on his favorite log, listening to the drip of melting icicles on the sodden carpet of dead leaves. He saw a bird fluttering from branch to branch.

He heard the distant rumble and whoosh of cars on the wet highway that curved through the potato fields. A large silence enclosed that sound.

Bentley shivered. The car noises reminded him of the night in November when Reverend Tally crashed into the wall of the freezing plant. And that, in turn, reminded him of a day, the year before, that he had seen a boy hit by a delivery truck on Main Street. Bentley's chest tightened as he remembered the boy flying off his bicycle and smashing onto the street. He was shrieking for his mother when they lifted him into an ambulance. It had been horrible.

After thinking about it for several days, Bentley figured that being hit by a truck scared him more than anything else. The cavern angel had told him that he would need superhuman courage to fulfill the purpose of his life. What he would face at that hour of his destiny was beyond imagination. He decided to test himself. He would practice being brave by confronting the most frightening thing he did know about.

In early April he started getting up before dawn

so that nobody could catch him. He put on a heavy sweater and rode his bicycle over to the highway in the flint-gray light.

The first few days he went there he stood among the new potato plants watching big trailer trucks burst from the tree line. Their headlights speared into the murk with the harsh glare of dragons' eyes. Smaller lights flashed and winked on the trucks' bodies. Their horns brayed across the sleeping landscape. Gears howled as the huge machines hurtled around the curve in the middle of the fields, exhaling bitter smoke. The trucks roared past Bentley and disappeared into the woods.

Every morning Bentley moved a little farther up the shoulder of the highway. He was trying to push down his fear so that he could stand right beside the pavement, with his toes on the edge of the macadam, as the trucks thundered by just a foot away from his nose. If he could bring himself to do that, he'd be equal to anything. As Bentley stood watching in the half-light, his mind would fill with chaos as he imagined those speeding tons of steel smashing into him and mangling his body under the double sets of wheels. He had to do it just right.

Finally, before dawn on a Friday, he was standing with one foot on the highway and another on the roadside grit. It was very cold, and Bentley was wearing his anorak. He tensed as he heard the rumbling of a truck approaching from the north. It got louder and louder. Bentley began trembling. He told himself to hold his ground. He closed his eyes and made two fists. Then he moved his other foot onto the pavement.

He opened his eyes. The truck exploded from the dark wall of forest at the far end of the potato fields. It tore across the flat country and hit the curve, gears shrieking, its headlights sweeping over the ground. Suddenly the glare of the lights was full in his eyes. He realized he was too close. The bellow of the truck's horn acknowledged him. His brain yelled at him to jump back. He froze.

In the cab, the driver had taken his eyes off the highway for a moment to glance at the speedometer. The needle was rising past 75 as the truck started around the curve. The driver hugged the inside to keep his load from shifting.

He looked up. His mind went white with shock. A small boy was standing in the full beam of headlights.

The driver pounded the horn once and wrenched the wheel to the left. The truck swayed like a drunken elephant and hurtled across the highway. It tore into the field, bucking and heaving. The driver frantically rammed the brakes and yanked the gears down, and brought the truck to a stop in a spray of dirt, rocks, and potato plants.

Bentley watched, horrified. He ran across the highway and into the field as plumes of dust were settling around the damaged truck.

The driver opened the cab door. The song of a lark trilled across the hushed morning. The driver unhooked the microphone of his CB radio and called the police.

He lowered himself to the ground. He didn't want to look at the highway for fear he'd see a crushed little body. He walked the length of the truck. The rear wheels were buckled inward. The stink of scorched brakes filled the air. Gears and parts of the transmission box littered the oily path gouged through the new growth. The driver walked past the end of the truck. He saw a brown-haired boy standing fifteen feet away, staring at him.

"I'm really sorry," Bentley said. "I didn't mean to . . ."

The driver looked back at him in the widening morning light. Any normal kid who'd caused a bad accident would have run like hell. This kid was weird. "Don't move," the driver said.

"Okay," Bentley answered. He was in shock. "I thought you'd gotten hurt or something."

Bentley nodded. He knew that he was doomed.

He and the driver were still standing in the morning light, looking at each other, when McGraw arrived. The police chief inspected the damage and radioed for a tow truck. He was elated because the driver's account of the accident gave substance to what McGraw had been saying for years. The Ellicott kid was crazy.

McGraw put Bentley in the front seat of his cruiser. Bentley didn't say anything on the way home. He was burning with humiliation.

It has begun!

The sun was splashing hot light on the sea as McGraw rang the doorbell of the Ellicott house. Helga clutched the top of her bathrobe and looked frightened when she saw Bentley standing on the porch beside the tall, heavy police chief. She went to wake Richard.

Bentley ate his breakfast at the kitchen table.

He felt small, stupid, and ashamed. He didn't answer when Helga asked him what had happened. He listened to the low decibels of male conversation coming from the living room.

After a while he heard his father and McGraw walk into the front hall. The police chief said, "I'm taking your word you'll do something about him, Professor. If you don't, the county will."

When McGraw had gone, Richard came to the kitchen door in his bathrobe and pajamas. Bentley saw the expression in his father's eyes. He looked down at a soggy cornflake floating at the bottom of his cereal bowl. His embarrassment got hotter as his father and Helga waited for him to explain.

He wanted to. But the cavern angel had warned him not to tell his secret unless he was offered love sealed with silence or unless somebody recognized what he really was.

Bentley knew that his father and Helga loved him. But he knew they wouldn't believe him. He tried to think something about the cornflake so that he could stop thinking about how alone he was.

Chapter Two

Bentley sat on a bench in a long hallway. He look-ed through glass doors at the spidery shadows of tree branches on a building across the street. The branches swayed in the fresh, spring wind.

A blond lady and a little girl were sitting on a bench across the hallway. The lady was reading a magazine. The girl stared vacantly at the wall above Bentley's head. Her face was narrow and pinched.

Bentley's father had brought him up to the university on Tuesday. For two days in this place call-ed the Kreistein Clinic they'd tested him, poked at him, and asked him questions.

First they'd made him take off his clothes so that they could peer at him and listen to his body. A doctor had rapped his knees until his legs jerk-ed. They made him close his eyes, extend his arm, and try to touch his nose with his finger.

After he got dressed again, they stretched him out on a table as a machine with winky lights like a spaceship rolled back and forth above him. Then they wired his head and arms and told him not to move while a needle traced grasshopper legs on a revolving drum.

A lady in a white smock showed him pictures and got him to make up stories about them. He played a kid's game of fitting wooden pieces into holes in a board. For two hours she asked him questions about himself and wrote the answers down with a fountain pen.

Bentley got the idea they didn't like him much. Nobody smiled at him. That made him feel even more ashamed about causing the truck wreck and being arrested by McGraw. It was almost as if he was being punished for keeping his secret and obeying the instructions he'd been given before he was born.

One doctor seemed to be trying to startle him into telling the secret. This man had some big cardboard sheets with blobs smeared on them in black ink. He told Bentley to say the first word that came into his head when a card flashed up. Mentally, Bentley stepped into his magic circles and repeated the incantation taught him by the horseshoe crabs. When the doctor flipped up a card, Bentley didn't say what the shape really suggested to him. Other words popped from his lips.

When they'd finished testing him, they told him to wait in the hall until Dr. Kreistein was ready to see him. Bentley stopped looking at the branch shadows on the wall across the street. They reminded him of spiders. Instead, he looked at the little girl sitting opposite him.

He figured she was younger than he was. She was thin and her whole body looked tight. Her face was pale as if she had a cold. She had tangled blond hair and large eyes that seemed to be telling the world that she was almost always scared. One of her hands was gripped so hard around the bench arm that her knuckles were white.

She must have felt him looking at her. She lowered her eyes, then raised them and stared at him. "Hi," Bentley said.

The empty expression on her face didn't change.

"What's your name?" Bentley asked.

The little girl looked up at the lady sitting beside her. Then she said, "Slally."

The lady lowered her magazine and smiled at Bentley. "Her name is Sally," she said. "She can't talk properly."

"How come?" Bentley asked.

His question seemed to encourage the little girl. She began to speak. The words tumbled from her throat in a beautiful torrent that sounded like sleet on the roof, a cat's purr, and the fluting chuckle of owls.

The lady's smile was sad. "See? Nobody can understand her. She feels wretched when people try to have conversations with her."

"She wants to know my name," Bentley said.

The wind rattled the doors at the end of the hallway. Somewhere deep within the building somebody was whistling.

The lady lowered her magazine into her lap. The expression on her face was a mixture of puzzle-

ment and doubt. She was pretty. Her hair fell over
the left side of her forehead. Her hands were long.
She was wearing a man's shirt, a black sweater,
jeans, and tennis shoes.

She put one hand under Slally's chin. "Is that
what you said, darling?"

Slally was grinning. She nodded. Then she turned back to Bentley and spoke to him again in a
whispery babble.

"What did she say?" the lady asked cautiously.

"She said you have a big white house with a
porch," Bentley answered. "She said it's close
enough to walk here, and her father hasn't lived
with you for a long time."

Slally's mother let her magazine slide to the
floor. She leaned forward, resting her elbows on
her knees. She folded her hands and drew a deep
breath. Bentley could feel her holding back excitement. "My name's Ellen Drake," she said. "What's
yours?"

"Bentley Ellicott," Bentley said. Mrs. Drake
made his ashamed feeling sharper. She was looking at him as if he was something that lived in a
tree.

"Are you Richard Ellicott's son?"

Bentley nodded. "Do you know my dad?"

"I know his name," Mrs. Drake said. "He
teaches here, doesn't he?"

Bentley nodded again.

"Can you *really* understand what Sally says?"

"Sure. It's easy."

Mrs. Drake sat looking at him for a moment.
"Nobody's ever understood her in her whole life,"
she said. "How can you do it, Bentley?"

Bentley shrugged. "I don't know. I just can."

Even though he was loud a lot of the time, Bentley was also a good listener. He had listened to all the wisdom and foolishness ever uttered. To him Slally's beautiful noises were a language she had made up for herself. He just listened to what she was saying.

Mrs. Drake had been looking at him as if he were a problem she had to figure out. Suddenly she stood up. "Will you stay with Sally?"

"Sure," Bentley said.

"I won't be long, darling," Mrs. Drake said to Slally. She walked up the corridor, pushed open two swinging doors, and disappeared into the testing part of the clinic.

Bentley liked Mrs. Drake. But her questions made him feel scrutinized and peculiar. He looked at Slally and made his chimpanzee face. She laughed as if she'd never laughed before. Then the expression of uncertain sadness softened her eyes again. She put her hands in her lap and linked her forefingers together.

"What's wrong?" Bentley asked her.

Slally said that now he knew why she had to come to the clinic. She hated it. But she couldn't talk.

"Sure you can talk," Bentley said. "You just don't do it like everybody else. This friend of mine who takes care of us, her name's Helga, she could only talk German when she came to live with us. Now she talks like my dad and me."

Slally said that was different. Bentley's friend had learned. Slally told him she'd tried to make the same sounds as other people. It was like almost sneezing but never quite doing it.

"How come you hate the clinic?" Bentley asked her.

Slally looked down at her hands and described all the indignities she went through three times a week at the Kreistein Clinic. Then she raised her eyes and asked him why *he* had to be there.

Bentley's face got hot. "They think there's something wrong with me," he said. "I wrecked a truck."

A *real* truck?

Bentley nodded. He lowered his voice and told her about riding his bike over to the highway every morning and what had happened on the last morning.

Slally smiled at him. She said she was positive he had a good reason for standing beside the highway. She knew how hard it was to make anybody understand.

"It sure is," Bentley said. "Even if you can talk."

Her large eyes looked at him anxiously.

"I can't tell the reason," Bentley said. "They made me promise I wouldn't. It's a secret."

Slally nodded.

"Hey, listen," Bentley said, feeling lighter and happier. "I'll bet there's a whole lot of stuff you've always wanted to tell somebody. You can tell me."

Slally smiled again.

"Go on," Bentley said. "What would you like more than anything in the world to tell about?"

She pressed her hands on the bench, hunched her shoulders, and looked at the ceiling. She said nobody knew she could read. They thought she couldn't because she hadn't been able to learn to write at this special school they sent her to. Sometimes, she said, her mother got mad at her when she was reading. Mrs. Drake thought she was pretending so that she wouldn't have to go outside.

"I'll tell her you can read," Bentely said.

Suddenly Slally seemed to fully grasp that he *could* understand her and that she could really tell him all the things that had been shut up inside of her all of her life.

She pushed herself forward on the bench and spoke quickly, almost breathlessly, in the rustle of birch leaves, rabbit warbles, and the night sound of water splashing drop by drop.

She told Bentley about her dreams, about what she saw on television, how she wished she could have another chance at learning to ride a bicycle— her uncle had tried to teach her when she was six. She told Bentley about swimming, being carsick, knowing she could play the flute if she could have lessons, feeling sorry for a lady next door who cried, about loving dogs. Bentley thought that her life seemed small as she described it, as if everybody treated her as special or invisible.

She was still telling him things when Mrs. Drake came back with the doctor who used ink blobs to try to make Bentley tell his secret. Slally immediately went silent.

The doctor looked down at her with an unmeant smile. "Now, then," he said, "what's going on here?"

Slally gazed at the floor and said they were just talking.

"She said we were talking," Bentley told the doctor. "Hey, would it be okay, when you ask her questions on the tape recorder, if she didn't have to talk about her birthday?"

The doctor stared at Bentley for a moment. "Why? Do questions about her birthday upset her?"

"She didn't have a party," Bentley said. "She doesn't know any other kids."

"*That's* why she cried on her birthday," Mrs. Drake said.

Bentley nodded. "She wants you to know that she can really read."

Mrs. Drake's eyes widened. Then she took Slally's face in her hands and raised it. "I'm sorry, darling," she said. "I didn't know."

Slally made a half-smile and touched her mother's hand.

"I don't have any immediate explanation," the doctor said to Mrs. Drake. "Let's carry on with Sally. Kreistein will try to find out what he can from the boy."

"Promise you won't make her talk about her birthday anymore?" Bentley asked.

The doctor nodded. "I promise. Thank you." He held out his hand to Slally. "Come on, sweetie pie. We won't do anything bad today."

Slally's hand tightened on the arm of the bench. She murmured a rivulet of protest.

"What's the matter?" Mrs. Drake asked Bentley.

Bentley felt embarrassed. "She's afraid I won't be here when she comes back."

"Of course she is," Mrs. Drake said. "Bentley, what are you going to do after you've seen Dr. Kreistein?"

"My dad's coming to get me," Bentley said.

"Would you like to have supper at our house if it's all right with your father?" Mrs. Drake asked.

"Yeah," Bentley said. "Sure. We could watch television," he said to Slally.

She slid off the bench, took her mother's hand, and told Bentley he had to make his father let him come.

"I'll try," Bentley said. "Then you can tell me more stuff."

Slally's face was glowing. In a rushed windsweep of words she said that if he told her his secret she'd promise never to repeat it.

Don't tell your secret unless you are offered love sealed with silence or unless someone recognizes what you really are.

Slally spoke again.

"What did she say?" the doctor asked.

Bentley got embarrassed again. "She doesn't want you to call her sweetie pie," he said.

The doctor started to answer. Then he put his hands in his jacket pockets and walked up the hall, talking to Mrs. Drake in a low voice. The double doors opened, and they took Slally into the testing section.

Bentley sat on the bench for ten more minutes. He was suddenly happy. Nobody had ever asked him to tell his secret. Nobody even knew he had one. Then he remembered again why he was in the clinic. He felt stupid again for trying to work on his courage by standing too close to the trucks. And he was still alone. There wasn't anybody grown-up and wise he could talk to about his destiny, about what the cavern angel had told him, and about how scared he was.

He was still thinking about Slally and his own bungled attempt to test his courage when a lady came out of the hallway and said that Dr. Kreistein was ready to see him.

She showed Bentley into a big office and closed the door behind him. It was messy and sunlit like his room at home. Papers and books were scattered all over the place. An old man with a wart on his bald head was standing behind a desk, glaring at a handful of papers, talking aloud to himself, and sucking in his breath between his teeth.

He was the ugliest human being Bentley had ever seen. He was short and lumpy. His warty head was huge and had tufts of white hair sticking up like weeds around a parking lot. His face sagged down to a turkey-wattle dangle of flesh on his neck. The skin below his eyes had drooped onto his cheeks. He had a big nose and a small, wet mouth. He was wearing a rumpled white shirt and a seersucker suit. His black necktie was twisted under his collar. His hands were like thick claws. "So," he said without looking up, "you are ze boy who iss creating all ziss few-roar."

Bentley didn't answer. He wasn't sure what he was supposed to do.

"Sit, sit, sit," the old man said, squinting at another piece of paper. He mumbled and tossed it aside. "Make some place for yourself. Sit!"

Bentley took some books off a large leather chair and sat down on the edge. Behind the desk the old man was still flinging papers around. Pretty soon he'd stop that and start asking Bentley questions about himself. In his mind, Bentley drew the three, magic circles and stepped into them. Silently he began to chant the incantation of the horse-shoe crabs.

"Ahah!"

Bentley opened his eyes.

The old man was standing behind his desk holding up a piece of paper. *"Now,* already, I find you!" He dropped the paper, sat down, folded his gnarled hands over his bulgy tum, puckered his lips, and looked at Bentley.

"How come you lose your papers?" Bentley asked.

"Because I am a messy man," the doctor answered in his thick accent.

"Me, too," Bentley said.

The old man nodded. "Now, maybe, you will tell me something. You have made an uproar in this place. How is it you can understand this little girl?"

Bentley shrugged. "I just listen to what she says."

"I am speaking English," the doctor said. "But I don't sound like other people speaking English. This is because I spoke another language first. German. I had to study English for a long time. You have never studied this little girl's language, but you understand it. Please explain that to me."

"I can't," Bentley said. Again, in his mind, he drew the three osprey circles and repeated the incantation. "I don't know," he said.

The old man looked through his office window. Outside, the spring sunlight had washed the air clean. The ground was wet. "Science," the doctor said, "thinks that this girl is sick in the brain. *Science* thinks she is speaking no language at all,

just"—he looked back at Bentley—"just making
mooky, mooky, mooky noises. What do you
think?"

"We're studying science in school, but they
haven't told us anything about that." Bentley said.

"Do you know my name?"

"I forgot," Bentley said.

"Kreistein," the old man answered. *"Kry—*
steen. Doctor. Now I am going to tell you something. Science doesn't know everything." He
wheezed suddenly. His body shook, and he took
out a handkerchief to wipe his eyes and blow his
nose. He stuffed the handkerchief in his pocket,
leaned forward, and opened a folder.

Bentley was feeling uneasy. He should have
been serene inside his magic circles, armed with
his chanted spells. But he wasn't. He couldn't understand it. He repeated the incantation twice
more to himself.

"I have talked to your father," Dr. Kreistein
said. "I have read these reports about you." He
picked up pieces of paper and squinted at them.
"Eccentric behavior—fighting, lying—jumping in
front of a truck." He raised his head and scratched
his nose with one crooked finger. "Maybe you are
angry because your mother died and abandoned
you?"

Bentley was warm with shame again. His
unease was growing. He shook his head. "My mom
didn't want to die. It wasn't her fault."

Dr. Kreistein's watery eyes stared at him. The
old man nodded slightly. "Ahah," he said softly.
He studied the folder again, breathing heavily
through his nostrils. "And I suppose you can ex-

plain to me why you did all of these things that everybody complains about?"

Bentley didn't answer. He stared across the office, silently, frantically chanting the words the horseshoe crabs had taught him. But the magic wasn't working. He felt as if he were out in the open, unprotected. He thought he was going to cry.

"Do you like stories?"

Bentley looked back at the desk. The slumped-over old man was still staring at him.

"I guess so," he said.

"Me, too," the old man said. "When you were having these tests yesterday, they showed you a picture of a woman in the snow and asked you to make up a story about it." Dr. Kreistein took out his handkerchief and blew his nose again. *"Ja?"*

"Ja," Bentley answered.

"You told the story of Sedna, the Eskimo maiden, only you used another name. Is this something you learned in school?"

Bentley didn't want to answer that. He didn't want to tell anybody that he listened to stories in the second air. But he was helpless.

"No," he said.

"Only scholars of northern folklore know the story of one-eyed Sedna who married the bird spirit and was sacrificed in the sea by her father," Dr. Kreistein said.

"I heard about this Indian who fell in love with her and died."

"Yes. The son of the Kitchki-Manitou." The old man coughed and cleared his throat. "Sedna had many suitors." He contemplated Bentley while all the clocks in the world pushed time before them.

Dr. Kreistein was having an unscientific thought about this boy. It was as if Bentley were a character from one of the stories that had obsessed the old man's life. Dr. Kreistein thought about all the children he had known—children in German hospitals where he had trained, children who sat in unquestioning silence among people waiting in the anxious gloom of a Portuguese refugee center. Children made up stories that embodied the figures and plots of classical legends; they lived in uncomplicated proximity to their dreams. There were mysteries and truths in these stories and legends. Dr. Kreistein wanted answers before he died.

He took a large card in one hand and looked down again at the diagnosis in the folder on his desk. The Ellicott boy was decidedly not like the disturbed children the old man usually saw. There was the business of the little girl, and the story of Sedna . . .

Dr. Kreistein whipped the big card around suddenly.

Bentley jumped in surprise at the ink blob. It was a violent splat of black that seemed to threaten all the white space around it.

"Quick!" Dr. Kreistein barked. "Who is that?"

Bentley's brain cried a warning not to tell. "Ombra!" he blurted before he could stop himself.

Dr. Kreistein put the card back on his desk. He looked out of the window again. The big office was profoundly still. Bentley's heart was beating hard. He had betrayed his trust. And he had been betrayed. His magic hadn't worked. This old man had penetrated past the circles, he had brushed aside the charm and made Bentley tell a name from the deepest part of his secret.

Dr. Kreistein turned his warty head back and looked at him. "I have played a trick on you," he said. "I am sorry. But I think you know something." Neither of them spoke for a moment while the world's clocks ticked some more. "Perhaps you would prefer not to tell me?"

"You mean I don't have to?" Bentley asked in wonder.

The old man shook his head. "No. I have secrets I would not wish to tell you or anybody else."

Bentley looked at the floor again. Maybe he hadn't done anything wrong after all. He had been given magic to protect himself against enemies and people who couldn't possibly understand what he was. Bentley raised his head and looked at the old man with curiosity. "It isn't that I don't *want* to tell," he said.

"There is, perhaps, some restriction on you?"

The sound and light of the grotto where life begins filled Bentley's mind. Once again he gazed up at the cavern angel and heard his voice like cherubim song telling him to keep his secret lest doubting mortals mock the eternal purpose of heaven.

Bentley blinked at the old man. "They told me that nobody would believe me."

"Ah," Dr. Kreistein said, folding his hands over his middle and squirming deeper into his chair. "Belief. Yes. That is a problem. People believe on-

ly those things which seem reasonable to them
from their own experience. Do you find this to be
true?"

"Uh-huh," Bentley said. The doctor was spinning a web of easy familiarity around them both.

"Me, too," the old man said. He twisted one side
of his sagging face and sniffed. "I am a doctor.
Children's minds. There is something *I* believe. It
is not my own idea." He sniffed again. "There is a
theory—you understand theory, *ja?*—that we are
born with memories of what happened in the
world before we were here. I believe this."

Bentley's wonder grew. "Not just what happened in the world," he said softly.

"Because I believe this," Dr. Kreistein said,
"this theory that we are born with ancient memories that only a few people can ressurect from
their minds, for me it is true until somebody proves
it is rubbish." His small shining eyes fixed on
Bentley. "What is your opinion, please?"

Bentley was awed. It had never occurred to him
that he would find the one who recognized what he
truly was, someone to whom he could tell everything. "I think you're right," he said in a small
voice.

"So," Dr. Kreistein murmured, "if you wish to
tell me about Ombra, it will be true because you
believe it."

And that was how, for the first time in his life,
Bentley Ellicott told a mortal being his secret.

Chapter Three

Willybill's pickup truck passed the low clutter of a shopping district on the eastern end of the university town. He turned at a stoplight. His jade eyes saw a playing field on the right side of the street. A one-story complex of buildings was on a grassy slope to his left. The stranger shifted down, slowed the truck, and swung it to the curb. He switched off the engine, took a toothpick from his shirt pocket, and stuck it in the corner of his mouth. He leaned back, folded his arms, and stared at four windows near the street entrance of the Kreistein Clinic.

"I remember stuff."

Bentley was sitting in the leather chair that was too big for him. His hands lay on the chair's arms. His dark eyes looked at Dr. Kreistein.

"I remember things that never happened to me," he said. "I know stories that nobody ever told me. But I remember them in somebody else's words. There are all these people. I know their names even though I never saw them."

Dr. Kreistein was still trying to recover from his astonishment. "Tell me the names," he said. Mentally, he was shifting his life back sixty-five years.

"Medea," Bentley said, giving the correct pronunciation, much to Dr. Kreistein's amazement. "Heimdall, Cassandra, Agamemnon, Arthur— that's King Arthur—Gilgamesh, Igraine, Bedivere, Merlin—everybody knows about him—this guy Modred." He frowned, as if puzzled by what he was saying. "It's like I memorized the names. But I didn't."

"They are the names of people in legends," Dr. Kreistein said.

Bentley looked at him for a long moment. Then he nodded. *"Ja,"* he said thoughtfully. "I guess you *would* know them. Maybe I *am* supposed to tell you the secret."

Deitrich Kreistein shook his head gently, The spectacle before him was astounding. *"Supposed* to tell me?" he asked. "What does this mean, please?"

"Maybe you're the teacher," Bentley said. "The cavern angel told me I'd find a teacher who'd help."

The old man pressed two fingers against the upper bridge of his nose and closed his eyes. The transformation in Bentley had happened too abruptly. Dr. Kreistein hadn't had time to assimilate it. The boy knew names from the world's mythology that few eight-year-olds would know. What was absolutely astonishing was the fluent German he had switched into when he began to tell his secret. He was speaking as Dietrich Kreistein had spoken as a child. Bentley was using a dialect of Schleswig-Holstein that had died out during the first decades of the twentieth century.

And now, suddenly, he was talking about some peculiar species of angel.

"I know a *lot* of other stuff I'm supposed to tell you if you're the teacher," Bentley said.

Dr. Kreistein took his hand away from his face. He looked at Bentley. "Whether I am this teacher or not is unimportant. Please. Continue with what you were saying."

Bentley turned his head and looked through the windows. The afternoon sunlight was golden. He saw the soccer players running in a streaming herd on the playing field across the street. The new spring growth was a startling green. Bentley saw a pickup truck parked at the curb. He saw sunlight falling on the face of the pickup's driver.

Bentley stiffened. His hands clenched the arms of the chair. Even at a distance of two hundred feet he could see Willybill's jade eyes as they watched the office windows—and him.

There was a tremor in Bentley's voice as he turned back to Dr. Kreistein. "There's this place I know about. It isn't in the world. It's farther away even than the stars." He glanced uneasily through the office windows and then looked back at the old man again. "I know all the words and names," he said as if he were truly whispering a secret that he didn't want anyone to overhear. "But I don't understand all of them. The place beyond the stars is called Te Kore-nui." He blinked. "I don't know what that means."

Dr. Kreistein was puzzled by the boy's sudden agitation. "Te Kore-nui," he said, "is a word used by the Maori people of New Zealand in their legends—you understand what it is, a legend, *ja?* —in their old stories, the Maori speak of Te Kore-nui, the great void. It means an empty space. Where did you learn this name?"

"I don't know," Bentley said. "It's always been in my brain." He glanced at the windows again. "Listen," he said to Dr. Kreistein, "it *isn't* an empty space. There's this huge hurricane in it. It's full of thunder and lightning, and the winds tear around faster and faster close to the center. The noise is awful." He had begun to tremble visibly. "That's where *he* lives. At the center of the hurricane. I didn't make it up. Honest."

Dr. Kreistein nodded. "Do not concern yourself with what I am thinking. Speak whatever comes into your mind."

"It's *always* been in my brain," Bentley said. "It's like you said—I know about a whole lot of stuff that happened before I was born."

The old man grunted. "This storm. It is, perhaps, something you dreamed about and it frightened you?"

Bentley shook his head hard. "I never dreamed about Te Kore-nui," he said, his voice low and conspiratorial. "I just *know.*"

Dietrich Kreistein nodded again. "And who is this person who lives there?"

Bentley sank back in the leather chair. His eyes

looked feverish with excitement. *Maybe it is fear,* the old man thought. *Perhaps he is frightened by what he is about to say, as if it were a taboo.*

Whatever had affected him, Bentley was being transformed yet again. His voice slid into the soft, rhythmic murmur of one reciting a liturgy he had learned by rote.

"He is the great blasphemy," Bentley chanted, his eyes fixed on Dr. Kreistein's face. "He is the bastard child of a love lost before the world began. Therefore, he hates the works of love. Since time first sprang from the vineyards of Creation, he has fought against all gods devoutly loved by men."

He stopped speaking. His dark eyes glittered as they looked across the office. Beads of perspiration had begun to show on his cheeks and forehead. The child in Bentley had become submerged beneath a message that had to be delivered urgently.

Dr. Kreistein watched him. *This,* he thought, *is what was once called possession.* He cleared his throat. "These gods you speak of—"

"Every god ever worshipped devoutly in the hearts of men is the one true god!" Bentley whispered.

Say nothing, Dietrich Kreistein told himself. *Do not question too deeply. What we have here is a child with an extraordinary imagination. And vocabulary.*

Bentley's gaze hadn't wavered. "This storm lord, the Dreaded One, is the poisoner of the world!" he chanted, the tempo of his voice increasing. "He is the author of our rages, our guilt and despair! No mortal escapes his wrath, because every mortal, aloud or in secret, beseeches a god.

"From his far kingdom at the center of Te Kore-nui, the Lord of Nightmares dispatches vile charms to blight the suicide's soul, lash the tyrant's mind with bloody fantasies, and inspires all fanatic schemes! He weaves the dreams of necrophiles. Every war, vow of revenge, and human cruelty is his work! His eye is the fire of cataclysm, his breath is the wind of immoral pestilence, and his stench hovers as shame in the house of fratricide!" Bentley was now sitting up straight in the leather chair. His whole body was shaking. His eyes were furnaces of fervor. "He is the poet of the hypocrite's sonnet! He composes catechisms for inquisitor and heretic alike! The blood of Medea's mother-murdered children is on his head! At his command the witches of Arras kissed the filth hole of a goat . . ."

Dr. Kreistein was becoming alarmed. He pushed back his chair, rose, and crossed the office. Bentley was trembling. His face was damp as he chanted his rhetoric in a swift flow of north German dialect.

"*Ko* is his hexagram, his number is the shunned thirteen . . ."

Dietrich Kreistein put his hand on the boy's shoulder and shook him gently. "Desist!" he commanded.

Bentley stared up at him. "The Roman poet called him *Umbras*," he muttered between clenched teeth, "the shadow the soul sees at birth. To the Greeks he was *Ombras*, the thunderstorm . . ."

"Enough!" the doctor said, shaking Bentley's shoulder again.

Bentley closed his mouth. His trembling began to subside as he looked at the sagging old face above him.

Dr. Kreistein took a handkerchief from his pocket, examined it, muttered something to himself, and handed it to Bentley.

Bentley mopped his face. "The war's beginning again," he said.

"I am not aware of any war . . ."

The boy got out of his chair. He went to the window and stared at Willybill sitting in the pickup truck. Bentley's whole body was taut. His mind felt as if the great storm, Te Kore-nui, was in it. The words of the stories he knew and had always known were swarming in his brain.

He turned around. Dr. Kreistein was standing at his desk, peering through the windows, trying to see what Bentley saw in the spring afternoon.

Bentley crossed the office and stood at the desk as the old man reseated himself.

Dr. Kreistein looked at the boy. He was shaking again.

And again the liturgical chanting began to flow from him, still in German. "A thousand times Ombra's power has swelled beyond its proportion in the cosmos," said the ageless voice coming from Bentley. "And a thousand times the seers have foretold his arrival in the world. Cassandra saw the plain of Troy darken as the armies of Agamemnon came from the sea. Ombra had taken mortal form and was among them, incarnated as a barbarian warlord. Merlin had a nightmare about ravens and castles. He interpreted it to mean that Ombra would soon appear and assault Arthur the Iron-Giver. Merlin's prophecy came true. King Arthur was a hero of the borrowed heart. Ombra is the lord of every nightmare . . ."

Dietrich Kreistein was about to calm Bentley again. But something made the old man pause. His instincts told him to let the transformed boy continue—and to interrogate the strange persona that had seized him.

The psychiatrist folded his hands and rested his arms on the desk. "A hero of the borrowed heart," he asked, "what does it mean?"

"A thousand times the sunless noon of heaven dimmed," Bentley chanted, "a thousand times the tides of sin and woe rose in the world. At such times the one god who is all gods summoned a soul to his service. This soul was endowed with the borrowed heart that beat in the breasts of legend's immortal heroes. It quickened in Hercules when he saw the Hydra. It cried warning to Gilgamesh as the smoke of Khumbaba rose about him.

"The soul made divine by the borrowed heart goes to the great grotto where the cavern angel gives him instructions for his life. The soul is born in a human body. This mortal must fulfill the destiny of heaven's cause—to summon Ombra to the world, fight him, and try to destroy him so that the balance of the cosmos will be restored to its equal proportions of the light which is god and the darkness which is Ombra's evil."

Dr. Kreistein was listening intently. "Very well," he said when Bentley had paused for

breath. "And the man with the borrowed heart—
how does he summon this Ombra?"

Bentley's dark eyes smoldered. He put both his
hands on the desk. "The warrior of heaven is given
the power of hearing what other men cannot hear.
He can enchant and be enchanted. He finds the
stone of Ra in the waters of the world—"

"Ra, the Egyptian diety?"

"At the moment the hero finds the stone, Ombra
reenters the world," Bentley continued as if he
hadn't heard the question. "Ombra comes at that
instant to attack the surrogate of god. He lays
temptations before the warrior. Ombra terrorizes
him and paralyzes him with the sorcery of mortal
circumstance.

"If the hero of the borrowed heart survives all
that Ombra does to him—and many have not—
Lord Ombra will incarnate himself. He takes the
form of that which his mortal enemy fears the
most! Then they fight until one of them is killed."

Dr. Kreistein leaned back in his chair. He had
passed from astonishment to fascination. What
the boy had invented in his fevered mind was in-
genious. It was a concept that every great hero
legend could be twisted to fit.

Bentley's fervor seemed to be draining out of
him. "It has happened a thousand times," he said
softly. "Now it is going to happen again."

Dr. Kreistein suddenly realized that he was *too*
fascinated. That part of him which was a scholar
of folklore was being seduced by Bentley's tale.
The old man reminded himself that he was also a
doctor. Children's minds. He felt a flutter of irritation at himself.

"It is an interesting story," he said, fixing Bentley with a stern look. "But it makes no sense. This war is *not* going to happen again," he said firmly. "If your bogeyman is killed by our friend the hero—" He raised both hands and shrugged. *"Kaput.* No more Herr Ombra—"

"He's a prince," Bentley said.

"—no more *Prinz* Ombra. Everybody lives happily ever after." He pulled a second handkerchief from his pocket and blew his nose. "Sit down," he said. He stuffed the handkerchief back into his pocket and looked at the dossier lying on the desk before him. "Sit. Now it is time we spoke English," he said in English.

"If Ombra is killed," Bentley answered in German," He will be reborn at the core of the hurricane. If the hero of heaven dies, the world will darken with evil and chaos until Ombra's powers of blasphemous invention are exhausted."

Dr. Kreistein was getting exasperated. The fantasy was going too far. "I have enjoyed the story," he said. "You will now please sit down and be calm so that we can discuss this behavior of yours that everybody complains about." He felt that Bentley was challenging him, daring the old man to try restoring him to reality.

"You don't believe me," Bentley said.

Dr. Kreistein contemplated him in silence for a moment. He couldn't gauge the boy's state of mind —whether he was still possessed by his story or had reemerged into reality. It could be risky to challenge Bentley's fantasy; it could make the boy retreat in distrust. Still, he had to be brought back to earth eventually.

"What you have said is difficult to believe," the old man said. "But for the moment, it is not important. Sit down."

"I know things about Arthur you don't know," Bentley said.

Dr. Kreistein was startled. It was as if the boy had somehow found out that Dietrich Kreistein had spent the last three years writing a major critical study of the many King Arthur legends. The scholar in the old man was tempted. It would be interesting to see how this boy's imaginative— maybe intuitive—mind would rework the great Iron Age myth to fit his Prince Ombra fantasy.

"Another time," the old man answered. "Someday we will engage in a discussion of—"

"Excalibur was the gift of iron," Bentley said.

Dr. Kreistein sniffed. It might be useful for Bentley's therapy to hear the boy's construction of classical legends.

"Very well," he said, giving into his curiosity. "One more story. But you will sit down and try not to excite yourself."

Bentley looked out the windows again. The pickup truck was gone.

He turned back to Dr. Kreistein. *"Na ja, gut,"* he replied quietly.

"And there is no reason to go on addressing me in the dialect of my childhood. I am perfectly capable of understanding . . ."

Bentley had returned to the chair. He slid back in it and put his hands on the leather arms. "Merlin made Niniane learn Welsh so that she could understand him when he taught her his magic," he said. "She was Cornish. Like Igraine."

"And you"—the old man reverted to German and used the intimate *du*—"are going to teach me some magic, hah?"

Bentley nodded. The feverish look had left his eyes. His face was somber.

Dr. Kreistein settled himself more comfortably in his chair and folded his hands over his stomach. "Proceed."

"I remember Arthur from the beginning," Bentley said quietly, slipping back into the timeless syntax he had used during his seizures. "My heart died his mortal death with him at Camlann."

And then Dietrich Kreistein suddenly understood everything. *It is why he became so agitated and afraid,* the old man told himself. *He believes he is a warrior of the borrowed heart in his story! He thinks he must fight this Ombra!*

Many are the faces that Prince Ombra has worn as he prowled the world, stalking the heroes of heaven, tricking them, tempting them, and, finally, dueling to the death with them if all of his sorceries failed. When he appears as a living being, it is in the form of that which his warrior-enemy fears the most. Ombra has been the monstrous Cyclops that made Odysseus weak with terror, he was the fire-headed axman who struck down mighty Cu Chulainn, the Hound of Culann, at the great carnage of Mag Muirthemne. Ombra was the multiheaded serpent slain by Hercules and by Susano, the divine Samurai. Once he turned himself into a knight of surpassing beauty to freeze the heart of a king. The knight's name was Modred.

From the moment of Arthur's birth, the borrowed heart that heaven had implanted in him knew
that Lord Ombra was watching him from the core
of the blasphemous vortex. Arthur was not yet a
man when the Lord of Nightmares beguiled fortune to lure Arthur away from the asceticism and
piety that formed his true nature.

Arthur Pendragon lived in a time of the world
when some of the Celtic tribes possessed the
secret of making iron and the other tribes did not.
All that these primitive Celts knew was that their
more powerful neighbors somehow got iron from
stones. When Arthur drew the sword from the
stone, his rememberer, the teller of his tale, was
making a poetic allegory to describe what really
happened. Arthur had discovered the secret of
making iron from stones. This is the real meaning
of the Excalibur legend. Arthur gave his people
power and, in return, they made him their king.

His deepest yearning was for holiness. But Ombra had enchanted his life. With his magic he had
guided Arthur to the act that made him a king.
When that was done, the Lord of Nightmares afflicted him with uncontrollable lust. Ombra's sorceries led Arthur to his half sister, Morgause.
Within the king, heaven's rectitude and the yearn-
ings of doomed flesh fought their senseless battle.
On the night that Arthur possessed Morgause, all
of his life's contentment was destroyed. God *is*
whatever devout men believe him to be. Arthur
knew that he had broken the laws of god and man
as he understood them.

Bentley looked at Dr. Kreistein. "I know the

words," he said. "But I don't know what it means.
What happened?"

"It means that King Arthur did a bad thing," the
old man replied. "He knew it was bad."

"But he was a hero!"

"And at the same time he was an ordinary man,"
Dr. Kreistein said. "Please, continue with the
story. Later, perhaps, I will explain it to you."

Arthur's fate gathered around him. Morgause
left him. At the court of another king she gave
birth to Modred, the whelp of their incestuous
coupling.

"I don't know what that means either," Bentley
said.

"Someday you will," Dr. Kreistein answered.
"Proceed."

Arthur had begotten his own, terrible enemy.
Ombra had returned to the world in Modred's
body. Modred *was* Ombra.

Thereafter, Arthur the Iron-Giver believed that
god had abandoned him. His borrowed heart told
him it wasn't true. But the king's guilt fought
against the light of divinity within him. He no
longer listened to his teacher, Merlin.

Arthur never knew happiness again. He inherited the great mandala that was called the
Round Table. But his most splendid knight, Lance-
lot, rose in rebellion against Camelot. He betrayed
the king with Queen Guinevere. Knight murdered
knight as the years of Arthur proceeded on their
terrible course. Bards sing of quests and adven-

tures. But Arthur was incapable of conceiving, with purity's imagination, the object of the greatest quest—the grail. A day did not pass—in barren winter or the glory of summer—in which he was free of his yearning for Morgause—and he despised himself for his obsession. Every hour of his hopeless love for his half sister was an affront to his god.

Meanwhile, far from Arthur's tormented existence, Modred grew to manhood. He was a knight endowed with great beauty and valor. His eyes were Morgause's eyes. His smile was his mother's smile. He was evil, and his grace was evil's disguise.

Then, in the last winter, the old king turned once again to the field of war to crush the revolt of Modred. Arthur went with his knights and army to the frozen battleground of Camlann to confront the throngs of his bastard son.

Great was the slaughter on the sward of mud and ice between the dark hills. All that day, as his knights—good men, failed men, men of no importance—fell about him, King Arthur searched for his own death. His borrowed heart sang of hope to him. But amid the clash and roar and the screams of the dying, Arthur, as he fought his way toward Modred, did not hear.

By twilight Camlann had become a quagmire of blood. Corpses lay everywhere, one with a frozen hand clutching the haft of a sword, another kneeling, bent over its disemboweled gut as if in prayer. Only four men remained alive in the cold dusk— Arthur the King, Modred, and two of Arthur's knights.

Exhausted, his body bleeding from a dozen wounds, the king confronted Modred at last. At last pure evil was face to face with a mortal who, for all of his imperfections, bore heaven's eternal heart in his breast.

Modred and Arthur were scarcely human. The great warhelms that covered their heads gave them slits for eyes. Their voices spoke from within those drums of hammered iron. Arthur stood with the sword Excalibur in his hands; it was the symbol of his tribe's power. In his leather belt wallet he carried a small black stone, the stone of Ra, which is the talisman of heaven's heroes. Arthur had found it in the waters below Dunpeldyr on the day that Modred was born. He knew what the stone was—but he carried it now only as a token of his lost faith.

Arthur saw Modred, armed with a short war ax, and the king rejoiced. He swung his great sword with both arms. Its gory blade flashed in the dull light. He saw Modred move—but, so dim was Arthur's eye, so eager was he for the final exchange, that he didn't realize that Modred had lifted his helm from his head and had cast it away from him.

Then, in his final moment, Arthur Pendragon's great strength was suddenly paralyzed. Adoration and hatred, yearning and revulsion possessed him as he looked upon that which he feared the most.

He looked upon the face of Modred. In it, he saw Morgause's face reflected—she was his greatest mortal passion, a love that had stained every day of his royal life. Modred smiled Morgause's smile as he raised his war ax for the kill. Arthur was overcome by the unholy love that had, in his mind, banished him from the blessing of the god he had been born to serve. His love for Morgause was his greatest terror.

Seconds became eternities as the king averted his eyes from that dreaded face. He glanced aside and saw the garden of death all around him. He saw the dark slopes of the vale rising to a cold winter sky.

And then, in an instant that redeemed his life, Arthur saw a strange, luminous figure. It was a knight seated on a gray horse at the edge of the forest of Camlann. His armor and unhelmeted head glowed with a silver nimbus in the twilight. This enchanted knight caught Arthur's gaze. It was the cavern angel who had given the king instruction for his life, and the angel's eyes burned with an unuttered demand: *Choose, son of Uther Pendragon and Lord of Camelot, choose now between the profane love of your mortality and the mission of your eternal soul!*

As he recognized the cavern angel, King Arthur knew, at last, that he was still the servant of heaven and that his worldly life was but a moment of torment. He heard the borrowed heart for the last time—crying to him that god had not abandoned him, pealing to him to acknowledge that his mortal love was the enemy of god. To regain the bliss of paradise he had but to rid the world of Ombra, who cursed it.

The Iron-Giver heard his heart. He swung Excalibur in a mighty slash across Modred's throat. Arthur Pendragon lived a moment longer; he heard Ombra's death-scream as Modred's ax came down in a blow that split the king's helm and crushed his skull.

Two survivors rode away from the bloody field of Camlann that evening. One was a knight named Bedivere who, according to legend, threw the sword Excalibur and the stone of Ra into a lake.

The story of Bedivere is true. The other knight was his brother, Lucan, an insignificant man in all respects save one.

This Sir Lucan was the rememberer of Arthur the King.

The cries of the soccer players were heard no more in the waning afternoon. The shadows lay longer on the wet playing fields and the street beyond Dr. Kreistein's windows.

The office was silent for a long moment. The old man grunted and reached for the wart on top of his head. "It is an old tale," he said. "You tell it in a different way. Very interesting."

"I know the words," Bentley said, "but I don't understand what a lot of the story means."

Dr. Kreistein didn't answer for a moment. The part of him that was a scholar of mythology had a dozen questions. The part of him that was a child psychiatrist warned him again not to enter too deeply into the boy's fantasies.

The scholar couldn't resist the desire to know more.

"This stone you speak of . . ."

Bentley was slumped back in the leather chair. His face was somber. "It's called the stone of Ra," he said. "A god left it in a sea."

"Nun," the old man muttered. "The sea is called Nun. It is part of an Egyptian legend, the first story about the creation of the world."

"Every one of those thousand guys found the stone," Bentley said. "It's a sort of protection. If they lose it . . ."

The psychiatrist part of Dietrich Kreistein nudged his mind. "It is, as I told you, an interesting story," he said. "But now we must return to—"

"I'm going to find that stone," Bentley said. "I think I'm going to find it pretty soon." He blinked. "I'm scared."

The old man folded his hands. He pursed his mouth and contemplated the boy in silence.

Perhaps, Dr. Kreistein said to himself, *what we have here is a business of multiple personalities.* He immediately dismissed the idea; none of the psychotic personalities could know more than their eight-year-old creator.

"Maybe *I'll* do something bad," Bentley said.

Dr. Kreistein raised his eyebrows. "Are you suggesting that you have done something which upsets you, something that would make you stand in front of a truck and nearly be killed so that your father would forgive you?"

"I mean like *Arthur,*" Bentley said. "He did something bad and Ombra nearly beat him."

Dr. Kreistein pushed away his irritation at the boy's stubborn hold on his fantasy. The old man felt the need to retake control of the conversation. He looked down at the dossier on the desk and began scanning it once more, searching for facts that would help him bring the boy back to reality. "It is natural to make up such stories as yours," he

said as he read. "Everybody your age does this."
He switched into English. "But it is important to
understand the difference between—"

"Anna," Bentley said, suddenly but softly.

Dr. Kreistein jerked up his head. There was an
astonished look on his face. "Please?"

Bentley was still slumped in the chair. His
hands still rested on its leather arms.

"Anna," he said again. "Ombra has already
come to the world once in your lifetime, and you
know it." Bentley was still speaking German. His
eyes shone, and he resumed the chanting in which
his altered personality had first addressed Dietrich Kreistein. "It was many years ago. For the
thousandth time Ombra burst from the tempest,
carrying the darkness with him. A warrior of god
rushed to confront him. Ombra had incarnated
himslf as a fanatic man with many followers. He
tempted the hero with power, he terrorized him
and then destroyed him and his rememberer in a
holocaust of fire and death. Thereafter, Ombra became a ferocious leader. He spewed forth a
madness. Anna and millions of others perished in
it."

Dietrich Kreistein was stunned. He felt violated,
as if Bentley had stolen a fact of the old man's life
that was only bearable if nobody knew about it.

"Avenge Anna!" Bentley whispered, leaning forward in the chair, his eyes burning. "Believe me!
Help me!"

"These events you speak of were the result of
history!" Dr. Kreistein snapped. "Politics! Eco-
nomics!"

"My heart was there," Bentley said.

"Me also!"

"You heard the voice of Ombra!"

"I was *really* there!" Dr. Kreistein said in a rush of angry German. "I heard no voices! I saw no bogeyman!"

"You heard Ombra," Bentley answered. "You can still hear his voice!"

Dr. Kreistein slumped in his chair. He was shaking. It was the guilt, he told himself. It was the rush of insupportable recollection from the chambers of his own mind.

There was a new urgency in Bentley's eyes. "You heard Ombra making the promise that drove a nation mad with joy! Remember!"

Heute Deutschland! Morgen die Welt! When Dietrich Kreistein lost control over his memory, when memory burst from the darkness within him, carrying darkness to the surface of his life, it always came first as sounds—the terrible, rhythmic, marching in the streets of night, the breaking of doors, glass smashing, the screams, and the music blaring from the felt-covered speakers of radios. One sound, above all others, followed him when he left Germany. It was that hypnotic voice shrilling its prophecy. He read its words in the headlines as newspapers reported the madness. He heard it on overseas broadcasts. *Today Germany! Tomorrow the world!*

The old man closed his eyes. He reminded himself again that he was a healer of children's minds. It was both absurd and terrible that his own mind could oppress him so after all these years.

He felt a hand touch his arm.

He opened his eyes. Bentley was standing beside

him. His round face looked anxious. "Are you okay?" he asked in the small voice of an uncertain eight-year-old boy. He was speaking English.

Dr. Kreistein forcibly drew away from the memory.

"You came over all funny," Bentley said. "I thought you got sick or something."

The old man pushed himself upright in his chair. "I am this okay you speak of," he mumbled. The onslaught of grief was receding in him. "You will excuse me," he said. "I was having another thought while you were speaking. Believe me, this happens frequently even when we are engaged in discussions that are very interesting."

He flapped his hand at Bentley. "Go sit. We will continue the conversation." He blew his nose as Bentley crossed the office and sat down in the big leather chair again. As order returned to the old man's thoughts, he decided there were too many questions to consider. For the present he would consolidate a relationship with the boy.

Bentley was looking at him reproachfully. "I bet you think I'm goofy."

"It is not important," the old man said. "What is important is what *you* believe. This is what we must discuss." He settled himself comfortably in his chair again. "Perhaps, to help me understand, you will now explain why you were standing in front of a truck on this road?"

"I was trying to make myself brave," Bentley said. "I wanted to see if I could do it."

"To prepare yourself for Prinz Ombra."

Bentley nodded.

Dr. Kreistein sniffed. "In your story you say this

Ombra will make himself into the shape of what
you are most afraid of. And which shape is that
going to be?"

Bentley looked across the office at the late afternoon sunlight on the wall. "I don't know what I'm
scared of most," he said.

"Ahah," the old man said softly. "So. This is the
problem. To find out what it is, your deepest fear."

Bentley nodded. "So I can be ready when Ombra
comes."

"For this reason, for that reason. This discovery
is something I can help you with."

Bentley stared at him. "Did you really know
what I am?"

Dr. Kreistein shoved some papers around on his
desk. "We know something. We don't know something. It isn't important." He raised his head.
"What is important is this riddle of yours. To find
out what it is you are most afraid of."

Bentley nodded.

"Then you must come back so that we can discuss it."

"Okay," Bentley said. "I have to come back anyway. If I don't, MrGraw will arrest me again." He
looked anxiously at the old man. "You haven't said
yet if you believe me."

The question made Dr. Kreistein feel oddly un-
comfortable. There was a conflict beginning
within him whose opposing forces he hadn't yet
identified. "It is too early for me to tell you this. It
depends."

"On what?"

"I must think about it."

"Okay," Bentley said.

"A few questions, please. There is a German woman who is housekeeper for your father. She is old? Like me?"

"She's a girl. She goes to the university."

"So," Dr. Kreistein said. "Then where did you learn the German language you have been speaking here this afternoon?"

Bentley shrugged. "It's like I told you. I just know things. I knew it."

"When did you know it?"

Bentley was silent a moment. "I didn't know how to speak it before. It came into my brain after you started talking to me."

"And the Drake girl, the mooky-mooky talker. You just listened to her, her talk became intelligible in this remarkable brain of yours?"

Bentley nodded.

The old man looked down at the dossier on his desk. His inner conflict was beginning to take shape. He was confronted with something totally unfamiliar to that part of him that was a medical scientist. What shook Dietrich Kreistein was that, as a mythologist, he understood Bentley perfectly.

The old man closed his dossier. "It is time for you to go away. I must think. Somebody will telephone your father to arrange for the next time you will come and see me."

Bentley slid off the chair. He stood in the middle of the office for a moment. "Does this mean you're going to be my teacher?"

Dr. Kreistein's sagging face studied the boy for a moment. The old man had learned long before never to make promises to disturbed children. He was surprised to hear his own answer.

"Yes. This means I will be your teacher."

Dietrich Kreistein walked home slowly in the dusk—a thick, stooped old man wearing a brown fedora. He carried a leather briefcase with a broken strap. His own doctor had told him to walk as much as he could because of his heart. He had been sick with it for half the winter.

He was so engrossed in his thoughts that he didn't notice a battered pickup truck rattling past him in the spring evening.

His younger associates at the clinic had been excited after the Ellicott boy left with his father. Bentley had tested out as a pre-schizophrenic, a child torn between reality and an incomprehensible fantasy. What excited the testing psychologists at the Kreistein Clinic was the possibility that the Drake girl was also schizoid. That raised the possibility that schizophrenics might transmit thoughts to each other in some way.

Dr. Kreistein was unimpressed. *They are grasping at small straws,* he told himself as he proceeded along the sidewalk in the dusk. *Science thinks altogether too small.*

The old man knew a vast range of theories about the emotional illnesses of childhood. None of them could explain Bentley Ellicott.

Science was unable to explain how the boy's altered personality could know more than even an eight-year-old genius would know. Science couldn't explain the boy's flawless command of a German dialect that hadn't been spoken for sixty years. Children take stories literally. They are not analysts. Yet the Ellicott boy had come up with a brilliant explanation of what the Arthur legend really meant.

Above all, there was no psychiatric theory that could explain how Bentley Ellicott knew a secret so deeply buried in Dr. Kreistein's heart that he had never discussed it, not even with his wife, who had died six years before.

It was a secret poisoned with the guilt of the survivor. Dietrich Kreistein had fled alone from Hitler's Germany. He had come to America, finished his studies, married, and, from the safety of a university campus on the northern coast, he had read the newspapers and listened to the radio as ruinous armies smashed their way across Europe. Cities burned and Jews like himself were annihilated without even the dignity of being accused of a crime.

That insanity couldn't be explained by science, either.

He stopped to catch his breath, setting his briefcase on the sidewalk. He looked at the fading light in the western sky and saw Mercury, or perhaps it was Venus, gleaming at him as the evening star.

Darkness and light, the old man thought. *It is what every hero legend is about. The darkness which is more than death, the light which is love, like our friend Venus here, or perhaps this star is Mercury, the messenger of Olympus, the bringer of hope.*

For fifty years the old man had studied mythology—first as an avenue into the recesses of the unconscious mind, eventually to discover what ancient men knew and modern men have all but forgotten. To him, this was not unscientific or fanciful. Baby chicks are born knowing that the hawk's silhouette in the sky threatens them. Man is born with the innate knowledge of a shadow, too. For centuries legends spoke of it, and of the war between the shadow and the redemptory powers of light in the human soul.

Dietrich Kreistein had stood in the caves of the Dordogne valley and Ariège, where the walls glow with polychrome symbol paintings of primitive men. He had seen opaque splendors shimmering in the friezes and stelai of ancient Egypt—and a threatening darkness surrounded them. The old doctor had read deeply in the wanderings of Assyrian hero-kings, and he thought he knew what the sophisticated mind of prehistoric Greece was trying to say to him. The mysticism of the Celts and the god-demon stories of American Indians were repeating the same, timeless tale of war between a darkness profoundly sensed in human intuition and its opponents, the heros of legend who served the power of light. Dr. Kreistein had become as famous for his critical studies of the world's mythology as he was for his work with disturbed children.

He adjusted his fedora on his head, picked up his briefcase, and moved on toward his house, which stood tall and frilled with Victorian trim against the twilight.

Science is nothing more than facts we have learned, he told himself for the hundredth time. *What we have learned has made us forget what we were born knowing.* That was the conclusion the old man had finally come to.

Now, in his eightieth year, Dietrich Kreistein's

private conclusion seemed to be confirmed by a small boy who could not be explained by the facts of science. All that was needed was for the old man to surrender himself to belief. Then the boy could be easily explained; he was telling the truth—he was what he said he was.

Dr. Kreistein turned in at his front walk and stopped at the foot of his porch steps to let his heart decelerate.

He looked up. A figure was standing in the deep shadows of the porch. The old psychiatrist could just make out the shape of a man, legs spread, thumbs hooked into a wide belt. A sheepskin vest dangled from his shoulders. What startled Dr. Kreistein were the jade green eyes that stared down at him, burning in the gloom.

Chapter Four

Bentley lay on the floor, trying not to move. Light from the kitchen beamed up through the floor grate in Slally's bedroom. Its silvery rays were broken apart by the grate's ornate ironwork; cigarette smoke drifted up through the light. He could hear his father and Mrs. Drake talking in the kitchen.

Bentley and Slally had been talking, too; he had turned down the TV sound when they'd begun. Slally had fallen asleep, worn out by talking, with her head on his arm. His arm had gone numb, and he was trying to figure out how to wiggle it free without waking her up. On the TV screen a bunch of men were having a silent gunfight on a brushy hillside. Bentley watched absent-mindedly and thought about everything that had happened since he'd left Dr. Kreistein's office.

Richard Ellicott had been standing in the hall of
the clinic with Mrs. Drake and Slally when Bentley's interview with Dr. Kreistein was over. They
had all driven to the Drakes', with Slally and Bentley in the back seat. Bentley was surprised at the
way his father was talking to Mrs. Drake. She was
really pretty. The collar of her shirt was turned
down over her black sweater; her blond hair fell
over one side of her forehead, and once in a while
she brushed it back. Richard Ellicott kept turning
toward her. His thin face, slender nose, and short-
cropped hair were outlined by the afternoon light.

Halfway there, Slally's mother said she was
divorced. Bentley was amazed when his father
then told her Bentley's mother was dead. Richard
Ellicott never talked to anybody for very long.
Bentley was used to seeing him make polite conversation for a few minutes and then slip back into
his silence.

When they got to the Drake house, Slally went
upstairs to change her clothes. Mrs. Drake took
Richard out into the kitchen. Bentley stood in the
dining room, listening to her light, gay flow of talk
as she cracked open ice trays and got out bottles
and glasses. Bentley's father kept answering her
in his soft voice.

Slally had put on dungarees and a sweat shirt.
She came downstairs, struggled into her anorak,
and took Bentley outside. There wasn't much day
left. The last sunlight was burning low in the
western sky, its light coming through the budding
branches of bushes. The air was cold and the
ground wet. Slally took Bentley around to the
back of the house. There was an orchard of old,

small trees, a compost-covered garden, and a pen
made out of chicken wire. Slally and Bentley
crawled into the pen. She pulled a large brown
rabbit out of its hutch. It lay trembling in her
arms, twitching its nose.

"What's his name?" Bentley asked.

Slally wasn't tight or scared anymore. She said
the rabbit was named for her uncle Grover, who
had tried to teach her to ride a bicycle.

"Do you still have the bike?" Bentley asked.

She nodded.

"Let's get it."

Slally locked the rabbit pen and pulled up the
garage door. She wheeled out a red girl's bicycle
with a rack fastened to the rear fender. First Bentley got her to sit on the rack. He took her to the
end of the street and back up the Drakes' driveway. Then he made her get on the bike herself, sit
on the seat, hold the handlebars, and think hard
about riding instead of falling off. She wobbled
down the driveway, scraping her boots on the
gravel, her large eyes larger than usual. Bentley
limped along beside her, yelling at her to relax.
When he let go of her shoulders, she rode across
the front lawn and into the hedge. She looked
scared as she plunged off the bicycle with both
arms stretched out in front of her. But she got up
grinning.

They wheeled the bicycle back up the driveway.
Bentley saw his father and Mrs. Drake standing in
a bay window, martini glasses in their hands,
watching.

The air got colder as evening began. Slally
pedaled down the driveway eight times all by her-

self, with Bentley hopping along shouting instructions. Each time, she bumped across the lawn, hit the hedge, and fell off. It became a sort of game. Bentley took a turn. He sped down the driveway, shot across the muddy grass, and hit the hedge so hard he nearly went through it. He fell off on his back while Slally clapped and cheered. She still hadn't learned to ride the bike when it was too dark to see anymore. But she liked falling off.

She was red-faced and breathless when they went inside. Lamps had been lit in the living room. Professor Ellicott sat on the sofa with his jacket off. Mrs. Drake was in a low chair. Slally stood between her mother's outstretched legs and jabbered excitedly. Bentley sat beside his father, translating for her, as if that were something all of them had acknowledged as natural all of their lives.

When Slally stopped talking to take off her anorak, Ellen Drake raised her eyes to Richard Ellicott and murmured, "See?"

Richard was looking at Bentley as if he'd never seen him before. "Amazing," he murmured. He leaned forward. "You're a pretty smart kid, you know."

Bentley grinned. "Nah."

"How come you understand her?"

Still grinning, Bentley shrugged. Richard was still halfway out of his sadness. But Bentley had figured that as soon as they got home, everything would be as it always had been for as long as he could remember. He didn't want to hope that his father would keep on holding conversations and not hiding in himself.

"How'd it go with Dr. Kreistein?" Richard asked.

"Okay," Bentley said.

The happiness of the afternoon had made him forget his wonder at being recognized, his own rush of words and stories in German, and Dr. Kreistein's agreement to be his teacher. The specter of Prince Ombra had been far from Bentley's mind. He had dismissed the fearful certainty of what lay ahead in a clutter of bicycles, hedges, and cautious enjoyment of his father's lifted mood.

"He'd rather tell about Dr. Kreistein when you're alone, Richard," Mrs. Drake said. She held out her hand. Bentley was embarrassed, but he took it. "Your father and I have been talking about all of this, lovey," she said. "About how marvelous it is that you can understand Sally. We think it's best not to make too big a thing out of it. Do you understand?"

"Yeah," Bentley said, turning to look up at his father, "but what if she wants to say something and I'm not here?"

"You'll see her again," Professor Ellicott said. He actually smiled.

"Really?" Bentley asked.

His father nodded. "You told her mother that Sally can read. What about writing?"

"She can write numbers but not letters," Bentley said. "She's tried."

"Well," Mrs. Drake said, squeezing his hand and letting go of it, "maybe someday she'll learn how to write. Then she can send notes to everybody."

"Maybe." Bentley answered. He tried to imagine

not being able to talk or write. The imagining
made him feel ignored or desperate, as if he'd been
locked up in a box.

At supper in the kitchen they talked about
things that real families talk about. Slally got a
piece of paper and a pen and wrote numbers for
Professor Ellicott. He drew boxes on the paper
and taught Slally a game he played with other
mathematicians. Once she understood the rules,
she began to beat him at it. Bentley played and
Slally beat him, too.

Upstairs in her room after dinner, they watched
television while Professor Ellicott and Mrs. Drake
talked in the kitchen. Then Bentley and Slally talked. And then Slally fell asleep with her head on his
arm.

Bentley lay on the floor looking at the ceiling.
He listened to the voices from the kitchen below
Slally's bedroom. He could only make out a few
words.

Mrs. Drake said, "But why—"

Bentley's father said something about a rich,
vivid imagination.

Bentley knew they were talking about him. The
feelings of shame with which he had begun the day
started to come back. He'd never told his father
his secret or even hinted that he had one. But his
father didn't believe him anyway.

The shame Bentley felt led him back to remembering the episode that caused it. He had gone out
to the highway to dare the trucks because he knew
that he wasn't going to be able to postpone his
destiny until he was grown up. But he hadn't made

himself brave. He was just as scared as he'd always been.

His relief at being able to tell everything to Dr. Kreistein was fading. Bentley lay looking at the ceiling. The old man could teach him all kinds of stuff. But none of it would change the fact that he'd still have to face the timeless enemy of a thousand heroes, the executioner of many who had been strong and fearless.

Bentley remembered again that his life didn't belong to him.

Chapter Five

Beyond the shores of the farthest sea, beyond the molten rim where the sun sets, in a darkness that no starlight can penetrate, in cold that withers the wings of angels, Te Kore-nui, the hurricane of the cosmos, whirled on its concentric course. Its winds shrieked, thunder crashed in the black core, and the eye of the Storm Lord revolved on its stump of gristle. Prince Ombra was shapeless—save for that eternally watching eye. His seven brains, which radiate all the world's sin and grief, existed as conceptions of themselves. The second brain, which is the seer of all things, glowed with warning as it watched the turning of the world, the coming of spring to Stonehaven, and a boy limping in the sunlight. Lord Ombra's fourth brain, which is memory, heard the soft pealing of Bentley's borrowed heart, and the Dreaded One knew that war was nigh.

His revolving eye saw through all dimensions, past the icy light of a billion universes, and focused its baleful gaze on the boy, who knew his life did not belong to him.

Prince Ombra saw the village. He saw all the people who brooded, hoped, struggled with themselves, loved, and wondered in Stonehaven. Ombra's seventh brain, in which the fury of the cosmos is stored, brightened in the choleric anticipation of battle. Ombra saw that the sunless noon of heaven had dimmed.

He saw the stone of Ra rolling on the bottom of the sea as the tides took it closer to the shores of the northern coast.

He saw a pretty girl washing cups and saucers and laughing to herself.

He saw a gray-haired man striding up the main street of the village, choked with indignation as he clutched the folds of his overcoat to keep them from flapping in the wind.

Ombra saw a woman whose yearning to love struggled with her disdain and fear.

He saw a thin man squatting in a basement, yanking at a rusty pipe with a wrench. The pipe broke. Lord Ombra's third brain, the artisan, instantly crafted a rage. That mortal rage would become insanity, making the cursing man with a pipe wrench the Dreaded One's servant.

Ombra watched Stonehaven in the windy sunlight. He saw the vast uplands of forest, rivers, and granite ledges jutting above lakes carved by glaciers when the world was young.

The Lord of Nightmares knew now the ground on which he would fight his thousand and first battle. He saw the boy riding a bicycle toward the village. Ombra knew now who his enemy would be. He saw a seven-year-old girl sitting on the back of the bicycle, holding on, her hair streaming in the wind. Ombra knew now whom fate had cast as the rememberer for the thousand and first warrior of the borrowed heart.

Stonehaven understands some things about its life. It assumes other things to be true.

Everybody in the village knew why the Reverend Homer Tally was fired by his congregation. He had become a drunk and a public embarrassment. After he disappeared, his wife started referring to herself as a widow. Mrs. Tally was a striking-looking woman with gray hair who went around making instant judgments on everybody. Usually they were negative, and rarely could argument or evidence change her mind. Mrs. Tally expressed herself in a tart manner and was not good at listening. She made people nervous. Hardly anyone bothered crossing her. Nobody else in Stonehaven regarded her as a widow.

Mrs. Tally was Stonehaven't figure of righteous indignation. Charlie Feavey, who sat on the basement floor of his decaying Stonehaven House Hotel, swearing as brown water gushed from a broken water pipe, was the village's figure of contempt. He was a thin, hard man with a face like an angry bird. He rarely bathed. He was always broke. He was a morose, unrelenting drinker, a skillful deer hunter, and a quarreler with almost everybody. Most people in Stonehaven assumed that Charlie Feavey was one of nature's mistakes, and they could see no reason for his life.

Mrs. Tally and Charlie Feavy were the village's moral extremes. They were obsessed with each other but rarely exchanged a word. They reinforced each other. Mrs. Tally said that a man who showed depraved tendencies was going to end up like Charlie Feavey. When reproached or argued with, Charlie snarled that his critic had caught a dose of whatever it was that made Old Lady Tally a bitch.

Everybody in Stonehaven knew that Polly Woodhouse, the soda fountain girl in the drugstore, was the illegitimate daughter of Chief McGraw's father and Grace Woodhouse. Polly had been born in one of the house trailers that littered the road leading south out of the village. Her mother and father had left town without her when she was eleven. There had been scandals over debts, drinking, and Mrs. McGraw's suicide. McGraw and his wife tried to adopt Polly, but the state went to court for her custody. She was raised in foster homes, and her dreams were haunted by the memory of her parents being driven away. Awake, she was a merry girl with a voluptuous figure. She was now eighteen and lived alone in her mother's dilapidated house trailer. Men and boys sometimes visited her at night.

Stonehaven assumed that she was wanton. Like mother, like daughter.

On that windy May morning Polly was behind the soda fountain in the drugstore, washing coffee cups and chortling to herself. She had a slangy

way of talking and ribald laughter. Polly's face
was round and her eyes were almost always bright
with good feelings; her blond hair was tied up by a
blue bandanna she wore as a scarf. She had on a
gray T-shirt and a white apron over her large
breasts.

Mrs. Tally had long since decided that the gleam
in Polly's eye was wickedness. Secretly, the self-
designated widow of Reverend Tally wanted to
take Polly home, scrub her with a brush to cleanse
her of sin's odors and bruises, and turn her into a
lovely girl. But, since fear allies itself with anger
to wage war against love in the troubled heart,
Mrs. Tally couldn't stop herself from needling the
girl and expressing her motherly instinct by disapproval.

Polly grinned and raised her head, remembering
the expression on Elias Cutter's face. She looked
through the drugstore windows. Bentley Ellicott
was riding by with a little girl on the fender rack
of his bicycle. Polly wiped her hands on a dish
towel and walked over to the windows.

The child riding behind Bentley wasn't familiar.
Polly saw her blond hair streaming in the wind.
The little girl was holding onto Bentley's belt,
dragging the tips of her sneakers along the ground
and looking anxious as if she was afraid she'd fall
off. Polly was glad that Bentley had a new friend.
He hadn't been himself since he fought with dopey
Joe Persis.

Elias Cutter glanced at the Ellicott boy as he
walked up the street from the drugstore. He had
just finished his morning coffee and was deciding
all over again that Polly Woodhouse was a per-

fect example of what was wrong with young people. Polly sometimes called this last, surviving
member of the Stonehaven aristocracy "Pappy."
She'd just done it again. As the lean, gray-haired
banker got up from his counter stool, Polly had
grinned at him and said, "Have a sexy day,
Pappy."

Mr. Cutter went into his bank and carefully closed
the door against the blustery day. The marble
floor and carved woodwork of the interior hadn't
been altered since the time of Elias Cutter's grand-
father. The bank's hushed, dignified setting
always soothed him. He hung up his overcoat and
sat down at his desk. Spring sunlight streamed
through the windows. Mr. Cutter saw Mrs. Tally
getting out of her car and crossing Main Street
toward the drugstore.

The woman, he thought to himself, was a fool—
going around calling herself a widow when everybody knew her husband was alive and probably
getting drunk somewhere. Mrs. Tally still blamed
Cutter for what had happened. Elias Cutter was
president of the Congregationalist committee that
had voted to fire Reverend Tally. But his cons-
cience was clear. He'd tried to save the wretched
clergyman's job.

He thought about Polly Woodhouse's offensive
remark. A little outrage still tingled within the
sixty-three-year-old bachelor. He wondered why
everybody was flawed. He didn't wonder why he
saw flaws first whenever he looked at someone.

Polly dried the last saucer and put it on top of a
stack. She looked through the drugstore windows
again and saw Mrs. Tally coming up the street.

Polly tried to think about something pleasant.

Bentley stood in the middle of the playground holding the handlebars of his bike. He was watching Slally wrestle herself onto the lowest branch of an old maple tree. He'd told her about climbing with Joe Persis. Slally had said she'd never climbed a tree in her life. She was hesitant when Bentley told her to see if she could get up into the maple. He said he'd help. Slally said no. She walked across the playground and jumped until she grabbed the thick, low branch. Now she was almost sitting on it.

Bentley held his bicycle and watched her. His father and Mrs. Drake had talked on the telephone four times since Tuesday, as far as Bentley knew. Maybe they'd talked some more when he wasn't around. On Thursday Richard told Bentley that the Drakes were coming down for lunch on Saturday. Bentley began to plan all the things in Stonehaven he was going to show to Slally. His father had become more talkative and cheerful.

Bentley listened to the wind in the sunny morning. He heard hawk's whistle and crab chant in the second air. He felt an anticipatory shrinking in his middle. Something was about to happen.

Slally was sitting on the tree branch grinning. She'd managed to climb up there without any help. She waved.

"Come on down," Bentley yelled. "There's a place I want to show you on the way home!"

Slally lay down on the branch, slid her legs off, grabbed with both hands, dangled, and dropped

onto the grass. She looked less scared than she
had when she'd arrived with her mother at 10:30.
She was still grinning as she walked across the
playground toward him.

Bentley suppressed his apprehension. He was
determined to have fun with Slally. "There's this
creepy old hotel," he said. "We can go look in the
windows. It's really *old*."

Slally said okay. She didn't seem to be worried
about going to see a creepy old hotel. When she
seated herself on the fender rack behind Bentley,
she put her arms around his waist.

Polly crushed out her cigarette and tried to
laugh. She'd been having a running joke with herself all morning because a car had driven past her
trailer after midnight the night before. The headlights had swept over McGraw, who was standing
talking in the door of her trailer. Anybody who
didn't know they were half brother and half sister
would have thought that the police chief was leaving after a high old time.

Polly was certain that everybody—and especially Mrs. Tally, who had stopped to look at the window of the wool shop—thought that the soda fountain girl was sleeping with all the men and boys
who visited her trailer in the evenings. She wasn't.
Polly Woodhouse was a virgin. She had a lure
more powerful than sex. She was a rapt listener
because her mind was uncluttered with thoughts
about herself. Men started talking to her in the
drugstore and then followed her home, where they
told her their troubles and dreams. So did some
women. Sometimes Polly thought it was funny

that people assumed that she was a slut. But if
anybody said it directly to her or even hinted at it,
she got angry.

The bells over the front door jangled. For a moment Polly could hear the wind banging a shutter
somewhere outdoors in the bright morning and
whipping through the rigging of a scalloper tied
up at the town wharf. Then Mrs. Tally closed the
door.

Mrs. Tally looked at cartons of soap lying in a
glass case. She moved to the shelves and scrutinized the denture cleaners. Polly leaned against the
mirror at the back of the soda fountain with her
arms folded and watched.

Mrs. Tally turned around and looked at her. The
midmorning silence hung between them.

Mrs. Tally said, "A girl whom Nature did as well
by as you ought to wear a brassiere."

Polly's face flushed. She looked at Mrs. Tally's
chest. "Poor old flatty," she said. "Some people
Nature likes, some people she doesn't."

The bells jangled hard and the glass shivered as
Mrs. Tally slammed the door on her way out.

Charlie Feavey stood in the moldy shadows of
the hotel basement. The wrench was still clutched
in his right fist. Oily water from the broken pipe
widened in an oozing pool across the cement floor,
gathering up dust and turning it to mud, moving
around the legs of a workbench and spreading
toward a rusty furnace that hadn't worked for
years.

Charlie was hung over and thought he heard a
prophecy sounding in the morning wind. The

premise of his life had always been that the universe was presided over by some malevolent god whose chief pleasure was arranging fate so that nothing ever worked for Charlie Feavey—the money never came when he needed it, pipes burst when he wanted to go fishing, crazed spells hit him when he was drinking and made him feel belligerent toward some guy who was twice his size, motors broke down. During his three-day benders, Charlie would wander the empty corridors of his hotel shouting curses at the thwarting god.

But as he stood in the basement that spring morning, Charlie had the exhilarating sensation that the god had suddenly embraced him like a father who recognizes one of his children. He listened to the wind. The god was telling Charlie that they both had an enemy.

The terrible deity promised Charlie Feavey that all of his dreams were going to come true. It told him to find the enemy.

Late in the morning Bentley rode back up Main Street. He waved at Polly as he pumped his bike past the drugstore. He skidded onto the sidewalk and let Slally off.

He laid his bicycle on the grass and led her along the path between the growths of long grass in front of the Stonehaven House Hotel. Slally followed Bentley up onto the porch. "This place is *real* old," Bentley told her again. "All kinds of stuff happened here. I know about a lot of it."

Slally stood with her hands shoved into the back pockets of her dungarees.

She looked across Main Street. The blue water of the harbor was ruffled. A tanker was moving down the horizon, disappearing behind one of the pine-crowned islands. She turned back to Bentley and asked if they were doing something wrong by coming up onto the porch.

Bentley wiped the dust off a window with his sleeve. "Nah," he said. "This place belongs to Mr. Feavey. He's weird!" He cupped his hands onto the glass and peered inside.

He saw a long mahogany reception desk, a fireplace, and a broken sofa. On his left there was a hallway littered with dusty pieces of timber and wallboard. The sunlight that poured through the windows turned a strange, translucent yellow that Bentley had never seen before.

Slally rubbed off a clear circle on another window and looked inside. She said she hoped that Mr. Feavey wouldn't mind them being on his porch.

Bentley looked away from the window. "It's okay," he said. "I *told* you, he's weird!"

"Who's weird?"

Bentley's heart quickened. He looked around, Charlie Feavey was standing on the porch steps. He wore baggy, stained trousers and a red shirt with the sleeves rolled halfway up his hairy arms. His hatchet-blade face came to an edge on a line down his nose and chin. He hadn't shaved for a couple of days. His black hair was plastered across his forehead by sweat. A pipe wrench was clutched in his left fist.

"You calling me weird?" he said to Bentley.

Slally's eyes were wide as she, too, stared at

Charlie. She whispered to Bentley that he ought to apologize for trespassing.

Charlie looked at Slally. Then back at Bentley. "What's she making that noise for?"

"She can't talk like other people," Bentley said. He was scared.

Charlie looked back at Slally. "A goddamn idiot."

"She isn't an idiot," Bentley said. "She just doesn't talk like—"

"You and this moron better clear off my property," Charlie snarled. "If I catch you around here again, I'll take a shotgun to the both of you." He gestured with the wrench. "Bastard!"

Bentley stared at him. The same peculiar yellow light seemed to be burning in Charlie Feavey's eyes. Being called a bastard made Bentley feel soiled and grown up. "Climb down," he said to Slally.

Slally swung one leg over the porch rail, grasped it, and lifted the other leg over. The rotted banisters broke under her slight weight and the rail collapsed beneath her hands. Slally teetered on the edge of the porch.

"You goddamn idiot!" Charlie shouted.

Slally's face was white. She jumped down into the tall grass and ran for the sidewalk.

"You come back here!" Charlie Feavey yelled. He thundered down the porch steps after Slally.

"Mr. Feavey!" Bentley cried. "Hey, Mr. Feavey, you sure are *weird!*"

Charlie whirled around on the cement path. He glared up at Bentley. "Why you—little—*bastard!*" He bolted back up the steps, two at a time. Bentley began to chant his incantation. Charlie was half-way across the porch when his right leg suddenly went out from under him as if he'd stepped on a patch of ice. He crashed onto his side with a yowl.

"Bastard!" he yelled. "I coulda broke my back!"

Bentley went on chanting and looking into Charlie's eyes.

"Bastard!" Charlie shrieked. But he didn't try to stand up. He sat spread-legged on the porch, swearing and threatening.

Bentley walked past him and went down the steps. He crossed the grass and picked up his bicycle. "I guess you were right," he said to Slally. "We shouldn't have gone up there."

Slally was wide-eyed with wonder. She looked at the porch. Charlie Feavey was still sitting, shouting swear words at a boy who wasn't there anymore.

At 12:45 somebody telephoned the police station because of the racket Charlie Feavey was making. Dick Amberstam, McGraw's second deputy, walked up to the hotel, collared Charlie, and threw him in a cell for the afternoon to sober up.

Charlie was dazed. But he wasn't drunk. He sat in the cell beneath the police station, thinking about what had happened. He felt his new power and the unworldly promise swelling around him in the cool basement.

Then he knew. The Ellicott kid was the enemy of Charlie Feavey and Charlie's god.

Chapter Six

Summer comes to this coast with warm winds and dancing clusters of gnats in the afternoon light. It posts notice of itself in bright sparkles on the morning sea and lines of cars driving up from the hot cities of the south. On their way to Stonehaven the outsiders pass through towns where white houses and churches stand among tall, stolid trees. Vacation homes are then unshuttered, and suddenly the village is full of station wagons and men wearing madras trousers who follow their wives around the grocery store.

For some of Stonehaven's people the new season brought an imprecise malaise: it was as if one among them were infected with a pestilence of the heart that was contagious.

The great antagonists of the cosmos, who were recognized in the older, wiser time of the world, had begun to wreathe their sorceries of light and darkness about Stonehaven and contend for the souls of everyone who lived there.

Charlie Feavey was the carrier of Prince Ombra's plague. He drank harder and got into four fistfights in the bar on Main Street.

McGraw sat in the police station looking through the screen door at the village, the town wharf, and the islands scattered across the bright sea. He was filled with a sense of foreboding; he didn't know what was going to happen—but odd symtoms of it were all around him. McGraw despised the supernatural because it implied God. He decided to keep a closer eye on his half sister, Polly, who was turning hard and flippant. McGraw also decided to watch Charlie Feavey. McGraw and Charlie had been friends of a sort—they went fishing together—and he could sense a change, a new confidence, in Charlie.

Polly Woodhouse surprised herself. She'd never known how angry she could be. Her ire was focused on Mrs. Tally. Polly was fed up with the woman's needling and sarcasm. She spent her idle hours trying to figure out how she could shock the old bat. This obsession smothered Polly's usually cheerful nature.

Mrs. Tally made up her mind to take Polly firmly in hand. But every time she went into the drugstore, she ended up having a contest of barbed remarks with the girl. Mrs. Tally always lost. She was infuriated, because other people in the village never dared stand up to her.

Elias Cutter decided, ruefully, that he was getting old. Disdain for everybody was hardening in him.

Willybill went his silent way around the village and the countryside in his pickup truck, thinking his impenetrable thoughts and speaking to no one. McGraw and his deputies kept the stranger under surveillance.

Something, the police chief told himself, was going wrong with the world. Then he told himself not to be a damned fool.

The trees thickened with foliage and the air grew brighter, and Bentley Ellicott was happier than he'd ever known it was possible to be—even though the certainy of his destiny lay before him like the autumn that would follow the summer.

As the damp evaporated from the forests, Slally and her mother began coming down to Stonehaven every weekend. They slept in a guest room across the hall from Bentley's room. On Tuesdays Richard Ellicott took Bentley up to the university to see Dr. Kreistein. Sometimes the old man got Bentley to tell him stories whose words he knew but whose meaning he didn't understand. Then Dr. Kreistein explained the stories to him. On other Tuesdays they talked about what Bentley's greatest fear might be.

After these visits to the clinic, Bentley and his father drove over to the Drakes' house for supper. One evening when Richard Ellicott and Ellen Drake came up to Slally's room to collect Bentley, they were holding hands. On other nights of the week that spring Richard got home very late. Sometimes he didn't come back to Stonehaven at all. Bentley asked Helga if she thought everything was all right. Helga laughed and told him everything was fine.

Helga and Ellen Drake became instant friends. They bullied Richard into letting them repaint the ground floor of his house. The next weekend Helga's boyfriend and two other university students moved all the furniture out of the living room, the hall, and the dining room. Then Helga and Ellen put on coveralls and began to paint. The students spent the afternoon rearranging closets. That night Slally slept alone across the hall from Bentley. Ellen had moved into Richard's room to share his bed.

One Tuesday afternoon Dr. Kreistein was sitting at his desk, looking disheveled and wrinkled as usual, when Bentley arrived. There were books all over the office. "Sit," the old man said when Bentley had closed the door.

Bentley took some books off the big leather chair and sat on the edge. "What have you been doing?" Dr. Kreistein said without looking up.

"Building a raft," Bentley said.

"With the Drake girl? The mooky-mooky talker?"

Bentley nodded.

Dr. Kreistein raised his head. "It is only May. If you go out on a raft, you will fall in the ocean and freeze to death."

Bentley grinned. "Nah. I've built rafts before. Me and Joe Persis—"

"And what happened to that raft, please?"

"It busted up."

Dr. Kreistein grunted. "What else?"

"I had a dream," Bentley said.

"So," the old man answered softly. "Tell me this dream."

Bentley looked at his sneakers. "It was weird. It was a story I heard. Only the guy in the story was me."

Dr. Kreistein nodded. "Proceed, please."

So Bentley spent the next forty-five minutes putting books back into Dr. Kreistein's shelves and telling him an Algonquin Indian legend he had heard in the second air.

The story was about the man-son of the Kitcki-Manitou, mightiest of all Algonquin gods. It was told by Indians who visited the wide Stonehaven cove to feast on berries and clams before the white men came and built the town. In the smoky dusk the Indians recounted the tale of Hosop, the half-divine warrior who had many adventures as he wandered the world looking for the Great Enemy, his father's rival. One day Hosop found a stone in a shining river and used it to kill the Dreaded One, who had returned to the world and assumed the shape of a monstrous wolf. Then Hosop traveled two hundred walking days north to the land of white bears and ice islands. He was searching for Sedna, the Eskimo maiden whose beauty was famous in the world. Sedna spurned Hosop the Wolf-Killer, and he died of a broken heart. She reigns over the underwater world where the souls of the dead do penance for the sins of the living.

When Bentley had finished telling the story, Dr. Kreistein studied him in silence for a long moment.

Bentley returned to the leather chair. "That's

how I knew about Sedna the first time I came here," he said.

The old man nodded. He scratched his nose again. "You say you *heard* this Indian story. It was not something you found in your head like the others?"

"I heard it."

"Where did you hear it?"

"Out in the woods."

"Somebody tells stories in the woods?"

"It isn't exactly *somebody*—well, yeah, it is. I go out to this place I have, and I can hear the talk. You know. Before."

"Before what?"

"I'm not making it up!"

"Be quiet. There is no need to shout. What talk do you hear?"

Bentley looked out of the office windows and told Dr. Kreistein about listening to the second air. When he had finished, he turned his head back to the old man.

"Very well," the doctor said. "Now. You dreamed you were this man, Hosop, *ja?*"

"Yeah. I dreamed I was looking for something. Then I found it."

"The stone?"

Bentley nodded.

"And what happened after that in your dream, please?"

Bentley looked at his sneakers. "I dreamed I had the stone. I knew this huge wolf was coming. I didn't *see* it or anything. I just knew it was coming to fight me."

"Did this frighten you?"

Bentley raised his head. "No," he said.

"You were not frightened at the prospect of fighting a very large wolf?"

Bentley shook his head. "In the dream I was scared before I found the stone. Then I wasn't. What does it mean?"

Dr. Kreistein frowned and looked out of the window. Then he looked back at Bentley. "I must think about it. Now, please go away."

By the middle of May Bentley had taught Slally so well that she could ride his bicycle from one end of the lawn to the other without falling off. They climbed trees, and Bentley showed her his school. On weekend evenings they watched television and talked.

The fear Bentley had first seen in Slally's eyes went away. The more she talked—for the first time in her life, to somebody who could understand her—the more her personality began to show. She thought about things more than most kids Bentley knew. But she wasn't bossy. When she made Bentley clean up his room, she helped him.

Richard taught her to play chess. He told Ellen that Slally was a genius. He liked to get her to play chess with his friends from the mathematics department who came down for Sunday lunch.

Bentley was amazed by his father. He'd never asked his friends to visit them before. It had never occurred to Bentley that he even had any friends. Richard's eyes became bright, he gained eight pounds, and he didn't act as if he was thinking about something else all the time. One weekend Richard and Ellen went down the coast to the city.

When they came back, Bentley's father had a whole lot of new suits, shirts, and ties.

On the Saturday after Bentley's school closed for summer, Richard took them all to a sporting goods store on the town wharf. They bought a fiberglass dinghy and arranged to have an eighteen-year-old boy named Steve Slattery give Bentley and Slally sailing lessons. At lunch on Main Street, Ellen told them that she and Slally were going to close their house and spend the summer in Stonehaven. For once Slally didn't have anything to say. She just grinned at Bentley.

The next Monday Ellen and Richard brought everything down to the Victorian house on the point. That afternoon Bentley and Slally rode their bikes up the dirt road to the stone wall where the overgrown meadow sloped to a cliff above the sea. Slally only fell off her bike once.

Bentley limped up the meadow ahead of her, pushing down the brittle stalks of grass that had survived the winter and the strong, new growth of summer. Behind them, the first cicadas buzzed in the trees. The sun was a silvery-white blast of light in the sky. The smell of kelp and the taste of salt came on the inshore wind.

Don't tell your secret unless you are offered love sealed with silence . . .

Bentley and Slally sat on the edge of the cliff, dangling their feet. The warm wind was in their faces. The crash and hissing retreat of the waves forty feet below them was so loud that they couldn't hear the cicadas anymore.

"Listen," Bentley said, "there's something I have to tell you."

They couldn't hear the cicadas anymore. But Willybill heard them. He had stepped out of the woods after Bentley and Slally left their bicycles. The stranger stood on the dirt road with his thumbs hooked into his belt, a toothpick jutting out of the corner of his mouth as he watched the two small figures silhouetted against the sun on the top of the cliff.

Slally's hair blew back from her face. She heard the gravity in Bentley's voice and turned to look at him.

"There's something I've got to do," Bentley said. "It might be dangerous."

Slally looked puzzled.

And that was when, for the second time in his life, Bentley Ellicott told a mortal being his secret.

"See," he said when he was finished. "I'm afraid something might happen to you when I fight him," He turned his head and looked at her. "You're my best friend now."

Slally asked if he was trying to make himself brave when he stood on the highway in front of the trucks.

He looked down at the sea swirling and foaming among the rocks far below. "Yes," he said. "But I'm not brave. I'm scared."

Slally took hold of his arm. She looked out at the horizon. For a moment her eyes filled with tears and her mouth quivered. Bentley thought she was going to cry. Then her face changed. Bentley had seen that expression before—when she made him clean up his room.

She let go of his arm. She said he had to promise to tell her when Prince Ombra was coming.

"I don't want anything to happen to you—"

Promise! Slally said fiercely.

Promise! glittered a command in Willybill's jade eyes on the road below.

"Okay," Bentley said. "I promise to tell you when Ombra's coming."

On the dirt road, Willybill took the toothpick from his mouth and snapped it in two between his thumb and forefinger. He grinned, spat in the dirt, and sauntered back along the road and around the curve.

As he limped down the meadow in front of Slally, Bentley decided he'd never be able to figure girls out. Slally was chattering away merrily as if the only thing she'd heard was Bentley telling her she was his best friend.

Most days Bentley and Slally rode their bicycles into the village.

They took sailing lessons from Steve Slattery, the teenager. Bentley learned faster than Slally.

They bought clam rolls with their lunch money and had picnics on the town wharf. The poison that had come to the village from afar hovered around them. But Bentley sat in a radiance of happiness that was the armor of heaven, and it protected Slally, too, because she was near him.

McGraw looked through the drugstore windows and said that the nutty Ellicott boy had found himself a nutty girlfriend and have you heard that kid try to talk?

Steve Slattery slouched across the marble counter of the soda fountain and grinned. He said Bentley claimed he could understand her.

It takes one to know one, Charlie Feavey snarled.

Putting away washed glasses, Polly Woodhouse said they were all terrible. Then, giving Charlie Feavey a look, she laughed, too.

God speaks to man through man. Ancient men speak to us in myths. Above the brown river waters of Egypt, sluggish in the burning sun, the first story of the world's creation lingers in the second air.

At the beginning of this legend there was no world. Neither were there suns, stars, mortals, nor air. In the emptiness, the great sea of chaos, Nun, held within its waters all that would eventually come to be.

In those profound depths lived he who would never die. His name was Atum, which meant "the sun at its setting."

He dwelt in the primordial sea, keeping his eyes closed so that his light would not be extinguished. He hid himself in a lotus blossom so that his nature would never be known.

Tiring, at last, of his solitude, the god transformed himself into a stone obelisk. He changed his name to Ra-Harakhte, which means "the sun at its noon zenith." This name also means "the creator."

The god burst from the depths of Nun, breaking through the surface with a great turmoil that made the first tides. The obelisk rose into the sky and filled it as the sun at noon. All the world was illuminated for the first time and, thus, came to be.

Ra made his shrine at Heliopolis and there, without wife, he bore his divine children, their children, and the children of those children. Their names were Shu and Tefnut, Geb and Nut and Osiris, the gentle king and world-conqueror who governed Egypt with his sister-wife, Isis. Their brother was the wicked, pale-skinned Prince Set, and their sister was Nephthys, keeper of the palace at Heliopolis beside the great river Nile, which brings life to the land.

These eight descendants of Ra inhabited his shrine. They were the divine company called the Ennead.

All things were in them—the light and the darkness, wisdom and tyranny, good and evil.

Their ancestor had left a piece of himself in the depths of Nun, the primordial sea. This fragment of Ra, the obelisk, is black, with specks of quartz and silver glinting on its surface. At the moment of the Creation it was washed from Nun into the waters of the world. It is called the stone of Ra, and a thousand heroes have found it.

At the moment of its finding by a smooth-lipped one, Prince Ombra is summoned from his kingdom of dark winds and reenters the world to resume his war with god the nameless who is all the gods ever worshipped by the devout of heart.

No mortal prophet, no god, not even Ombra himself knows why he returns when the hero finds the stone of Ra. The war between good and evil must be. Ombra's coming to earth has always been since the world began.

It was 3:02 on a bright, windy afternoon. Bentley and Slally were poking along the shore, waiting for the tide to get lower so that they could pick mussels for Helga.

Ellen was in the attic rearranging the storage room. She opened a closet. A question was taking shape in her mind.

Polly Woodhouse put the last dried glass on a shelf at the rear of the soda fountain. Charlie Feavey disgusted her. But if she could make it look as if she were having an affair with him, Mrs. Tally would be horrified. Polly hated the new perversity in herself. But she couldn't help it.

McGraw turned a corner in his police cruiser. The street was empty except for two dogs romping across the sidewalk and over the curb. McGraw drove past the Congregationalist church and muttered, in disgust, as he always did, "Goddamn."

On the starless perimeter of the cosmos, the energy of primal negatives sung in the mighty void storm. The vortex, millions of miles wide, whirled faster upon its center, sucking up the plasma of darkness. Jolts of energy intensified the gravity at the core, drawing wind and thunder in upon the heart of the hurricane. Gloom became matter in that terrible weight, and the storm molded it.

For the thousand and first time, Prince Ombra, Lord of Nightmares, the Dreaded One of every heart, was taking shape.

Universes trembled and comets veered off course as they entered the force field of his monstrous re-creation. An archangel trumpeted warning, and heaven looked upon earth, watching its warrior turn toward his timeless destiny. Enchantments flickered as lightning in the tumult of Lord Ombra's new being, and their blinding flashes challenged the illumination of god.

Ombra roared in the agony of his solidification. His pain swelled as his fourth brain, which is memory, cast up a panorama of his thousand previous lives. His death wounds burned within him. The faces of his warrior enemies looked upon him with scorn, and Prince Ombra cursed heaven with every blasphemy ever uttered.

His second brain is the seer of all wars, tears, and plagued epochs. It showed the Dreaded One a vision that lay beyond the dense glitter of a billion universes and the fire of their billion suns. He saw again the curve of coastline, uplands rising, and, beyond them, the wilderness of forests and rivers. Ombra knew this place. Centuries before he had met death here at the hand of Hosop, the Algonquin wolf-killer. Now, upon that coast, another mortal hand was about to close on the stone of Ra. Another of the loathed warriors was about to embark upon his mission in the world.

The shrieking of winds and the cascades of thunder were drawn into Prince Ombra's throat. He bellowed them forth as a warrior's challenge in the tongue of desert kings. The mighty sound rolled before him as he burst from the tempest and strode across the cosmos toward the world.

Ellen Drake came down from the attic and told Richard Ellicott he ought to give away his wife's clothes that were hanging in the storage room. Richard put down his newspaper and pulled her to him. They rubbed noses and he kissed her. He said no.

Steve Slattery, the teenage sailing instructor, went up to the loft above his mother's garage. He

locked the door, climbed on a chair and took a
brown paper bag from its hiding place at the end
of a rafter. He sat down on the floor. He began taking photographs from the paper bag and studying
them. They were pictures of naked little girls.

All the world's clocks ticked past the quarter-
hour. Slally had her dungarees rolled up and was
standing barefoot in a little pool of water, watching crabs scuttle in and out of the waving strands
of kelp. Watching her, Bentley began to get nervous about a crab pinching one of her toes.

He looked down the beach. He thought something had gone wrong with his eyes. What he saw
was the reverse of what you'd see if you turned on
a flashlight in a dark room. A shaft of shadow was
beaming up from a cluster of bolders. It was nearly black at its pinpoint bottom and became a dirty
gray where the top of the beam dissolved into the
sunny sky.

Bentley closed his eyes. Then he opened them
again. The shaft of shadow was still there, motionless—a ray of darkness in the sunlight.

He heard Slally murmur behind him. He looked
back at her. She was standing in the water with
her mouth open, gazing at the high spread of
shadow.

She looked at Bentley.

"I don't know," he said. "You stay here. I'll go
see what it is."

Slally splashed out of the shallow pool and
grabbed his hand.

"It's okay," Bentley said. He pried her fingers
loose and limped toward the cluster of boulders.
The dark shaft didn't waver.

Elias Cutter sat stiffly in his drawing room. He looked through the windows at the bright afternoon. It seemed, to the aging banker, that a storm was coming and that he was a part of it. He had just realized that disdain had taken complete possession of him and was focused upon Polly Woodhouse. Mr. Cutter thought she embodied everything that was wrong with Stonehaven.

Ellen Drake straightened up, laughed, and brushed back her hair. She looked down at Richard and wondered if he really loved her.

Bentley leaned on the sun-baked surface of the largest boulder. The beam of shadow was a foot from his eyes. He poked his finger into it. He didn't feel anything. He put his hand in the shadow. There was no shock or burn.

Bentley's heart was beating with an alien excitement. Nowhere in the ordinary world could darkness beam like light, and he knew it. Only a supernatural power could make that happen.

He felt dizzy as he lay on the hot boulder. He thought about dinghy sailing and watching television with Slally. But his life didn't belong to him. He wished he was older than eight. Everything was happening too soon.

He inched his body over the top of the boulder and looked down. The shadow was radiating from a small black stone lying among the pebbles of the shore. Specks of quartz and silver flashed on it in the afternoon sun.

Then Bentley Ellicott did what he was born to do. He reached down and picked up the stone.

His brain exploded, as if all his senses had broken loose at once. The beach and the forest whirled and tilted around him as he slid off the boulder. From his stomach to his brain he was filled with an exaltation he had never known before.

His fear was blasted away by a new vision of himself standing in the center of a protecting nimbus. His size and age no longer mattered as the knowledge of a power that could conquer armies and transform the world churned through him. In that instant, Bentley's borrowed heart took possession of him with the searing light of a divine realization; he rejoiced because his life belonged not to him but to a benevolence, and he was its servant. Standing in the afternoon sunshine he was overwhelmed by his release from the supreme mortal affliction: he knew that, even though he might be killed, he would never die.

Then, in the haze of the summer afternoon, the voice of Prince Ombra broke upon the world, bellowing the words it had spoken as Goliath the Philistine: *Come unto me and I will give thy flesh unto the fowls of the air and the beasts of the field!*

As Slally watched in wonder, Bentley threw his head back, and his voice pealed the reply that a shepherd boy had cried within sight of the gates of Ekron: *This day will the Lord deliver thee into my hand!*

In a tongue of the dry, ancient world, Prince Ombra had flung his challenge to the borrowed heart. And Bentley had answered him in the words of David, who had once borne the heart among men.

The first impact of Bentley's exaltation passed. Shaking and disoriented, he put the stone in his pocket and sat down on the beach.

Slally crouched before him, peering into his eyes. Her face was white with anxiety. Bentley raised his head and looked at her. He knew that he had to become himself again; he had to contain the rapture and overpowering confidence that filled him.

Slally asked him if he was all right.

Bentley nodded. He was shivering and thought that maybe he was going to be sick.

Charlie Feavey stopped on the ground-floor hallway of his hotel. He kicked aside a piece of broken timber. The power in him was getting stronger. The summer afternoon creaks and settlings of the ruined old building seemed to be telling him that his bad luck was over forever. He could have anything he wanted. The god of his dreams was suddenly all around him. Charlie vowed his devotion, went out the front door, and walked down the street to the drugstore.

Polly was leaning against the soda fountain mirror smoking a cigarette. She raised her head when Charlie came in. He stopped by the candy counter. "I was thinking," he said in his voice like a rasp on hard wood. "Maybe you and me could have some fun."

Polly's revulsion at his gaunt, unwashed body was overpowered in her mind by a bitterness she had never known before. She wanted to take out her resentment on Mrs. Tally.

"Maybe," she answered.

On the shore, Slally squatted in front of Bentley, her arms wrapped around her legs. She asked him what he'd screamed when he found the stone.

Bentley raised his head. "Did you hear the thunder?"

Slally said no.

"It was Ombra," Bentley said, his eyes shining. He was still trying to control the exhilarating sense of power that was surging through him. He was still shaking. "He's coming," Bentley said.

Slally looked at him with sympathy. She put her hand on his cheek.

Gently, despite his trembling, Bentley took it away. "I'm going to fight him," he said in an intense whisper. "He can't hide from me! I'm going to kill him!"

Chapter Seven

Dr. Kreistein stopped his car at the junction of the Stonehaven road and the highway. It was almost dark. He opened the door to light the car's interior and fumbled in his pockets for his glasses and a scrap of paper. Muttering imprecations about people who lived in the woods, he reread the directions Ellen Drake had given him over the telephone.

He put his glasses back into his pocket, closed the door, and drove across the highway. He followed the road until its tarred surface turned into packed dirt; then it curved through trees, which thickened the darkness.

Dietrich Kreistein could see the stars through breaks in the black foliage overhead. The evening seemed innocent and ordinary. The flavor of late spring's cool nights was fresh in the air. The old

man saw a glint of house lights among the trees
and the silver splash of moonlight on the water.

So, Dietrich Kreistein, he told himself as he
steered along the dark road at ten miles an hour,
*you needed an extraordinary experience to make
the final proof that this boy is what he says he is,
that what you have come to believe is true.* He
thought again about his encounter with Willybill
on his porch. *Proof, proof, proof. It comes from being too much a scientist of facts and not listening
to what you were born knowing.*

"Dummkopf," he said aloud.

There was a small white sign with ELLICOTT
painted on it in black letters. Turning the steering
wheel as carefully as if he were maneuvering an
ocean liner, the old man bumped into a driveway
and stopped in front of a brightly lit porch.

He picked up his black medical bag from the
seat and adjusted his brown fedora on his head. As
he climbed, grunting, out of the car, a screen door
slammed and Richard Ellicott walked across the
porch.

He came down the steps, holding out his hand.
"We're awfully grateful, Doctor," he said.

Dr. Kreistein shook hands. *"Ja,"* he murmured.
"It's a nice night for driving in the automobile."
He sniffed and looked across the lawn at the
moonlight on the water. "You must be healthy
people. All of this sea air."

"Come in," Professor Ellicott said.

The old man labored up the steps behind him
and walked into the house. The screen door closed
behind him with a little bang. He took off his
brown fedora and shook hands with Ellen Drake

and Helga, who were both standing in the living room.

"Have you had dinner?" Ellen asked him.

Dr. Kreistein put his bag on the floor beside a flower-patterned chair and sat down. "No dinner, thank you," he said. "A glass of water, perhaps."

Ellen went out to the kitchen. Dr. Kreistein looked up at Helga. "Where in Germany do you live?" he asked.

"Munchen," she answered. *"Und Sie?"*

"Schleswig-Holstein," Dr. Kreistein answered. "It was a long time ago. For now we will speak English. The boy has told me about you. What do you think has happened to him?"

Helga sat down on the sofa. "I don't know," she said. "They were playing on the beach this afternoon. Sally came back very—" She looked up at Richard Ellicott. "How do you say it?"

"Upset," he answered.

"Very upset," Helga said. "She was trying to tell us something. Richard wasn't home from the university. Ellen and I found him—" She shrugged.

"What was he doing when you found him?"

Helga folded her hands and looked at the old man. Richard was leaning against the wall by the screen door. Insects sang in the darkness beyond the porch. "He was—" Helga paused. "I don't know the right words. I forget."

"Speak German," Dr. Kreistein told her.

Helga told him she and Ellen had finally picked up the alarm in Slally's prattling. They had run across the lawn and out onto the pebbled beach. Bentley was sitting doubled over, his arms wrapped around his stomach. He was shaking and sweating. His eyes were only half open; he was talking between clenched teeth.

Ellen and Helga had had to half carry him to his room. When they put him on his bed, he wouldn't lie down. He kept jerking into a sitting position and babbling.

Ellen came back with a glass of ice water. She handed it to Dr. Kreistein. "Has she told you?"

Dr. Kreistein took a sip of water. "About finding him on the beach, yes. What happened then?"

"I took his temperature," Ellen said.

"And?"

"It was normal," Ellen said. "The children had lobster salad for lunch. So did Helga and I. There wasn't anything wrong with us, so Helga called Dr. Leon in the village. He's taken care of Bentley all his life."

"And he knew the boy was having therapy at our clinic, yes?"

Ellen nodded.

"Dr. Leon came about five," Helga said. "He made Bentley—you know—barf."

Dr. Kreistein looked puzzled. "What is this barf?"

"Throw up," Ellen said. "Dr. Leon couldn't find out what the matter was. He thought it might be some sort of trauma. He suggested—that's when we called you."

"This was the right thing to do," Dr. Kreistein said. He put down the empty water glass and folded his hands over his stomach. "Now, a few questions, please. Does he understand you when you talk to him?"

"He seems to understand," Richard Ellicott

said. "But whatever's done this to him has most of his attention."

"You have asked him what is wrong?"

"He won't tell us," Ellen answered. "He keeps saying it's a secret."

Dr. Kreistein nodded. He scratched the side of his head, sniffed, and folded his hands over his midriff again. "When he speaks, does he always make his words and sentences in English?"

"Yes," Richard said. "Why shouldn't he?"

"When he makes this—what do you call it?—babble, what does he say?"

"He talks about fighting somebody," Richard answered.

A breeze rustled in the trees beyond the porch.

Dr. Kreistein pushed his lips out in a thoughtful pout. "Nothing else?"

"No, he just keeps saying he's going to fight and kill someone," Richard said. "What does it mean?"

"He's having a nightmare wide awake," Ellen said.

Dr. Kreistein nodded. "And where is the little girl?"

"She's upstairs with Bentley," Ellen said. "She won't leave him."

"Herr Doktor," Helga asked softly, "how does Bentley understand Sally?"

Dietrich Kreistein took a handkerchief from his inside jacket pocket and blew his nose. "It is not important at present," he answered. He stuffed the handkerchief back into his pocket. "Now I am going to talk to him."

He picked up his medicine bag and rose from

the chair.

"Doctor," Ellen said, "have you *any* idea—"

"We will see what we will see," the old man answered. He moved across the living room toward the hall. He stopped for a moment in front of Helga. "Your parents bought an airplane ticket so that you should come here and learn English," he said. "Did they do this so that someday you would be able to say *barf*, hah?"

Helga flushed. *"Nein, Herr Doktor."*

Dietrich Kreistein grunted. "I am not Mister Doctor here. Just Doctor."

"Ja, Doktor Kreistein." Helga giggled.

"Good." He nodded to Ellen and Richard, crossed the hall, grasped the banister with one arthritic hand, and began to climb the stairs. He glanced through the window as he proceeded.

In the soft darkness, it seemed to him, the buzz of the insects was more insistent. He didn't know that a voice was speaking in their buzz and chirp. Only one person could hear the words, and he wasn't listening.

He was lying down. When Dr. Kreistein opened the bedroom door, Bentley was curled up like a caterpillar on his bed. One small lamp burned in the room. Slally jumped off a chair and stood beside the bed, looking at Dr. Kreistein. Her eyes were large, and though her face was as frightened as it used to be in his clinic, she looked defiant, too.

The old man stood with one hand on the half-opened door, his medicine bag in the other. "Good evening," he said.

Bentley rolled over and looked up at him. Slally didn't move.

"May I come in?" Dr. Kreistein asked.

Slally told him to go away.

"Thank you," Dr. Kreistein said. He came all the way into the room and closed the door.

Louder, Slally told him to leave Bentley alone.

The old man put down his medicine bag. He looked at Bentley, who hadn't said anything. The boy's face was pale. He had both hands clasped tight. His forehead gleamed with perspiration in the lamplight.

Dr. Kreistein took the handkerchief out of his inside pocket. He looked at it. "No," he mumbled, "that one is for me." He put it back and pulled another, neatly folded, from his hip pocket. He started to lean over to wipe Bentley's forehead when Slally suddenly rushed at him.

She pushed the old man with both hands on his stomach. Caught off guard, Dr. Kreistein staggered back and sat down in a chair. "Enough!" he barked. "Enough, enough!" He looked across the room at Bentley. "Will you be so kind as to tell this lady that I am not a lion that is going to eat you?"

"It's okay," Bentley said in a voice so small that it was barely a voice at all.

Slally remained standing in front of Dr. Kreistein.

"Did you hear?" he asked her. "He says it is okay. Go away."

Slally didn't move.

Dr. Kreistein handed her the folded handkerchief. "Here. Wipe off his face."

Slowly, Slally extended her hand, took the handkerchief, and went over to the bed. She tugged at

Bentley until he was lying on his back. Then she mopped his face and sat down on the side of the bed. She looked at Dr. Kreistein.

"He knows about Ombra and everything," Bentley said.

Slally said she was sorry and explained.

Dr. Kreistein didn't understand her. But her face had softened and her voice was gentler.

"I am not as clever as he is," he said to Slally. "You will have to be patient if I do not understand immediately."

"She says she doesn't like the clinic because they're mean to her," Bentley said, still looking at the ceiling. "She thought you were going to do something mean to me."

Dr. Kreistein nodded.

Slally handed back the handkerchief.

Dr. Kreistein took it from her. He sat with the handkerchief in his hand, watching Bentley.

"He's come," Bentley finally said.

"Yes," Dr. Kreistein answered. "I assumed from the dream you had that this would happen soon."

Bentley's face was pale. His eyes were bright with an almost manic gleam. "First I found the stone," he said. "Then I heard him in the thunder."

Dr. Kreistein took a black leather notebook from his pocket and opened it. "And what happened after that, please?"

Bentley sat up straight. *"You're writing things down because you think I'm crazy!"* he yelled.

"Shush," Dr. Kreistein said. "I am not a police chief who has a bad opinion of you. I have been persuaded that everything you have told me is true."

Bentley was still bolt upright on his bed, glaring at the old man.

"And, since it is true that Prinz Ombra has come, we must make a plan."

"I don't need a plan!" Bentley blurted. "I'm gonna take that stone and smash his head in!"

"If you would be so kind as to lower your voice—"

"I don't need you!" Bentley yelled, his eyes shining brighter. "I don't need anybody! I can—"

"—so that everybody in the county won't know this secret you are supposed to keep secret!" Dr. Kreistein said loudly.

"I'm not scared of him!" Bentley shouted. "I'm—"

"Desist!" Dr. Kreistein bellowed.

Bentley looked startled and closed his mouth. Slally jumped off the bed and stood glowering before the old man.

"Sit down," Dr. Kreistein said peevishly to her. He looked back at Bentley. "By your foolish behavior you are inviting Prinz Ombra to dispose of you so quickly that he will be back home in time for breakfast."

"I'm not scared of him!"

"Your dream also told us this would be your reaction," the old man said. "In it you found this stone and were not afraid, not even of a wolf. Do not be deceived by this first burst of courage. You know very little about Herr Ombra. But he knows a great deal about you. He has met people like you many, many times before. He knows that when his enemies first find the stone they are made foolish with their new power. He knows that this is the most dangerous moment for you—and he would like very much to fight now because you are reckless and ignorant."

Bentley flushed with anger. "I'm *supposed* to fight him after I find the stone! All those other guys did!"

Dr. Kreistein nodded. "And many of them were destroyed by Ombra. It happened to one during my lifetime." He sniffed. "Others, like Susano the Japanese made themselves wise as well as powerful. Then they defeated Ombra."

"I never heard of Susano," Bentley said.

"If you will make this dangerous girl who punches people in the stomach sit down and behave herself, I will tell you about him," the old man answered. "And from the story of Susano you will learn something that will make you more sensible."

"C'mon, Slally," Bentley said. "Leave him alone."

Slally retreated to the bed and sat down.

Beneath the starlight on the northern coast, the shadows and moonlit places of the night were heavy with a new presence. Prince Ombra had dispersed himself into a molecular infinity as he entered the world. He lay, vast as the dark sea, his breathing the rise and recession of the tides. His seven brains glowed in the forest rot of foxfire, and his eye was the Dog Star. It watched a dimly lit bedroom overlooking the water in the moonlight. Lord Ombra no longer spoke in the myriad small sounds of the night. He listened. He remembered. In his thousand lives he had met many warriors who were accompanied by magicians. These had been foes full of guile and subtle strategies. Already, Ombra could feel the rash excitement fading in the boy. The Dreaded One's Dog Star eye focused on the old man who sat in a bedroom chair with his hands folded. This magician was an enemy. Ombra cursed him.

"Susano," Dr. Kreistein said again to Bentley, "was a Japanese god. But he was such a nuisance that the other gods sent him to the world. There he became a great warrior and had many adventures."

"What'd he do?" Bentley asked. He was still pale and trembling. But the old man's soft voice and the promise of an interesting story were distracting him from his new power.

Dr. Kreistein took off his hat and put it on the floor beside his chair. "Like you, Susano came to the world knowing the reason for his life. He had not just been banished from heaven. Like you, he was born as a mortal to undertake a terrible task." Dietrich Kreistein listened to the night. He looked back at Bentley. "Susano knew that his enemy would appear in a form that was very frightening. So he decided to prepare himself."

The old man sniffed. "As he went about his mortal life, Susano gave much thought to what frightened him. He paid attention to his dreams and nightmares. He tested himself. Finally he discovered his greatest fear." The old man raised his eyebrows, looked at Slally, then back at Bentley. "A snake. This is what frightened the mortal part of

Susano more than anything else. A snake.

"To discover this great fear, it took Susano a
long time and great patience. After that, he protected himself with his magic while he took more
time to find out everything he could about a snake.
He became very wily in dealing with these reptiles. He did not immediately rush off to make a
quarrel with Prinz—"

"That's because he hadn't found the stone yet,"
Bentley said.

"I'm coming to it," Dr. Kreistein said. "That
part. One day Susano was traveling in the pro-
vince of Izumo. It was summer and very hot. Our
Samurai friend stopped to refresh himself in a
clear stream. While he was drinking, he found this
stone of yours. Then he knew the hour of his
destiny was near. He proceeded on through the
valley, and finally he came to an old man who was
weeping and wailing and beating his fists on his
head. Susano told the old gentleman to stop making such a noise and tell what was wrong. The old
man said that once he had eight daughters." Dr.
Kreistein paused. He looked at Slally. "I don't
think they punched anybody in the stomach."

Slally giggled.

"So. This old man told Susano that every year a
terrible, eight-headed serpent came on such-and-
such a day and ate up one of the daughters. There
was only one daughter left, and this was the day
the monster was coming to eat her."

The manic gleam was receding from Bentley's
eyes as he listened.

"Then Susano knew that his enemy was

nearby," Dr. Kreistein said. "He had spent years preparing himself for this battle. Years." He looked at Bentley.

Bentley blinked.

"Now, then. In his long time studying reptiles, Susano discovered something very interesting about them. A snake is a drunkard. If permitted, it will intoxicate itself with alcohol—especially in warm weather."

On the dark shore beyond the bedroom, a breath of wind stirred. Memory fluttered in Prince Ombra's fourth brain, where all of his lives are forever recounted. He remembered a day of baking heat on the dry, Japanese landscape. He cursed again the memory of furious Susano.

"The warrior made a plan. First he took the old man's daughter. With his magic, Susano turned her into a comb, which he put in his hair. This was to protect her. Then he found eight bowls and filled them with strong rice wine. After placing these bowls carefully in the road, Susano removed his sandals, made an offering to his gods, and hid himself in a thicket of bamboo. He waited in the heat of the day.

"Finally, he heard a terrible sound."

Slally murmured a question.

Dr. Kreistein looked at Bentley. The old man's eyebrows rose again.

"She wants to know what the sound was," Bentley said.

Dr. Kreistein pursed his lips. "Hissing," he said. "It was, in fact, several hissing noises happening all at the same time. Susano looked out from his hiding place. He saw the fearful serpent writhing up the road toward him. Its eight heads were looking this way and that. Its tongues were coming in and out. Each head was making a hiss.

"When this frightful creature arrived at the eight bowls of wine in the road, it stopped. Three of the eight heads stared with red eyes at the bowl. The snake heads hissed some more. Then one head lowered and took a taste. After that the other seven heads came down. The serpent drank all the wine.

"For a moment the snake felt very brave and glorious. Then, in the next moment, it felt very drunk and dizzy with the heat. One head flopped on the ground and began to snore."

Bentley grinned.

"Two more began a nasty fight and tried to bite each other. At that precise instant, Susano leaped from the bamboo thicket, roaring and drawing his sword. With a great oath, he stamped twice and his sword flashed in the sunlight as he chopped off all eight heads. The terrible snake writhed and lashed in the dust of the road and then slithered into the ditch. It was quite dead. Ombra had turned himself into this snake to terrify and kill Susano. He did not succeed."

In the forests of the night, foxfire glowed as Lord Ombra lived again his reptilian folly and the eight slashing strokes of Susano's mighty sword, Kusanagi.

The bedroom was silent. In the dim lamplight

Bentley looked down at his sneakers.

"I don't feel like I did this afternoon," he said.

"Yes," Dr. Kreistein replied. "This new power the stone brought to you, this is already becoming quieter in you. If it did not, it would be impossible for you to live your ordinary life."

Bentley raised his head. "But I'm still not scared of him. I'm not scared of anything anymore."

"If you fight now before you are ready, Ombra will turn your magic against you," Dr. Kreistein said. "You would not only be putting yourself in great danger, but this lady here as well. Also, me." The old man rubbed his nose. "We know your secret. I think some danger comes with such knowledge. We will, therefore, follow the example of Susano; we will learn much, and then we will make a plan."

Bentley looked across the bedroom. Then he looked at Slally. "Okay," he said to Dr. Kreistein. "I have this thing I can do—I have these fish hawks that fly around me, and I know this kind of song. If I stand inside the circles and sing the song, Ombra can't get me."

"Good," the old man said. "I think you will be like Susano and the other warriors in the old stories. I think you will have many adventures before the day comes that you face Prinz Ombra. But we, too, will be busy. We will find out what it is you fear." He looked at Slally. "Be so kind as to hand me my bag."

Slally slid off the bed, picked up the black medicine bag with both hands, lugged it across the room, and set it down at the old man's feet.

"Thank you," Dr. Kreistein said. "Now, please, a glass of water for our friend here."

Slally opened the bedroom door and disappeared into the hall. Dr. Kreistein poked around in his bag. He sat up with a bottle of pills in his hand. "So," he said, "these circles that protect you and the song—where did you learn it?"

"If I tell you you'll think I'm—"

"If you please. No more talk of goofy."

"From the horseshoe crabs," Bentley said.

"Very well," Dr. Kreistein answered. "This magic of yours—as we will call it—gives us time to prepare."

"Yeah," Bentley said, "but I can't hang around inside those circles forever. They told me I *had* to fight Ombra. And I'm ready!"

"A little time is not forever," Dr. Kreistein said.

"But you live all the way up at the university," Bentley said. "I'd have to—"

"It is almost summer," the old man told him. "I think the sea air will be good for me."

"You mean you're going to come down *here?*"

Dr. Kreistein nodded as Slally came back with a glass of water. The old man stood up and handed Bentley a pill and the glass. "It is for sleeping," he said. He picked up his medicine bag. "I will see you in the morning." He looked down at Slally. "You go to sleep, too. Otherwise, you will grow up with baggy eyes like me. Where is this stone?"

"In the toy box," Bentley said heavily.

Dr. Kreistein crossed the room and lifted the lid of the box. Even in that dim light he saw the small black stone lying in a corner. Toys and bits of seashore treasure had been pushed away from it. As he looked at the stone, the old man tried to encompass, in his mind, all the hands that had held it in the history of the world. He closed the box and turned back to Bentley and Slally. "Go to sleep. Both of you," he said.

Bentley was already asleep. Dr. Kreistein went downstairs. Richard, Ellen, and Helga were in the living room. "He is better," the old man said.

"What *was* it?" Ellen asked.

"Please," Dr. Kreistein said. "He told you it was a secret. It is better that his problem stays a matter between him and me and this little girl."

"But I'm his *father*," Richard said. "I have a right to know."

"If you will be patient," Dr. Kreistein answered.

Ellen laid her hand on Richard's arm. "Perhaps he's right, darling."

"These are interesting children," Dr. Kreistein said. "I would like to make an arrangement to spend the summer months with them."

Helga looked at Ellen. "The what's-their-names —they are going to rent their house."

"The Salisburys," Ellen said.

Helga nodded. To Dr. Kreistein she said, "They live next door, just through the *Wald*—"

"Woods," the old man said grumpily. "Forest. Very well. I will look at this house in the morning. Now I am going to take a walk and breathe the sea air. I have told these children to go to sleep."

Ellen stood up. "We'll put them to bed." She looked at Richard. "Please, darling. Let's at least try—for both of them."

She went upstairs, followed by Helga. Richard

Ellicott remained on the sofa, his elbows on his knees, looking up at Dr. Kreistein. "I don't think I understand this at all," he said. "Why would you leave the clinic for a couple of months just to work with two children?"

Dr. Kreistein pushed his lips out in his serious pout. "My dear professor. Children have been teaching me for over fifty years. Always there is something new to learn. If you can find the right children."

"And you aren't willing to tell me what's wrong with my son?"

"This is correct," Dr. Kreistein said. "If there is, as you say, something *wrong* with him."

"But he's *my* son!" Richard said.

"Please. That is only one of the facts which make him a person. This person who he is wishes to keep his problem a secret. I respect this and you must, too."

Richard Ellicott looked at the floor. "I still don't understand." The insects were busy with their speaking in the suddenly enchanted darkness beyond the screen door. "All right," Richard said, raising his head, "we'll do it your way."

Standing in the middle of the living room, Dr. Kreistein contemplated him for a moment. "I have some sense of you, Professor," he said gently. "Is there a misery you have suffered that you worry is going to return to you?"

"It's nothing," Richard answered, wondering why he had even conceded that much.

"A secret," Dr. Kreistein said.

"The guest room's the third door in the hall upstairs," Richard said, getting up. "Helga will have the bed turned down and some towels laid out when you get back from your walk."

Dietrich Kreistein crossed the porch and went slowly down the steps. He walked across the driveway and grass to a place where the lawn ended in a tangle of tree roots and rocky shingle. Beyond that the shore began.

The old man stood with his hands shoved into the pockets of his rumpled jacket. His brown fedora was on his head to keep off the night chill. The first fireflies of the season burned as phosphorescent specks in the dark shrubbery on either side of him.

Beyond the sea lay Dietrich Kreistein's past— the Germany of his childhood, the Germany that became a fuse to ignite the world with horror.

He was irritated that life had played a trick on him, confirming his belief in his last years when there was so little time to learn more.

"So, Prinz Ombra," he said aloud, "the shadow we are born knowing about is real after all, hah?" He raised his head, looked at the stars, then at the sea again and the distance of his own life. "Before you face the boy, you and I will have a confrontation, Herr Prinz. It was intended I should be the boy's teacher. I know the old stories, and I will try to make him a wise and strong hero." The old man paused. "Naturally, you will try to push me out of the way." He took his handkerchief from his jacket pocket. "I wonder if you can hear me?"

The slight waves of a spring night washed on the rocks and the sand. The insects sang in the dark forest. *I hear you, old magician. You have read the legends well, and you know. But this knowing will crush your heart!*

Dr. Kreistein blew his nose. "You have a problem I think, Herr Prinz. You cannot fight the boy until he chooses to come out of his circles and stop making noises like a crab. This means I have time to teach him something, unless you stop me. But there is not much you can do to me, Ombra. Old men are too feeble to be tempted. We have seen so much of life that even you are not very frightening. *Jetzt*, already, we are making friends with death. A few months more, a few months less of living, it isn't important. So. I will settle an old score with you—and you know what it is. After we have finished, the boy will kill you."

He put the handkerchief back into his pocket. "This is a good task to end an old man's life, Prinz. It will not, I think, be so good for you."

He looked again at the dark sea, strolled back to the house, and went to bed. The sounds of insects were shrill in the trees, but no one heard the words in them.

No one except Willybill. He hadn't sung his songs in the roadhouse that night; he was standing in the moonlight on the dirt road that led to the Ellicott house.

He listened to the infuriated buzzing of the cicadas and spat in the dust. Then he climbed into his pickup truck and drove back to the sleeping village.

Chapter Eight

The fires of remorse burned in the nimbus of the rising sun. The coast and granite hills were drenched with light the colors of gold and blood. In Bentley's toy box the stone glittered as if it, too, had caught the burn of the new day.

Prince Ombra was shapeless, diffused in the haze and glow of morning. His essence was alive on the northern coast; his vaporous poison spread from there throughout the world. Foreboding trembled in a dawn, a noon, a sunset, and a midnight as the planet turned. Ombra sang a temptation to heroes in a voice as sweet as the first lark song of the day. In his fourth brain, he searched the charnel house of memory for spells to stun magicians. His second brain had made a strategy in the hours of the night.

He watched.

He listened as a screen door slammed and the boy-warrior limped across the lawn to the beach followed by his rememberer. Two fish hawks rose from the stump of a dead tree and cruised in the bright air.

Lord Ombra saw that the boy was surrounded by an aura of divine protection. That was the circle the magician had spoken of. The Dreaded One watched Bentley limp. He heard the residue of the warrior's dreams. From fact and dream he had devised his first plan.

Ombra watched his enemy's rememberer trailing him across the rocky beach. She was talking to him, but in gibberish. Mirth burst from Ombra like a wave crashing on the shore. This one would tell no tale, repeat no saga for the world's store of legends. There would be nothing worth remembering when Ombra was finished with his crippled enemy. The prince of all melancholies saw dewdrops glistening on stalks of grass as the jewels of his victory.

Bentley picked up a skipping stone. Slally found another. "Watch how I do it," Bentley told her, holding the stone between his curved forefinger and thumb. He threw the stone. It sailed out over the choppy water, flicking spray into the shining light as it skipped from wave to wave.

Slally threw her stone. It arched against the sky and fell, slipping sideways into the water without a splash.

Bentley stood for a moment, looking at the place where Slally's stone had plopped into the waves. Never, it seemed to him, had a morning been so beautiful. His new power nestled in his mind like a miraculous potion that filled him with happiness and confidence. He heard the song of the lark and believed that he could do anything he wanted to do. His protective magic shone around him as if extra light had been added to the day just for him.

He picked up another flat rock. The lark trilled again. Bentley threw the skipping stone, suddenly willing it to circle the water and return to the shore.

Ombra decreed that this would be.

The stone skittered over the water in a curve; spurts of spray marked its wide course. It leaped from the breaking crest of an inshore wave and skidded across the flat, gleaming sand, stopping at Slally's feet.

She looked at Bentley wide-eyed and asked him how he'd done that.

Bentley was as astonished as she was. "I just decided to make it come back," he said.

Slally told him to do it again.

Bentley found another flat stone. He curved his finger around it, willed it to return to the beach, and threw hard.

The stone flashed in a straight line out over the water, skipping four times. Then it sank.

A fresh wave crashed onto the sand, its hissing foam spreading up to where Bentley and Slally stood. *Your magic was given to you because of me,* Prince Ombra hissed. *It is not yours until you have dealt with me.*

Bentley frowned. "You're a liar!" he said loudly. "I had magic before you came!"

Slally asked him what Ombra had said.

"He says I only have magic because of him,"

Bentley told her. "He's a liar. I could do all kinds of stuff before."

Slally grabbed his arm and said she was scared.

"C'mon," Bentley said. "He can't do anything until I decide to fight."

Slally said he didn't know that for sure. She told him to go back to the house and talk to Dr. Kreistein about what happened with the skipping stones.

Suddenly Bentley's confidence turned to irritation—as if she didn't believe in him. "I don't need to talk to Dr. Kreistein," he said. "It's okay."

Slally stared at him for a moment. Then she walked back to the house with Bentley following her.

Richard had left for the university. Ellen and Dr. Kreistein were talking to a real estate lady in the dining room. After Helga gave Bentley and Slally their breakfast they followed the three adults along a path through the woods to a two-story Victorian house painted a mustard color. It had a porch running around three sides and large rooms that smelled musty.

A shadow the size of a rat slipped along the baseboards and up the stairs as Dr. Kreistein inspected the house. *Remember!* said a wooden beam in a creaking whisper as the old man stepped on it. Dr. Kreistein told the agent the house would do.

Bentley stood on the porch railing and grabbed the edge of the roof. He swung his sneakers up into the cobwebby ceiling. He was still irritated. He was also filled with excitement at the way he'd been able to make the skipping stone do what he willed it to do. He had begun to imagine all the wonders he could perform once he'd gotten rid of Prince Ombra.

Slally was inspecting a pair of rusted andirons lying in the rubble at the end of the porch. She hadn't spoken to Bentley since they'd left the beach.

Bentley jumped down off the porch railing. "People used to hide treasure in old houses like this," he said.

Slally told him to stop being silly. She said he ought to have told Dr. Kreistein what happened on the beach.

"I don't *need* to tell him!" Bentley said loudly. "He doesn't know everything."

Slally said she was afraid for him.

"Listen," Bentley said. "You're just scared because Ombra said I didn't have any magic. I'll prove it to you that he's a liar."

Slally asked how.

"I know where there's some treasure," he said. "Nobody else in the whole world knows. Real jewels and stuff."

Slally looked at him in doubt.

"I'll show you," Bentley said.

In the village Ellen dropped them off at the wharf and then drove Dr. Kreistein to the real estate office. The old man's hand shook slightly as he signed the lease. His mind was dull that morning, as if it were burdened with something heavy and indistinct that sleep had not disposed of. He wrote a check and handed it to the real estate agent. "I will come back Saturday, perhaps Monday," he said. "There will be many books with me."

"Fine, the woman answered. "I'm sure you'll be very happy working in the library on the ground floor."

Driving back to the point with Dr. Kreistein sitting beside her, Ellen Drake thought how absurd it was to say that a room could make someone happy.

For her, happiness was freedom from the curse of memory. She had been in a white shimmer of bliss with Richard Ellicott until the day before when he refused to give away his wife's clothes hanging in the attic. Hearing that one-word refusal, Ellen had felt the sting of pain that had struck her on the day her husband left her to marry a younger woman. Now she felt incapable of competing—even with the vestiges of Richard's loyalty to a dead woman. She had treated him at a distance for the rest of the day and had rejected him when he'd tried to make love to her. She hated herself for her behavior and the insecurity that inspired it.

She turned the car into the driveway and switched off the ignition. For a moment she considered asking Dr. Kreistein if she could talk to him professionally. But the old man seemed preoccupied. "Is there anything we should do for Bentley while you're gone?" she asked.

Dr. Kreistein took out a little pad and scribbled a prescription. "For if he cannot go to sleep," he said, handing her a slip of paper. "If he has another nightmare when he is awake like yesterday, you should call me immediately."

"His father is upset because you won't tell him what's wrong with Bentley."

Dr. Kreistein nodded.

"What about Sally?" Ellen asked.

Dr. Kreistein put the prescription pad back in his pocket. "I think now we will stop her visits to the clinic for a while. She doesn't like it."

Ellen felt a slight and inexplicable irritation stirring within her. "Will you work with Sally this summer, too?"

Dr. Kreistein nodded. *"Ja.* Of course." He looked through the windshield at the azalea bushes swaying at the edge of the lawn in the warm wind.

Ellen felt dismissed. "If Bentley can understand her, doesn't that mean that the clinic's original diagnosis of her was wrong?"

"Science doesn't know everything," Dr. Kreistein answered.

Ellen's irritation became a burst of rage. "That's a stupid and evasive answer!" she snapped. "I think we ought to take both children away from you!"

Dr. Kreistein turned away from his contemplation of the sunny morning. He looked at her. "From you, I expected something, perhaps, more subtle," he said as if he were addressing someone else.

Ellen looked dazed.

"Mrs. Drake," Dr. Kreistein said quietly, "you did not say these words you have just spoken. Do you understand me?"

Ellen was bewildered. Something terrifying had passed through her like a voltage that had momentarily altered her. She was searching for herself.

"And you will have no more thoughts about removing these children from my care." Dr. Kreistein's old, accented voice was edged with a determination that was almost harsh. "If you did this, your daughter would never speak. I am the only one who knows, maybe, what is really wrong with her."

Ellen stared at him. "Are you telling me you can cure her?"

"Without me it is impossible," Dr. Kreistein said. "With me—" He shrugged. "We will see what we will see."

Ellen bowed her head and put one long hand over her face. "I'm sorry," she said. "Of course we won't take the children away from you." She raised her head. Her eyes were filled with tears. "I don't know what got into me a moment ago."

The old man patted her arm. "We will tell each other something got into you," he said. "If it happens again, we will remember this morning, hah?"

Driving inland toward the university in his car, Dietrich Kreistein passed through the remnants of an old village on the bare crest of a ridge. A boarded-up church and a deserted store stood forlornly against the sky.

Swift as the cloud shadows that pass over sunny landscapes, Prince Ombra raced ahead of the old man. The Lord of Nightmares' strategy against the boy had begun; its premise was embedded in Bentley's mind. Now this magician needed to be immobilized so that he couldn't interfere. Ombra broke an ampule of old, crippling doubt in that part of Dietrich Kreistein's soul where secrets were held.

Remember! wheezed the car's decrepit engine.

"Ombra, Ombra." The old man sighed aloud.

"Are you trying to trick me by doing something so stupid? This woman loves her child. I used her love so that she would not take these children from me.

"Maybe you don't understand about love, Herr Prinz. Permit me to instruct you. It is a very strong business. Stronger, I think than sorcery."

Remember! whispered the wind from the north.

Dietrich Kreistein tightened his grip on the steering wheel as the car swayed in the gusts. "I wonder if you can hear me, Ombra."

A mottled bobcat burst from a tree line. It streaked across the road and stopped, one paw raised. It looked at the approaching car with feline loathing in its eyes. Ombra had touched the animal's brain and possessed it.

Dietrich Kreistein barely noticed the bobcat. He was telling himself that he had to become a detective in a mystery story. Now that he believed the boy, he had to deduce what was happening. He had awakened early in the morning determined to spend the day thinking about the little girl. Where she fit in. He had already concluded that her appearance in the boy's life was no accident.

But the dullness in his mind kept her at a distance. It smothered his power to think.

Mrs. John Rutherford Hackett was crazy.

When she first came to Stonehaven in 1917 with her servant, a reticent man named Lafcadio, Mrs. Hackett seemed to be nothing more than a self-indulgent rich lady. Every summer she rented five rooms side by side on the fourth floor of the Stonehaven House Hotel. She put herself in the center room, Lafcadio in an outer one, and left the others empty. She spent July and August surrounded by emptiness, taking her meals alone in the dining room and being driven around the countryside by Lafcadio in her large black touring car. She was plump in appearance and distantly dignified in manner.

In 1922 she rented seven rooms. The year after the stock market crash, Mrs. Hacket rented the entire fourth floor for herself and Lafcadio.

Charlie Feavey inherited the old hotel from his father. He remembered as a boy asking Mrs. Hackett why she insisted on having empty rooms around her. "I don't want *them* near me," she said.

As Stonehaven and its hotel declined, the New York dowager grew madder and madder. She stopped speaking to everybody except Lafcadio. He stood behind her chair in the dining room. She would look at the menu and tell Lafcadio what she wanted, and he told the waitress as if he were translating from another language.

In her last years she was the sole support of the Stonehaven House Hotel. She rented the whole place from mid-June to Labor Day and lived on the fourth floor. No one, not even the Feaveys, were permitted to go upstairs. Lafcadio swept the halls and changed the beds. At night people heard the insane woman and her servant making noises. Lafcadio died in the spring of 1937. A month after that, Mrs. Hackett was put into an institution, where she died three years later. The Stonehaven House Hotel closed for good.

Charlie Feavey knew a lot about this strange dowager. He liked to tell Mrs. Hackett stories around the village.

Bentley Ellicott knew much more than Charlie Feavey. Every word that Mrs. Hackett and Lafcadio had ever exchanged in Stonehaven remained in the second air. Their conversations were mysterious and absorbing—whispers, mutters, and instructions. Bentley listened to them over and over. He had never thought of Mrs. Hackett's secret as important. He knew so much about the Stonehaven past that nothing said or revealed by the dead voices in the second air astonished him.

But now, suddenly, Mrs. Hackett's insane secret *was* important to Bentley. He was going to use it to impress Slally and become the leader again after a half-morning of feeling both amazed and angry.

"C'mon," he said to her when Ellen had dropped them at the town wharf. "I'll show you something."

Slally shoved her hands into her dungaree pockets and followed him up Main Street. They crossed it and waded through the tall grass that grew around the shuttered hotel. In the rear, the wet, punky boards of a back porch were shaded by tall bushes.

Bentley climbed up onto a propane gas cylinder that, in winter, provided fuel to heat the one room Charlie Feavey occupied. Bentley braced himself as Slally watched, pulled back a flaking shutter, and opened the window to Charlie's room.

Slally said that Mr. Feavey would catch them.

"Nah," Bentley said, stepping carefully over the window and climbing in. "He's gone fishing with Mr. McGraw. I saw them." He disappeared inside.

"Every kid in town's broken in here," said his voice from the room.

Ten seconds later he unlatched the back door and pulled it open. Slally climbed up onto the decrepit porch, teetered her way over to the door, and peered inside. It smelled dry and slightly burned. Slally saw a long hallway. Sunlight came through the grimy windows and lay in square patches on broken floorboards. Everything was covered with dust.

She looked at Bentley.

"It's *okay,*" he said. "It isn't like breaking into a regular house where you're going to steal stuff."

Slally stepped inside. She shoved her hands into her dungaree pockets again.

Bentley picked up a small crowbar that was leaning against the wall.

Slally said that was stealing.

"What's the matter with you?" he demanded. "I'm just going to *use* it for a minute to show you something. Come on!"

He went down the hall and started to climb the stairs. After a moment's hesitation, Slally followed him, doing what he told her to do.

Chief McGraw and Charlie Feavey came out of the woods at the end of the point. They often went fishing together in the mornings now. They were wearing chest-high rubber waders. They carried casting rods and tackle boxes. McGraw had an eleven-pound striped bass slung over his shoulder. Its head was crushed; a stevedore's hook pierced its gaping mouth. The two men broke down their rods, stored them in the police cruiser's trunk, and threw the dead bass in on top. They drove down the dirt road toward Stonehaven.

They passed a turning into the town dump. Willybill was sitting in his parked pickup truck. He had one booted foot propped on the dashboard, a toothpick in his mouth. His gaze followed McGraw and Charlie as they drove by.

"See your weird buddy on the dump road?" Feavey asked.

McGraw grunted.

"I'd give a hundred bucks to know why he's hung around here so long."

"If he pulls something, he'll get his ass kicked," McGraw answered.

"Still watching the Ellicott kid, is he?"

"That's another one could use a kick in the ass," McGraw said.

The cruiser crossed the highway and slowed as it rolled into Main Street. McGraw parked in front of the hotel.

"I expect I've got a couple of beers in the cooler," Charlie said.

"I should hope," McGraw answered as they mounted the steps.

Charlie unlocked the front door. They walked through the door. They walked through the cool, littered ground floor to Feavey's bedroom. "Crap," he said, looking at the open shutter. "Damned kids have been breaking in again. If I catch one of 'em—"

"You ought to either get locks or burn the place down," McGraw said. "What about that beer?"

Charlie Feavey opened a red cooler that had COCA-COLA painted on its side. He bent over and then straightened up.

"You hear something?" he asked.

McGraw raised his head. "Sounds like some-body's upstairs."

They mounted the stairway, paused at the sec-ond floor, and listened. The sound of splintering wood came from above them. Quietly they climb-ed to the third floor and heard the murmur of voices. McGraw and Feavey went up another flight of stairs. They stood in the dusty hallway.

"That's just one," they heard Bentley's voice saying. "She hid jewels all over the hotel."

Slally's incomprehensible voice replied in the soft sound of wonder.

McGraw and Feavey walked down the hall and kicked open the door of the room. Bentley and Slally looked up with frightened expressions on their faces.

Slally was sitting and Bentley was kneeling on the floor of the room. The crowbar and a floor-board lay beside him. Something sparkled in the dark, narrow crevice between the two children.

Charlie walked across the room and looked down. "Son of a bitch," he murmured. He squat-ted and took a piece of jewelry from the exposed place beneath the floor. He stood up as Bentley and Slally watched in silence. Charlie blew dust off a diamond bracelet. "Son of a bitch," he repeated softly.

McGraw crossed the room. "How did that thing get there?" he asked Bentley.

"The rich lady had it hid," Bentley answered in a small voice.

"What rich lady?"

"The one who used to come up here in the summer," Bentley said.

"That's crap," Charlie Feavey snapped. "That old lunatic died forty-three, forty-five years ago." He grabbed Bentley by the arm and lifted him to his feet. "You stole that bracelet and put it down there!"

"Cut it out!" Bentley yelled. "I didn't steal anything! She made that guy Lafcadio hide it!" He was half off the floor, dangling in Feavey's grip, and his arm felt as if it was going to break. "Lay off!"

"I'll give you lay off," Charlie shouted, shaking him. "How would a little bastard like you know—"

"Let him go," McGraw said.

"Mind your own damned business!" Feavey said. He was getting into a frenzy of excitement and anger.

McGraw took Charlie's wrist and twisted it. Charlie released Bentley, who collapsed on the floor in a heap. Feavey cursed at McGraw.

"Let's see that bracelet," McGraw said.

"It's mine by rights," Charlie snarled.

"Not until we find out where it came from," McGraw told him. "Hand it over."

Charlie gave him the bracelet. Bentley was less scared than he was amazed. McGraw and Charlie Feavey went fishing together. Neither of them liked Bentley. Now they were acting like enemies.

McGraw stepped over to the window and held the bracelet up to the light. "Looks like it's been down there a time," he said more to himself than anybody else. "Got grime all around the stones." He turned the bracelet over and ran his thumb

along the inside of its silver rim. "M.R.H. from
J.R.H., July 1915," he read slowly. McGraw put
the bracelet into his shirt pocket.

He turned to Charlie Feavey, who was standing
in the middle of the floor, glaring. "Mrs. John
Rutherford Hacket," Charlie snapped. "It's mine."

"That the rich lady?" McGraw asked.

"That's her," Feavey said. "Crazy as a barn
owl." He looked at Bentley sitting on the floor.
"Where's the rest of the stuff she hid?"

Bentley didn't answer. Sitting opposite him,
Slally watched with anxious eyes.

"Goddammit!" Charlie shouted. "You're gonna
tell me where she put the rest of it if I have to—"
He lunged at Bentley. McGraw brought his big fist
up suddenly. It hit Charlie in the face. Feavey staggered sideways and fell onto an old, rusted bed.

"Bastard!" Charlie screamed, holding his hand
over his face. Blood trickled between his fingers
from a broken nose.

McGraw went over to the bed and pulled Charlie
up by the back of his collar. "Now, you hear me,"
he said in a deep voice. "If I catch you bothering
either of these kids, I'll run you in for child mo-
lesting." He shook Feavey. "You know what they
do to child molesters, Charlie?"

"Bastard," Feavey said bitterly. Blood was
smeared all over the lower half of his face.

McGraw released him. "You remember," he
said. He picked Slally up and set her on her feet.
"C'mon," he said to Bentley.

With his arm around Slally's shoulders,
McGraw took them out to the cruiser and put
them in the front seat. He got in beside them,

crossed his arms on the steering wheel, and gazed out across the sunlit harbor. Sea gulls wheeled over the pier. "Care to say how you knew the bracelet was under there?" he asked.

Slally said Bentley ought to tell.

"I can't," Bentley answered.

McGraw told himself to take it slow. There were a lot of rooms in the old hotel. It would take Charlie weeks to tear them apart. Once McGraw got the boy's confidence, he could lock up Charlie on a drunk charge and find the stuff in the hotel in one night. Charlie was half drunk most of the time anyway.

The police chief looked down at Bentley. "You kids ride your bikes into town?"

"Her mom brought us," Bentley said.

"Guess I'd better take you home," McGraw said, switching on the ignition.

Bentley was bewildered. McGraw hadn't bawled him out for not telling. Now he was going to give them a ride.

McGraw drove to the end of Main Street. Going up the hill toward the highway, he switched on the siren. It made a wavering howl as they crossed the potato fields, turned into the woods, and turned again into the Ellicott's driveway. Bentley and Slally were delighted. McGraw stopped the cruiser and flipped off the siren.

The screen door slammed and Helga came out onto the porch. She looked frightened when she saw McGraw getting out of the police car.

"Brought a couple of friends of yours home," the chief said.

Slally ran up the porch steps and started telling

Helga about riding in the cruiser.

Helga put her arm around Slally and told her to be quiet. "What did they do?" she asked McGraw.

"Nothing," McGraw said. "You folks like stripers?"

"Please?" Helga asked.

"Striped bass," McGraw said. "Caught a good one about an hour ago." He walked around and opened the trunk of the cruiser. He took the hook out of the fish's mouth and handed it to Bentley. "Both arms," he said. "That's some heavy bass."

Bentley stood in the driveway, holding the striper in his arms and looking at McGraw. He didn't understand. He was pleased that the police chief didn't think he was crazy any longer. But he didn't want to say anything in case McGraw changed his mind.

McGraw looked down at Bentley. "If Charlie Feavey gives you any trouble, you just let me know."

"Okay," Bentley said. He was both elated and puzzled as the dust settled after the cruiser had gone.

Helga came down the porch steps. "What did you do?"

Bentley looked up at her. He shrugged. The bass was heavy in his arms.

"But you must have done *something* to make him change so!"

"I don't know," Bentley said in wonder at himself.

Ombra rose as steam from the shining streets. *Remember!* murmured the pelting rain.

Steam clouded the windows of Dietrich Kreistein's library, and he could not see out into the
world at evening.

Remember! whispered the whoosh of distant
traffic, the rumble of cattle cars swaying and
jostling their human cargo in the winter dawn.
The young women to Ravensbruck, the old to
Belsen, mothers and children to Dachau. *O mein
Bruder!* cried a girl's voice across the gray void of
decades. *Wo bist du?* Ombra spread a bitter mist
of accusation as the light went down. His fourth
brain, which is the memory of all things, all pain
and remorse, cast its heat in the darkened library
where Dietrich Kreistein sat alone, imprisoned in
his helpless remembering.

*O my brother, where are you? Do you know what
they have done? All are gone save me. Brickmann
came an hour ago to say that, tomorrow, I will go,
too. He will do favors if favors are given him. But I
have nothing more to give, Dietrich!*

Dr. Kreistein sat facing the window's disappearing light. One hand held the letter in his lap; the
paper was dry, its creases split from a thousand
unfoldings through the years. "What do I tell you
now, my Anna, to make easier your passage to dying so long ago? What could I have told you then if
I had been able to speak to you?"

*When they came for Papa and Mordecai we had
no men left in the house. Only Hilde and me. You
cannot know how barren it is in a house with no
men, Dietrich. Once Brickmann questioned me
about you. He did not believe you were in America.
Jews have had no permission to leave for a long
time. I could not explain that we had paid money*

*so that they would allow you to go to the confer-
ence in Lisbon . . .*

"Do you accuse me, Anna? Do you make my safety shameful by telling me of your peril? I do not
believe that is what you intend. I think you must
speak to me in one last letter because there is
no one else. Hilde is stupid and is herself terrified."

*Is it a green place where you live? I wish I had a
letter from you. We have not had one since May,
two years ago next month . . .*

"It is not my fault, Anna, I wrote. My wife,
whom you never knew, wrote also to her German
family. All my letters to you came back. *Adresse
unbekannt,* they are stamped. They are still in the
desk drawer right here, my letters to you. You
would believe that I wrote if you could see them."

Ombra descended as poisonous nightfall. He
drenched the air with the waters of bitter vulner-
ability which drown the time-healed heart in old
recrimination.

"Anna, Anna, the eldest of us all who became the
mother after Mama died. So certain and strong. I
thought that all the world's wisdom was in her.
She made Mordecai and me learn the Kaddish by
heart when Grandpapa went to his grave. We are
Jews, she told us. God has given us this gift as a
special way of speaking to Him for the comfort of
Grandpapa's soul. It is commanded that Papa and
the boys say Kaddish, and you will not read such a
wonderful thing from a book. You will stand up
and say it as a Jew and as a man, from the heart."

Mordecai was eight in 1922, the year Grandpapa
died. Anna was only fourteen.

*I have given Brickmann everything we owned. I
have given him everything else. Now I am to have
his child and he no longer wants me. He is afraid
he will get into trouble for being the father of a
Jewish child. He did not try to protect us. I think he
is the one who gave the order to send us away . . .*

"Thin, sallow-faced Brickmann pumping himself on you? Why do you tell me this, Anna? A
coughing village policeman they made an *Unter-
führer* so that he could lie on top of you and then
take away your life? You reproach me with all the
indignities you have suffered. You tell me exactly
how it is and, in this way, damn me for living in
peace!

There is no auf Wiedersehen, *Dietrich. There is
only farewell. I love you. Already, I am proud of
what you will be. Remember me . . .*

Old men are doomed to remember everything.
Old men weep like children. Dietrich Kreistein
folded the brittle paper and put it back into its
envelope. The delivery of the letter almost forty
years before had been the final cruelty.

If Dr. Kreistein had not had it and others from
his sister, he might not have felt the helpless
shame of the survivor. He might have felt only immense grief.

The evening darkness thickened. The rain became a pounding torrent on the roof of the porch
outside his library window. The dullness in
Dietrich Kreistein's mind had hardened into despair and self-hatred. He was incapable of thinking about anything except the oblivion of sleep.
He had been repossessed by years that had long

since blurred into subsequent years of work, thought, happiness and sadnesses.

He took a handkerchief from his breast pocket and looked at it, crumpled and white in the final light that remained. *"Ja,"* he said to himself, *"this one is for me."* He wiped the tears from his face and lowered his hands.

That handkerchief was for him. He always carried two. Sometimes children cried when he talked to them. In the corner of his mind he remembered giving the other handkerchief to Bentley. This boy had not been crying. He had been gripped by emotions he did not understand. But he hadn't cried.

Neither had Susano, the snake-killer. Nowhere in the great stories had a hero wept in fear. *History is the history of murder,* Dietrich Kreistein told himself; *men brutalize each other. But all passes and there is light again, because some come forth who do not weep when they confront the enemy of the soul.*

Dietrich Kreistein raised his head. He sniffed. *Dummkopf!* he said to himself. *After so much time you sit crying for what cannot be undone. Do you think this happens to you by chance? You feel bad because you are alive, and so you are going to go to sleep and try to forget? Maybe this is what somebody wants you to do—go to sleep and forget about everything, including the boy.*

He stood up and moved across the library to a long table. He switched on a lamp. The room glowed with warm, comforting light.

The old man put his handkerchief back in his pocket and went into the bathroom. He opened the medicine cabinet and took a pill. "Just in case somebody has a plan I should have a heart attack," he said aloud.

He turned off the bathroom light and went into the front hall.

Thunder split through the storm, crashed, and rumbled away toward the sea.

"I hear you," Dietrich Kreistein said. "And now I know that you hear me."

He opened the front door. The freshness of the wet evening washed over him. The oppressive weight in his mind had vanished.

"Listen to me, Ombra," he said in the rainy darkness. "Hardly anybody believes in you anymore. You are too easy an explanation for so much that is wrong with the world. To people nowadays the idea that there is a perfect evil is very frightening. If we accepted such a thing again, we would need to believe in a perfect good, too. Then everybody would feel inadequate and have to take a tranquilizer for the nerves."

He moved to the center of the porch where Willybill had stood in the dusk weeks before. "You know what I know, Herr Prinz. I have seen your face in the old stories that our ancestors left behind—hoping to teach us." He grunted. "It was the boy who finally made me believe what I knew. Now I will teach *him* what *his* heart already knows."

A gust of wind drove the rain in slanted sheets through a pool of lamplight.

"I don't think you are just amusing yourself by making me miserable, Ombra," Dietrich Kreistein said. "The world is suddenly full of you, Prinz. I have seen you like this before—in the newspapers which print the arguments leaders make to justify wicked things they do . . . in people's lives. Perhaps you have attacked me because I recognize that you have come back. But I don't think so. I think you are afraid to fight this boy and have a plan to corrupt him before you need to make a fight. But first you must get me out of the way." He breathed deeply. A profound calm was within him. "You have gone about it all wrong, Ombra. You have just reminded me of my sister, who is the personal score I will settle with you. You have made me realize that the purpose of my life is to teach the boy what others who came before him knew."

The wind whirled a heavy splatter of rain onto the porch and sidewalk. "Now I am going to go inside, drink tea, and think about what this plan of yours may be. Good night, Prinz Ombra."

He went back into the house and slammed the door.

"Sleep, Anna," Dietrich Kreistein muttered. "This one who made the poison that destroyed you will regret it a little bit, I think, when I am through with him."

He went into the kitchen and made a pot of tea. He was no longer tired. He was filled with exaltation because he had found the purpose of his life almost at the end of it. The old man carried his tray back to the library. Thunder crashed down the night sky, and the wind shook the house. Dr. Kreistein spread a napkin on his desk and carefully set down the tray.

Then he made himself comfortable in his chair,

folded his hands across the bulge of his stomach, and began to think.

Slally sat on Bentley's bed, looking at him in bewilderment. They were both wearing their pajamas. The day was ending as it had begun; Slally was full of disbelief.

"I don't want to talk about it," Bentley said.

He wanted her to go away. He wanted to be alone with the daydream that had burst in his mind with the coming of the storm.

Slally's eyes were bright. Her thin face was flushed and her mouth was set in a straight line. Bentley was angry at her. She was trying to boss him around.

He looked down at his feet. His right pajama leg was drawn up. Bentley looked at his withered calf. He had always accepted his deformity. He had always limited his fantasies about himself to accommodate the fact of his weakness. Now, suddenly, he could dream that both of his legs were strong.

It was really going to happen.

He listened to the storm. Within the dull drumming of the rain, he could hear other sounds. They'd begun when he and Slally were sent up to bed. *Throw the stone away!* cried the gravel as it clattered across the beach with a receding wave. *Run, Ellicott, run!*

Slally said that Prince Ombra was talking again, wasn't he?

Bentley raised his head. "Yeah," he said. "He's talking."

Slally demanded to know what Ombra was saying.

Bentley grasped both his ankles and looked down at his right foot.

He wanted to dismiss from his mind all the turmoil that had disrupted the house as the darkness approached from the east and the storm from the west. Bentley wanted to blot it all out and replay the daydream that Ombra had delivered to him.

Both Bentley and Slally could hear the uneven sounds of argument floating up from the living room. Ellen's strident voice and Richard's mumbled replies cut through the repeating eruptions of thunder, the rain's drumming, and the gusts of wind that battered the house. *Throw it away!* cried Ombra the Omnipotent, spreading his poison across the stormy night sky. *Throw the stone away and our battle will be done!*

"Why can't you admit it?" Ellen cried angrily.

Then you will perform wonders without end, murmured Prince Ombra in a torrent of water gushing from a pipe onto the sodden ground beneath Bentley's bedroom window. *Run, Ellicott, run!*

Richard's reply was too low for Bentley and Slally to hear the words. It was a defensive undertone, spoken and then dismissed by Ellen's resentful voice.

Slally's expression changed as she lifted her face to listen to her mother and Richard. Bentley watched her. He thought she was going to cry. She almost had when they came upstairs. The argument had started in the sunlit hush of midafternoon. Helga had kept out of the way in the kitchen. As Bentley and Slally watched the evening news on television, Richard and Ellen had been continuing their fight on the porch.

Violent pictures had appeared on the TV screen in grim sequence. Angry men contradicted each other in Washington. Tanks and truckloads of soldiers crossed a ruined landscape. Airplanes roared down the sky. People wept as a coffin was carried from a building and then threw themselves on the ground. Bursts of smoke rose from the entrails of a city as the airplanes wheeled in the sky above it like vengeful birds.

Ellen's piercing accusations and Richard's dull answers were as threatening as the scenes on television. The grownups had eaten dinner in heavy silence. Bentley turned on the TV again. He switched from one dopey program to another. Then the rain started, and, with the arrival of the storm, the daydream brightened in his mind—as if it followed logically on the events of a remarkable day. Bentley had never stopped marveling at his power—to make McGraw and Mr. Feavey have a fight, and to will a skipping stone to flash over the waves and return to the shore.

When I am gone, your wishes will come true, Lord Ombra had announced in the distant thunder. *Throw away the stone of the accursed Ra and our quarrel will be over,* whispered Ombra in the first gusts of storm wind that passed through the treetops. *Then your magic will serve your dreams.*

Ellen cried out in scorn. Richard's voice rose.

The storm's violent core approached the coast.

Bentley watched Slally's eyes. They were magnified by tears. Her mouth trembled.

"Listen," he said, "I could make them stop." He let go of his ankles and took hold of Slally's arms. "You're scared your mom's going to take you away, aren't you?"

Her cheeks were wet and her mouth was curved into a weeping grimace. She nodded.

"Listen!" Bentley said urgently. "I can fix it so they'll make up and you'll *never* have to go away!" His heart cried a warning to him. Its voice of rectitude within him said he was wrong, that he was betraying the very purpose for which he had been born.

But Bentley willed himself not to hear. In Slally's tears he saw a chance to get her to agree with what he had to do to make his fantastic dream come true.

Slally wiped her eyes on the hem of her pajama top. Her voice broke as she asked Bentley how he could get their parents to stop fighting.

Self-reproach rose in Bentley, but the sounds and vision of the daydream overpowered it. When he answered Slally, his voice was full of excitement. "If Ombra goes away, I'll have my magic to use for whatever I want! I can make anybody do anything!"

Slally looked startled. She wiped another tear from her cheek with her fingers.

"All I've got to do is take that stone out of the toy box and throw it in the sea!" he said. "That's what he's saying! If I throw away the stone—"

He abruptly stopped speaking as he saw her face change. Her eyes were still wet, but they were angry.

"What's the matter with *you?*" Bentley demanded, feeling the hot flush of embarrassment spread across his cheeks.

She told him he shouldn't even *think* of throwing away the stone. Dr. Kreinstein would be ashamed of him, and she would be, too.

"You don't want everything to be all right again!" Bentley said. "You're not the one who has to fight him."

Rain slashed against the western side of the house. Thunder rolled across the sky. *Run, Ellicott, run!* shouted thousands of people in the daydream. *I will give you the world!* roared the Lord of Nightmares. *Throw away the stone!*

Slally told Bentley that he couldn't do anything until he talked to Dr. Kreistein.

Bentley looked at the windows. The storm was moving. He saw jagged flashes of lightning reaching for the sea's horizon like stiff, electric fingers.

He looked down at his thin foot again.

The house shuddered again with a new buffeting of wind and rain. Ellen's accusing voice rose relentlessly above the drumming of the storm on the roof over Bentley's room.

Slally slid off the bed. She said that she was going downstairs to get a Coke.

"Get me one, too," Bentley said without raising his head. "I've got to think."

Slally went out into the dark hall. She looked back at Bentley. He was still gazing at his toes. His eyes beneath his thatch of brown hair were unfocused and full of dreams.

That afternoon Ellen had come home with Bentley's sleeping pills in a bottle. She put them in her bathroom, told Slally what they were, and said not to touch them.

Downstairs, Richard said something Slally couldn't hear. She flinched as lightning made everything in the hall vivid for a moment. Thunder broke, rattling windows. She heard her mother say, "Christ, can't you acknowledge *anything?*" Slally pushed open Richard's bedroom door and went into the bathroom. She climbed up on the toilet seat, switched on the light, and took the bottle of pills from the medicine cabinet.

She turned off the light and went downstairs with a sleeping pill in her hand. Everything frightened her. The argument in the living room had gone on for hours. The weight of the air told her that Prince Ombra was everywhere, that they were drowning in his presence.

She groped her way into the kitchen. Prince Ombra was power and death. She knew how scared Bentley had been before he found the stone. She wished more than anything that she could protect him. But a wordless voice within her said that she was part of the war, too—in a way she didn't understand. She had to make Bentley keep the stone.

Slally put her forehead against the smooth, cool refrigerator door and began to cry.

Thunder broke over the house like a load of black gravel. Its shattered fragments echoed in the forest and dissipated on the rolling sea.

Willybill raised his head and looked at the

storm-swirled sky. He was leaning against a tree on the edge of the lawn with the forest at his back. His arms were folded, and water dripped from the brim of his hat. He heard the voice of Ombra thundering across the world. He saw great Ombra's shape sprawled from horizon to black horizon. The Dreaded One had become air and flint. He reeked in the drenched earth and flung ninety-nine storm-spewing arms across the billowing heavens. *Throw away the stone!* he thundered in the churning darkness. *Make the dream come true!* The Lord of Nightmares' sorcery filled the air with another sound, the acoustics of a fantasy, and Willybill heard that, too—the roar of thousands, the voices roaring as one voice. *Run, Ellicott, run!*

Willybill shrugged himself deeper into his sheepskin jacket and grinned. He tightened his arms around his body and looked at the house. He saw bright lights in the living room, the orange glow of Bentley's bedroom windows. Willybill saw a faint, swift waxing and waning of light in the kitchen as Slally opened and closed the refrigerator door. He laughed softly and made a rasping sound as he cleared his throat. He watched with the anticipatory grin still on his face.

Slally ripped the seal off a soft-drink can. She poured half into a glass and dropped the sleeping pill into the can. She pulled down a dish towel and wiped her eyes. She was frightened of Prince Ombra, but she hated him, too.

She took the glass and the can back upstairs. She heard her mother crying as she walked along the dark hallway, trying not to spill the drinks.

Bentley was still sitting on his bed, one hand clutching his thin right foot.

Slally climbed up beside him, handed him the can, and asked if he'd made up his mind about throwing away the stone.

Bentley nodded. "I'm going to do it." He drank from the can. "It's going to be okay," he said without looking at Slally. "You'll see." His face was somber.

Carefully, so that he didn't get mad again, Slally began to argue with him. She said that Bentley wasn't supposed to make deals with Ombra. They would have told him if that was all right.

Bentley drained the can. "He promised me something," he said softly.

Slally asked what Ombra had promised him.

Bentley put the can on the bedside table and lay on his back. "I don't want to talk about it," he said thickly, looking at the ceiling. "I'm going to throw away the stone. I'm going to do it tonight. In just a minute."

The storm rumbled on the sea. Then it seemed to turn back. A clap of thunder broke close to the shore, and the hard pelting of the rain resumed.

"In just a minute I'm going to get up," Bentley said.

Lightning flashed across the lawn, illuminating the swaying trees for an instant.

"I'm just resting my eyes."

Slally didn't move or answer him until he was asleep.

And when his sleep was so profound that he could no longer hear Prince Ombra, the rage of the storm burst over the house again. Slally was afraid as she listened to the bangs of thunder and the slashing of wind and rain against the glass. But she felt triumphant, too.

She hopped off the bed and went to the window. She stood watching the lightning sear the world and make the waves' spume look like white flame. She stood her ground as rain pelted the house. Her mother and Richard were slamming windows downstairs.

Slally heard the winds that Prince Ombra had captured shrieking his curses at her. She looked up at the place in the darkness where, she hoped, Prince Ombra's glaring eye would be. Then she stuck out her tongue.

Chapter Nine

"*Run! Run!*"

"*Run, Ellicott, run!*"

Thousands scream in anticipation. Their voices rise like dust in the hot afternoon as Bentley Ellicott strides to home plate. He is tall and sinewy. His famous swatch of brown hair dangles below his hard hat. He lashes the bat back and forth, pretending he doesn't hear the shrieking frenzy in the stadium.

He lowers the bat and leans on it as the catcher and pitcher confer on the mound. He pretends that he doesn't know that voices are hushed before millions of television sets. He watches the outfielders—three figures backing up, putting distance between themselves. The whole world is focused on a sun-baked stadium. The whole world is watch-

*ing Bentley Ellicott leaning on a baseball bat and
waiting.*

Mist lay low in the forest and the afternoon light
was pale gray. The sea, at full tide, lapped against
the sloping rock where Bentley sat with the stone
in his pocket.

Ombra spun dreams from the silence of ocean
and air. Every soul in Stonehaven was soiled by
him.

McGraw sat alone in the police station and
thought about getting his hands on a million dollars' worth of jewelery.

In the hushed cool of the bank, Elias Cutter was
overwhelmed by bitterness at the emptiness of his
life. Prince Ombra had decreed that the banker
and Mrs. Tally—enemies at the time Reverend Tally was fired—would come together in a contamin-
ated alliance. He had given them a common scape-
goat, Polly Woodhouse. Mr. Cutter was trying out
phrases to brutalize the soda fountain girl.
"You're a whore, Miss Woodhõuse. We have to
close your brothel, Miss Woodhouse, in the name
of common decency."

In the guest room of her impeccable house, Mrs.
Tally alternated righteous indignation with tears.

Charlie Feavey lay on his unmade bed in the
Stonehaven House Hotel. His broken face throbbed.
He was having revenge fantasies about McGraw
and the Ellicott kid.

Bentley gazed at the flat sea. But he was really
seeing a daydream that had taken vivid shape and
color in his mind. He heard its voices.

*"Ellicott is now two for three in this game with a
homer and a double," says the television announ-*

cer. He speaks softly as the manager of the opposing team walks out to join the conference on the
pitcher's mound. "And in the series so far, Ellicott's
got six RBIs and three homers . . . wait a minute.
They're going to change pitchers! Yes! They're
bringing in Jones!"

The caterwauling of anticipation rises again
from the thousands in the stadium. They want
blood. Ellicott stands motionless and waits.

The low, damp afternoon pulsed with goblin
music for those who could hear it.

Bentley sat on the rock and listened, a small
figure huddled against the soupy sky and the flat
water.

Bentley Ellicott hasn't moved. He looks into the
eyes of Cannonball Jones. The rawboned Arkansas
pitcher shifts the wad in his cheek and spurts a
stream of brown juice into the dust. He pounds the
ball softly in his mitt and stares at Ellicott with
eyes like ice drops. Jones has said publicly that if
he comes up against Ellicott in the series, he'll
finish the career of the great slugger—one way or
other.

Ellicott raises the bat, spreads his legs slightly,
and goes into his stiff-backed crouch. The crowd in
the stadium is quiet. Ellicott, with his brown hair
falling over his eyes, waits for Jones. Slally sits in a
box with Richard and Ellen. She wears a flowery
summer dress. Her pretty face, shining in the summer heat, is anxious as she looks down at Bentley
waiting for Cannonball Jones's first pitch.

Jones's eyes dart to first base. Bentley's team-
mate sidles two quick steps toward the bag. He is
wary of this morose southerner who can throw

*faster, harder, and more unpredictably than any
pitcher in the majors.*

A car pulled into the Ellicott driveway and
stopped. Dr. Kreistein heaved himself out, grunting. He slammed the car door.

The sun burned above the haze. Ombra ignited
Steve Slattery's mind with lust as Steve drifted in
a dinghy on the breathless sea.

Dr. Kreistein shoved his hands into the pockets
of his rumpled raincoat and looked around. The
brown fedora was tilted at an angle on his head.
He gazed up at the house. "Here," he said to himself, "nobody is at home." He walked acros the
driveway onto the lawn.

A sandpiper was captured by Ombra's will as it
tripped with flickering legs across the flat shine of
sand at the water's edge. The bird stopped. It saw
the distant figure of the boy on the rock. It saw the
old man trudging across the lawn toward the
beach.

Bentley reached into his pocket. His fingers
closed on the stone. The pull of the fantasy had
captured him. Bentley looked at the dark green
strands of kelp waving just below the surface of
the black water. But his mind was watching Cannonball Jones wind up for the first pitch.

*Jones's arm uncoils with a snap. The ball floats
toward the batter. Bentley rises slightly onto the
spiked toes of his shoes. The bat leaves his shoulder
in a precise, even swing. His body tightens into itself as his left leg bends. The television cameras
catch the muscles rippling as his body twists, stiff-
armed, and the bat slams into the speeding ball. A
sharp ash wood crack breaks across the hushed*

*stadium. The ball soars toward the right field as
thousands of mouths open to scream. Ellicott's
eyes are on the ball. He spins. The bat flips end over
end as it leaves his outstretched hand. Ellicott's
head goes down as he sprints toward first base.
"Look at him run!" shouts the television an-
nouncer. "Look at that man run!"*

Dietrich Kreistein had nearly reached the
beach. Prince Ombra cursed.

The bobcat trotted across the bare uplands
toward the coast. It stopped on a rock jutting out
from the coarse grasses of a meadow. It looked
down on the forest, the village, and the islands in
the sea. The bobcat had been called from its hunting ground by a command as powerful as instinct.
Incapable of reasoning, it had obeyed.

In the pallid afternoon light, Ombra cast his
spells. He watched the boy and the old man. He
looked through McGraw's eyes at Main Street, deserted except for a stray dog. Ombra's touch ran
through Steve Slattery's cortex and traveled down
the myriad nerve roads of his body. Swift as the
passage between life and death, Ombra put his enchantment upon the ghosts of Stonehaven who
spoke in the second air.

Do it now! Quickly! cried the Indians through
the smoke of autumn fires.

Throw that stone away this instant! barked an
ancestor of Elias Cutter's.

Or your dream will never come true! shouted
mad Mrs. John Rutherford Hackett.

Dr. Kreistein had almost reached the shingle
where the beach began. As he approached, the
sandpiper left the beach with a flit of its wings. It

tore across the rocks toward Dr. Kreistein at the
height of the old man's eyes. He yanked his hands
from his pockets and revolved them in the air
before him. "Shoo!" he said loudly as the bird
sped past his head, nearly knocking his hat off.
The bird swooped between two trees, wheeled,
and attacked again.

The forest, the beach, and the sea echoed with
phantom voices. All of Stonehaven's history had
suddenly entered the present and told Bentley Ellicott that his last chance had come.

"Go away bird!" roar Dr. Kreistein, flapping
his hands.

Run! Run!

Run, Ellicott, run!

*Bentley rounds second, driving two other players
across home plate. The score is tied. The ball col-
lides with the right field wall. Kotz scoops it up and
makes a wild throw at the infield. Bentley is sprinting toward third. Jones dashes off the pitcher's
mound as the ball makes a skidding bounce, kicking up dirt.*

Dr. Kreistein adjusted his hat on his head.
"Homicidal birds," he muttered. "Somebody, I
think, is trying to distract me." He put his hands
back into his raincoat pockets and breathed deeply of the sea air. He looked at the beach. He saw
Bentley sitting on a rock slanting down into the
water. "Ahah!" the old man whispered. "So."

*Ellicott breaks for home on his powerful legs.
Jones catches the ball on the tip of his glove, whirls
around, and throws hard. He has lost control of
himself. He hasn't thrown to the catcher. Jones has
tried to bean Bentley Ellicott! Dust billows in the*

*hot light as Bentley goes into a slide. The shortstop
runs for the baseline . . .*

Bentley got to his feet, holding the stone in his
hand. He heard the screaming of the frenzied
crowd. He heard the cry of the sandpiper and the
voices of the past warning him that he must throw
away the stone immediately or no crowds would
ever cheer for him, he would never know the jubi-
lation of winning.

*Ellicott gets to his feet, brushing dust from his
uniform. The stadium is in bedlam. Bentley takes
off his hard hat. Out on the pitcher's mound the opposing team's manager is shouting at Cannonball
Jones and pointing to the dugout. Jones slams his
glove to the ground and walks off the field to a
swell of booing from the stands. His career in the
majors is over. Bentley's teammates smother him
with hugs and pound his back as he walks toward
his own dugout. High above the field, Slally stands,
clapping and cheering, her face flushed with pride.*

A breeze from the sea tossed Bentley's hair. He
looked over the flat water for a spot to throw the
stone. He didn't hear the old man walking past
him, down the sloping rock. Bentley saw Dr. Kreistein only when he stopped at the edge of the water.

"Open your hand, please."

Bewildered, drawn abruptly from his fantasy,
Bentley unclenched his fist. The stone lay in his
palm. Its quartz and silver specks glittered even
though the light was dull.

"This is what I thought," Dr. Kreistein said.
"Now. Please. Pay attention very carefully. Prinz
Ombra has been speaking to you, *ja?*"

Still half mesmerized, Bentley nodded.

Ombra watched from the forest floor where he lay in a billion droplets of ground mist.

"Where is Sally?" Dr. Kreistein demanded.

"She's taking a sailing lesson," Bentley answered. "I didn't feel like it."

"So," Dr. Kreistein said. "And now Ombra wants you to throw away the stone."

Bentley nodded again.

"This means you won't be a hero anymore," the old man said. "You are refusing to be a hero?"

Bentley looked out over the water. The afternoon was hushed. The ghost voices were dimming in the second air.

"You were not given this stone to throw it away," Dr. Kreistein said. "Put it in your pocket."

Bentley went on searching the water's surface for the shadow that would show where centuries of currents had carved a deep hole on the bottom.

"Put it in your pocket," the old man said again. "Whatever Prinz Ombra has offered you, it is a lie."

Bentley looked back at him.

"No," he said.

Silence.

The silence of the sea was a bowl placed over the cloudly afternoon. Ombra's power wreathed through the vast hush.

Slally sat in the cockpit of a dinghy with her orange life jacket pulled up around her ears. She had undone the ties that held the jacket together at the front. Watching her pull each ribbon, one by one, to release the bow knots, Steve Slattery was reminded of a woman undressing.

Slally looked up at the sail. It hung limply from the mast. The boom rocked slowly back and forth. Steve burned with a heat that was more than the heat of the day. Slally's sleeveless blouse was unbuttoned halfway down. Her body would be as dry and smooth as a freshly ironed sheet.

She felt his gaze. She lowered her head and stared at him.

Steve was sitting on the gunnel at the stern of the dinghy. The tiller shaft lay across his legs. Three fingers of his right hand barely touched it.

"No wind," he said.

Slally shrugged.

Every heart in Stonehaven tightened with compulsion and self-mystery. Polly Woodhouse turned in at the path leading through the tall grass in front of the Stonehaven House Hotel. Mrs. Tally had just been in the drugstore. She was tight-lipped and unspeaking in her disapproval as she paid for soap and a bottle of cheap eau de cologne. She had slammed the door as she left.

Polly's hatred of Mrs. Tally overpowered her disgust at Charlie Feavey's dirty body and coarse mind. She had called the substitute counter girl, made a ham and cheese sandwich, and capped a container of black coffee. She mounted the steps of the ruined old hotel and pushed open the front door.

Mrs. Tally walked up the steep pavement toward her house. She felt imprisoned by the habits of a lifetime. That morning she'd rearranged her guest room. She had intended to ask Polly to move in with her. But when Mrs. Tally got to the drugstore and looked at the girl's round face and unconstrained breasts, compulsive scorn rose in her. Mrs. Tally had the notion that if she suddenly became loving, she would put herself in Polly's power.

She went into her house, slammed the door, and threw the soap and eau de cologne she'd bought into the kitchen waste bin.

Polly went down the dark, littered hallway of the hotel, stepping over a broken two-by-four, and opened Charlie's door. He was lying on his bed.

"I brought you something to eat," she said.

Charlie stared stupidly at her. He was half drunk.

"I heard you weren't feeling too good," Polly said. She looked around the room. Soiled underwear and socks lay where Charlie had thrown them. The bedsheets were filthy. Flies swarmed over a smear of grease on the table. The floor hadn't been swept for months.

Polly thought she was going to be sick. She had to forcibly remind herself that she was going to make it look as if she were sleeping with Charlie in order to enrage Mrs. Tally.

"What else you got in mind?" Charlie said.

Polly put the paper bag she was carrying on a table littered with tools, crumpled cigarette packs, and old magazines. "Cleaning up this dump," she said. She looked at Charlie lying on his bed in stained trousers and an undershirt. His face was swollen and had two bloody scrapes. "I'll be back after work. While I'm cleaning you can talk to me."

The hot contamination hung over Stonehaven.

Lord Ombra released the sandpiper and turned his willl on a person who drove out of the village toward the forest beyond the potato fields.

"So, if you throw away the stone, no fight with Prinz Ombra?" Dr. Kreistein asked. He was standing, back to the sea, with the heels of his shoes in the water. His hands were deep in his raincoat pockets, and his hat was tilted down over his forehead.

Bentley's thumb was hooked into his belt, just to one side of the big brass buckle Ellen had given him. "Yeah," he said, trying to sound nonchalant, "no fight. It's dumb."

"Look at me," Dr. Kreistein said softly.

Bentley raised his head.

"Now," the old man said. "Tell me again that you are going to throw away this stone and give up your life."

"And I'm *not giving up my life!*" Bentley retorted. "You're just like Slally! Both of *you* can hardly wait for *me* to fight Ombra. Big deal!"

"Maybe we both know that, sooner or later, you *are* going to fight him, and so we wish you to give up this monkey business," Dr. Kreistein said.

Bentley gazed out across the water again. "I'm not kidding around," he said. "Ombra doesn't want to fight, either. He told me."

"Very interesting. Fate has made a terrible mistake, hah? What else did you discuss with Prinz Ombra?"

"You said I didn't have to tell anything I didn't want to."

"Correct." The old man said. "You are free to do

as you please. I am free to think what I please.
Now I am thinking that you are ashamed of this
bargain you have made with our bogeyman
friend."

"I never *said* I made a bargain with him!"

"You are right. You didn't say it. It is my *opinion* that you have made a bargain with him."

"He's going to fix my leg!" Bentley yelled. *"He's magic! He can fix it!"*

"I have read all the information about your leg,"
the old man answered quietly. "I have sent a
report to my colleague. Your leg doesn't need
magic. It needs to go to a hospital in Boston,
Massachusetts, and have three operations. I
have spoken to your father and Mrs. Drake about
this."

Bentley stared at him. "When?"

"When what?"

"When am I going to the hospital?" Bentley demanded.

"You will go when you are fourteen years old if
you behave yourself and take minerals."

Bentley turned his head away. He unhooked his
thumb from his belt and held the stone in two
hands. He looked down at it.

"This must go back in your pocket immediately," Dr. Kreistein said.

Bentley studied the stone. He turned it over a
couple of times.

"No," he said.

Steve Slattery wondered if it was true.

He wondered if the Ellicott kid could *really* understand her. He looked at Slally's profile. She
was sitting five feet away in the cockpit. Her fore-

head curved down to the bridge of her small nose. Her lips were slightly parted as she stared at the empty sea.

Steve perspired in the heat of Ombra's eyes. He could smell the damp fervor of his own body. He looked at Slally's legs and wished she'd take her sneakers off so that he could see her bare feet.

If the Ellicott kid *couldn't* understand her, there would be no way she could tell.

A cabbage butterfly wobbled and soared above the green blur of foliage. An old wagon with rusted wheels lay half-tipped into a ditch that was hidden by tall grass. The sound of trickling water came from somewhere among the trees. Tiny asters and buttercups grew in the oil-splattered grass ridge between the ruts of the road that wound through the forest. Ahead, the road curved, became a diminishing splinter of itself, and vanished into the curtain of brush. No birds were singing.

The bobcat had heard the footsteps on the road when the human being was still a half-mile away. The beast had made itself invisible; it crouched near a boulder. It was far from the territory where it lived and hunted alone. The impulse to cross the dangerous open country, skirting an abandoned village on the uplands, had possessed its mind like the first sense of winter's coming. The bobcat had traveled for a day and a half toward the coast. It was starved.

A twig whispered as hairs brushed it. One brittle rib of a dry leaf cracked. The bobcat turned its head. Its tufted ears twitched. The large, luminous eyes fixed on a rabbit browsing ten feet away. The

distance was perfectly suited for the sudden
sprint and savage grab that were the cat's killing
style. It contemplated the unheeding rabbit, nose
quivering. Then it turned its head and watched the
road.

White flashed through a gap in the brush. The
footsteps were loud in the bobcat's hearing. The
human being came around the bend and stopped
in the middle of the road.

Prince Ombra's eye had become many eyes in
the overcast afternoon. He looked through the
dazed vision of the mortal whose mind he had
seized. He saw the bobcat among the hues and
shadows of the brush beside the road.

The bobcat raised its head and said wordlessly:
*What is Lord Ombra's business with the flesh-
clawer who hunts alone?*

*The magician makes spells to stop the boy from
throwing away the stone,* replied the human being.

You wish the magician killed, then? asked the
cat.

No. You will kill another when I command it.

The bobcat's slanting eyes stared up at the
human being in the road. The cat heard Lord Ombra's voice in the second air. It was unable to
resist him. *And when will this command come?*

If the magician triumphs over me, I will depart,
whispered Ombra from the mortal brain he had
entered. *This old sorcerer will stop making
strategies against me. The boy will return to happiness, and his warrior's heart will be lulled within
him. At the moment of his greatest bliss, when he
revels in his mortal life, I will return and destroy
him. It is then that I will summon you again.*

The bobcat's eyes narrowed. It stared at the human face that returned its gaze without seeing. *And whom will I kill at your command?*

The person who now stands before you, murmured the voice in the poisoned afternoon. *Look well.*

The bobcat watched without moving as the human being turned and walked back along the road, vanishing around the leafy bend.

Dr. Kreistein stood with his lumpy hands on his hips. He suppressed his exasperation as he looked down the coast. The water lapped quietly on the pebbled beach. Its moving edge curved around a pile of glacial boulders; a tall stand of black pine above the rocks shimmered as a reflection on the glazed surface of the sea. To distract himself from his irritation at Bentley, the old man considered briefly whether bathing in this freezing water would be good or bad for his heart. He had a sudden image of himself in a bathing suit and dismissed the idea. He looked back at the boy.

"So. You have made up your mind and no sensible discussion can change it," he said coldly.

Bentley glowered at him. He was feeling bad. He remembered the cavern angel telling him the reason for his life, but he was unable to think why he shouldn't throw away the stone. He wasn't even sure he wanted to throw it away. But everybody was telling him he shouldn't, so he was going to. He was angry again.

"You better stand behind me," he said. "I'm a pretty good thrower, but I might make a slip and hit you."

The old man nodded. "If you throw the stone
when I am standing in front of you, you will
definitely hit me."

"I said I might by *accident!*" Bentley retorted.

"If somebody can make you give up your whole
life, he can also make you throw stones at his
enemies." Dr. Kreistein said. He pushed his hands
back into his raincoat pockets and straightened
himself as if he were posing for a snapshot. "Now.
Proceed. With a stone of that size you might have
the good fortune to kill me."

Bentley rolled the stone to the tips of his fingers
and yanked back his throwing arm. He glared at
Dr. Kreistein, his eyes wide with defiance. The old
man stood calmly looking back at him.

"You aren't his enemy!" Bentley shouted. "*I*
am!"

Down the shore line sea gulls wheeled and
screamed against the dark afternoon sky.

"Everybody is Ombra's enemy," Dr. Kreistein
said. "You most of all, because you threaten him.
Me because I am your friend. Last night he attacked me."

Bentley lowered his arm. "What'd he do to
you?"

"He made me cry," the old man answered.

Bentley stared at him. The screeching of the
gulls floated across the still water.

"Cry?" Bentley asked in soft amazement.

"This is one of the things our friend Ombra does
very well. Inside everybody there are feelings we
do not wish to show, even to ourselves. Ombra
makes such feelings so strong that we think they
are shameful."

Bentley tried to imagine Dr. Kreistein crying. He couldn't. Suddenly his own defiance and anger seemed dumb. He was sick of feeling guilty and trying to pretend that wrong was right.

"It is easier to walk down this rock than walk up it," Dr. Kreistein said. "Meanwhile, the tide is still rising, and if I get wet feet it means rheumatism. You do not know about rheumatism, but, I assure you, it is a very bad business." He held out his crooked hand.

Bentley put the stone in his pocket, braced himself, and grabbed Dr. Kreistein's hand. He hauled the grunting, muttering old man up to the top of the rock and steered him over the smaller boulders until they were safely on the beach.

"You ought to wear sneakers if you're going to horse around on the rocks," Bentley said.

Dr. Kreistein breathed heavily. "When I decide I am going to engage in this horsing around, I will consult you about footwear," he said, gasping.

Bentley grinned and followed him back to the house.

Ellen stood on the wharf and watched the dinghy crossing the harbor. A fresh breeze had come with the waning of the afternoon. It had thinned the haze. The sun cast a yellow light across Stonehaven and the water. The dinghy turned up into the wind.

Ellen shaded her eyes with her hand and tried to see who was holding the tiller. But the sail blocked her view of Slally and Steve.

Ellen had begun to regret the cruel words she

had uttered in the argument with Richard the night before. He had become monosyllabic and then mute as thunder shook the house and rain poured in the windows on its eastern side. Ellen knew how fury could paralyze the mind and tongue. She had experienced that paralysis in confrontations with her cool, controlled husband. All afternoon she had ached with the fear that Richard's undispensed anger would strangle his love for her.

Her eyes followed the sailboat. Remorse and anxiety filled her heart. Sally had been made whole by Bentley. The little girl was happy for the first time in her life. So Ellen realized as she raised her face to the breeze, was she. *Please, God,* she murmured to herself, *give us another chance.*

The dinghy came about, its sails fluttering again. The mast bent before the gentle pressure of the wind, and the boat headed for the wharf.

Ellen cleared her distracted mind for a moment and watched. Slally was sitting on the edge of the cockpit in her orange life jacket. She was gripping the tiller. Steve sat on the gunnel, holding the sheet.

The dinghy plowed toward the float tied at the end of the wharf. Steve gave Slally an order. She pushed the tiller away and the little sailboat headed up and slowed. Slally steered for the landing. The dinghy stopped, sail flapping, four feet away.

Ellen walked down the ramp to the float. She picked up a boat pole lying on the planks and extended it to Steve's outstretched hand. He pulled the dinghy into the float.

Slally jumped out and threw her arms around

her mother's waist. She grinned and talked in an excited prattle.

"Yes, I saw you," Ellen said, touching Slally's face. "You're a very smart girl."

Steve finished tying the dinghy. "She's doin' pretty good," he said. "Couple more lessons and she'll be taking both sheet and tiller."

Slally looked at Steve and said something in an excited whisper.

"You get that?" Steve asked Ellen.

Ellen shook her head, looked down, and put her hand on Slally's cheek. "No, only Bentley understands her. I imagine she's trying to thank you."

"Does he really know what she's saying?"

Ellen raised her head. Smiling, she nodded.

"It's about dinnertime," Steve said. "So long, Sally."

Slally waved.

Driving home, anxiety took possession of Ellen again. The late afternoon sun had burned off the haze. Its golden light flickered through the trees as Ellen drove along the dirt road in the forest. The ache within her heightened her awareness of how much she had come to love the Ellicott house and the life she and Sally had briefly lived there.

She turned into the driveway. Richard's car was parked in front of the garage. Helga was going up the porch steps with two bags of groceries. "Bentley is over at the doctor's," she said. "They are unpacking books."

Ellen looked down at Slally. "You can go help them," she said. "But tell Bentley you both have to be back in a half-hour."

Slally ran across the lawn and into the path that

led through the trees to Dr. Kreistein's house.

"Thank you," Helga said as Ellen held open the screen door for her.

Ellen walked into the cool, dark hall. Her heart was beating hard. Richard wasn't in the living room. She went upstairs. The door of the main bedroom was closed.

Ellen stopped in the upstairs hall. She put her palms together and touched her fingertips to her lips. She stood, trying to compose herself for a moment. Then she lowered her hands and opened the bedroom door.

Richard was standing by the window reading a letter. The rest of the mail lay on a chaise lounge. He looked up.

Ellen pressed the door closed behind her. She took a deep breath. "There are probably a lot of things you want to get off your chest," she said quietly. "I didn't give you much chance to talk last night. I think you'd better do it now."

Richard's gray eyes studied her. He lowered the letter. "When you're angry, you've got a mouth on you like Niagara Falls," he said.

Ellen stared at him.

Richard smiled. "And I love you more than I've ever loved anybody in my life."

Ellen started to cry as she walked across the room. "How did you find that out?"

"By living through today," he said. "I thought it was all over. I didn't know what I'd say to you when I came home."

She put her arms around him. Through the blur of tears she looked at the sea. The water was deep blue. "Just say it again."

Richard kissed her on the forehead and said it again.

"Me, too," she said, weeping.

"I've invited Kreistein for dinner," Richard said.

"He can come to dinner every night for the rest of our lives," she said.

The sounds of an ordinary summer afternoon hummed and washed around them.

In the second air only the voices of animals and all the people of Stonehaven's history spoke.

Prince Ombra had vanished from the world.

Chapter Ten

The northern coast glowed in the sun-baked hush of July. The narcotic of contentment numbed every heart, banishing regret and apprehension. At the cool ending of each day Bentley and Slally watched the television news. Powerful men in the capitals of mighty nations weren't shouting at each other anymore; they sent messages congratulating each other for stopping the war. People in the dry, distant country rebuilt their houses and resumed their lives. As Bentley and Slally watched television, Richard, Ellen, and Dr. Kreistein talked on the front porch in a flowing murmur that was periodically interrupted by soft laughter.

They had dinner on the porch as each evening's light turned lavender-gray and night moved in from the sea. Chamber music floated from the open windows into the velvet darkness. Dr. Kreis-

tein had given Richard and Ellen a set of Mozart
recordings to thank them for feeding him every
evening. Often Helga carried his lunch on a tray
through the woods.

For Slally those halcyon days would be forever
symbolized by two memories—the announcement
and the party.

Richard and Ellen had contracted a new understanding in the aftermarth of their worst quarrel.
Both of them knew how close they had come to losing each other. They were restrained and at peace
with themselves.

Dr. Kreistein was baffled. Every morning
Bentley came over to his house. They sat in the
musty library and talked about Bentley's life
before he was eight. The old man was probing
through Bentley's childhood memories and daydreams, trying to discover the darkest core of
dread within the boy. But he could see no pattern
that would lead him to what Bentley feared the
most. He had questioned him about his handicap,
his relationship with his unforthcoming father,
feelings about other children, his nightmares.
Bentley seemed to have an inner resilience that
made him impervious to trauma.

One sunny morning Dr. Kreistein sat, hands
folded over his stomach, watching the boy on the
window seat. Bentley was poking at a wasp that
buzzed frantically up and down the window
screen.

"Proceed with what you were saying," the old
man said. "This insect will not hurt you."

Bentley turned back from trying to steer the
wasp toward a gap in the bottom of the screen

through which it could fly to freedom. "I'm not scared of it hurting me," he said.

"Go on."

"About what?" Bentley said. He grinned. "I forgot."

"If you would learn to pay attention, you would be of great assistance to both of us," Dr. Kreistein said. "We were discussing your mother."

Bentley looked back at him. "Oh, yeah, I remember. I guess she must have been terrific. My dad was all sad about her until he met Ellen. And that was a long time after."

"After what?"

"You know," Bentley said.

"Is it that you dislike saying that your mother is dead?"

Bentley shook his head. "Nah. You *know* she is, though. She died when I was born."

"What if somebody were to tell you that your mother was not, as you say, terrific? Perhaps that she did something bad?"

Bentley stared at him without answering for a moment. He was about to tell Dr. Kreistein not to be dumb. But the old man's words had shaken him. Bentley kept the mother he had never known as a blurred image of perfection within him. He felt a heaviness rising in his heart. For a moment he thought he was going to get mad or cry.

"Nobody has ever suggested such a thing," Dietrich Kreistein told him gently.

"Then how come you said it?" Bentley said, trying to push down his grief.

"Try to understand," Dr. Kreistein answered. "It is important that I know your feelings about your life, even about matters that are not necessarily true."

Again Bentley stared at him for a long moment without answering. "Are you sure nobody said my mom did something bad?"

"I assure you," Dr. Kreistein said. "From all I can gather, your mother was a very gentle and good woman. Also beautiful, judging by the photograph of her in your father's living room."

"Yeah," Bentley said, "she was beautiful." The heaviness was vanishing. "You're trying to find out what I'm most scared of, aren't you?"

"It is the most important thing for us, to discover what this is."

Bentley straightened up on the window seat. "Ombra's gone," he said.

The old man nodded.

"Maybe he's given up," Bentley said hopefully.

"No," Dr. Kreistein said. "Not while you are alive and have the stone. Ombra couldn't make you throw it away. He couldn't make you come out of your hawk circles and stop making these noises the crabs taught you—"

"I bet you don't believe me about the horseshoe crabs," Bentley said.

"Desist!" Dr. Kreistein barked. "Enough of these questions. I believe you. Already we have had a few adventures. We know that Prinz Ombra has appeared in the world again and you must fight him. This being true, whether you talk to crabs or dance a jig with a fish is not important. Our friend Ombra has just changed strategies."

"To what?" Bentley asked.

"It is not clear yet," the old man said. "Go away. I must think."

Bentley went outside. He was relieved not to hear Prince Ombra speaking to him in the sounds of night and morning.

In the library, Dr. Kreistein rose from his chair and picked up a fly swatter. He crossed the room, slid up the screen, and shooed the desperate wasp into the sunlight. "Next time, maybe, you will be more careful where you take yourself," he said.

He returned to the table he had arranged for himself as a working desk. It was cluttered with papers, books, and notes. The old man felt a foreboding in the hot day.

Prince Ombra had not departed permanently. Dietrich Kreistein knew too much to believe that. Every one of the old stories had a final ending— sometimes the bloody death of the hero, sometimes a new redemption for the world.

During the tranquil days of early July, Charlie Feavey went insane.

First he sold his pickup truck to get money for a chain saw, a sledgehammer, and a larger crowbar. Then he spent his days and nights obsessively tearing apart the fourth floor of the Stonehaven House Hotel. People walking past the ruined building late in the evening saw lights upstairs and heard the sounds of wood splintering, glass shattering, and disappointed curses being shouted in the empty rooms. It was fearsome. Only Polly Woodhouse visited Charlie now. Her resentment against Mrs. Tally had faded to almost nothing. But, during the time it had inspired her to clean up Charlie's room, Polly had begun to feel sorry for the despised hotel owner. He belonged to nobody.

One day Polly made some vegetable soup, poured it into a thermos jug, put on her oilskin jacket and hat, and set off for the village through a light rain. The islands beyond the harbor were dim abstractions of themselves: the road glistened and the boulders above the shore were stained a darker gray by the rain. Polly walked along, swinging her thermos by its handle and wondering if Charlie had reached the point that most men reached—if he was now more interested in talking to her than trying to go to bed with her.

A horn sounded lightly in the fog behind her. She stopped and watched as Mrs. Tally's car approached her and stopped. Mrs. Tally opened the door. "Get in," she said.

Polly hesitated. She wasn't mad anymore, but a flicker of reserve remained in her.

"You'll catch your death walking in the rain," Mrs. Tally said. "Get in."

Polly slid onto the front seat, put her thermos on her lap, and closed the door. "Thanks," she said.

Mrs. Tally put the gear into drive and moved the car down the road toward the village. "Even old bats can be nice on rainy days," she said.

Polly glanced at her. She couldn't be sure but she thought the set of Mrs. Tally's mouth was a smile. "C'mon," she said softly, "I never called you an old bat."

Mrs. Tally actually smiled. "No," she said, "but you were thinking it."

"Everybody knows you've had a hard time, Mrs. Tally," Polly said softly.

Mrs. Tally watched the road in silence for a moment. "What's in the thermos?"

"Soup," Polly said. "I made it for a friend of mine. I don't cook very well."

"Shouldn't think you'd have a chance to learn *any* cooking on a house trailer stove." She took a slight breath and steeled herself. "Why don't you come over to my house tomorrow after work? I've got a full-sized kitchen. I'll teach you to make *real* soup."

Polly was astonished. "Jesus, that's nice. I can't tomorrow night, though. I work the late shift Thursdays and Friday."

Mrs. Tally closed her eyes for a half-second. She opened them and wondered if she would be able to stand a second rejection from this girl who filled her with uncontrollable dreams of motherhood. "Then come around Monday after you finish work. And stop calling me Jesus."

Polly laughed. "You've got a deal, Mrs. Tally. About four-thirty. That's when I get off."

Mrs. Tally couldn't remember the last time she had felt such a spurt of happiness. She suppressed it. "Good. Where does your friend live?"

Suddenly Polly didn't want her to know about Charlie Feavey. "I've got to go to the drugstore first. If you could let me off there, that'd be just fine."

When Mrs. Tally had driven to the center of the village, she stopped in front of the drugstore. "Your sneakers are soaking wet. Haven't you any rubber boots?"

Polly shook her head. "Just my fur-lined ones for winter."

"You'll catch your death," Mrs. Tally said again.

Polly opened the door and grinned at her. "Thanks for the ride. See you Monday."

Polly went into the drugstore glad that she had stopped being mad at Mrs. Tally. She made up some small tasks for herself that took fifteen minutes, and then went out into the rainy afternoon again.

She looked up and down Main Street. Mrs. Tally's car wasn't in sight. Polly walked quickly to the hotel. She ran up the path and over the porch and banged the front door behind her, hoping that nobody would notice her.

Charlie was standing in the hallway. He was sweaty and caked with grime, and had a crowbar in his hand. "I was just thinking about you and me," he said.

Polly took off her rain hat and shook the water from it. "Well, you can stop thinking foolishness. I brought you some soup. You don't eat right."

Elias Cutter had seen Polly walk past the bank. His contempt for her had been like a twist of nerves in his solar plexus. He got up from his desk, walked across to the windows, and watched Polly run up the path and into the hotel. Suddenly his dislike was replaced by worry. Somebody, he thought, ought to protect that girl from Charlie Feavey.

The next afternoon, Ellen and Richard stood on a sloping rock at low tide, looking down through the green water at the sand on the bottom. A crab crept sideways on its unknowable journey. The sun seemed to warm Ellen's soul.

Richard released his hand. "I meant it when I said I love you more than I've ever loved anybody," he said.

"I believe you," she answered, looking into the water but seeing the large, unfinished shape of her life. "I didn't tell you that afternoon, but I will now. You've made me happier than I've ever been in my life."

Richard touched her face and turned it toward him. "Then stay happy. Marry me."

She had wanted desperately to hear that since she had stood on the wharf, watching the sailing dinghy and wondering if she'd lost him. But a lance of doubt quivered in her mind. She worried, suddenly, about her own feelings of inadequacy and the unpredictable eruptions of her rage.

"Don't say no," he told her.

"Of course I won't say no, darling Richard," she answered. She raised her head and looked into his eyes. She remembered how stricken with the pain of abandonment they'd been when she first met him. "It's a yes-but. Yes, but first I'm going to get my confidence back so that I can be the wife you deserve."

"We could ask Kreistein about someone to help you," he said.

"That's what I thought."

She slid her arm through his, and they walked back across the beach to the lawn. Ellen put her head on his shoulder.

Bentley and Slally were in the living room watching the evening news. Nothing unusual seemed to be happening in the world. There were scenes of plowing contests at fairs, a story about a summer music camp for inner-city children, and pictures of beaches with people sunning themselves and playing with Frisbees.

Richard sat down on the sofa. Ellen crossed the living room and rumpled Bentley's hair. "I'll *get* it cut!" he yelled. Slally grabbed her mother's wrist.

Ellen switched off the television and sat down on a footstool. She looked at Bentley. "Have you ever heard stories about wicked stepmothers?"

"Sure," he answered. "Cinderella. That's for kids. Dr. Kreistein knows stories—"

"If you let me be your stepmother," Ellen said, "I promise not to do anything wicked."

Bentley was sprawled in an armchair. He stared at Ellen. Slally held her breath and watched him. He suddenly sat up straight. *"You're gonna get married!"* he shouted. Slally made a small shriek of delight and threw her arms around her mother's neck.

Ellen smiled and nodded.

Bentley jumped out of his chair. "Then you'll never go away!"

"Never," his father said. He was smiling, too.

"When?" Bentley demanded.

"Not for a while," Ellen said. "Okay with you?"

"Let's tell Helga!" Bentley said to Slally. They tore out of the living room, across the hall and into the kitchen.

A few moments later they followed Helga back into the living room. The brown-haired girl kissed Ellen on the cheek and held her arms. "This makes me very, very happy," she said. She crossed the room and kissed Richard. "May you live many good years."

"We ought to have a party to celebrate," Bentley

said.

"Not yet," Richard told him. "For the time being, this is our secret, sport."

"But you're never going to go away?" Bentley asked Ellen again.

"No, darling," she smiled, "we're never going to go away."

Richard had waited to hear those words, emphatically spoken, since the terrible day after the quarrel.

"Speaking of parties," Helga said, looking at Slally, "somebody is having a birthday next week."

"She's never had a birthday party," Bentley told Dr. Kreistein. "She doesn't know any other kids except me."

The old man closed the pages of a large book he had been trying to show Bentley. It was an illustrated encyclopedia of northern European mythology.

He looked up at the boy standing beside his desk. "What has a party got to do with these pictures, which I am showing you in order that you should understand yourself better, hah?"

"Slally's going to be eight next week, and she's never had a party," Bentley said. He tossed his ninth paperclip at the wastebasket. It was another bright, bee-humming summer morning, and Bentley was distracted.

He is content, Dietrich Kreistein told himself again. *He feels that the imperative business of his life is far away.* He looked up into Bentley's face. Their eyes met. "So," the old man said softly.

"You have proven to me that you are, perhaps, the most expert thrower of paper clips in Stonehaven." He stared.

Bentley stared back. Then he grinned.

"You will now go get these useful pieces of wire and bring them back." He sniffed. "I need them to clip together all the bills I am going to send your father for spending many hours with you while you practice throwing things at dust bins."

Bentley chortled. He knelt beside the wastebasket and began rummaging around in it.

He came back to the desk and dumped his handful of paper clips in Dr. Kreistein's half-opened desk drawer. Then he went to the window seat and sprawled on it. "I said that Slally doesn't know any other kids except me, and next week's her birthday."

The old man gave a slight shrug. "I do not see the problem. If you wish to have a party, ask your friends from school."

Bentley looked down at his sneakers. "I haven't been hanging around much with kids from school since I had the fight."

"With your friend Joe."

Bentley nodded.

"So," Dr. Kreistein said softly. "Maybe now it is time for you to make up this quarrel."

"He started it," Bentley said.

Dr. Kreistein turned to the window. "Let us think about what happened in a different way. This boy is your best briend. Then, just before Ombra comes, he turns into your enemy."

The library was still. Bentley raised his head, looked at the ceiling and then at Dr. Kreistein.

"You mean *Ombra* made it happen?"

Dr. Kreistein pondered him for a moment. "This seems likely, since we presume that every evil thought we have originates with him. This is something else the old stories imply."

"Hey," Bentley said softly, "if I made up with Joe—"

"Yes," Dr. Kreistein said. "This would be a victory over Ombra. It would strengthen you. Odysseus, Gilgamesh, and these other heroes of the legends we have been discussing conquered this *verdammten* Prinz Ombra with their wisdom and insight, not their muscles. They were what they wished to be—not what Ombra tried to turn them into. They did not permit themselves to become lost in despair, rage, or fear like birds flying in smoke and striking everything in their path." He took out his handkerchief and blew his nose. "This is why I have persuaded you to be patient until you learn a very important lesson about this existence of ours." He stuffed the handkerchief back into his pocket. "The facts of life cannot be changed. The person who lives with them successfully must change the way he thinks and feels about these facts of life. People with your special capacities who manage to do this are heroes."

Bentley stared at him, forgetting, for a moment, the power that lay within him. "Me?" he murmured.

"Du," Dietrich Kreistein said to the boy who—despite all his magic—was the boy the old man had once been.

Joe Persis pounded the softball in his glove and

looked at Bentley. Bentley stood in a slight crouch, the bat raised, and waited. Everyone on the lawn and the porch had stopped talking. Ellen sat beside Mrs. Tally and crossed her fingers.

Joe turned and looked to his left. McGraw was standing, hands on his knees, behind the fourth-grader who was playing first base.

"Whattya think you're doin'?" Joe demanded.

"Base coach," McGraw answered, grinning. He was enjoying himself. When Bentley had asked him if he'd come to the girl's birthday party, McGraw was surprised, and even more surprised that he quickly accepted. He was glad. His wife was sitting in the sun beside Helga.

"You can't play and be base coach both!" Joe yelled.

"Ask the ump," McGraw retorted.

Joe looked at Elias Cutter standing behind home plate. "Can he? They already got ten players!"

"Nine players and a substitute runner," said Mr. Cutter. "Play ball."

Joe looked at Bentley, shuffled his feet, and pitched the ball.

Bentley chopped at it and connected. The ball shot over Joe's head and past the shortstop. Slally dashed from home plate toward first base. Everybody was yelling at her to run. In left field, Richard lunged for the ball, missed, and nearly fell over Mrs. Tally.

Slally streaked across first. McGraw grabbed her, spun her around, and shoved her toward second.

"No fair!" Joe yelled ferociously from the pitcher's mound. Forty grownups and children on

the lawn, porch, and front steps of the house
cheered as Richard picked up the baseball and
threw it at Polly, who, with her blond hair flying,
was playing second. She caught the throw and pir-
ouetted, touching Slally as she fell across the base.

"Out!" yelled Joe.

"Safe!" Richard and Steve Slattery shouted
from the outfield.

Elias Cutter stood with his hands on his hips,
squinting at second. Polly sat on the base with her
arm around Slally. They were giggling. Everybody
else was cheering or shouting.

"The runner is out," Mr. Cutter said.

"She was safe by a mile!" Bentley yelled at him.

"Out," Mr. Cutter repeated firmly. "Mr. Persis's
side wins four to three." He looked down at Bentley. "That's final, Mr. Ellicott."

"Boo!" Bentley retorted.

The baseball players moved toward the porch to
finish off the birthday cake. McGraw stood with
Richard, drinking lemonade and wiping the sweat
from his forehead. Mr. Cutter walked across the
lawn to where Mrs. Tally and Ellen were sitting.
He picked up his seersucker jacket. "You're blind
as a bat," Mrs. Tally said to him.

Mr. Cutter looked down at her. He felt a peculiar mirth stirring within him. "You could be sent
to the showers for a remark like that," he said in
mock hauteur.

"Don't be a pompous old goat," she retorted.
"Sit down here and talk to me and Mrs. Drake."
Polly was coming off the baseball field still wear-
ing her second baseman's glove. "Would you be a

lovely child and get Mr. Cutter something to drink?" Mrs. Tally asked.

Polly's face was flushed and wet with perspiration. She smiled. She liked being called lovely. Even more, she liked Mrs. Tally calling her "child." She had spent five evenings at Mrs. Tally's house and had learned how to make moussaka and real apple pie. "Sure," she said. "What'll it be, Mr. Cutter?"

Mr. Cutter took out his handkerchief and dabbed at his forehead. "If there's any lemonade, that would be fine."

Mrs. Tally held out her hand. "Give me that baseball glove," she said. "I'll keep it for you."

Polly handed the glove to her and trotted off toward the porch. "Sometimes I ask myself about her," said Mrs. Tally. "Do you suppose she'll catch the right sort of young man by playing second base?"

Ellen laughed.

"I shouldn't wonder," Elias Cutter answered. "Did I ever mention to you that I played second base for the varsity?"

The sun descended on its westward course. Dr. Kreistein was standing on the lawn with his hands clasped behind his back and his brown fedora tipped forward on his head. One of Richard's colleagues from the mathematics department was discussing cars with Helga's boyfriend. Dr. Kreistein pretended to be absorbed in the conversation. He didn't have the wildest idea of what they were talking about.

On the beach Bentley and Joe had found a board

lying in a mess of brittle, dried seaweed and tiny
flakes of flinty sand. They had balanced it across a
rock and put stones on one end. Then they took
turns jumping on the other end to show Slally how
they used to make catapults when they were best
friends. The shadow of the forest lay over the
beach and small waves expiring in the sand. The
tree line was silhouetted on the water. "Whoom!"
Joe yelled as Bentley jumped on the board and a
stone arced high into the day's last light.

Slally asked if she could try.

"She wants to jump on it," Bentley said.

"Sure she can," Joe said. He put a stone on the
downward end of the board and held Slally's hand
while she climbed onto a boulder.

She hopped onto the board.

"Whoom!" cried Joe Persis as the stone flashed
into the light.

"I forgot," Chief McGraw said to Richard. "Picked up your mail on the way over." He opened the
door of his cruiser and handed Richard letters and
a small package.

"Thanks," Richard said. "Mrs. McGraw, I hope
we'll see you again soon."

Mrs. McGraw looked at Richard and Ellen
standing together on the driveway. They were a
handsome couple. Seeing them made her feel glad.
She hadn't felt glad in a long time. "That'd be real
nice," she said.

Almost everyone had gone.

"This has been a busy afternoon for you and
Mrs. Drake," Dr. Kreistein said to Helga. "Tonight
I will have soup in my house and go to bed early. A
party is hard on the feet and the listening."

"Ach nein!" Helga said. *"Wir wollen—"*

"Speak English," the old man said to her gently. "Maybe you will go home and marry a lawyer. Then you can speak German for the rest of your life."

"We are all going to have clams, Herr Doktor," Helga said, "and it is planned that you should come with us. The children would be disappointed."

"You are doing this sitting down?"

Helga laughed and nodded.

"Then I will eat clams," Dr. Kreistein said.

"The package is for you," Richard said, handing it to Helga.

She looked at it. "From my mother," she said. "Excuse me. I will just go see what it is." She crossed the driveway and went up the steps into the house.

"I could get my father or my stepmother to drive us over," Bentley said.

He was sitting on the beach with Joe and Slally. The shadow of the forest stretched farther out on the water. The light was softening. Joe and Bentley were talking about going to the movies together the next Saturday.

"I didn't know she was your stepmother," Joe said.

Slally told Bentley it was still a secret.

"She's *sort* of my stepmother," Bentley said. "Just as good as."

"That's neat," Joe said.

Slally pointed and told Bentley to look.

He looked. The two fish hawks had burst from the tree line. Their bodies were murky brown blurs as they swooped through the shadow. The two birds emerged into the last glow of the sun above the water. With powerful beats of their wings, they rose in the clear air. The children on the beach watched them climb high into the light. At two hundred feet the ospreys broke their ascent and began to cruise in a wide circle.

Slally asked Bentley why they were flying above him.

Bentley looked up at the hawks, a solemn expression on his face. "I don't know," he said.

McGraw took his wife home and then drove down to the police station. His first deputy, Mike, was on duty. "How was the party?" he asked McGraw.

"Nice," the chief answered. "Seemed like everybody in town was there except you and Charlie Feavey."

"Don't think I didn't get asked," Mike said. "The Ellicott kid came all the way out to my house."

"I expect he didn't ask Charlie," McGraw said.

Mike laughed.

McGraw pushed open the screen door, walked down the wooden steps, crossed the street, and passing the boathouse and the freezing plant, strolled out to the end of the wharf. It was the clearest moment of the day. The sun had dropped behind the village ridge, but a lucid brilliance was still on the outer bay and the distant islands. McGraw took a few deep breaths.

He had two, separate feelings. The afternoon at the Ellicotts' had relaxed him more than he'd been in years. He thought he must have been out of his

mind trying to befriend Bentley Ellicott as a way
of finding out where the rest of the jewelery was in
the hotel. The kid probably didn't know, anyway.
In a sudden, new appreciation of who he was and
where he lived and what he did there, McGraw
told himself he didn't need a million dollars.

The second feeling was symbolized by nothing,
it had no precise situation to which it could afix
itself: The old uneasiness he'd felt at the end of the
winter was back in McGraw's heart. All it told him
was that something was about to happen.

As he thought these things, his operating senses
had heard someone come onto the wharf and walk
toward him. He was abruptly aware that the
walker had stopped and was standing behind him.

He turned his head and looked.

Then he turned his whole body and faced Willybill. McGraw was startled.

The stranger was only ten feet away. He had a
toothpick in his mouth. It was nearly dark, but
McGraw could clearly see his beard, the long hair
tied with a rolled bandanna—and the eyes.

Willybill's jade eyes glowed in the dusk that was
about to become a new night.

Helga sat on her bed with the open package in
her lap. Behind her the shade was pulled down
over the open window. The shade was an oblong of
light in the sunset. A smile touched Helga's lips as
she finished reading her mother's letter.

Wearing the oncoming night on his shoulders,
Prince Ombra stood on the farthest horizon of the
sea.

Helga laid the letter on the bed beside her. She

unwrapped blue tissue paper from a handful of old photographs. Her smile broadened as she looked at pictures of herself taken when she was seven. It was like seeing another child.

There she stood, holding her cat, Putschke, in her arms.

There she stood with her mother and father on a summer holiday in the Schwartzwald.

There she knelt, crying, on the edge of a picnic blanket.

Lord Ombra appeared before her in the hot, still room. He was armored in the golden light. He offered Helga memories and dreams.

Such grief! Helga laughed softly to herself. *Such weeping for a cat lost in the forest!*

She put her hands over her face and wept. The photographs slithered from her lap and fell in a cascade to the floor. *O mein Putschke!"* she sobbed, bewildered at the sudden onslaught of mourning but unable to control herself.

The bedroom door opened.

"Helga!" Ellen said in astonishment. She sat down on the bed and put her arms around the weeping girl. "Helga, darling, what *is* it?"

Helga shook her head.

"Tell me," Ellen said softly. "Come on, sweetheart."

"It is nothing, something so silly—"

"Here," Ellen said, releasing her. "Your photographs are all over the floor." She gathered them up, put them in Helga's lap, and got her a tissue from the dresser.

Helga wiped her eyes. She picked up the snapshot of herself weeping as a child. "This is me," she said softly, trying to smile. "Such a sad little girl. We were on holiday in the Black Forest, and I lost my cat. He ran into the woods. Have you ever seen such grief?"

Ellen looked at the photograph, then back at Helga. "I think you're homesick, love."

Helga dabbed at her eyes. "No. I am very happy here." She laughed in the last residue of her weeping. "I think I will be really homesick when I have to leave you and the children."

"It was a marvelous party," Ellen said. "Sally's never had one before. She's thrilled. Thank you for doing it."

Helga shook her head again. "It was Bentley. Imagine riding his bicycle all over the village and inviting everybody. Even Joe Persis. And they didn't have a fight."

Ellen laughed. "I think they've made it up. I guess Bentley apologized. Joe doesn't strike me as the apologizing type."

"He is a nice boy, but not intelligent," Helga said. "Between them, Bentley was always the leader."

"All right now?" Ellen asked.

Helga nodded. "Of course," she lied. "It was just a memory. Thank you."

She stood up, went to the mirror, and ran her fingers through her brown hair. She appeared composed again. But the memory burned like new pain. The heartbreak of a seven-year-old cried in her soul. She didn't understand.

But she knew with a bitter conviction that happiness would never return to her life until she had found her cat.

Chapter Eleven

And her rag doll.

The shade in Helga's bedroom billowed slightly in the predawn breeze, then sank back against the window frame. The darkness in the sleeping girl's mind was coagulating into a shape. She lay on her back in white, short-sleeved pajamas, her hair coiled on the pillow. Her arms were spread like those of a supplicating victim. Her face was turned toward the window.

Ombra, the craftsman, lifted a rag doll from the rubble of Helga's half-remembered childhood and laid it upon the stage of her dreams. The bit of wool that had pinched the body into a neck was gone. So was one of the eyes, made from an overcoat button. But the remaining eye, black as coal, stared at her. The doll lay in a corner.

Helga whispered a name and rolled over. Her long, supple body bent into an S. Her hands were gathered close to her mouth.

Ombra murmured an old love song. *Du, du, liegst mir im Herzen . . .* The song came from behind the closed door of her parents' bedroom on a sultry evening.

Bentley rode his bicycle in the bright sunshine. He stopped and invited Helga to a party.

Bentley and Slally sat on Bentley's bed. The black-eyed doll was in the toy box. When Helga got the doll, it would lead her home.

A young man named Kurt raised his hand to her face as they lay with no clothes on. Helga tasted the tip of his thumb.

She opened her eyes and took the tip of her thumb from her mouth. She was awake. But her dreams went on. Wearily, she remembered that she had to find her cat and her rag doll to get back her happiness.

She rolled over on her stomach and lay for a moment holding the pillow. Slowly, she raised herself to her hands and knees.

The rag doll waited in the shadowed corner, a one-eyed promise. Putschke mewed for her in the forest where the sun was rising. Morning was coming and she gently shook Kurt. *"Liebes Herz,"* she whispered, *"wo ist . . ."*

Bentley leaned against the handlebars of his bike and said to her, "It's in the toy box."

Helga nodded and moved to the edge of the bed. She put her bare feet on the floor and threw her hair back with a toss of her head. For a moment she sat still, remembering the face of her cat peering from the shrubbery and the doll's one black eye.

Du, du, liegst mir im Herzen . . .

Helga walked slowly down the hall so as not to awaken her parents. "It's in the toy box," Bentley said again, giving his bicycle a shove and pedaling away in the hot afternoon. Helga loved him and reached out to touch him. Kurt slept on. Somewhere in the blaze of sunrise she heard Putschke crying.

She walked past Bentley's bed. She gathered up his rumpled sheet from the floor. She held it against her breast and looked down at the sleeping boy, curled in upon himself. Gently, she unfurled the sheet and watched it float down, covering him. She bent over and kissed him good-bye. "Now I am going to be homesick for you," she murmured. "But I must go back. They are waiting for me, darling child."

To go back. It was the commandment of God. Back to the twisting streets of Munich and the spring fragrance of the English Garden. They were calling her from the lakes, the green hills and pure forests of Bavaria, where the Isar ran more swiftly than any other river and seraphim sang in the bells of Easter against the foggy sky.

Bentley stirred. Kurt, her first love, stirred, calling her away from the land where the shore faces east, calling her back to rapture and the country where the clocks had stopped and peace had come at last. There she would find the cat and her lost happiness. The one-eyed doll would show the way. This, God promised her.

She crossed the room silently on bare feet and

opened the toy box. The doll's eye stared at her, black, but glittering with the light that would lead her home.

Helga reached into the toy box and picked up the stone.

She recrossed the bedroom and gently closed the door. Walking softly, she went downstairs, one hand sliding along the smooth banister, the other clutching the stone. She went through the living room and pushed open the screen door.

The world spread new before her as if she had just been born. She heard the chorus of awakening birds. She saw the splendors of Creation in the green of high summer. The thick foliage of the forest and the stalks and branches of shrubbery glistened as the rising sun touched a billion droplets of dew.

On the perimeter of the cold sea, the real sun was the color of a bleeding wound.

Helga went down the porch steps. The grass was wet beneath her feet.

She heard her cat calling in the woods where it had been lost long, long ago. Helga looked toward the path that ran through the forest.

The sun was glowing on the perimeter of her vision, but, despite its brilliance, she saw the cat's face. Its large eyes stared at her from the tall grass at the edge of the forest. Its mouth opened in a low yowl. It looked starved.

"Putschke," whispered the girl.

The cat turned and vanished into the brush, leaving only a quivering milkweed that scattered droplets of dew.

She walked, then ran toward the brush line. The

forest floor was rough. Her feet pressed upon stones and roots. Branches tore at her, ripping her pajamas and scratching her flesh.

"Putschke!" she cried.

The cat stood between two pine trees on a flat shelf of mossy rock. Its starved eyes beckoned her forward.

Helga threw out her arms to it, one fist still holding the stone. The cat crouched, trembling as she walked toward it. "Putschke," she said softly, trying to persuade it not to be frightened.

The bobcat leaped.

The pain of Helga's yearning became the pain of death. The promise had been false. God had not made it. As the bobcat's claws tore her head and its teeth sank into her neck, she fell. A monstrous being filled the forest. It watched with a blood-red eye that shone through the foliage. The last thing Helga saw was the eye of the promiser, the hideous god.

The last thing she felt was the bobcat's jaws crushing her fist and snatching the stone from her broken fingers.

Dietrich Kreistein stood in the forest clearing. McGraw was opposite him, on the other side of the blanket-covered body. Dr. Kreistein wore pajamas and a heavy bathrobe. He raised one gnarled hand and idly fingered the wart on the top of his head.

McGraw's cruiser was parked on Dr. Kreistein's back lawn. Its red roof light whirled and flashed. Another Stonehaven police cruiser was parked behind it. An ambulance was in the driveway. People from neighboring houses had gathered on the road. Ellen and Slally and Bentley were halfway down the path that led through the woods to Dr. Kreistein's house.

McGraw finished writing something in his notebook. "Anything else?"

Dr. Kreistein pused his lips. *"Ja,"* he said quietly. "Secondary lacerations on the right arm. The right hand has been partially destroyed." He looked at McGraw. "I am not a pathologist. But I think you will find it is as I have told you. The wounds on the head and throat caused her death."

"Was it quick?" Richard asked. He was standing near them with his hands shoved into the rear pockets of his blue jeans.

Dr. Kreistein looked at him.

"I'm sorry," Richard said. He lowered his head so that the old man couldn't see the tears in his eyes.

"It is a natural question," Dr. Kreistein said. "Do not feel embarrassed. I think she died very quickly."

McGraw closed his notebook and put it in his shirt pocket. "Seems like it was a bobcat, all right," he said. "A hunter was killed by one last year."

Dr. Kreistein turned to him. "Please. What is this bobcat?"

"A wild cat," McGraw said. He looked down at the blanket draped over Helga's body and remembered his sense of foreboding the evening before. "Don't see too many of them around here. They're loners, usually stick to their own hunting territory."

"And such an animal is large enough to do"—the old man bent and pulled the blanket over Helga's extended bare foot—"this?"

McGraw nodded. "Yep. A bobcat can kill somebody. A big cat weights, oh, thirty, thirty-five pounds. I expect this one went off its head."

"But what was Helga doing out here at five-thirty in the morning?" Richard asked for the third time.

"This," said Dr. Kreistein, "is a very interesting question. Please, Professor. Take the children away from here. They have already seen too much." He flapped his hand. "Go. Now. I will visit them later."

Richard nodded. He went back up the path through the woods, taking Ellen, Slally, and Bentley with him.

"And you didn't hear anything?" McGraw asked Dr. Kreistein.

The old man shook his head. "No, and this is curious. I am a very light sleeper. I always wake up at sunrise. Something kept me asleep this morning until you knocked on the door."

McGraw was about to ask him what he meant by "curious" and "something." Then the police chief remembered his encounter with Willybill. Never again would McGraw react with instant scorn to anything that smacked of mystery. "Okay, Eddie," he said to one of the ambulance men standing in the driveway, "let's get her out of here."

Dr. Kreistein climbed the porch steps of his house, holding his loosening bathrobe belt. He hadn't needed to see Helga's body to know what had happened. He'd seen it in Bentley's face as he

stood beside Ellen on the path. The boy knew that
Prince Ombra had reentered the world.

Breathing heavily, Dr. Kreistein stopped on his
porch. He turned and looked at the malicious
sparkle of the sun through the high foliage. He
gasped several times until his breathing was
easier and his heart had slowed. "Poor, poor
child," he muttered. He squinted at the pinpoints
of sunlight. "So, Ombra, you have returned in an
even more terrible form. The slayer of the mighty,
vanquisher of Cú Chulainn, the fire-headed, you
have this girl destroyed as part of a new plan, I
presume. You do not even consider this a murder.
To you, it is just a first move." He took a handkerchief from his bathrobe and cleared his throat.
"But to us, the mortals who live a life that is
shorter but more complete than yours, this is the
slaughter of an innocent, and you will suffer for it.
Already, I know why it was done." He spat in contempt, turned, and walked slowly into his house,
letting the screen door bang behind him.

Suffer? taunted a voice in the depths of the sea.
*What suffering will you deliver on me, Magician? I
am the pontiff maximus of all suffering!*

When Dr. Kreistein had bathed and dressed and
made a pot of tea, the lawn, forest, and sea had
resumed their normal pattern. But, as he stood
with a cup of tea on the porch, he felt the other,
menacing presence within the pattern.

He heard yelling. He looked into the woods.
Bentley was running toward him on the path.
"You gotta come quick!" he cried. "Something's
wrong with Slally!"

The old man put his teacup down carefully.

Bentley stopped at the bottom of the porch steps. "And something else has—"

"Calm yourself," Dr. Kreistein said. "Already one terrible event has happened today. We must prepare ourselves for more. I know that your stone is gone."

Bentley's eyes widened. "How did you know?"

Dr. Kreistein hesitated for a moment. Then he decided that it was best the boy be told. "Helga's hand," he answered quietly. "The fingers were broken. This means she was holding something in her fist and the animal did considerable damage getting it." He looked closely at Bentley. "How do you feel?"

"Terrible," Bentley said. "Helga's dead." He brushed one eye with his fingers.

"It is a good thing to cry," Dr. Kreistein said, coming heavily down the porch steps. "It is one of the reasons why our eyes were given such equipment. You have lost somebody dear to you. It is proper that you should cry."

Bentley raised his head. "I'm not supposed to."

"And who told you this, please?"

"I just know," Bentley said, a miserable expression on his face.

"What is wrong with Slally?"

"She can't talk," Bentley said, his mouth trembling. "She can't make a sound!"

The old man nodded. "So. The ripples widen, and somebody else is injured." He took his clean handkerchief from his pocket. "If you are not supposed to cry, you can still wipe your eyes and blow your nose. Go inside. My medicine bag is in the library. There is no rush."

Bentley went into the house. Dietrich Kreistein stood looking toward the woods where Helga's body had been found. *What does it mean,* he thought, *that he no longer has this stone? To find it was to give him supernatural powers. What happens to him if he loses it? Does he cease to be this eternally returning person? It is important to Ombra that the boy be separated from the stone. Why?*

Bentley came down the porch steps carrying the medicine bag in both hands. "Ombra made it happen, didn't he?"

"Yes," the old man answered.

"But how did he make a bobcat—*why?*"

"We will see what we will see," Dr. Kreistein answered. "Now. Let us go attend to Sally. First things first."

Richard was sitting in the living room when they came in. He rose. "I don't know what's the matter with her," he said. His face was taut and frightened.

"I will find out," Dr. Kreistein said quietly.

"Christ! What an awful day!" Richard said, suddenly on the perimeter of panic.

"We must bring order back to it. Where is the little girl, please?"

"With her mother in the kitchen. I can't get any sense out of Ellen."

Dr. Kreistein crossed the hall and went into the kitchen with Bentley and Richard following him.

Slally was sitting on a straight-backed chair, holding a glass of orange juice in both her hands. She wore shorts, a striped T-shirt, and sneakers. She was jerking in uneven spasms. The orange juice had spilled and was running in two narrow streams down her leg. Ellen knelt beside her, stroking the little girl's perspiring forehead.

They both looked up as Dr. Kreistein came into the kitchen. Slally's eyes were wide and her teeth were clamped together. Her upper body convulsed twice.

"Doctor—" Ellen said.

Dr. Kreistein pulled back a chair, turned it to face Slally, and sat down. "Now," he said. "Look at me."

Slally looked at him with terrified eyes.

"You are clever at numbers," the old man said to her. "We have already discovered this. Now. Please. Tell me how much is seven times seven?"

Slally took a small breath and opened her mouth. She strained as if she were trying to eject the answer from her throat. Her body twitched. Then she began to cry soundlessly.

"Shush," Dr. Kreistein said, leaning forward and patting her knee. "Do not be afraid. You will talk to Bentley again. We will try another problem. If you cannot speak the answer, perhaps you will hold up some fingers to show me what it is. How many times does twelve divide by four, please? Show me the answer."

Slally took her left hand off the orange juice glass. She raised it. Her fingers were crumpled into her palm. She looked at her hand. Then she began to cry again.

"Oh my God," Ellen whispered. Tears were running down her cheeks as she gazed at Slally sitting on the chair.

"Please," Dr. Kreistein said calmly. "We will not make a big fuss over a business that is going to pass." He turned to Bentley. "The bag, if you please."

Bentley set it down beside him.

"Now," the old man said, bending over and rummaging among the bottles and instruments, "we will speak frankly about what is happening." He straightened up with a brown plastic pill bottle in his hand. "You have seen something terrible this morning. Do not think about what you saw. Just realize that it was terrible."

Slally stared at him. Her eyes were large and filled with tears.

"When anybody sees such things, they are shocked," Dr. Kreistein continued, looking at her. "We understand much about shock but not everything. It does strange things to us. Do not feel bad that you cannot talk. It is not your fault. It is the shock doing it to you." He shook out two pills and handed them to her. "If you go to sleep, your mind and body will relax. Sometimes this stops what the shock has done. Swallow these, please."

Slally tried to hold out her hand. Ellen took the pills. She put one in Slally's mouth and helped her drink some orange juice. Then the second pill.

"Very well," Dr. Kreistein said. "These will make you go to sleep all day. When you wake up, I will come see you, and you will do some multiplications and divisions for me."

Ellen took Slally up to her room. When she came down, Richard and Dr. Kreistein were drinking coffee in the kitchen and talking about Helga. Bentley was slumped across the table, his face pushed to one side by the hand he leaned it on.

Ellen sat down. "She's mute," she said.

Dr. Kreistein nodded. "Perhaps because speaking is so important and sensitive a matter with her, the shock affected her there first."

"But will it wear off?" Ellen asked.

"Yes, I believe so," the old man said. "Violence in its true manifestation is alien to children. What took place today was violent. But, terrible as it is for her and Bentley, who were close to Helga, this is impersonal violence. It is something that happened to someone else. Her capacity to absorb such things is great. For this reason I do not believe she will be mute permanently. If something violent had happened directly *to* her—" He shrugged.

"I've called Helga's family," Richard said. "Her brother spoke English."

The old man looked at his hands. "There are no words to change what has happened." He looked up. "But we continue and must do our best with our lives."

He went upstairs with Bentley. When they had gone, Ellen said, "It's *all* changed."

"What's changed?" Richard asked.

"Poor Helga," Ellen answered, staring at the wall. "Last night she had a letter from her mother with some photographs. It made her cry."

"Nothing's changed," Richard said. "Nothing between you and me."

Ellen didn't answer him.

Dr. Kreistein stood in the middle of Bentley's bedroom looking at the open toy box. "The taking of this stone is very important." The old man paused. "You remember hearing nothing early in the morning?"

Bentley shook his head. He was sitting on the edge of his unmade bed. "How come you asked me how I feel?"

"Because I wish to know how you feel," Dr. Kreistein said.

Bentley looked at the toy box. "I feel different," he said. "It's kind of weird."

Dr. Kreistein lowered himself onto a chair. "Describe this weird as precisely as you can. It is important."

Bentley pulled a loose thread on the edge of a rumpled sheet. "I feel awful about Helga. But that's not all." He looked at Dr. Kreistein. "I really hate Ombra for what he did to her."

The old man nodded.

"But I can't do anything about it." The house was silent. "At least I don't *think* I can."

"Go on."

Bentley shrugged and pulled at the thread some more. "It's like—I don't know—" He looked at Dr. Kreistein. "I'm scared," he whispered.

Dr. Kreistein moved to the bed and sat down.

"I still hate Ombra. But—"

Suddenly, for the first time since Dietrich Kreistein had known him, Bentley Ellicott began to cry. It was not the weeping of despair, but an outburst of fury. "I want to *kill* him for what he did!" Bentley sobbed, grabbing handfuls of the bedsheet. "I want to kill him for what he did to Helga and Slally! But I *can't!* I'm *scared!*"

"You know the reason for your life," the old

man said gently. "Perhaps—"

"That was *different!* That was just what some-body said I *had* to do! He's a—a—" Bentley re-membered the ugly name Charlie Feavey had call-ed him "—*bastard!* I want to *kill* him! I really want to do it now, and I—I—can't!" He rolled over onto the bed, grabbed a pillow, and sobbed into it. "I *hate* him!" wailed his muffled voice.

Dr. Kreistein put his hand on Bentley's heaving shoulder. "My friend," he said, "we must deduce the meaning of what has happened."

Bentley turned onto his back and clutched the old man's hand. "They've taken something away from me," he cried. "They gave me all that magic and power and stuff so I could fight that—dirty—*bastard* and kill him! Now that I really want to do it, I'm scared!"

Dr. Kreistein squeezed his hand. "Compose yourself. It is Ombra who has taken something away. We will now find out precisely what it is you have lost."

Bentley lay weeping for a moment. Then he pull-ed his hand from Dr. Kreistein's hand and sat up. He sucked in air and swallowed a few times. "How?" he asked.

Dr. Kreistein stood up, moved back across the room to the chair and seated himself again. "These noises and voices from the past that you can hear," he said. "You will listen."

Bentley sat on the bed wiping his eyes with a corner of the sheet. He looked at the far wall of the bedroom. His sobbing had stopped.

Dr. Kreistein studied him. "What do you hear?" he asked.

"Helga."

"Good. What is she saying?"

"She's crying."

"What else?"

"She's—she's talking to Ellen." He swallowed hard. "She's talking about memories."

The old man contemplated him for a moment. "So," he said. "Already we have established something. Your magic has not been taken away from you."

Bentley lowered the sheet. His urge to cry had passed. "Yeah, but I still feel weird." Suddenly he erupted all over again. "I'm gonna *kill* him!" he yelled, slamming his fist into the pillow. "I don't care if they take *everything* away from me! I'm gonna find that stone and then kill the bastard!"

"Shush," Dr. Kreistein said. "The situation is too serious for such theatrics." He regarded the ceiling for a moment. *"Ja,"* he said. "Now we know why he tried to make you throw away this stone. Without it, you have lost the supra-will."

Bentley looked puzzled.

"I don't know what that means."

Dr. Kreistein took off his brown fedora and held it on his lap. "In the old stories," he said, "the heroes took many winding roads. They made mistakes. They committed wrong, sometimes wicked acts. Some of them you wouldn't want to have as a friend. All of this was, I think, the ordinary mortal in them acting out his life."

The old man wiped his brow with his handkerchief. "Today," he said, "it is hot." He sniffed. "Even though they lived as ordinary people, the heroes in the old stories knew what most people never know—they understood the purpose of their lives. They moved steadily toward their rendezvous with this terrible Prinz. That was their destiny. Only they and the people closest to them were aware of this secret."

Bentley looked at the windows, then back at Dr. Kreistein. "If I'd been an ordinary kid, Helga wouldn't have died, Slally wouldn't—"

"You have been given a great burden. Also a great gift. To know why we live is a miracle in itself. This capacity of the heroes of legend to see what lay ahead of them and bend their fates toward it was the part of them that was terrible, beautiful and unafraid. It was their supra-will. Death did not concern them because these men knew that only the mortal part of themselves would die." Again, he stopped speaking.

Bentley stared at a crack in the pale blue wall that he had studied countless times before. It was a series of lines like a mosquito's leg. "I'm scared," he said softly and fiercely, "but I'm going to get that stone back."

"It is a very small object," the old man answered. "The world is a very large place."

Bentley nodded. His anger was replacing the power that Prince Ombra had stolen from him.

"You will have to use your own, very ordinary will power. This will not be easy."

"I'm still going to find it," Bentley said.

"Our friend Ombra will do anything he can to stop you," Dr. Kreistein said. "We know that he is capable of horrible acts."

Bentley turned his head and looked at the old

man. In his eyes, Dietrich Kreistein saw a fury that he hoped would last. "I cannot go with you," the doctor said. "I am too clumsy and feeble."

"I'll go by myself," Bentley said.

"Very well," Dr. Kreistein said. It was the decision he both hoped for and dreaded.

A great lassitude seizes the northern coast at midafternoon. Tree branches extend without moving. The ocean tides drift imperceptibly beneath the surface. Only birds of prey high in the air and creatures on the bottom of the sea make sounds. No ordinary human ear can hear them.

Bentley crouched in the tall grass, looking at the place where Helga's body had been found. He saw weeds pressed down all around a shelf of gray rock. He looked at the moss, thick on one end of the ledge. Helga's head had rested there. He couldn't see any blood. But blood spoke in the hot hush of day all around him.

The power of the borrowed heart has left you! whispered the voice of the death-dealer. *You have lost the stone. You are no longer fit to live in legend with great Arthur and Susano!*

Bentley's solar plexus tightened with fear. He felt small, stupid, and humiliated. He got angrier.

"Shut up," he said aloud. "When I find that stone, you're gonna pay for what you did!"

He turned his head and gazed at the sea through the forest. "Help me," he whispered to the sky.

The two fish hawks rose from their nest in the dead tree at the end of the lawn. They soared to the great height from which the hawk's eye sees all that moves in the fields and forests below. *Listen!* cried one osprey. *It is he whom you seek!* cried the other.

The sun penetrated the shallows of the harbor at half tide. The horseshoe crabs spoke from inside their curved, brown shells. *Hear our deceived brother!* they chanted.

He is dying! shrilled the fish hawks in the whistle of the diving predator bird. *All beasts detest the one who has tricked him!!"*

Bentley concentrated hard on the second air. The echoes of all human time on the northern coast were rising and receding in waves. Then Bentley heard a new sound that hadn't been there before.

Some living thing was panting in the heat. A stricken heart thumped slowly. Bentley heard an animal life ending somewhere in the vast interior beyond the village.

"The bobcat!" he said. "It's Ombra's bobcat!"

He scrambled to his feet. He stood listening again to the heartbeats and the labored panting. Then he dashed up the path through the woods, across his father's lawn, and up the porch steps, two at a time.

Inside, the house was cool and quiet. Bentley started upstairs. He heard Ellen talking on the telephone in the kitchen. He tiptoed up the stairs.

As he got to the top, he saw the door of Slally's room open. She came out into the hall. She looked pale and bewildered with sleep. She said she was thirsty.

"Hey!" Bentley whispered. "You can talk again!"

She looked at him sleepily for a moment. Then she nodded.

"That's great!" he said. "Listen, I have to—"

Slally asked him why he was whispering.

Bentley grabbed her by the arm, took her into his room, and closed the door. He went into the bathroom and got her a glass of water. Slally drank it. She sat down on the bed. Her eyes looked awake.

"Ombra stole the stone," Bentley said. "I'm going to find it."

Slally stared at him a moment. She asked if Prince Ombra had killed Helga.

Bentley nodded. "Yeah," he said quietly, "he did. And I'm going to make him pay for it. He's a bastard."

Slally told him he shouldn't use rotten words. She slid off the bed and told him to wait a minute until she got her sneakers.

"You *can't* go," Bentley said. "You've been sick. Besides, I've got to—"

Slally said she was fine. Anyway, he couldn't stop her from coming with him.

"Listen!" Bentley said, forgetting to whisper. "You might get hurt."

But Slally had already opened the door and was crossing the hall to her own room.

Bentley scowled at the door for a moment. Then he rummaged quickly through his toy box. He took out his fishing knife and his poncho. He tiptoed past Slally's door and went downstairs. Ellen was still in the kitchen talking on the telephone. Bentley crossed the front hall and closed the screen door quietly behind him.

Outside, the afternoon shadows were getting longer. Bentley went around to the back of the house. He strapped his rolled poncho onto the fender rack of his bicycle. He rode as fast as he could across the lawn, out the driveway and along the dirt road.

When he got to the potato fields and the highway, he stopped. The day's last heat simmered around him. He listened hard. The sound of the panting bobcat was a little louder. He knew that he was heading in the right direction.

He rode west along the side of the highway. Cars and trucks passed him. In the shuddering air they left behind them, Bentley's fear was renewed. He remembered the morning the truck nearly hit him.

The sun was dropping toward the horizon. It was becoming a round ember of wrath as it sank into the world's haze and pollution.

Willybill got out of his pickup in the parking lot of the roadhouse where he sang his songs. He cupped his hands around a flaring match and lowered the cigarette in his lips to the flame.

His eyes went up as Bentley rode past on the highway. Willybill blew out the match, snapped it in two between his thumb and forefinger, and watched.

A few minutes later Slally rode past, going west, pumping hard to catch up with Bentley.

Willybill took the cigarette from his mouth. He dropped it on the asphalt and crushed it out with one twist of his booted heel.

Then the life-soiled stranger got into his pick-up. He switched on the ignition, started the engine, swung in a circle around the parking lot, and turned west onto the highway as the night rose, steeped with Prince Ombra's poison, from the rim of the world behind him.

Chapter Twelve

The land was dry. Dust whitened the brush along the dirt road in the forest. As the sunlight gave way to shadow, the aroma of the exhausted earth and scorched foliage hung in the motionless air. It was as if a plague were murdering the world by sucking all moisture from it.

West of the potato fields Bentley had veered off the highway onto an unpaved road. His bicycle rattled so loudly on the bumps and ruts that he had to stop periodically and listen to the second air with his eyes closed. If the heartbeats and panting of the dying bobcat were louder, he rode on. If they got fainter, he backed up and tried another road. The woods grew darker; the sky turned a soiled ochre.

He had ridden about two miles into the labyrinth of forest roads and paths when he skidded his bicycle to a stop at a fork. A road curved off sharply to the left. He closed his eyes again. The gasping breath and labored heartbeats were strong in the second air. Bentley turned his bike and rode up the new road to the bend. The panting of the bobcat was no longer just in the second air. It was part of the subdued murmur of the wilderness—the faint trickle of water in a ditch, the pulsing chirp of crickets. He laid down his bicycle, stood in the middle of the road, and listened again for the bobcat's sound. It was somewhere near him.

Bentley was suddenly seized by an urge to get out of there before it was night. He whirled around, and looked back down the road.

He saw nothing except the dusty tracks and the low, unmoving forest.

He recalled Dr. Kreistein's words about relying on his own will power. He told himself he was being dumb. There was nothing to be scared of.

Unpersuaded, he knelt on the road and peered under the bushes. He saw darkness on one side. He saw a wall of granite. His heart was beating fast. He saw some spreading ferns in front of the rock. Then, as his eyes grew accustomed to the dim light, he saw the bobcat.

Bentley shivered. He looked up at the pallid sky. The ospreys were circling so high above him that they were mere dots of light, but he could plainly hear them. *The lord of all treacheries bestows our brother's death!* they whistled. Their shrilling penetrated the forest.

Still kneeling on the road, Bentley looked at the bobcat again. It lay panting among the ferns. Bits of tree bark and twigs were tangled in its sickly fur. Bentley saw the emaciated ribcage rising and collapsing beneath the unkempt pelt. The cat's tufted ears twitched slightly. Its dull eyes stared back at Bentley.

Twice he summoned me from my hunting ground, whispered the voice of the doomed animal in the second air. *I was powerless and could not resist him.*

Bentley put his arms around his legs and shivered again.

At his command, I have not paused to hunt or eat for many days. I am starving.

"You killed Helga for him," Bentley said softly.

The bobcat closed its eyes. *Child, child, this is the way of our kind. We have no names. We have no deaths. We exist to beget and die so that we may come again in a new season as our own progeny.*

"How did he make you do it?" Bentley whispered.

The bobcat opened its eyes and gazed up at him. *He grasped my will, and I did not serve myself. I killed and took the stone to a distant hill. Even in death he commands me. I returned to this place because it was here I first saw him.* The eyes hooded again.

Bentley stared at the animal. He didn't hate Helga's murderer. He realized that the bobcat was as helpless as he was.

"Where did you take the stone?" he asked gently.

The bobcat's eyes remained closed. Its nostrils spread its pink nose apart as it inhaled feebly. *I traveled to the deserted village, across the windy highlands, north around the lake.* . . . The eyes half opened. *There were hares for the taking, water snakes to be eaten.*

Bentley nodded.

The bobcat's body suddenly convulsed. Its legs jerked inward toward the hollow belly, then slowly unfolded. *Beyond the marshes, a hill rises that was sacred to ancient men. He commanded me to put the stone there, among the roots of the oldest flowering tree.*

I know where that is," Bentley said, his heart filled with pity and fear. "Our class went there once. It's called Indian Hill."

The bobcat's eyes looked up at him. *The land has no names. I left the stone where mice sleep beneath the roots. So great was his power, I did not touch them. Avenge me.*

Bentley reached out slowly to stroke the head of the dying animal.

The bobcat's eyes flew open wide. *Do not touch me!* it hissed. *I will rip you as long as instinct lives within me! I will mangle you with the power of my last heartbeat as long as the betraying lord possesses me—may the hatreds he scrapes from the husks of lost love strangle him!* The eyes grew dim again. *My night is coming, and there will be no dawn to stalk the ground pig in his dewy meadow.* The eyes looked back at Bentley. *Avenge me.*

"I'm going to get back the stone and make him pay," Bentley said. "I'm going to make him pay for everything."

Behind you . . .

Bentley spun around so violently that he sat down hard in the dust.

Slally stood at the bend of the road, holding her bicycle. Its wire basket was stuffed with a brown paper bag.

"Don't sneak up like that!" Bentley called in a desperate whisper. He wondered if he should warn her about the bobcat.

Slally put down her bike. She tugged the paper bag out of the basket. She said Bentley was the one who had been sneaking—right out of the house without waiting for her.

"I *told* you I had to do it alone," Bentley shot back. "Even Dr. Kreistein said so." He was still trembling and his stomach was clenched.

Slally walked over and sat down beside him.

Bentley looked beneath the ferns. He could just see the bobcat. Its body was stretched out flat and seemed longer. Its ribs weren't moving any more. It was dead.

"I found out where the stone is," he said. "A place they call Indian Hill." He stood up. "It's getting too dark to go home. I'll make a lean-to. I wish I'd brought some matches so we could have a fire."

Slally dumped out the brown paper bag. A loaf of white bread, a packet of salami, and a box of kitchen matches slithered out onto the road.

Bentley inspected the provisions. He was still furious at her for following him and scaring him. But he was glad she was there. The trees and bushes were turning black. Bentley could protect her instead of trying to protect himself all alone. "Okay," he replied to her unspoken question. "But cut out the sneaking."

A half-mile away, Willybill eased his pickup

truck onto the side of the road. Low branches
scraped across the metal roof. Willybill switched
off the ignition and stepped out onto the ground.

He looked up at the new moon. Then he spat in
the dust.

The moon rose, and the scorched day poured its
sere brilliance into the sunset. The air of the
northern coast reeked with human wrath. Prince
Ombra possessed Charlie Feavey completely.

Charlie lay flat on his back on the fourth floor of
his hotel. He wasn't hurt, but he couldn't move. A
wall Charlie had been demolishing had fallen on
him, pinning his left leg in the knee-deep rubble.
He was gasping hard from his last floppings and
writhings like a beached fish. All around him there
were heaps of timbers, window frames, doors, and
broken plaster. In weeks of frenzied wrecking,
Charlie had turned the fourth floor into a vast,
barnlike space. But the torn-up walls and floors
had yielded nothing except dust and rat drop-
pings. He found no jewelry.

He lay wheezing, looking at the ceiling. It was
getting dark. The wall toppling on him was the ultimate indignity. Bentley Ellicott had claimed that
Mrs. John Rutherford Hackett had hidden a fortune in jewels all over the hotel. He had inflamed Charlie's hopes. But there weren't any jewels.
Bentley was the enemy of Charlie Feavey and
Charlie's god.

He shouted curses into the gloom around him.

Downstairs, somebody slammed the front door.
Charlie tilted back his head and shrieked profan-
ities anew. Then he yowled for help.

Ombra, lord of all misapprehensions, enchanter who alters mortal minds from hopeful to hateful visions, had turned his full power on Polly Woodhouse.

In recent weeks Polly had come to understand Mrs. Tally's brusque way of expressing affection. Polly liked the older woman's manner. Their mutual understanding of the snappish phrases and the appearance of irritation bound them together.

Earlier that day, when Polly arrived for lunch, Mrs. Tally had presented her with a pair of rain boots. Polly didn't know how to accept presents. For a moment she had hesitated in embarrassment. "Don't be a fool," Mrs. Tally had said. "Here. Take them, you silly girl."

Suddenly, inexplicably, Polly was filled with an indignation that came from nowhere. She walked out of Mrs. Tally's house. She lay on her bed in the trailer all afternoon, getting angrier and angrier at Mrs. Tally's assumption of a maternal role in her life. Polly didn't want another mother. She'd gotten along just fine without one.

Toward evening she got up and walked into the village. She passed the drugstore and went up the front porch of the Stonehaven House Hotel. She hadn't been there for weeks, for fear of upsetting her new friend. Now she hoped that everybody in town would see her.

Elias Cutter did. As he locked the bank, Mr. Cutter watched Polly cross the porch and slam the hotel door behind her. She made him feel that all of Stonehaven was soiled.

Polly stood in the dim front hallway of the hotel. She smelled dust and decay. Then she heard Charlie screaming and swearing somewhere above her. She went up the stairs to the fourth floor.

She looked across the rubble and saw Charlie pinned to the floor. "*Now* what've you done?" she demanded.

"Get if off me?" Charlie barked at her. "Lift the fu—"

Polly found a light switch. She flipped it and the ceiling bulbs filled the wrecked space with glare. Polly climbed over the mess. Charlie was wearing an undershirt and grimy trousers. His face was dirty and streamed with sweat. A new, yellowish light was in his eyes. "Lift it offa me!" he yelled.

"Keep your shirt on," Polly snapped.

She grabbed a side of the wall that lay across Charlie's thighs. She strained as she tried to lift it. The other side of the wall pressed down on Charlie.

He howled. "You're breaking my goddamn legs!"

Polly let go of the wall. It dropped two feet. Charlie shouted and cursed again.

Polly looked down the length of the wall. "It's jammed between those studs," she said. "Where's your wrecking bar?"

"How the hell do I know?" Charlie snapped.

Polly pulled a small crowbar from beneath some splintered lath. She climbed over the rubble, falling twice and scratching her arms. She wedged the crowbar between the edge of the fallen wall and an upright stud. She pulled hard. The wall wouldn't move. She tugged harder, popping two buttons on her shirt. Her hair tumbled down, and she took off her bandanna. She was perspiring.

"What the hell are you folks playing?"

Polly turned around. McGraw was standing almost at the top of the stairs. His revolver hung low on his hip. His bulk seemed to fill the stairwell.

"Get this goddamn thing offa me!" Charlie rasped. "She's as useless as tits on a bull."

McGraw climbed across the littered floor, took the crowbar from Polly, stuck its tip between the wall and the stud, and yanked once. The broken wall collapsed, tilting off Charlie. Charlie howled. McGraw helped him up. "You all in one piece?"

"You coulda broken both my legs," Charlie said, feeling his scrawny thighs.

"I could've done a lot of things to you and didn't," McGraw said. "We've got two kids missing, Charlie. Looks like Willybill's gone, too. We need men who know the country back yonder. I thought you'd like to join up. God knows you've hunted enough deer—" He looked at Polly. "And laid enough women out there."

"Which kids?" Charlie demanded.

"The Ellicott boy and the Drake girl."

Charlie began to gather up his tools. "You and them can all go to hell."

"There's talk of a reward," McGraw said.

Charlie's mind filled with new fantasies—about the uplands, about Bentley Ellicott, about finding Bentley out in the empty country and killing him, about reward money. "How much?" he demanded.

"Everybody's meeting at the police station in a

half hour," McGraw said. "Be there." He turned to Polly. "I want to talk to you."

Polly followed him back down the stairs. The last daylight was fading. Through the dust-caked windows of the downstairs hall she could see the streetlights turning on.

"I ought to kick your ass for hanging around with Charlie," McGraw said. "You've got more brains than that, Polly."

Again, Polly wondered at herself. She couldn't explain. She didn't try.

"I'll drive you home," the police chief said to her.

"I don't want to go home," Polly answered. "Those kids are my friends." She hesitated, fighting down an impulse to start crying. "Please, McGraw, let me help."

McGraw nodded. "Okay," he said. "You're a class act when you get your head screwed on right, Polly. Use your sense and stay away from Charlie. Now, c'mon, let's get out of here."

Mrs. Tally parked her car on Main Street near the Stonehaven House Hotel. As she got out, she saw Polly and McGraw coming down the steps. Polly was holding her shirt together where the two buttons were missing. Her hair was disheveled, and perspiration still gleamed on her round face. She stopped when she saw Mrs. Tally.

"If you're staying in town, there's a spare shirt in my locker," McGraw said to Polly.

"Okay," Polly said. She was looking at the expression on Mrs. Tally's face.

McGraw tipped his cap and walked down toward the police station in the deepening dusk.

Mrs. Tally didn't acknowledge him. Her eyes moved from Polly's hair to the hand that held her shirt together. She looked into Polly's face. "Did you go into the place *with* Mr. McGraw?" she demanded.

"No," Polly answered. She was starting to get angry again.

"Mr. McGraw *found* you in there?" Mrs. Tally snapped.

"That's right," Polly answered coldly.

Mrs. Tally turned and walked away. Her back and her grip on her handbag expressed the outrage that Polly had once wanted to provoke.

Charlie Feavey stood in the back of the crowded police station. His imagination was full of reward money, jewels, and murder. McGraw stood down front, looming over everybody else. He ran his finger across a geodetic survey map pinned to the wall.

"Lee, you take your guys south—along here. Don't forget the empty houses on Massassoit Road. You've got the granite quarry. Take some rope and a grappling hook—"

Ellen Drake stifled a cry. She and Richard were sitting together against the wall.

McGraw's finger swept across the map and stopped on the wooded point sticking out diagonally into the bay. "Mac, this whole area's yours. Don't forget the cliff up on Rawling's meadow. Mrs. Drake tells me the kids sometimes go there."

Memory. For a fleeting moment Richard's mind brightened with memory of the blustery Sunday

afternoon he and his wife had walked up the
meadow, hand in hand. "Pretty soon we'll be a real
family," she had said happily. Six days later Bentley was born and she was dead.

The screen door next to Charlie slammed. Dick
Amberstam, McGraw's second deputy, took off his
cap and wiped his forehead on his sleeve.

McGraw looked over the heads of the men
crowding the room. "Anything on Willybill?"

"His pickup's gone," Dick said. "Ellie Natcher
says she saw him in the parking lot of the roadhouse. She saw him leave."

"Which direction?" McGraw asked.

"West," Dick answered. "It was long 'bout sunset," she said.

Polly was standing against the wall. She glanced
across the room. Mrs. Tally's face looked like a
mask of ice.

McGraw turned back to the map. "I'll take
everything west of here," he said, pointing to the
area between the village and the rise of the uplands. "That's all woods. Most likely they went in
there." He glanced at Richard and Ellen. "Now
we're in pretty good shape. The Coast Guard's got
a description of them. The state police are sending
in a helicopter soon as it gets light—and they've
put out a bulletin on Willybill. Remember. The
girl's wearing a striped T-shirt, shorts, and sneakers. She's blond and about yea tall. She can make
noise but she can't talk. Bentley's wearing a blue
sports shirt. You all know him.

"Thanks for coming out," McGraw said. "I know
the kids' parents—"

A chair scraped as Ellen stood up. Charlie could

just see the shine of her hair in the overhead light. "My former husband," he heard her say in a voice that trembled, "Sally's father—I've talked to him on the telephone, of course—he has asked me to say that we'll pay a reward of five thousand dollars to anybody who finds our daughter."

There was an embarrassed silence.

"All right," McGraw said quietly. "Let's get to it. Mike comes with me. Dick'll take over here at the station house. Phone in to him every two hours."

Our daughter, Richard thought bitterly as he and Ellen followed the crowd of men out into the humid evening. She hadn't said a word about Bentley, whom she professed to love. Richard felt the new web of intimacy between him and Ellen fraying under the stress of the day's terrible events.

McGraw walked out onto Main Street. Men were throwing gear into pickup trucks and cars. The roar of starting engines filled the street.

The situation was too familiar to McGraw. Willybill was a total puzzle—but he could be just the type. The men around the police chief on the street and sidewalk were hard-bodied locals—lobstermen and scallopers, packers from the freezing plant, machinists and farmers. They'd done things like this before. They wouldn't be unnerved if they found two ravaged little bodies. They wouldn't try to lynch Willybill, either. If he was somewhere out in the empty country, they'd find him and bring him in. And yet . . . McGraw's sense of foreboding was greater than the components of a potentially grisly tragedy warranted.

Charlie Feavey walked over to him, carrying a shotgun.

"What're you doing with that?" McGraw demanded.

"I'm not going out there without it," Charlie said. "Like you say, I know the country."

McGraw was silent for a moment. "All right. But you're riding with me." He turned to Polly. "If you want to do something, stay in the station with Dick. He may need an errand run."

"Sure," she said.

She looked past McGraw. Mrs. Tally had stopped on the sidewalk and was glaring at her. Polly's indignation rose again. She patted Charlie on the shoulder. "See you when you get back, honey," she said.

She turned and went into the police station.

McGraw crossed the street. Richard and Ellen were getting into their car. "All right, folks," McGraw said, "you go home and sit tight until you hear from me." He saw the expression on Ellen's face as the headlights of a car swept over her. He reached in and squeezed her shoulder. "We'll find 'em. They're just stuck up a tree somewhere. Don't worry about Sally, Mrs. Drake. She's with Bentley, and he's some smart little kid."

He watched them drive off into the darkness. *Maybe*, he thought, *it's because they're living together without being married.* Something, sure as hell, was all wrong.

Charlie was standing on the street behind him. "Smart little kid, my ass," he said. "You're sucking up to him so he'll tell you where the stuff's hid in my hotel."

"Shut your damn mouth, Charlie," McGraw said, "and get in that cruiser."

He led the motorcade out of town. With Mike,

his first deputy, driving the police car directly
behind him, McGraw turned left on the dark highway. It seemed to him that the day had been a
thousand years long. The discovery of the German
girl's body that morning had been rendered into a
remote event by the disappearance of the two
children. And just before *that* report came in, the
news on the radio had been enough to make a man
wonder if he lived far enough from where the
nuclear fireballs would hit if the two world
leaders didn't stop their new round of quarreling
and accusation.

McGraw felt that a putrid fury was boiling inside of Charlie Feavey.

A half-burned stick tumbled into the heap of
glowing coals, and sparks rose. Bentley watched
them extinguish one by one against the bed of cold
starlight. He looked back across the fire at Slally.
"Okay," he said resignedly, "*we* have to get to Indian Hill and find the stone before anybody catches us." He poked at the fire with a stick. "I still
think you ought to go home when it gets light.
Your mother's going to be mad as stink at us for
staying out all night."

Slally nodded.

In the deep tangle of the forest, an owl made its
throaty trill; the night's hunting was about to
begin. Beyond the owl, on a dirt road banked by
tall, black walls of growth, Charlie Feavey's eyes
gleamed in the lights of the dashboard. "Stop," he
said.

McGraw braked the cruiser to a halt. Charlie
opened the door and got out. He folded his arms

on the smooth roof of the police car and listened. He heard the owl. He sniffed. A light breeze carried another faint whiff of the smoke Charlie had smelled in the car. He opened the back door and pulled out his shotgun. "Wait here," he said.

"Hold it," McGraw said, leaning with one arm across the seat back. "Where do you think you're going?"

"Place I know up the road we just passed," Charlie answered. His narrow face gave no sign of the murderous excitement that had flared in him.

"We'll drive in," McGraw said.

"Deep ruts," Charlie said. "You'd get hung up. I remembered a place back there a couple of kids might crawl into."

"What do you need the shotgun for?" McGraw asked, not taking his eyes from Charlie's eyes.

"Saw a moose cow and calf up here two summers ago," Charlie answered. "I'm not walking around without protection. If you're smart you'll do the same. Gimme a light. Won't be but a moment."

McGraw handed him a long flashlight.

Charlie trudged back to the left fork. He walked up the branch road. He breathed Ombra's poison in the close night air. The visions of jewels were coming clearer in his mind. But now he knew that he had to earn the fulfillment of his dreams. He had to kill Bentley Ellicott first. He broke the shotgun as he walked and flicked on the flashlight to check the two brassbutted shells in the chamber.

"I don't know what'll happen *first* when I get the stone back," Bentley said. "I guess Dr. Kreistein—"

Slally wasn't looking at him. The firelight glowed on her face as she stared past Bentley. Her mouth was slightly open. Her fists closed slowly.

"Stand up," whispered the voice of Charlie Feavey.

Bentley jerked around and swallowed a yell of fright.

Slally scrambled to her feet and sidled halfway around the fire.

"Now you," Charlie snapped at Bentley, gesturing with the shotgun.

Bentley got up and moved to the middle of the road. "How come you're holding a shotgun on us?" he asked. He was trembling all over.

In Charlie's demented mind the reason the good life had always eluded him stood before him. His realization, that Bentley had put a curse on him, was so immense and simple that it didn't need explaining.

Bentley stared at Charlie. Bentley didn't know if his hawks were in the sky anymore. He wasn't even sure he still had his magic. He was so scared he couldn't remember the incantation of the horseshoe crabs. He knew that Charlie was really going to shoot. "Hey, listen," he said loudly. *"Listen,* Mr. Feavey—"

Charlie yanked the shotgun up to his shoulder and aimed its barrels directly at Bentley's eyes. He flicked off the safety catch. Suddenly Bentley's stomach clamped tight and he bent his body, trying to duck. Slally streaked past him and jumped, grabbing the shotgun barrels with both her hands, swinging her body clear of the ground. She screamed at Bentley to run. As he dashed for the bushes, he heard Charlie Feavey roaring curses; he had nearly fallen into the fire.

Bentley yelled at Slally to follow him. He fell over the bobcat's body and rolled among the ferns. The shotgun went off with ear-cracking thunder. Pellets smashed into the granite wall a few feet above Bentley's head and ricocheted off in every direction.

McGraw threw his cruiser into reverse and gunned the engine. He hit the brakes at the fork, dust billowing in the red taillights. He yanked the wheel to the left and put his foot on the accelerator, the siren howling. As he drove, he grabbed his radio microphone and shouted for help from the other cars searching the forest roads.

He went around the bend on two wheels and saw the fire. Charlie was holding Slally by one arm. She was pummeling him with her free fist and screaming. McGraw slammed on the brakes and, opening his door, threw himself out on the car's momentum. He pulled his gun as he stumbled into the beam of the headlights. "Let her go, Charlie!" he bellowed, holding his revolver before him with both hands.

Charlie let go of Slally, who was yelling *Murderer* and *Run, Bentley, run!*

McGraw slid his gun back into its holster, stepped forward, and put his arm around Slally's shoulders. "Okay, Charlie," he said, "what'd you shoot at?"

"I didn't shoot at a goddamned thing!" Charlie barked. "The little bastard grabbed my shotgun and took a pop at *me!*"

Slally screamed he was lying.

McGraw looked down at her. Then he looked back at Charlie. "Sounds like she saw it another way."

"She's a half-wit!" Charlie yelled. "Listen to her! Blah, blah, blah!"

"Where's the boy?" McGraw asked quietly.

Charlie pointed at the bushes by the granite wall.

McGraw led Slally back to his cruiser and helped her into the front seat. The headlights of other cars were jouncing up the dirt road. McGraw stood beside the closed front door on the driver's side. He switched on the cruiser's searchlight and played it across the bottom of the granite wall. The ferns and stones were like people staring in a flash photograph.

McGraw tilted the light up. He swung it back and forth across the ledges, cracks, and crevasses where saplings grew. McGraw told himself that an energetic kid in sneakers could go up that rock face like a monkey.

He raised the searchlight higher. For an instant he saw Bentley, forty feet up, looking at the fire, the people, and the cars. Then the boy vanished.

"Bentley!" McGraw bellowed. "Bentley Ellicott! Come on down from there, kid!" He cupped his hands around his mouth and shouted again. "It's Chief McGraw, Bentley! Nobody's going to hurt you!"

He lowered his hands and put them on his hips. "I saw him," he said. "He's up there. What the hell's he doing?"

"I get the five grand!" Charlie shouted. "I found her!"

"Ah, shut up," McGraw grunted. He opened the car door and got into the front seat beside Slally. He looked down at her. "Is Bentley going someplace?"

She stared up at him. Her eyes were large and her mouth was a little circle.

"Can you tell me where he's going?" McGraw asked gently.

Slally turned her head and looked through the windshield at Charlie Feavey standing beside the fire. Car doors were slamming in the darkness and men were walking past the cruiser toward Charlie.

Slally looked back at McGraw. Her lips were trembling. She shook her head.

McGraw sighed and picked up his radio microphone. "Dick, do you read me?" He turned a switch.

The radio sparked and spluttered. A voice said. "I read you."

"We've found the girl," McGraw said, holding his microphone close to his mouth. "The Ellicott kid's okay, but he's running someplace. We lost him. Call the family first and tell them both kids are all right. We're bringing Sally in. Then get ahold of Lee and Mac. Tell them to call it off where they are. I want every man out here in a half-hour. We're on Coppermill Road, three, four miles north of the highway. Got it?" He turned the switch again.

"Got it," said Dick's voice on the receiver.

"Great news. Where do you want Mac and Lee to meet you?"

Before McGraw could turn the switch back, Polly's voice came over the speaker. "God bless you, McGraw," she said softly.

The police chief opened his microphone. "I want everybody up at Pensionville. We've got a lot of territory to cover tonight. And make sure you send out every walkie-talkie we've got."

"Shall do," Dick said.

McGraw hung up the microphone. He got out of the car. As he walked toward the cluster of men around the fire, he thought of what Polly had said. *What the hell does God have to do with it?* he asked himself. Then he wondered.

He stopped at the fire and hitched up his trousers. "Charlie," he said, "I don't believe that an eight-year-old kid can grab a twelve-gauge shotgun from a grown man, much less turn the thing on him and shoot."

"Are you calling me a liar?" Charlie snarled.

The men around the fire were looking at him.

"I'm calling you a liar," McGraw said. "I don't believe the boy could climb that rock face holding a shotgun. He didn't have any weapon in his hand when I saw him. I think you took a shot at him. Where's the gun, Charlie?"

"He took it," Charlie answered. "Grabbed it from my arm. Ask *him* where it is. I want my five thousand."

McGraw looked at the men around him. "You guys looked for the gun?"

Several heads nodded.

"T'aint in the ditch," a man said.

McGraw looked back at Charlie Feavey. "I haven't got time to fool around with you. If you want five thousand dollars, you walk yourself back to Stonehaven and we'll talk about it. I don't want you hanging around here. Go on home. And stay away from that boy."

Charlie walked down the dark road until the last car had backed past him. Then he returned to the fire. He stepped over the ditch, pushed his way three feet into the brush, and drew the shotgun from the crotch of a tree.

He walked back down the road to the fork. He stopped. The moon was a cool radiance above the treetops. Charlie heard a slight sound to his left. He crouched and crept up the road on the center strip, raising his boots so that they wouldn't whip through the grass.

In the pale cast of moonlight he saw a pickup truck parked by the side of the road. A man, shaped in shadow, was standing on the road one hundred yards beyond it.

Charlie inched along Willybill's pickup. He reached inside, ran his hand down the steering shaft, and felt for the ignition key. It was there. He jumped in, cranked the windows, locked the door, and switched on the lights. He gunned the engine, backed to the fork, swung the truck around, and lurched ahead, gathering speed along the bumpy road. He hit the highway and turned west, the speedometer rising to seventy.

West was the direction the boy had gone.

Chapter Thirteen

Elias Cutter drove through the village in the soft summer night. He had done what was expected of him. He had offered whatever assistance he could provide. McGraw had done what Mr. Cutter expected he would do. He politely declined with thanks.

As Elias Cutter drove home he impulsively counted lighted doorways in the houses he passed. He would never admit it to anyone, but he was superstitious. He believed that his life was governed from afar by alternating periods of good and bad luck. One day as a young man, while he rode a streetcar to propose to the only girl he had ever loved, he had paid attention to the stop lights. Each one turned red as the trolley arrived at it. The girl had laughed in his face and told him to stop pestering her. On the desperate afternoon when his bank's reserves were far below the legal minimum and the inspectors were due, everything had come to Elias Cutter in twos—telephone calls, letters, visitors. He had seen swallows swooping in pairs across the harbor. Just before the close of business, the two new owners of the freezing plant walked in with a very large deposit and told him they had decided to bank locally.

Elias Cutter felt that he was, to an unknowable degree, helpless in determining his own fortunes. He was carried back and forth on the surgings of a remorseless struggle that was taking place in a dimension beyond his comprehension. Elias Cutter was a secret, involuntary believer. By the time he turned into the driveway of his mansion, he had counted thirteen lighted doorways.

He got out of his car and stood in the darkness, looking at the stars and listening to the night sounds as Mrs. Tally parked her car beside his. He had never known so ominous a time. The struggle — which his inner self recognized even though his intellect would never acknowledge it — had become one-sided. The triumphant dealer in all misfortune was squatting, unimpeded, on the world. Elias Cutter had the eerie sensation that Stonehaven was the epicenter of a trembling presence.

Mrs. Tally walked across the driveway. "I need to speak to you about . . ." She groped for words. Her face was set and grim. "Something must be done."

"Come in," Mr. Cutter said.

"Can't," Mrs. Tally said. "I have to go home and count the silver. She may have stolen something while my back was turned."

"Who?" Mr. Cutter asked, feeling pleasure at the anger and indictment in her words.

"That disgusting Woodhouse girl."

Elias Cutter raised his eyebrows. "I thought you were trying to civilize her. I must admit I wondered—"

"There's no fool like an old fool—or a sentimental one," Mrs. Tally snapped. A car sped past on the dark road. "The girl's been conducting a place of prostitution."

"She's taken up with Charles Feavey," Mr. Cutter answered. "I've seen her going in there."

"That's known as home delivery of what she offers," Mrs. Tally said. She stood with her purse clasped in both hands. "Now then. What can we do about it?"

Elias Cutter looked down at the village. Its lights shimmered in long, broken streaks on the black water of the harbor. "Citizen's complaint," he said. "Somebody can go to Mr. McGraw and make a formal charge. I'd say she qualifies as a public nuisance."

"Will you go with me?" Mrs. Tally asked.

Mr. Cutter turned and looked at her. He remembered her sarcastic wit at the birthday party. He liked her spunk. "I will indeed," he said. "Mr. McGraw will have to investigate, even though she's kin."

"At the very least, that should get her out of the village."

"I should think so," Elias Cutter said. He was full of pleasurable anticipation. His desire to pay

Polly Woodhouse back for her impertinence was great. "We'll have a word with Mr. McGraw as soon as this search business is finished."

Mrs. Tally unclasped her gloved hands from her purse. "I've never seen such a hullabaloo over two unpleasant children," she said. "That girl is feeble-minded. If her mother had any sense, she'd put the child in an institution. And I've always said that Bentley Ellicott was peculiar." She walked back to her car. She opened the door. She looked at Mr. Cutter in the dim light. "It wouldn't surprise me a bit if they found them both dead."

Elias Cutter listened to the creatures of the summer night chanting devotionals to the omnipresent evil that ruled it. He knew he should be shocked at the bitter words Mrs. Tally had just spoken. But he wasn't.

Through the circuitry of enchantment that carries dreaded foreknowledge, the intention of Elias Cutter and Mrs. Tally came to Polly as a vague, constricting sense of threat.

She sat in a swivel chair, watching Dick Amberstam hand out walkie-talkies to the men who had come in from the search along the point. The lights of the small police station were bright; the radio speaker erupted with bursts of talk as if it were alive.

Polly swung around in the chair and propped a foot on the table beside the radio. She put her chin in one hand and stared at the shining dials and switches before her. She had been so happy about McGraw's finding the children. Now, for no appar-

ent reason, that pleasure had faded, and her irritation at Mrs. Tally had turned into a clutch of
alarm in her breast.

The old bag would talk about her all over the village. That would widen Polly's reputation as a
slut. The thought of people she'd known all her life
gossiping about her and being smirky-polite to her
face was unbearable. She saw everybody at the
drugstore. She considered quitting her job.

Then she wondered where she could find
another job. Polly was still thinking unhappily
about that problem when the search party left to
join McGraw in the forest west of Stonehaven.

Anxieties multiplied in the hot night. Polly
began to recall all the times she'd rumpled old
man Cutter's dignity with her kidding.

She wished that she'd behaved herself. She took
her foot off the table and sat up straight. Maybe
they'd gang up on her and *make* her go away.

Prince Ombra rose with the moon; his unshaped
nebula rolled west with the revolving of the
night's curved canopy of stars. As he moved, he
left his smear of soul plagues across the village
and the coast. He did not speak. The night sounds
had become a babble of all that he did not need to
say for his presence to be proclaimed. The shrilling of cicadas in the trees gave voice to furies fer-
menting in mortal minds; the hollow croaking of
frogs echoed as grunts of unloving lust; the loon's
cry summarized all despair in the darkness, and
the hiss of waves dying in the sand expressed
every cruel insinuation.

The world beyond Stonehaven inhaled his essence. The proximity of him suffocated rejoicings, turned pity into contempt, and so altered the minds of the powerful with the passions of the moment that they cast aside caution and charity.

Ombra's seven brains exchanged sight, knowing, and strategies between themselves in voltages of excitement. He saw Bentley clawing through the dark forest. The warrior was alone and afraid. His rememberer and his sorcerer had abandoned him.

Ombra entered the dreams of a madman blubbering and snoring in a dark place.

Snakes.

Bentley couldn't see the ground as he pushed his way through the underbrush. Low branches and whips of vine snared his legs and ankles. He was sweaty and scratched and nearly out of breath from the effort to get out of there before he stepped on a snake, dreading with every step that he would feel one writhing beneath his sneakers and fangs stabbing into his leg.

Suddenly he came to the end of the forest. With a final stumble through a bed of nettles he fell onto short, rough grass. Immediately he scrambled to his feet and ran up a slope to an outcropping of rock. He climbed it and felt safer. He didn't know whether snakes came out of the woods and chased people.

Bentley had only two things on his mind, now that he knew Slally was all right: getting as far away from Charlie Feavey as he could and heading for Indian Hill.

He lifted his head and looked at the forest. It

was like a vast pit.

Bentley was scared of what had already happened—nearly getting shot by Charlie Feavey—and he was scared of what was *going* to happen to him. He knew that the immobility of the nocturnal landscape around him was an illusion; Prince Ombra permeated it and was watching. Bentley wished Dr. Kreistein were with him. The old man had a comforting way of reducing fears to ordinary problems and annoyances.

Bentley looked down at the pit-black forest. He looked up at the cold, dead sky. He tried to pretend that Dr. Kreistein was beside him. "I know he's all around me," he said aloud to the old man. "I don't know what he's going to do to me." He sat staring at the forest, trying to make his pretend real. But Dr. Kreistein was too real to be pretended. Bentley couldn't make up words for him to say.

He tried, instead, to remember some of the things the old man had told him.

Dr. Kreistein had made him feel bad only once—the day they were talking about his mother. But the old man had fixed it quickly: "From all I can gather, your mother was a very gentle and good woman. Also beautiful, judging by the photograph of her in your father's living room."

Bentley's mother always seemed to be gazing directly at him when he was anywhere near that photograph. She had dark hair, and there was the beginning of a smile at the right corner of her mouth. Her eyes, gazing at him, seemed as if they might have been gray.

They had never known each other. But she was

still a presence. He knew that every soul returned to the place of its other childhood. She hadn't been much older than Helga when her mortal life ended. He had never tried to talk to her in the second air.

He got to his feet. He looked down at the village where he'd spent his whole life. He could see the headlights of a car moving along Main Street. "Remember the drugstore and the wharf?" He stopped speaking for a moment. He didn't know what to call his mother. He decided not to call her anything.

He saw a line of headlights coming up the highway that curved to the top of the ridge. "They're looking for me," he said aloud. "I can't let them find me yet." He turned and saw the deserted village on the rise of land behind him. All he could see was the steeple of the church. But he'd gone past there every time his father or Ellen drove him up to the university. He began climbing the slope again. He was so absorbed in talking to his mother for the first time, and making her come real, that he wasn't scared anymore. His father must have really loved her to be so sad for so long after she died. She must have really loved him, too. In the fusion of that good and gentle love, Bentley had been given his mortal life.

Suddenly he felt happy. He told his mother all about Slally. "She saved my life back there," he said. "Mr. Feavey's crazy. He was really going to kill me. I would have stayed to help Slally. But after Mr. Feavey shot at me, I heard the car coming, so I figured it was okay."

He stopped. A hundred yards away the empty

church loomed against the night sky. Its white
paint was peeling: The bare places, visible on the
moonlit side, were sores inflicted by time and
neglect. The windows stared into the evening as
tall black oblongs. Pieces of timber stuck out of
the cupola.

Bentley stood watching two cars pass on the
highway between the church and a tumbledown
store on the other side of the road. He walked toward the church. There was an old barrel beside
one of the windows. For a moment, Bentley was
tempted to climb up onto it and have a look inside.
Then he got a little nervous. If he peered through
the glass, he might see a face peering back at him,
like the faces that burst onto the TV screen in horror movies after somebody opens a mysterious
door. He started toward the back of the building.

He heard car engines slowing down. He heard
tires crunching on gravel.

Bentley took a panicky look around him. He was
standing a few feet away from a small open window just above ground level. He heard a car door
slam. Then another. His heart began to beat faster.

"You take the other side of the road," said a
man's voice on the far side of the church.

Bentley hesitated for a moment, the way he did
before jumping off the rocks into the cold water.
"I've gotta hide in there," he whispered to his
mother. "If I don't, they'll find me!"

He scuttled into the open window. He fell
through cobwebs and landed on all fours in the
dark, bruising his knees. He scrambled away from
the window and bumped into a wall. Bentley
crouched, brushing at the cobwebs that stuck to

his ears and face. The basement of the church was pitch black despite the square patch of pale light in the window; it smelled of old dirt and mold.

Bentley started groping his way along the wall. Maybe he'd find a box or barrel to hide behind in case the guy looking for him beamed the flashlight through the window. He stopped and rubbed his back up and down against the cinderblock wall; he was worried that a spider might have been in the mess of cobwebs and dropped down his collar. He edged to the right, his hand waving in the darkness before him.

Prince Ombra struck.

Bentley's hand froze in midair; he couldn't move. Something alive was in the cellar with him! He suddenly had heard its breathing. It drew in air with a clotted rattle, then gave a lip-flubbering exhalation. Slowly Bentley brought his hand down.

He heard the bubbling intake of breath again. The creature was less than three feet in front of him! The spent breath was warm on Bentley's face, and sour with the stench of vomit.

His heart thumping, Bentley clenched his teeth and drew back. He pressed his lips together to keep himself from yelling in incoherent fear, and slid along the wall on his rear end. The hoarse breathing was just as loud, but the stink was fainter.

He got to his feet fast, looking at the windows on the opposite wall, calculating the run and the sprint up the wall that would get him a grip on its sill.

"Well, let's see," said a man's voice outside, speaking as if to himself, "let's have a look here, kid. Maybe you got yourself into a church.''

Bentley was about to screech for help. In his
swarming mind he realized that his mother would
hear him yelling like a baby. His heart was pounding so hard that it pulsed against his eardrums. He
wiped his brow. He saw a pair of legs appear in the
square frame of moonlight. The man outside
began to squat. Bentley moved a foot to his right,
groping frantically with his hand. His knuckles
cracked on something, and he had to swallow a cry
of pain.

He groped again. He'd hit a board fixed to the
wall. He lifted his hand. There was another board
above it. Stairs.

He could see the searcher's head and shoulders
silhouetted against the pale moonlight. The flashlight blazed for a moment. Bentley grabbed the
stairs and swung himself around so that he was
facing them.

Prince Ombra watched.

The flashlight's beam spread on the cellar wall
and moved toward the place where Bentley was
standing. Thoughts of rescue from the creature
slobbering in the dark tossed for a second in his
brain. Then he thought of being brave for his
mother. He scrambled up the stairs on all fours.

His head butted into a door at the top. It swung
open and he sprawled, exhausted and half numb
with dread, onto the church floor.

Prince Ombra contracted his incorporeal persona. Intangible, he filled the dim, dry interior of
the church.

Bentley lay on the floor, trying to calm himself.

He thought of the man with the flashlight outside; that man was real, he was somebody who was trying to rescue Bentley; but he had no idea of what terrible things he was rescuing Bentley from.

Bentley felt something tickling his neck. He was re-electrified into frenzy by the idea of a spider crawling on him. He grabbed his collar and felt something squish between his fingers. He sat up, yanked off his shirt, and flapped it frantically in the air.

‹ He sat panting on the floor, holding his rumpled shirt in his hands, and decided to give up. He was sitting on a side of the church, near the altar. He could see part way down the cavernous length of the wall. Weak light was coming through the tall windows. It glowed dimly on the backs of the pews. Everything smelled of dust and ghosts.

Bentley heard a car door slam. He jumped up, struggled into his shirt, and ran down the center aisle of the church. The car's engine started and roared twice.

"Wait!" Bentley yelled. "Hey, you guys, wait!"

He ran to the tall front doors of the church. He could see a slit of light between them. He pounded on the doors. "It's me!" he shouted. "I'm in here! Wait!"

He was still beating with both fists, the doors giving a little under his pressure, when he heard the car drive away.

He stopped pounding. He turned around.

The church stretched before him, its shapes in shadow. High above him, among the eaves, he heard a brief, dry twitter of bat wings. Bentley sat down in a pew. A sliver of moonbeam lay on the dust-covered wood beside him. He was lonely, and frightened.

He felt his heart bumping in his chest. His mind wasn't frantic any longer. It was filled with one hopeless realization. He didn't know how to get out of the church except through the cellar. The windows were too high for him to climb up to even if he broke one of them. The doors were locked. And he wasn't going back to that cellar for anything.

What was down there was probably going to come up to where he was. He tried to pretend that his mother was sitting beside him. He didn't want her worrying that he couldn't take care of himself. "I'll get a stick somewhere," he said. "See, it can't get at me because of my circles and stuff." He knew that wasn't true, because the creature in the basement was real, not an idea or magic. "So . . ." he said, his voice trailing off as the pretend of his mother disintegrated. "I'll get a stick and hit it. When it comes up here."

The dark nimbus of Lord Ombra stood between Bentley and his mother's presence.

He looked around the church. People had locked it up a long time before and walked away from it. Bentley wondered if god was sore about that. The chamber that towered above him seemed filled with mute resentment.

Something clattered at the bottom of the basement stairs. Bentley jumped. Rockets of panic arced through his brain. He heard the something mumbling. Then it barked.

Bentley skidded along the pew, pushing a pile of

dust before him. He dropped into the shadows of the wall aisle and put his hands over his face. He crouched like that for ten seconds. Then he opened his eyes behind his hands. The mumbling, self-absorbed sounds of a beast came from the cellar stairs. Bentley spread his fingers slightly and saw orange light.

He lowered his hands. His eyes widened. The light was getting brighter, flickering on the dusty walls and the black placard that held white numbers announcing the last hymns ever sung in the church. Bentley heard a new and terrible singing.

Two sputtering fistfuls of flame emerged from the cellar door. Bentley ducked and put his hands over his face again. He tried to flee into himself because he had no place else to go. He heard staccato, nasal singing as if a great bird were chanting through its resonant beak.

The singing turned into a croak, a gargle, as if the singer were strangling on his song. It wasn't a bird of some hideous breed—the voice was human.

Bentley lowered his trembling hands, opened his eyes, and raised his head.

A man was scraping up the aisle toward the altar. He was holding a bottle with a flaming rag stuck in it.

He was a ruin of a man. His hair was tangled and filthy. There was an oval patch on the side of his head where scabs had taken the place of hair. His eyes were sunk deep into his skull, and his cheekbones were covered with broken, red splotches. His nose was smashed in; his mouth, surrounded by the dirty chaos of an unkempt beard, opened and closed as he tried to force out the words of a hymn. But the rasping chant that came from him was just guttural noise studded with words—"Father," "mercy," and "peace." Even when he wasn't saying words, the mouth opened and closed mechanically, as if he were doing a grotesque imitation of a hymn singer.

He wore a black suit. His body was shriveled within it. His chest, Bentley saw, was bare. The ankles above his cracked and wrinkled shoes were naked, too.

The strange creature—a human shape reduced to a rubble of filth and bruised flesh—shuffled toward the altar. The flame danced on the church wall. Bentley gasped.

A grotesque crucifix cast bizarre shadows. A piece of board had been tied diagonally onto a twisted tree branch that leaned against the wall. A child's doll, unclothed and wigless, had been nailed by its hand to one end of the board. It dangled lifelessly, its inanimate eyes staring into the gloom of the church.

The broken man put his flaming bottle on the altar. He clasped his hands and lowered his body in supplication before his votary. One leg crumpled and collapsed. The man fell on his side with a thud. He made no effort to unclasp his hands and cushion the fall. His head hit the floor, but he neither cried out nor winced. It was as if his body were so corrupted that it no longer interested him.

He lay on his side, his eyes shining in the torchlight as he gazed up at the altar. His voice rattled from his throat. "Why won't you send the sign?"

he begged. "Whaddya *want?* Penance?" He raised his clenched hands and struck himself on the forehead three times. "Repent!" he barked after each soft blow. He raised his eyes to the flaming altar again. "Nobody can do it all by himself! I need a sign!" He unclasped his hands, rolled on his stomach, and raised his head. His toothless lips curled into a grimace of disdain. He spat upward. His saliva glistened on the wall behind the cross. Then, as quickly as his rage had flared, it subsided. His head fell forward, slamming against the floor, and he began to sob. "I didn't mean it! It's j-j-just that you won't *send—the—sign!*" The black shoulders jerked up and down, and a low wailing came forth.

Bentley stood up. His mouth was half open and his heart was torn betweeen dread and pity. "Mr. Tally," he whispered. "Mr. Tally—it's me—Bentley!"

The apparition of the Reverend Tally was not interrupted. He rolled over on his side again, and the face his craning neck lifted toward the flame was blotted with tears. "You could do a miracle," he rasped. "You could make it so there would be a little place for me somewhere! A hospital!" He looked eager. "Comfort the sick—preach thy word—a hospital with a place for me! I wouldn't do it anymore then—not a drop—I promise. Please . . ."

Bentley barely recognized the man lying on the floor. Fear suffocated his pity for a moment. In the wreck of Mr. Tally, Bentley saw the inexorable power of Prince Ombra. The clergyman hadn't known that, years before, he was tempting disaster when he had gathered a lonely boy into his care. In those days, when Bentley was little, the Reverend Tally's selflessness and Christian love had been manifest in every hour of his life. Bentley remembered how *clean* Mr. Tally had once been—his white surplice, his shining hands. Now Bentley saw the result of a long struggle; Prince Ombra had penetrated the holy light around the clergyman, and the human devastation he had made was terrible.

Bentley began to move down the side aisle. The gloom in the great cavern of the church seemed untouched by Ombra's triumphant fire flickering on the altar. As he approached slowly, brushing the rounded back of each pew, Bentley was afraid that Mr. Tally would suddenly turn on him. Then he wondered if, by being spoken to, Mr. Tally could become his former self.

Bentley stood behind the rail at the front of the church, watching and listening as Reverend Tally's beseeching continued. Even at the distance of ten feet the reek of stale alcohol and body musk was unbearable. Bentley crept toward the derelict as he would toward a dangerous beast. "Mr. Tally," he whispered again. "Mr. Tally—it's Bentley!"

Reverend Tally abruptly stopped pleading. One eye, a drop of flame shining in it, peered over his shoulder. It stared at Bentley.

"Don't you *know* me?" Bentley asked.

Mr. Tally's eye gleamed with fear. "You're green!" he rasped.

"No I'm not."

"Dead green of the sea!" Mr. Tally exclaimed, hugging his ribs. His shoes made a frantic scraping and thudding on the floor as he shuffled to get away from Bentley. "Sea and wind! Cold! Go away!"

Bentley took a cautious step toward him. "Mr. Tally, I'm not going to hurt you. It's *Bentley Ellicott!*"

Reverend Tally uncoiled his body and slithered backward on all fours toward a space between the altar and the wall. He was spitting and hissing. His face was white beneath its grime. "Lucifer!" he cried.

Bentley shook his head. "Listen, Mr. Tally—you've gotta remember me—Bentley. We used to go fishing and take walks and stuff. Please remember!"

Mr. Tally crouched, staring. Then, suddenly, a new hallucination possessed him. He lunged, and before Bentley could jump out of the way, Mr. Tally had grabbed his belt with both hands. The filthy, quivering face was six inches from Bentley's, exhaling its stench. "The sign! Thou art Gabriel and Michael! The sign sent to me!"

Bentley grabbed one of the clergyman's dirt-caked wrists and tried to wrench himself free. "I'm *not!*" he yelled. *"Let go!"* But the creature that once was his friend held him fast.

"The messenger of God!" Mr. Tally prattled. "He has not forsaken me!" The hands yanked urgently at Bentley's belt. "He has heard my prayer and He has sent thee to tell me what I shall be given." The insane minister scrabbled closer to Bentley on his knees, his face uplifted, his mouth with cracked teeth and coated tongue gaping wide in a demented grin. "Tell me, tell me, telltelltell,

Michaelgreatarchangel! Wrestler of Satan! Conqueror of sin! Michael, tell, tell poor child Homer—"

"Mr. Tally, I haven't got *anything* to tell you!"

"Michael!" Mr. Tally whispered, his face still spread in its idiotic grin. He wriggled closer, and Bentley stumbled backward. But Reverend Tally held him "Michael, listen, listen, Michael, I'll make my confession again, perhaps He didn't hear it all, I'll do it again—" His whispering had become a frantic babble. "Lust! Lust, drunkenness, and fornication! I am guilty of all these, Father, and I repent me of my sins!"

The grin disappeared. The cracked lips curved down into a child's weeping grimace. "You saw into the soul of Abraham, Father!" Mr. Tally bawled. "See into mine! I lusted for my neighbor's wife and committed fornication with her! You know my penance is sincere, Father! See into my heart! I prayed most sincerely for her soul when she died! I was a friend to her child! I tried to love him, Father!"

Holding onto Mr. Tally's wrists, Bentley stared down in horror. He didn't understand all the words, but he knew who and what they were about.

Reverend Tally's eyes closed. His body jerked with his sobs. "I did not love the boy! You know it, Father! But I *tried!*" Tears tracked down his face's grime that had been turned to mud by previous tears. "You saw my soul burn as I hated the boy because he was the flesh of her greater love!" He yanked several times on Bentley's belt. "Tell him, Michael!"

He let go. As Bentley straggered back, the clergyman crumpled onto the floor. "I *tried* to love the boy, Father! He *thought* I did! Doesn't that count for something, the *wanting?* I am Abraham, Lord! Read my heart! I only drink because of the loneliness!" His voice broke and he beat his forehead on the dusty boards. "See my remorse, God . . . pleeease forgive me . . ." Flame from the bottles threw the shadows of his heaving shoulders. "Please, Lord, just a little place . . . in thy . . . great . . . world. . . ."

Bentley fled. He fled from the terrible light into the darkness below. Shock stunned him and broke his thinking into pieces. Like a frenzied animal he leaped over and over again in the gloom, tearing his clothes and skin as he scrambled through the window, as he ran and ran beneath the cold stars. He beat his hands on his ears, trying to drive the words of the madman from his mind. Bentley wanted to pound it all out of his head before he had to think and feel. He stumbled, sprawled, and hurt his arm. He jumped up and ran, limping and shouting, but shouting no words, just making noise so he couldn't hear Ombra's jubilant cackle in the ranting of Mr. Tally. Bentley ran beyond all sense and knowing, and when, at last, he collapsed with the sweet aroma of grass and earth in his face, he slept instantly, because he didn't want to be awake anymore.

Chapter Fourteen

Silence is the delusion.

From a distance we see the city. The life of men thunders in it, but watching from far away, we hear nothing. The soul passes from life, through death, and arrives at its Elysium to welcoming song; but standing in the shadowed room, watching the old woman's last gasp into her oxygen mask, we hear no music.

Prince Ombra had become the silence.

McGraw stood next to his car on the curve of highway above the forest and coast. He could see the full nocturnal panorama of a new moon and the stars, scattered and frozen, where the power of Creation had cast them. The police chief looked at the aurora borealis. It was a veil of phantom colors. "Mike," he said.

McGraw's deputy raised his eyes from the police cruiser's dashboard. Through the radio speakers he could hear the soft walkie-talkie chatter of men searching the forest below.

"Ever see the northern lights so early in the year?" McGraw asked him.

Mike leaned out of the police car and peered at the sky. He gazed for a moment at the curtain of pale, shifting light. "Never did," he said.

McGraw raised his Styrofoam coffee container and drank. "They *never* show before September."

Mike continued staring at the northern sky. "Here it's only July," he said. "Funny."

"Some strange," McGraw murmured.

Mike turned back to the radio's crackle and the voices of forty-six Stonehaven men talking to each other as they proceeded in a line through the forest and across dirt roads in the darkness below, searching for Bentley Ellicott.

Richard Ellicott arrived at McGraw's command post on the edge of the uplands at two A.M. He talked to Mike, listened to the radio voices, and questioned the searchers who came up for coffee and a break.

McGraw watched him as he sat in the cruiser. The college professor was struggling to fight down a bitter fury. The effort showed in Richard's eyes and the nervous setting and resetting of his mouth. McGraw understood the strain the man was under. But why the rage?

The dead light is a foretelling of what will be.
The traveler raises his head in the forest at evening. He sees the dull shine of an eye as the panther

*watches him. It is a glint of murderous intention.
Asleep, the king dreams of the sun's death. He
awakes to a bleak morning, and his soul is as heavy
as all the stones of his realm. The moon shines on
great machines beneath gaunt towers, energizing
them. When the machines roar to life again, they
will kill.*

Prince Ombra had become the dead light.

Richard stood on the edge of the highway in the
waning of the night. The aurora borealis was fading. Richard watched the last of the phantom radiance in the northern sky. He was helpless against
the anger that rose in him like black tidewater rising in the hull of a wrecked ship. He had been trying to suppress it since the moment he and Ellen
had realized that the children were missing. They
had still been disoriented with shock over Helga's
death. Richard was as frightened by Ellen's fear as
he was anxious over Bentley and Sally. He had
begun to get angry when Ellen went out to the kitchen to call her ex-husband after McGraw left the
house. Richard had sat in the living room for forty
minutes, listening to the flow of Ellen's voice behind the closed pantry door.

When she finally came back to the living room,
she said that Rupert Drake was on his way east.
She sat on the sofa, the fingers of her right hand
clenched into her palm. "God, I wish he were here
right now."

Richard had tried to reassure her about the
search that McGraw was organizing. Ellen didn't
want to be reassured. "That horrible animal tore
Helga to pieces!"

"That was an aberration," Richard said. "Bob-cats don't usually attack people."

Ellen stood up abruptly and crossed the room to the screen door. "There's one bobcat out there that *does* attack people, and my darling child is lost . . ." She began to weep.

Richard went to her and tried to put his arms around her. But the angle of her body made it impossible. He touched his hand to her shoulder. "I'll get Dr. Kreistein to give you something," he said.

"I don't want that old freak to give me something!" she had screamed, bursting from grief into fury. *"I want my daughter!"*

"You'll get her back—"

"You don't know that!" she cried, turning her wet face to him. "Don't tell me things that may not be true!"

"Listen!" he retorted. "I feel—my *son's* missing, too!"

"He's a boy! He's lived here all his life! *He can talk!*"

"And Sally's with him."

Ellen had turned her face back toward the rising night. She put her forehead against the screen. "I never should have brought her here," she said, as if to herself. "I put myself first. My *big romance* came before my child." She rolled her head from side to side. "Stupid. Selfish. Stupid. I wish Rupert would come."

Richard's own bitter anger flared at that moment. "Finally found a way of getting him back, didn't you?" he snapped.

"Don't be an ass!" Ellen screamed. "I don't *want*

him back! He's coming because his child . . . our child . . ." She was overpowered with weeping for a moment. "He's doing what *any* father would do! God, you're so weak!"

Richard tried to tell himself that she was being unfeeling because she was distraught. But as the night filled his house, another darkness was filling it, too. It hissed at him from shadowed corners. It spat acid on a hurt buried so deep in his past that he no longer knew what it originally had been. It taunted him with the prophecy that Ellen was going to leave him when this was over. Fear took possession of him and he could not help himself.

They went into the village and Ellen made her reward offer to the search party. Then Richard knew that never again could he think of Sally as his child. She was Rupert and Ellen Drake's child.

When McGraw and Mike had brought the little girl home at nine-thirty, Ellen's anger and anxiety hadn't been appeased. She took Sally upstairs. To Richard the child seemed to be all right—just oddly undemonstrative.

He had sat alone in the living room waiting for Ellen to come down, repentant, and apologize. He wanted her to be with him and share his anxiety about Bentley — so that he'd know again that she thought of Bentley as her son, too. She didn't come.

At midnight Richard had gone upstairs. Ellen was lying asleep on Sally's bed with Sally curled up beside her. Sally was the reason she was going to leave him.

He stood on the highway watching the northern lights end with the night. He tried to put Bentley

first in his mind. Through the dark hours he had
returned again and again to the police cars parked
on the highway just below the deserted village.
Richard tried to focus on the reality that his son
was lost somewhere in the forest or out on the uplands. But his thoughts kept returning to the abandonment and failure he would feel when Ellen was
gone.

McGraw sat in his police car with the doors
open, watching Richard. Funny, McGraw thought,
the professor's reaction to his kid being missing.
The whole night had been strange.

The police chief looked through his bug-spatter-
ed windshield. A streak of red lay like a knife edge
on the horizon of the sea, announcing the beginning of dawn.

He got out of the cruiser. He put his big hands
on his upper butt and arched his back. He was
tired, but he was filled with an urgency about
Bentley.

He looked west. Up on the crest of the ridge the
church and store of the deserted village of Pensionville had caught the first fiery dawn light.
McGraw didn't know why the village had been
abandoned years before. But he had a presenti-
ment that some power that saw far into the future
had drained the place of people and life as a
preparation for the coming day.

In the emptiness we see our fate.
We gaze through the window at the landscape ly-
ing under a shroud of frost. Nothing moves on the
frozen marshes or at the edge of the distant forest.
We feel eyes looking back at us. In the knowing of

*dreams, we know that the specter which will clasp
us to its cold breast waits in an empty room. We
awake and it is true.*

Prince Ombra had become the emptiness.

McGraw rested his hands on the hood of the
cruiser. It was eight A.M. Richard stood beside the
police chief with his arms folded. McGraw studied
the map spread out on the hood. "We'll split into
two shifts," he said. "Anybody real tired can go
home and get some sleep." He looked around at
the men sprawling on the grassy edges of the highway or watching him from cars and trucks. "Who
wants to work until four o'clock?"

Tired hands raised. Wind-burned faces nodded.

"Okay," McGraw said. "Mike'll decide who goes
home and who stays." He turned to a state police
lieutenant standing with one booted foot on the
cruiser's fender. "What about it, Barney?"

The lieutenant squinted at the sky. A helicopter
was parked on the slope fifty yards away. The lieutenant looked north. "We can cover west and
south pretty good," he said. "Won't be much use
to take the chopper up yonder, not with that fog
hanging in. Can't see a goddamn thing out there
until the wind comes up."

"Tough," McGraw said, returning to his study of
the map. "North of here is where the kid's probably gone."

"Why?" Richard demanded suddenly. "Why not
inland? Why not south down the coast?"

McGraw looked at him. Richard's curt manner
was a part of the day's strangeness. "We don't
know whether your boy's going *toward* someplace

or away from something. An eight-year-old kid
hasn't much of anyplace to go. My guess is he's
panicked and he's running away."

"From what?"

"That character Willybill's been missing since
about the time the kids disappeared." McGraw
answered him quietly. "We don't know what it
means. Maybe Bentley's running away from
Charlie Feavey. Charlie's 'bout half crazy anyway.
He's got a grudge against Bentley and tried to hurt
him last night."

"Why in hell didn't you tell me?" Richard demanded.

"I'm telling you," McGraw replied. "The boy
knows this country around here. He knows if he
goes south it's all brush and woods. If he goes
north there's open spaces *besides* the woods.
That'd attract him." He looked down at the map.
"It's wide open a couple of miles north." The
police chief pointed to the map. "He could stop at
this lake here. He could go to the old Cogshall
place. There's lots of places for a boy to hide from
whatever's after him—whatever he *thinks* is after
him."

"What's that?" Richard said, indicating a spot
on the map.

"Indian Hill," McGraw said, "That's where
civilized territory begins again. Emson's stone-
crushing works is just beyond. And Tysonville."

"His school class went to Indian Hill last fall,"
Richard said.

"If he's in a panic like I think he is," McGraw
replied, "he'll head for someplace he knows. We'll
work the ground search north toward Indian

Hill." He folded the map. "Professor, go home. You look like one beat man. We'll call you when we find him."

"*If* you find him," Richard said.

"We found the girl," McGraw said. He turned to the men resting beside the highway. "Tell Mike which shift you want to work. Barney, if you're willing, maybe the chopper can start covering the highway going west."

"We're all yours until we find him," the lieutenant said. "Dead or alive."

Richard barely took in the state police lieutenant's words. He was incapable of thinking of Bentley as dead. All he was capable of was feeling his rage. He drove back to Stonehaven, the unresisting victim of his fury at Ellen, which was the twin of the pain she had caused him. In his imagination he heard her calmly explaining that she was leaving for Sally's good—and asking him not to try to see her for both their sakes. Richard wanted to injure her, to shatter her calm. "Just shut up and go!" he snapped at her in his imagination.

Ellen sat at the kitchen table in her bathrobe. Slally put down her fork and looked at her mother.

"Please," Ellen said. "Darling, you're the only one who knows where Bentley's gone. You've *got* to help."

Slally looked at the uneaten bits of scrambled egg on her plate. She shook her head.

"Darling, you *love* Bentley—"

Slally couldn't look at her mother. She was afraid Ellen was going to start crying again. "*I* love Bentley," Ellen said. "Oh, *please,* Sally. Can't you just nod or show no if Mr. McGraw asks you some questions?"

Slally began to cry softly.

Ellen got up from her chair and pressed the little girl's head to her waist. She looked out the kitchen window. The sun was burning above the mist, but the light beneath it was dead and cold.

Dietrich Kreistein stood on his porch, looking through the forest at the blur where the sea melted into the petrified sky. He had just come back from the Ellicott house. In the few minutes he'd had alone with Slally, the little girl had answered with an emphatic nod when Dr. Kreistin asked her if Bentley had found out anything about the stone. "Has he, perhaps, discovered where this animal took it?" Slally had nodded again. Ellen Drake told the old man that Polly Woodhouse had telephoned from the police station to report that the search for the missing boy was moving to the uplands, beyond Pensionville.

So, Dr. Kreistein said to himself. *We will hope that these good men do not find him too soon.* Every droplet of mist, every gleaming leaf in the forest, and each bird cry that splintered the morning's silence conveyed an ephemeral sense of waiting and expectancy. "For once, Herr Prinz, you and I are both doing the same thing," Dietrich Kreistein said. "But we do not hope for the same conclusion."

Ellen bent over and kissed Slally on the top of her head. "Don't cry," she whispered. She took Slally's face in both of her hands. "It's a secret, isn't it?"

Slally nodded.

"If you won't cry anymore because you can't tell, I won't cry anymore because I was horrible to Richard and because I'm worried sick about Bentley."

Slally wiped her eyes on the edge of Ellen's robe.

"They're *going* to find him," Ellen told her. "We'll make a bet. I'll bet that Bentley's home before lunch."

She heard Richard's car turn in at the driveway. Slally slid off her chair and went out into the living room. Ellen ran her fingers through her hair and prayed for such grace that never again would she have to practice sentences to convince the only man she'd ever loved that she loved him.

Richard's footsteps sounded on the front porch. The screen door banged shut. Ellen tightened the belt of her bathrobe and went out into the hall.

Richard was standing in the living room. He looked exhausted. "They haven't found him," he said to Slally.

Ellen's heart ached for him. He was beaten. She couldn't remember the words that would make everything all right again. But she tried. "Richard, darling—"

He raised his head and looked at her. "Just shut up and go," he told her. Then he went upstairs and slammed the bedroom door.

Ombra was the delusion, the foretelling, and their fate.

Bentley opened his eyes.

He was lying with his cheek on the grass. An ant was struggling along, a few inches from his nose,

tugging a morsel as big as itself. Thoughts started
to brighten in Bentley's mind like the foggy day
around him. He watched the ant stagger over a
broken stalk of grass. Its legs flailed as it hauled
its burden through a tangle of fibers and dust. It
was oblivious to anything except its destination.

Bentley's brain began to fill with memory. He
sat up. He didn't want to watch the ant anymore
because it made him feel ashamed about giving
up. He didn't want to remember, either; the
memory of Mr. Tally and what he'd said about
Bentley's mother was too terrible to think about.
Bentley sat on the grass, feeling an empty ache in
his stomach and a bitter taste in his mouth. He
raised his head. Mist was passing over him and all
around him, rolling in gentle, silent billows. He
squinted at the morning already partly gone. At
home they'd have finished breakfast by now. His
father and Ellen would be really sore at him for
running away.

He lowered his head. He was still a little stupid
with sleep. He sat staring at his sneakers out on
the end of his legs. He couldn't forget what Mr.
Tally had said.

He felt grief filling him. He sat in the white, billowing silence, looking at his feet. If he quit and
went home, Dr. Kreistein would probably give up
on him because he wasn't going to be a hero anymore. McGraw, who'd be responsible for finding
him, would go back to thinking Bentley was crazy.
Slally would be mad because he'd made her promise not to tell where he was going and that had
probably gotten her into a lot of trouble.

The stillness of the place where he sat pressed in

on him. The rolling fog passed through, taking
with it the minutes of the day and all the things
people were doing—and Bentley was being left
behind. His empty stomach hurt. The other emptiness swelled with a bleakness that made him think
of his house with nobody in it.

He sniffed. He wiped his eyes with the ends of
his fingers. He rubbed his nose on his sleeve and
raised his head, realizing he couldn't sit there on
the grass forever.

The wind that drove the mist sighed and
strengthened. As Bentley watched, the fog in front
of him began to thin out. He could see a jagged
wall emerging from the white—that would be a
stand of pine trees. He heard the wind fluttering in
his ears. He saw more of the grass stubble emerging from the haze beyond his sneakers.

He saw a human shape standing on a hummock
a hundred yards to his right.

Bentley jumped to his feet. Then he yelled.
"Hey! I'm over here!"

The figure didn't gesture or approach. It didn't
move. The smoky shape looked like a man standing with one hand on his hip as he watched Bentley. The mist was still too thick for Bentley to
make out the man's face or the color of his clothes.

Bentley cupped his hands around his mouth and
shouted as loud as he could, "I'm—over—here!"

The smoke man didn't move.

Bentley dropped his hands to his sides. The
figure on the hummock wasn't somebody out looking for a lost boy.

Bentley stared. His scalp prickled. The skin on
his face began to tighten. The figure stood motion-

less, staring back at him. A knot began to harden beneath Bentley's breastbone, above his stomach, as it dawned on him whom he was looking at.

"I'm not scared of you," he said in a small voice. "I've still got my magic and you—" He peered up at the sky. The sun was brighter in the dissipating mist. Bentley heard his hawks whistle twice as if to reassure him that they were there. He imagined their bodies circling close above his head.

He looked back at the man on the hummock. He hadn't changed his stance.

"You can't make me do anything!" Bentley yelled. "I've still got my magic! I don't have to fight or do anything else I don't *want* to do!"

Fog drifted past the silhouetted figure. It dimmed for a moment and then solidified again. Bentley remembered why he was out there all alone watching it. He remembered Helga lying in the forest. He remembered Mr. Tally in the firelight and the poison that had infected him years before. The same poison had turned Bentley's mother ugly. Now she was dead and the clergyman Bentley thought had loved him was worse than dead.

"Bastard!" he yelled suddenly at the smoke man. "I'm gonna find that stone! I know where it is! And when I find it I'm gonna kill you! Bastard!" He tightened his fists. He wasn't sad anymore. He was filled with the fury of getting even.

He ran.

He ran across the grass stubble toward the wall of pine trees. He dashed in among them, limping hard, jumping over logs and running faster on the springy floor of pine needles. He dodged around trees, going deeper into the woods. When he final-

ly stopped, he was gasping, his heart was pounding, and he was furious. He turned around and
pushed his brown hair out of his eyes. He couldn't
see the open country anymore. He couldn't see
anybody following him.

He turned back and started walking the way he
figured the bobcat had gone, toward Indian Hill.

Standing on the hummock in the open field,
Willybill looked with glittering jade eyes at the
facade of forest where Bentley had disappeared.

The sun grew stronger: It glowed with extra
power that was not its own. It murdered the low-
hanging vapor, and by noon the day was clear.
Heat shimmered on roads, distorting the images
that lay beyond them. The police station was
suffocating. Flies buzzed on the window glass. The
radio sputtered after McGraw had finished speaking. Dick Amberstam paused a moment before
replying. His face was sweaty and gray. He pressed the microphone button. "You got no choice but
to keep trying," he said.

The static on the radio grew louder. "That's
what we're doing," McGraw's voice answered
through the sputters and crackling. "As long as it
takes. Barney's gone north in the chopper."

Dick replaced the microphone on its hook. Polly
was sitting at the table beside him. Her round face
was flushed and shining in the heat. She put her
head on her folded arms and wept.

Mrs. Tally stood at her living room window,
watching Steve Slattery walk past her house,
down toward the wharf in the breathless noon.

Steve was a nice boy, she thought peevishly. Why couldn't Polly have taken up with a decent young man like him?

Ombra had disembodied himself. He had become earth, air, fire, and water.

With the Dreaded One commingled in its heat, the sun slid off its apex. It blazed and dazzled on the first curve of the afternoon. Steve stood on the wharf watching Ellen and Slally walk toward him. He could see Slally's upper body through her flimsy shirt as the sun burned behind her. Steve looked at her bare legs. The power that supercharged the sun had rendered Steve Slattery's mind, melting away everything he thought, knew, and believed, everything that restrained him; his desire had become flushed and irrational in the heat. He smiled at Ellen because he was grateful to her for producing a child who could never tell. "C'mon, Sally," he said, "today you're going to help me put on the sails."

"Are you sure you don't mind keeping her for the afternoon?" Ellen asked.

Steve picked up a sail bag and slung it over his shoulder. "It's a pleasure, Mrs. Drake. Me 'n' Sally get along fine."

Slally looked up at him.

"Thank you," Ellen said. "I'll pick her up about five."

She watched Slally climbing into the dinghy that was tied to the float. Slally had wanted to stay home. But Ellen had to get her out of the house. The situation with Richard was desperate, and Ellen needed to be alone with him.

She walked back to her car and started the engine. Her anxiety about Bentley, the dread that tightened in her each time the telephone rang during the interminable morning—everything was compounded and intensified by the stifling heat.

Richard, lying alone in their bedroom, had refused to speak to her—aside from his fierce command that she shut up and go—or even acknowledge her since he'd come in early that morning. When she went upstairs to dress, he had been lying with his face turned toward the wall. Ellen had gathered up her clothes and hairbrush quietly so as not to awaken him. As she'd left the bedroom, she'd seen that his eyes were open.

She drove through the village, crossed the highway, and turned into the dirt road that led through the forest on the point. The cicadas were shrilling in the thick foliage. They sounded infuriated.

Ellen understood that she had wounded Richard with her outburst of despair over Slally. Yet, surely, he knew she didn't mean it. After their quarrel during the thunderstorm, he had surmounted his own anger to be forgiving. This time it was different. He had been transformed. Ellen knew, intuitively, that the fury was coming from somewhere outside of him. Richard had become a lens that was focusing an inhuman rage on her. She was terrified by the malevolence that was expressing itself through him.

She parked her car in the driveway, crossed the porch, and went upstairs. Her hand was shaking as she opened the bedroom door.

Richard was tilted back in a wooden chair with his feet propped on a cold radiator. He was holding a cup of tea. A cigarette smoldered in the fingers of his other hand. His eyes, staring through the bedroom window, were inflamed with fatigue.

"Have they called?" Ellen asked.

Richard turned his head and stared at her. Love tried to assert itself from the boiling lava of his mind. But Ellen had assumed, for him, the shape of the abandoner and the personification of his failure. He wanted a flood of abject apology from her, a surrender. "What do you care?" he answered. "You've got your kid back."

"Darling," she said, "please. We *have* to talk about this."

Richard took a long pull on the cigarette. He exhaled and flicked the cigarette against the bedroom wall. It fell to the floor in a shower of sparks and ash. "Wait until your husband gets here," he said in a hoarse voice that was hardly his own. "You can talk your big mouth off to the son of a bitch."

Prince Ombra had become the earth and everything that grows or dwells upon it.

Hot, sweating, and dirty, Bentley climbed up from the shores of a lake. His sneakers were squishing and full of mud. His dungarees were soaked. He winced every time his arm throbbed with the bruise he'd given it the night before when he fell running from the church. He was so hungry that his stomach felt bloated. He stopped at the top of a hill, his whole body throbbing with fatigue.

He sat down in the tall grass and took off his

sneakers. He shook them and then scraped the goo
out of them with his fingers.

He wasn't angry anymore. He hadn't been able
to hold on to the driving force of his outrage at
Ombra as he toiled through the woods and along
the brushy shores of the glacial lake. He was sink-
ing into misery again.

He put down his sneaker and looked at the lake
below him. The afternoon sun glittered on the
water in sharp fragments that hurt his eyes. Going
around the lake, the bushes had been so thick and
strong that Bentley had had to wade out into the
water several times. Alarmed frogs had shot off
the bank. A fearless snapping turtle held its
ground on a log and glared at him. Once a heron
rose from the bushes, clattering its wings in Bentley's face. He had tumbled over into the shallow
water. Everything in the wilderness seemed to
hate him.

He looked up into the vast blue sky. His ospreys
were still with him. But they had flown so high
that they were almost out of sight. Their circle
looped far to the north, and Bentley was no longer
in the center of it. He didn't know what that
meant.

He looked at his wet socks. He thought about
forgetting the stone and just going home to all the
reproaches everybody would have for him. He quit
thinking about that because it made him even
more miserable. Again his memory began to
wander back to Mr. Tally and his mother—and he
forcibly stopped it. Ombra wanted him to be full
of grief.

He sat resting in the hot sun. He made himself

think, instead, about his best things—baseball. The fantasy opened its doors to him and Bentley entered, blotting out the world around him.

The locker room is full of laughing, cheering people, full of the exhilaration of winning the Series. Reporters, TV crews, and security guards crowd the locker room with the players who had poured champagne over each other's heads and then washed it off in the showers. The bright beams of TV lights fill the noisy space beneath a low ceiling.

Bentley finishes combing his hair. A girl sports commentator from a great TV network leans against the wall of the washroom with her arms folded. They've been rehashing the game. She's a terrific girl. She knows all about baseball. Bentley feels great. His muscular body is beginning to unwind from the peak of tension he brought it to during the game. He hit four homers. He can run faster than anybody. By being a good sport he triumphed over his enemy, Cannonball Jones.

The girl tells him to come look at a replay of the television interview she did with him for the evening news. He follows her out into the locker room. A huge cheer bursts from the babble of talk and laughter. Bentley's teammates don't mind him being the star. They like him.

The room goes quiet as the tape recording appears on a monitor. Bentley watches himself. He is tall. His brown hair falls over the right side of his forehead. There is a scar below his right cheekbone where Cannonball Jones once hit him with a pitch. He likes having that scar. It shows he's survived a lot.

On the tape the beautiful girl is calling him the

*hero of the Series. She talks about his four homers
and his speed. This is what he did it all for—driving himself, making himself become the fastest
runner in the majors on his fixed-up leg.*

*He is walking down an airport corridor with the
girl sports commentator. They pass a stack of newspapers whose headlines shriek ELLICOTT'S SERIES!
The girl straightens Bentley's tie at the boarding
gate. She tells him she'll see him at spring training.
She's terrific.*

Lord Ombra had become water as vast as the
seas.

The dinghy rocked gently a half-mile from the
shore. Steve Slattery stretched across Slally's
bare legs. He jiggled the tiller. "Too loose" he said,
looking up at her.

Slally leaned back, trying to get as far away
from him as she could, even though his body was
pressing on her legs. Suddenly she didn't like
Steve anymore. There was a yellow light in the
pupils of his eyes.

"I've got another rudder in the boathouse," he
said, raising himself from her legs. "We'll go in
and get it." He looked up at the sail. It was loose
and motionless against the afternoon sun. "Maybe
I'll have to paddle in," Steve said.

A light breeze riffled the water two hundred
yards from the dinghy. The sail filled and then
bulged as wind followed the breeze. The dinghy
heeled over. Slally brought it about and set its bow
toward the town wharf. Steve sat at the head of
the cockpit, holding the sheet and looking at her.

Ombra knew what Steve was going to do. Ombra, the sea, had become an avenue carrying Slally toward Steve Slattery's desire.

Bentley is walking up Main Street in the deepening dusk. Suddenly it is late autumn. Nobody in Stonehaven has come out to greet the returning hero. The village is empty. There are no lights in the windows.

Bentley is walking up the dirt road on the point. He turns in at the driveway. The house is dark. The windows on its west side reflect the day's last dull light. Bentley wonders where everybody is. He thought they'd have a big party to welcome him home. All he can hear are evening sounds—waves washing on the rocks and the solitary cry of a late-migrating bird.

Bentley raised his head. A small wind from the coast blew across the forest below him—swaying the treetops along its path, leaving the illusion that an invisible being was moving toward the grassy hilltop where Bentley sat. He didn't want to have the daydream anymore. But Ombra was afflicting him with the despair of shattered dreams. The vision compelled Bentley as if it were a prophecy.

Bentley walks across the porch and opens the front door. He smells dust. The closets of the house are bare. Sheets are draped over the furniture. Bentley is bewildered. Where have Slally, his father, and Ellen gone? Why isn't Dr. Kreistein there with grouchy cracks about people who make their living playing games? The television set is gone from the library. They aren't going to sit together and watch the replay of the game or his interview.

Bentley opens the screen door and goes out onto the porch.

His family and Dr. Kreistein are standing in the dusk on the lawn as if they were posing for a photograph, a memento by which he will remember them.

Alarmed, Bentley climbs over the porch railing, jumps to the grass, and walks toward them.

Slally shakes her head.

Bentley stops.

There is sorrow in Slally's eyes. "I waited for you. But you were with that girl."

"I was winning the series!" Bentley retorts. "Weren't you watching on—"

"And how, please, was your leg healed so that you could do this?" Dr. Kreistein asks.

"For Christ's sake, Bentley, where have you been?" his angry father demands.

"Sweetheart—if you loved us you wouldn't have run away," Ellen tells him.

"Listen!" Bentley yells. "Listen to me!"

He hears a voice hissing at him. He turns. His mother is leaning on the porch rail, looking down at him. Her gray eyes are mad, her hair is disheveled, and there are sores on her face. "Michael!" she whispers in the voice of the serpent, "I have sinned!"

"I'm not Michael!" he cries. "It's me! Bentley Ellicott!"

But he has grown up and become somebody else, a stranger to the child he once was and knew.

Bentley heard Ombra, the wind, hissing in the tall grass. Possessed by his desperation in the fantasy, he yanked his mind back to the sun-cooked afternoon, the empty landscape, and the sibilating sound of his invisible enemy surrounding him.

His heart was thumping in his chest once more as he put on his muddy sneakers and tried to tie the laces with his trembling fingers. He knew that Ombra was right beside him. He knew now that Ombra had blocked off any escape back into Bentley's ordinary life—the people he loved were being destroyed, like Helga, or transformed like his father and Ellen on the night of the thunderstorm when they had their terrible fight. Everything that Bentley had believed was eroding before the truth —his mother hadn't been gentle and good, Mr. Tally hadn't loved him.

He got to his feet. Bentley knew there was only one way for him to go—forward. He had to find the stone, feel himself full of power and confidence again, and then do what he was born to do before Ombra destroyed everything.

He saw his hawks flying over him. They turned against the blue sky and flapped toward the north. Bentley was right on the edge of their circle. "Wait up!" he screamed at them. He began to run down the side of the hill. "Wait!" he cried again.

Prince Ombra sang a victory song in the voice of the wind as he watched Bentley running through the tall grass toward the bait that would lure him to his death in the waning of the day. Lord Ombra turned away and aimed all the power of his sorcery against Slally, the rememberer. *Now!* whispered the wind. *Now!* Lord Ombra commanded—and Steve Slattery's flaming senses obeyed.

McGraw ran his big hand over his face. He

watched the sun burning on the uplands, the coast, the flat sea. Exhaustion was diminishing him. His brain wasn't working right anymore. He had conceived the idea that nobody else but him felt the strangeness that had grown and metastasized through the day, turning everything—the earth, the air, the sun's fire, and the sea—into menace.

He opened the door of his cruiser and sat on the front sea with his feet on the ground. McGraw knew that there had been some sort of change in him, but he was too tired to figure out what it was —or who had brought it about.

The engines of cars and pickup trucks were revving on the hot curve of the highway below Pensionville. McGraw looked at his watch. The day-shift men had searched the country longer after they were supposed to go home. The night-shift men were out there, still looking.

McGraw hadn't said a prayer since he was a boy. He couldn't decide whether to pray now or get somebody to kick him in the head and bring him back to his senses.

The helicopter sat on the field, its blades slowly rotating after the engine cutoff. Barney, the state police lieutenant, walked over to McGraw's cruiser, stuffing a pair of leather gloves into his hip pocket. "I figure we got maybe two, three hours before it's too dark," he said. "Where d'you want us to look now, McGraw?"

"Ask Mike," McGraw said, swinging his legs into the cruiser and slamming the front door. "He's had some sleep."

Cars and trucks were taking the day-shift searchers down the highway toward Stonehaven. A few men of the night shift were looking at maps and listening to Mike's instructions on the other side of the road.

Barney put his hands on the door of McGraw's cruiser. "I think he's dead," he said. "We sure as hell would have seen *some* trace of him by now if he was alive. Maybe he went south. Hell, maybe he drowned."

McGraw looked up at him through the car window. "The Coast Guard's been on the lookout since three hours after both kids disappeared. We found the girl."

"That doesn't mean the Ellicott kid didn't double back sometime during the night and fall in the water," Barney said. "Coast Guard can't see if he's thirty feet down." He spat in the dust. "You better call it off by morning, McGraw. You're beginning to waste a lot of people's time."

The state police lieutenant was giving substance to an anger that had been growing in McGraw all afternoon. Since the thing he was angry at was the same thing he sensed but couldn't define in the northern lights and the burning day, it was almost a relief to focus his rage on Barney.

"Take your goddamn flying machine and go where Mike tells you," McGraw snapped. "The Ellicott kid isn't dead. I'll be back before dark." He started the engine, swung the cruiser out onto the highway, and drove the winding way down to Stonehaven with the anger almost choking him.

The late afternoon breeze flapped the pennants of sailboats moored against the town wharf. It

blew in Slally's hair as she followed Steve toward
the boathouse. He looked at her once and smiled.
Slally didn't smile back.

Steve unlocked the boathouse door.

Now you can do it! whispered the wind and the
heat.

"C'mere," Steve said.

Slally walked over to the boathouse door. She
peered into a low-ceilinged room cluttered with
tackle and a rack of masts in the middle of the
floor. She smelled rope.

"Over there," said Steve's voice behind her.
"Against the wall."

Slally saw a green sailboat rudder leaning
against the wall on the far side of the room.

"Go get it," Steve said.

Slally hesitated. She didn't look at him. She
didn't know why she was frightened. She couldn't
think of any reason for not obeying.

She stepped down into the room and climbed
over the rack of masts. She lost her balance and
fell onto the floor.

She heard the door slam shut. She raised her
head up over the masts. Steve was locking the
door. Then he turned. He wasn't smiling anymore.

Charlie Feavey hunkered in the brush beside a
road, his arms propped across his bent knees. The
road led past Emson's stone-crushing works to Tysonville. In his left hand Charlie clutched a pint
bottle wrapped in a brown paper bag. He looked
up at the hill. The confidence that the whiskey had
brought to him was giving way to stupor. Charlie
looked at the stunted trees on top of the hill; he

saw a party of blueberry pickers on the lower
slope. They had waved as a state police helicopter
flew over fifteen minutes earlier.

Charlie had driven through the night and the
long day with the same desperation that had im-
pelled him through the striving, hoping, disap-
pointing years of his life—and he had found
nothing. He had searched every back road, lake,
and ruined farmhouse he knew of in the directions
the boy had gone. But there were no signs of the
damn Ellicott kid.

He raised his free hand and swatted at a swarm
of gnats that danced in the heavy air before his
face. His brain was getting numb. His vision wobbled like the jigging insects a few inches from his
eyes. The late afternoon sunlight burned through
the leaves and shone in a green halo around the
place where Charlie squatted. Willybill's pickup
truck was parked behind him, its front end pointing down into the brush.

He lifted the bottle and tried to shake a few last
drops into his mouth. He wanted to feel the singing of the whiskey because it kept his brain clear.
The bottle was empty. He threw it across the road,
trying to smash it against a stone wall. The bottle
sailed over the stones and whished into the woods.

Charlie put his head in his arms. The bed of glittering jewels dimmed in his mind with the fading
of his drunken senses. All he needed to do to get
the jewels was to kill the Ellicott kid. But he
couldn't find the little bastard. He fought off sleep.

He lifted his head and tried to focus his swirling
eyes on the jumbled stones of the collapsed wall.
Charlie Feavey worshipped a god of desperations,

and the god heard his silent lament.

He sensed a movement to his right. He swayed forward and looked down the road.

He saw Bentley Ellicott crawling out of the bushes. The kid stood up slowly on the road. His clothes were torn and he was dirty. He looked scared. Bits of twig and grass were matted in his hair.

Charlie rolled backward and scrambled down the embankment behind him. He grabbed for the pickup truck's door handle. The shotgun was right inside, leaning on the seat.

Then he remembered the blueberry pickers on Indian Hill. They'd sure as hell see him if he blasted the little son of a bitch away in broad daylight. Charlie wriggled up through heavy covering brush. He peered through the leaves.

Bentley was limping toward him. The kid's mouth was half open and his dark eyes were fixed on the brushy rise of Indian Hill.

Charlie drew back in among the branches and roots. He covered his head with his arms as Bentley walked past above him. A car came down the Tysonville road, going the other way. It left a swirl of dust that drifted down through the green light surrounding Charlie Feavey.

Charlie lay still. His reawakened mind cast up what it would be like when he had the little bastard between the barrel ends of the shotgun. Charlie would splatter the kid's brains all over the landscape. Thinking about it was almost as pleasurable as thinking about the sapphires, rubies and mountains of diamonds that Charlie's god would give him when Bentley Ellicott was dead.

People running. People poised just before running. The whole of Main Street had been shattered by the screaming. As McGraw drove past the hardware store, his weary brain took in everything as if he were watching a slow-motion movie.

Polly in her drugstore apron, her blond hair flying behind her, as she leaped across a pothole; Elias Cutter standing beside his car, staring at the boathouse where the screams had come from; Nick Matos running down the wharf from the freezing plant; Dick Amberstam sprinting from the police station, the screen door banging wide and Dick's elbow jutting out behind him as he reached for his .38 in its leather holster.

In the same bloat of time and vision, McGraw accelerating his cruiser, nearly hitting Polly, passing Elias Cutter, McGraw twisting the steering wheel hard to the right, his weight slamming into the door as the tires spit gravel, the police car skidding onto the stone approach of the wharf, heading directly toward the boathouse door; Dick Amberstam floating into his field of vision as McGraw hit the parking brakes and simultaneously threw open the cruiser door and swung himself out, thinking it was funny that a young fellow like Dick should be going bald; McGraw turning his body so that the back of his shoulder would take the impact of his body on the boathouse door.

The door split apart under the force of McGraw's two hundred and forty pounds, and McGraw went with the broken pieces into the gloom, seeing the yellow eyes of the beast, smelling rope as he hurtled across the rack of masts, grabbing Steve Slattery by the hair, taking the trouserless adolescent with him over the masts and hard against the wall, with tackle and ironware showering down around them.

Steve tried to bellow as McGraw lifted him, but one big hand choked off his windpipe and the other was gripped around his leg. He was rising against the ceiling and was about to be flung across the room so that his back would be broken and the devil in him murdered when Dick Amberstam's revolver barrel smashed across McGraw's forehead.

The boathouse exploded with the dead light of the northern sky and the yowls of the teenager as McGraw took Steve, stinking of evil, into the red pain where the rage and the weariness stopped.

Someone weeping. Someone trying to weep and a terrible, dry choking noise taking the place of sobs.

McGraw leaned the back of his head against the stone wall of the boathouse. His eyes were open and he saw solicitous figures hovering over him with the oblong light of the door behind them. He knew that one of the figures was Dick, and McGraw said it before Dick said it. "You had to, hell, you had to do it, don't worry about it, you had to do it because I must have gone off my head for a minute there. It's not having any sleep did it."

"Could've happened to anybody," Dick said in front of him. "I'm sorry, McGraw."

"You had to do it," McGraw said again. He wanted to cry.

The dead light receded and McGraw began to see. Dick, Nick Matos, and Elias Cutter crouched before him. To one side of him he heard the weeping and the strangling noise.

McGraw moved his eyes and looked at his deputy. "What was it?"

"He tried to rape her," Dick answered quietly.

"Sit still, Mr. McGraw," Elias Cutter said. "Doctor Leon's on the way."

"Who?" McGraw asked.

"The Drake girl," Dick said.

McGraw closed his eyes because the fearfulness of it blinded him anyway. *And I looked and, behold, a pale horse, and his name that sat upon him was Death, and Hades followed with him. And power was given them over the fourth part of the earth . . .*

The dead light had dimmed, but it wasn't gone. It hovered over the world, sickening it with the revelation of the archdemon that was nourished by the light. McGraw knew that he had to see it all. He opened his eyes and looked to his left. He saw Polly holding Slally against her breast, rocking and crying. The little girl's eyes were wide; her mouth was open as if she were making a scream that McGraw couldn't hear.

Polly looked back at him. Her grief was his own, but he didn't know yet what they grieved for. "She can't make a sound!" Polly wailed. "Oh, God, McGraw, she's been struck dumb!"

And, having done this, Prince Ombra rose from the shadows as McGraw's heart wept. The Lord of Nightmares turned toward the uplands where his enemy had stopped. The pale light became the shape of a horse, and Prince Ombra mounted it and rode to the place where the day was dying and gunfire would herald death in the night.

Bentley opened his eyes. The western sky looked as if a bloody hand had been smeared across it. He was sitting at the end of a grassy track that led off the road, down to a picnic table and benches at the foot of Indian Hill.

Bentley had sat down to rest with his back against a tree. He realized that he must have fallen asleep.

He got to his feet, yawned, and shut his mouth. His bruised arm ached. He didn't feel hungry anymore—just scared. The afternoon sunshine was gone. He looked at Indian Hill above him. A towering rock was on his left. The people picking blueberries he'd seen when he got there were gone. The red streaks of sunset disappeared into the top of the hill, where he could see low trees growing. *He commanded me to put the stone there,* the dying bobcat had whispered, *among the roots of the oldest flowering tree.*

Bentley listened. He heard, in the distance, the roaring sound of earth-moving machinery. He heard three sharp whistles. He looked up into the sky.

He had been following his hawks all through the afternoon, trying to catch up with them. As he stood at the foot of the hill they were circling directly above him, high in the waning fire of the sun. Suddenly the ospreys tilted their wings and swooped toward the earth. Bentley raised his arms to them. The birds cruised in a wide sweep around him, forty feet from the ground.

Then, with a whistle, the fish hawks rose again

into the red flare of the sun. They beat their wings and were gone toward the east where a new night was gathering.

Bentley Ellicott had lost his magic. Heaven's light was dimming before the power of Lord Ombra.

Chapter Fifteen

McGraw and Dick Amberstam saw the empty husks of Pensionville against the sunset. McGraw was driving at seventy miles an hour up the highway from the coast. Dick clamped together the ends of his seat belt. "If I were a praying man—"

"Pray anyway," McGraw said. His head was throbbing. He had told Dr. Leon there wasn't time to get the gash in his forehead stitched up.

The cruiser bounced over the top of the hill and tore past the deserted church and store, its speedometer needle rising. McGraw switched on the headlights as he hit the straight stretch going west.

The Ellicott house had been a graveyard of the happiness McGraw had seen in it on the day of Slally's party. Ellen Drake was beyond outcry or tears when the two policemen brought the little

girl home. As Dick carried Slally upstairs with
Ellen and Dr. Leon following him, Richard Ellicott
had come downstairs, passing them without a
word. He crossed the living room, slammed the
screen door behind him, and walked out to the end
of the lawn.

McGraw had been standing at the screen door,
watching Richard, when the telephone rang. It
was Mike at the police station. A woman had just
come in and said she saw a boy answering to Bentley's description walking along the Tysonville
road about a half hour before.

McGraw steadied the cruiser at eighty-five miles
an hour and turned on the red flasher. The police
car hurtled through the dusk, its revolving glass
dome crying havoc.

Charlie Feavey parked Willybill's pickup truck
on the road leading down to the stone-crushing
works. He took the shotgun, got out, and closed
the door quietly. He was cold sober and insane
with fantasy. He had watched the sun burning out
in the west. The voice of his god told him to find
the mountains of uncut, unpolished stones.
Charlie knew where those heaps of jewels were.
He walked down the road to Lewis Emson and
Sons, Graded Rock and Gravel.

The stone yard was a miniature universe of
lights. Large beacons shone from stark framework
towers; smaller lights sparkled as moving belts
carried rock to the tops of the towers where it
was dumped into crushers forty feet below. There
were street lamps standing among the piles of
size-graded gravel and stone.

Charlie stooped and ran across the parking lot. He slipped into shadow behind a one-story office building. He sat with his back against the wooden wall, holding the shotgun between his legs. The noise of the grinders and crushers nearly deafened him. But to Charlie Feavey that din was the croon of a supernatural being that loved him.

Slally saw yellow eyes staring at her in a dream. She tried to scream as she came awake. But she was mute.

Ellen laid a folded skirt in one of her suitcases on Richard's bed. Her emotions were suffocated beneath a pall of despair. She crossed the hall and opened the door to Slally's room. "Try to sleep, darling," she said to the wide-eyed girl. "Daddy's coming to take us home tomorrow."

Dietrich Kreistein sat in the messy library of his house with the lights off. He looked through the windows at Richard standing on the end of his lawn in the moonlight. "So heavy is the world with you tonight, Prinz Ombra," the old man muttered. "What you have done to this little girl shows, I think, how frightened you are to fight the boy. I now know what the girl is. If she cannot tell the story when this is over, I will do it. I think you are afraid that soon the boy will find the stone. Then you will have to confront him as you confronted the greatest of his brothers in all the ages of the world." He took a handkerchief from his pocket, checked to make sure it was the right one, and blew his nose.

Prince Ombra's essence hovered on the uplands where his enemy stood, frightened and alone.

I hear you, Magician, Ombra whispered, *but you are old and do not understand. There are no mortals remaining worthy of calling themselves brother to David, Arthur the King, and Susano. I fear nothing. I will never meet this crippled whelp in combat. Tonight he will go obediently to his death.*

Sorcerer, sorcerer, you do not even know the name of the last chosen warrior who perished at my hand. You only remember the calamities that came after he and his rememberer died. When this night is done, old magician, you will see such a burning of the world that you will yearn for the sorrows of your youth!

Dietrich Kreistein could not hear him. Through the library windows he could see the aurora borealis wreathing again like smoke in the northern sky, its tendrils the pastel colors of glacier ice.

Dr. Kreistein turned his head and looked at the television set in a corner. He liked the symphony orchestra program. But announcers kept interrupting with news bulletins about the distant war, the hotlines chattering across the world's darkness, and all the other symptoms of a crisis the old man could have foretold. He had finally switched off the set in disgust when a voice broke into a Brahms concern with the news that the President would address the nation within twenty-four hours.

"So," he said softly, settling himself more comfortably in his chair, "now we will see what we will see."

Bentley watched until he couldn't see the ospreys any longer, until their bodies blurred into the evening and the rising of the moon. His hawks were gone. He turned and looked up at Indian Hill. Suddenly the slope seemed too steep for his tired legs to climb. His chances of following the bobcat's instructions and finding the stone seemed suddenly remote. Suddenly he knew he couldn't win even if he did find it. His will was gone, too.

He went over to a picnic table standing on the grass. He sat down on a bench. He looked north and saw the aurora borealis. Somewhere in the distance Bentley could still hear the sounds of the earth-moving machinery. He was scared.

Now that he'd lost his magic, all that remained of his divine mission was the memory of where he had lived before he was born. The memory reproached him. He didn't deserve it because he'd let Ombra steal the stone of Ra that a thousand heroes had carried in the world. Now Bentley was ordinary, just like everybody else.

He itched in his dirtiness. He ached all over. He was ashamed of being frightened.

The moon rode above the hills and forests. Its silver shivered on the surface of the lake. Bentley thought he could see the lights of Stonehaven beyond the last rows of hills. But he wasn't sure. He wished he was home.

The only difference between him and everybody else was that he had his memories—and he knew what made all the bad things happen in the world. Other people didn't.

Giving up when you knew something important that hardly anybody else knew was, he suddenly realized, letting down the whole world.

He got off the bench. Memory of the perfect place he'd been before he was born brightened in him.

He raised his head in the moonlight. They *wanted* him to remember. He felt what every mortal can feel if he chooses to acknowledge it—the eternal warmth of hope.

Bentley put his right foot on the bench and retied the sneaker's lace tightly. He crossed the grassy place and began to climb Indian Hill. His heart was lighter. Maybe, he thought, he still could win.

Elias Cutter finished writing. He picked up two sheets of paper and read them in the lamplight. "I'm not a lawyer, of course," he said, "but I believe this is the proper form."

Mrs. Tally got up from her chair and crossed Mr. Cutter's library. She took the papers from him. She stood in front of his desk, reading the citizen's complaint against Polly Woodhouse he had composed.

As she read, Mrs. Tally suppressed the knowledge that she had thought Steve Slattery was a nice, decent young man.

"I'd say that will do the job very nicely," she said, handing the sheets back across the desk. For a moment she saw the loneliness in Elias Cutter's eyes and had to resist the impulse to take him home and give him supper. She repeated to herself the old saw about people who've made their own beds and have to lie in them.

"I expect they'll call off the search for the Ellicott boy by morning," Mr. Cutter said. "I'll go along at lunch time and give this to Mr. McGraw."

"How is he?" Mrs. Tally asked.

"He took a nasty crack in the head," Mr. Cutter said. "It didn't seem to slow him down much. The man's a plowhorse."

Mrs. Tally stood in Elias Cutter's driveway for a moment after he'd closed the door behind her. The undeniable truth that she'd thought Steve Slattery, a rapist, was suitable for Polly wouldn't go away. But it didn't persuade Mrs. Tally to relent. She just got angrier at the slut who'd made her so unhappy. She dismissed the notion that if she'd been mistaken about Steve, she might also be mistaken about Polly. She got into her car. Resisting self-doubt was her only comfort. She worked hard at getting angrier as she drove home. The anger gave her a savage pleasure. She could hardly keep from bursting into tears.

Bentley trudged up the slope in darkness. The sound of machinery was getting louder. A diesel shovel was roaring and clanking on the other side of the hill. The lights of the digging crew made silhouettes of old trees standing twenty yards above Bentley.

He stopped beside a big boulder to catch his breath. The trees on the ridge looked as if they'd once been an orchard. He tried to figure out which was the oldest one.

Then he saw it. Its trunk was the thickest of all the trees. Its lower branches were twisted like unnatural elbows. Small apples dangled in leaf clusters; he could see them clearly against the lights of the earth-digging crew on the far side of the hill.

He saw a tiny glint in the grass around the roots.
He saw another, momentary sparkle as the tree
began to tremble with the vibrations of the diesel
shovel that was gouging out the earth below the
orchard. The stone of Ra flashed its specks of
quartz and silver as if to beckon Bentley.

The shovel's arm slammed hard into the bank.
At the crest of the hill the earth suddenly split into
a long crack. A wall of dirt and rock showered
down into the excavation.

Bentley yelled as the old tree began to sway and
shake. Apples dropped from its branches. They
bounced down the dark slope, hitting trees and
caroming off rocks and hummocks. Bentley flung
himself away from the boulder. He started running up the hill. He stepped on two rolling apples
and fell on his stomach with a thump. As he scrambled to his feet, he saw the tree's roots ripping out
of the ground; it fell away from him as another
slice of the cliff caved in.

Breathless again, Bentley dashed up the last ten
yards and dropped on his hands and knees. Below
him there was a wide, semicircular pit where the
other half of the hill had been. He looked down into the lights. Two trucks were parked in the middle
of the pit. The yellow-bodied diesel shovel was
directly below him. Its steel arm and bucket
thrust and gouged into the loose earth. Bentley
saw the old apple tree flung aside. The shovel's
bucket came up, showering dirt and pebbles. As
the arm swung through the trucks' headlights,
Bentley saw a speck of black on the top of the load.

He saw a brief sparkle. The bucket's jaw swung open and the load roared down into a truck bed, filling it.

Bentley leaped to his feet as the driver got into the truck and closed the door. The big six-wheeler jerked and began to back up.

The road out of the pit had been carved through the remaining wall of the excavated hill. Bentley dashed across the old orchard at the top. He jumped over fallen logs and bushes. The truck was driving slowly toward the exit road. Bentley ran, limping, down the slanting rim. He got to the opening just as the truck was lurching through, its headlights swinging across the thickets.

Bentley's body trembled as he waited for the precise moment. He looked down at the roof passing below him. He counted to three as the load of dirt rolled through the split in the hill.

He jumped.

Charlie Feavey crouched in the shadows, holding the shotgun. Twenty feet across the stone yard a mound of earth rose against the stars. A huge metal crusher at its foot was roaring and banging as it digested a load of boulders and earth that a truck had just dumped down the bank. Charlie had been watching the unloading platform at the top of the mound for a half hour. Three trucks had backed up and poured their contents down into the hopper of the machine.

All around him, Charlie heard the rattle and grinding of secondary stone crushers that chopped gravel into uniform sizes. Rock was carried on moving belts up to framework towers and tipped

into the crushers below. The bright searchlight on
the top of one tower had become Prince Ombra's
eye. The eye cast its overlord's beam across the
evening, and the fifth brain, the sorcerer, spun enchantments for Charlie Feavey.

Charlie saw the high mound of earth and the
first crusher bellowing and shaking below it. His
mind saw a bed of diamonds, gold, and rubies that
sparkled like the splattered blood of a murdered
boy.

Prince Ombra whispered to him in a voice more
powerful than the din of the stone yard's machinery all around him. Charlie turned his head and
gazed into Prince Ombra's glittering eye. He heard
the Dreaded One's promise—Charlie would be
rich beyond his own capacities to dream, once
Bentley Ellicott was dead.

Charlie nodded and turned his gaze back to the
top of the mound, where another truck was due.

McGraw cursed.

He pumped the brakes. The cruiser spun as its
speedometer needle dropped from seventy to fifty-
five. In the headlights' beam the Tysonville road
disappeared into a swirl of dust.

McGraw twisted the steering wheel. "Emson's
stone works," he grunted. "He might have gone in
there." The dust drifted off. McGraw bore down
on the accelerator, and the cruiser headed back
through the darkness from which it had come.

"There's two entrances," Dick said. "The main
one and one where the trucks go up—"

The rest of his sentence was drowned out as a
dump truck came around the bend, its headlights

breaking into McGraw's eyes. The truck thundered past them.

Dick looked back after it. "Dumb bastard's going too fa—*McGraw! Hold it!*" He wrenched his
body around. "*I saw him!*" Dick shouted. "*I saw
the Ellicott kid on the top of that load!*"

McGraw cursed again and hit the brakes again.
The cruiser turned completely around twice in a
plume of dust. Tree trunks appeared directly in
front of McGraw, and some colossal miscalcula-
tion made him stamp on the accelerator instead of
the brakes. The police car jounced hard as it shot
across a ditch. McGraw felt the violent impact and
saw cracks flashing in a dense spider-web pattern
on the windshield as his belly and chest slammed
into the steering wheel—and from the corner of
his eye he saw Dick hurtle as far forward as his
seat belt would let him go.

McGraw pushed himself back against the seat.
Dick was unbuckling his belt. "If one more thing
happens to you tonight, you're gonna be dead,
McGraw."

"Shouldn't wonder," McGraw muttered. He
leaned on the door handle. The door groaned as he
pushed his weight against it. It gave with a screech
of twisted metal.

He got out of the tilting cruiser. Its grill was
folded around a tree trunk. The hood was sprung,
gaping like the mouth of a creature whose heart
had stopped in the middle of a death cry. Steam
drifted across the one headlight still shining.

McGraw pushed through the brush, jumped
over the ditch, and lumbered down the road with
Dick following him.

*   *   *

Bentley was still pawing frantically through the dirt when he felt the truck bump up an incline, swing in a wide circle, and stop. Bentley paused in his dog-digging as the lights of the stone yard brightened around him and the roar of its machinery broke through his frenzy. The truck was backing up. Bentley began to dig again, dirt flying from his hands and out between his legs. He saw stones rolling into the hole he was making, but none of them was black.

He was breathing so hard, pleading so hard for his stone to turn up beneath his fingers, that he didn't feel the truck bed begin to tilt until it was too late.

The load beneath him slid toward the rear of the truck, carrying him with it. Bentley yelled as he tumbled over, his arms flailing for something to hold on to.

He hit an iron bar at the back of the truck. He grabbed it and looked behind him. The truck bed was raising high against the stars. Bentley looked down. A metal trap on the back of the truck was swinging wide. Beneath it there was a drop of twenty-five feet ending at a huge, rattling machine with its mouth opened for the cascading rock and earth. The noise roared up at Bentley. The load poured out around him. Stones hit him in the back and boulders bounded past him. His legs were dangling in empty space, his hands were being torn away from the crossbar as the torrent spilled from the back of the truck, taking him out into the

air that was sparkling with light, down into the
hopper's grinding mouth.

He let go.

Charlie Feavey saw the rear trap of the truck
swing open. In the flow of yellow earth and gray
rock he saw the blue of Bentley's jeans. In the
lights of the stone yard he saw Bentley grab the
hinge bar on the back of the truck, saw the boy
dangle for a moment.

Now! roared a voice of metal and stone. *Now!
And the servant of Ombra shall have the riches
once granted to ass-eared Midas, king of Phrygia!*

Charlie gibbered like an ape as he darted back
and forth in the shadows. He saw Bentley's sneakers flailing in empty space. He saw the little bastard fall. Charlie saw the fall arrested. The boy
had grabbed something sticking out of the bank
above the crusher. Rocks and dirt showered down
in front of him. Charlie leaped into the light that
shone like diamonds. He raised the shotgun to his
shoulders, flipped off the safety catch, and
squinted down the barrels, trying to aim at the
kid's head, not his kicking legs or body.

Charlie saw McGraw climbing down the bank as
the last of the load poured into the crusher. He
saw McGraw lose his footing as he reached for
Bentley, who was dangling from a root. Charlie
saw McGraw's big body bounce off the side of the
crusher, hit a metal ladder, and land hard on the
ground.

Charlie heard Dick Amberstam's .38 go off—a
sharp crack in the din of machinery. Charlie heard
a window shatter behind him. He saw Dick standing at the top of the mound beside the dump truck,

legs spread, one hand holding the wrist of the hand that pointed the revolver straight at Charlie's head.

Charlie ran. He ran back into the shadow and around the corner of the wooden building.

Lord Ombra's seven brains signaled alarm to each other. The fantasist of dreams repugnant to gods and men smelled the reek of belief in the evening. It was heavier than the stench of Bentley's reviving will. Somebody else in the stone yard knew that Ombra was there.

The Dreaded One tasted the syrup of faith in his rock-swallowing mouths. His armor-plated shoulders of stone tightened to strike. His eye on the top of the tower searched the ground, trying to see the new believer; Ombra surveyed the chaos, pain, and madness he had created. He saw Bentley perched on the shuddering lip of the crusher, hanging on with both hands. Prince Ombra saw McGraw clawing at the bank as he tried to stand up; he saw the door of the wooden building fly open and the night manager of the stone yard run into the parking lot, heading for the switch box that would cut off the machinery. The Lord of Nightmares bellowed a command at his servant.

Charlie Feavey's brain sparkled with dreams of riches and death. In another dimension he saw the manager looking at him with astonishment as Charlie ran across the parking lot. Charlie didn't break stride; he pulled one trigger of the shotgun, felt the kick, and heard the explosion. He ran through a spatter of wet rubies. He ran toward the biggest diamond in the world. It was beaming at him from the top of a tower.

Bentley was holding onto the top of the stone crusher with all of his might. He had climbed down onto the machine after McGraw fell past him. The crusher was shaking Bentley so hard that he thought he was going to come apart. His hair flew as his head was jerked back and forth. His eyes were wobbling in their sockets, and he could barely focus on the belt rolling up from under the crusher. Bentley knew that Ombra's mouth was opening and crashing shut just below him. He knew that his enemy might eat him alive. But the stone's magic was flaring in the beam of the spotlight that glared down at Bentley. The stone of Ra was whispering its immortal summons to valor from inside the bucking, shaking machine.

That part of Bentley which was an eight-year-old boy was terrified that he might let go in a moment of panic and fall into the mangling throat of the hopper. That part of him which was being resurrected as a warrior of the borrowed heart commanded him to hold on until he saw the heroes' stone spat from the crusher onto the belt—and then risk everything to seize it so that his life would be restored to the purpose of god.

His head bobbing on his shoulders, his sneakers wedged into the steel ribbing of the crusher's body, and his aching hands gripping the top, Bentley held on.

He saw a disgorge of gravel spraying onto the moving belt. In it, he saw a momentary flash of light. As the load of gravel shivered apart, he saw the stone of Ra. Bentley crouched for one moment longer, trying not to see the snapping steel mouth beneath him. Then he threw himself with all his might across the hopper's opening, dropped onto the belt, bounced, hurt his knee, and started grabbing at his stone as he was carried up toward Ombra's angry eye.

For McGraw, time was splintering into micromoments, and the last ones were going too fast. He'd seen Bentley fling himself over the top of the giant crusher and land on the belt. So McGraw, who was still half stunned from hitting the ladder as he fell, had had to find it in himself to run, even though every bone in his body ached and his brain was numb. He ran parallel with the moving belt that was now high above him, remembering that he once thought that Bentley Ellicott was an eight-year-old lunatic who risked his life for nothing, and thinking it again for a tenth of a second as he yelled, *Jump, jump, in the name of God, Bentley, jump before you get carried to the top and dumped down into the next goddamn crusher.* McGraw was running toward the tower with the spotlight on top of it, trying to see the kid on the belt above him.

Charlie Feavey stepped into the center of the stone yard. His face and shirt were splattered with blood. He, too, had seen Bentley fling himself onto the belt. Enough connective reasoning remained in Charlie to know where everything on that conveyor belt was going. He was sane enough to know that the boy would appear for a moment at the top of the tower before he was dropped into the crusher.

Ombra saw with his searchlight eye. He roared a command with his voices in the machinery. Charlie raised the shotgun and pointed it at the

top of the framework tower. He steadied its aim
on a space between two slender uprights where
Bentley would have to appear at the last second.
Charlie's brain was filled with rapture.

He was standing thus in the middle of the stone
yard, a killer thrilled with what he had contracted
to do, when Dick Amberstam shot him from sixty
feet away.

McGraw couldn't look at the top of the tower
anymore because the eye of the demon that
bestrode the world was burning into his pupils,
trying to blind him. And so he looked up at the side
of the moving belt as he ran, pushing his heavy
body to its ultimate exertion as the demon beside
him thundered and devoured stone. Suddenly he
saw Bentley's face appear over the side of the belt
high above him, and McGraw thought he was a
funny-looking little kid, peering over the edge like
that, high and going higher, with an expression of
triumph on his round, dirty face as McGraw
shouted, *Jump! Jump! I'll catch you, kid! Its eye is
right ahead of you! In the name of our Lord Jesus
Christ, jump!*

Bentley's arms and legs appeared over the side
of the belt. He pushed himself off, kicking in the
air, falling thirty feet. The heart of McGraw, the
believer, nearly burst as he threw himself forward
and grabbed Bentley. His hurtling momentum carried them both into a pile of soft sand.

Dick's third shot, meant to stop Charlie for sure,
went wild. It hit the spotlight at the top of the
tower.

Ombra's eye went out.

He is the lord of all infamous burnings.

The hero Gilgamesh first sensed him in the heat of the day as he came up from the valley of the Euphrates. Ombra proclaimed his corrupt victory in the flames of Rome. His fiery hand caressed the martyred flesh of Saint Joan, the human torch of Rouen, and his breath was the atomic wind of Nagasaki.

Main Street lay like a deserted stage set. Spaced pools of lamplight shone on the low buildings that Charlie Feavey had known all of his life—the hardware store, the police station, the drugstore. Beneath the lights along the town wharf, Charlie's dying eye saw the freezing plant and the boathouse, pennants hanging on sailboat masts. The night wind no longer ruffled the water.

Charlie Feavey had slipped away, dying, from the stone yard. As the pain returned for the hundredth time, journeying down his body to his legs, radiating from the hole in his chest, Charlie wondered where the wind had gone. He gripped the side of Willybill's pickup truck in case he fainted with the pain. He didn't have time for that. There was one more task left to do.

Partly mad, partly a cogitator of last things, Charlie stumbled through the tall grass that grew in front of his hotel. He made it up the front steps and got across the porch.

Faithful, he did the bidding of the voice that murmured in the aura of pain around him. He leaned against the front door until it opened and made his way down the dark, rubble-strewn hallway, leaving his spoor as blood in the dust. He somehow managed to open the door of his room.

He didn't need to hold on to anything as he crawled up the stairs, dragging a five-gallon can of gasoline with him. Charlie's mind was living in the time before the burning. He knew that his dreams of wealth had their birth in fire.

If he burned down the hotel, he would find Mrs. John Rutherford Hackett's diamonds, emeralds, rubies, and gold and silver ornaments in the ash, among the charred timbers. He didn't know why he'd never thought of it before.

Moonlight filled the entire fourth floor because he had torn apart all the walls up there. Charlie crawled over the heaps of the two-by-fours and broken plaster on his hands and knees, dragging the red can. His body dripped blood, and the can slopped gasoline.

When he got to the end of the room, the dream was waning. But the being that possessed Charlie gave him one final chance. Charlie propped himself against the studs of a ripped-apart wall. He lit a match with his bloody fingers so that he could see his dreams. But they weren't there anymore. He threw the match into the middle of the room and died.

The Stonehaven House Hotel became a torch of proclamation for Prince Ombra. It was a pyre for Charlie Feavey's useless life. It was a conflagration for the furies to dance by.

Up and down the coast for miles and miles, people saw the fiery glow in the sky. The hotel's ghosts laughed and clapped as orange flame and black smoke soared through them toward the stars and the burning floors gave way beneath them. The spirits of mad Mrs. Hackett and all the thousands who had visited and loved there had returned in their dying shapes to sing songs of immortality behind the smoldering, shattering windows.

Ombra became heat and darkness. He listened to the legends of the world and knew that men had not forgotten him. He was weaker than he had been in all of his lives. He had failed to destroy the child hero without a battle. Now it was imperative to him to get the battle over and done with before the damnable memory of mankind further enfeebled him.

First the fire.

Ombra, lord of all infamous burnings, made his sign in the night so that the warrior who awaited him and the virtuous who despised him would know that he was still there.

Then the sword.

In the blazing radiance of the Stonehaven inferno, Prince Ombra proclaimed that when the sun came again, he would armor himself in the shape of his enemy's profoundest dread. Then he would go forth to combat with the thousand and first hero of the borrowed heart.

Chapter Sixteen

Late summer comes to this coast with stately swarms of sailboats on the bay and the buzzing of cicadas in the green domes of trees. Little children and old women dare the water's startling cold to swim. People lie sunbathing on towels spread across the rocks. Larks sing in the upland meadows.

Bentley woke up when a hand brushed the hair out of his eyes. He was lying on his stomach with his pajama top wadded beneath his chest. At the moment the hand touched him, he was dreaming about making a catapult with Joe Persis. They threw stuff into the sunshine and laughed.

He rolled over and opened his eyes.

Ellen was sitting on the side of his bed. She was wearing a white shirt. Summer had turned her hair light gold. Bentley saw the pain in her eyes.

"Hello," she said softly.

Bentley stared at her. "Hi," he said.

"Know what time it is?"

He shook his head.

"Half past eleven. Feel like getting up, darling?"

Bentley's arm and chest hurt. His legs were sore from having walked so far. But, the night befor, Dr. Kreistein had examined him and said he wasn't sprained or anything.

He yawned, stretching. Ellen put her arms around him and sat up, carrying him with her. Bentley held on around her neck. He could feel her trembling.

"Can Slally talk yet?"

She shook her head.

Bentley tightened his arms around her. He put his chin on her shoulder and looked at his room. Sunlight burned through the open space below the window shade. He heard a bird singing. *I'm going to make you pay*, he said in his mind.

He heard a wave rattling gravel on the shore. *What will be is not for you to say*.

His bedroom was dim. The lid of his toy box was closed. He'd put the stone back the night before after Ellen, his father, and Slally had hugged him, McGraw had told about him, and Dr. Kreistein had finished checking him over.

Ellen released him and stood up. "Hungry?"

Bentley nodded.

"By the time you've brushed your teeth and dressed," she said, "Sally and I will have breakfast for you." She stood looking down at him. Bentley was afraid she was going to start crying in front of him.

Ellen rumpled his hair. "We're going to have to do something about that before—" She didn't finish the sentence. She took her hand off his head. "Sweetheart," she said, "promise me you'll make your father get your hair cut before you go back to school."

"I promise," Bentley said. He gazed up at her. "My dad says you and Slally *have* to go. How come?"

Ellen took a deep breath. She wanted to question him about what Richard had said and how he had said it.

"Couldn't you just not have to?" Bentley asked.

Ellen was held by emotions too powerful to express. "Your father isn't home this morning, sweetheart," she said. "He had to go somewhere."

"Yeah, but couldn't you—"

"Come on, Bentley darling," she said. "Get dressed." She walked across the bedroom and closed the door behind her. She didn't weep until she was in the hall.

Bentley washed, brushed his teeth, and put on the last dungarees and shirt that Helga had ironed for him. Then he went out into the hall, too.

He stood in the door of his father and Ellen's room, looking at the packed suitcases lying on the floor.

When McGraw and Dick Amberstam drove him home the night before, he'd heard a man on the radio talking about a war.

Slally had been sitting on the sofa with her fingers locked together. Her face was pale and frightened again when she looked at Bentley. She didn't make a sound.

Bentley's father had told him, when he had put him to bed, that Ellen and Slally were leaving.

Bentley stood in the doorway of the sunlit bedroom. *You did it!* he whispered.

My works are as many as all the lives that have ever been lived, answered the voice in the humming of summer.

Today I'm going to make you pay! Bentley said fiercely.

There was no reply.

A layer of smoke from the smoldering ruins of the Stonehaven House Hotel lingered in the air over the village. The sun filtered through it, bathing Stonehaven in light as yellow as a demon's eye.

Prince Ombra's yellow eye watched the village. He had seen the depths of Bentley's soul, and knew now what the boy-enemy feared the most. All that was needed was a strategy to lure Bentley from the aura of the divine that protected him.

Lord Ombra's fourth brain showed him the memory of another summer, lost in the passage of centuries but remembered in the legends of the world. In the crushing heat of that year, the Dreaded One had stood, incarnated as a mortal, in the midst of a vast Greek army arrayed before the dusty walls of Troy. For nine seasons, the legions of Agamemnon had camped there, besieging the city of King Priam. The lads among them had grown to manhood, and men had aged, palsied, and died— or had been butchered in sorties as the gates opened and the Trojans poured out to slay their enemies, the men of Greece. Songs had already been made of the battles fought there. All that mortal existence holds within its brief span had been acted out in the lives of those who laid siege to Troy and those who defended her.

One day the Greek kings held a council and decreed the death of Troy's noblest warrior, Hector, son of Priam. When this faultless one was gone, they knew, Priam's heart would break and, with it, the will of the city to endure.

Standing among the king-commanders, Ombra spoke. "Hector, by rights, is mine," he said in the guttural, barbaric accent of the human being he had become. "My quarrel with him is old, older than the death of Patroclus, older even than this war."

Agamemnon, king of Mycenae and leader of the Greek invaders, frowned at the barbarian chieftan. "And how will you lure him out?"

"I will offer him single combat," Ombra replied. "None will assist him, nor me. He will have my promise." His hot eyes looked toward the Trojan walls. "He will not refuse me, Agamemnon. Hector and I have sought each other for a long time."

A messenger was sent to the city. Hector was in his chamber when the challenge and the promise of single combat were delivered. "All your life you have waited for me, Prince of Troy," the messenger said, repeating the words he had learned by rote. "Now come forth. Let us be done with it."

Hector's heart was heavy. He knew that the hour of his destiny had come—and shame burdened him.

"What is the name of your master?" he asked the messenger.

"I cannot give it, son of Priam," the man replied.

Hector took the stone of Ra from a jar. He lashed his shield to his left arm and clenched the talisman of heroes in his left fist. He took his sword
and went alone to the temple of Hermes beneath
the city's southern wall.

As he made sacrifice in the smoky gloom, he saw
a priestess watching him from the shadows. Her
eyes were those of the cavern angel who had given
great Hector instruction for his mortal life. Hector turned away from the angel. But its voice
spoke to him in that place sacred to Hermes, god
of luck, of music—he who watched over the fates
of young men and escorted the souls of the dead to
Hades. *Your cause is just, Hector,* said the cavern
angel. *You go forth this day not in the service of
Troy, but to save the world. Believe your heart!*

Hector tried to find comfort in those words as
slaves opened the gates for him. He tried to believe the importuning of his borrowed heart as he
stepped onto the scorching plain of Troy.

The gates groaned shut behind him. Above, the
army of Priam watched from the walls. Before
him the Greek kings stood in the front ranks of
their massed warriors. The silence was as if the
whole world had paused in its business to watch.

Hector looked from king to king. Menelaus, the
wronged . . . Agamemnon, the obsessed . . . the
crafty Odysseus . . . all stared back at him.

"One among you knows the secret of my heart!"
Hector called out. "Let him step forward, and I
will spill his blood upon this dust to make a
garden for scorpions!"

And one among the Greeks did know—that in his
heart Hector scorned the cause of Troy, and that

he feared, more than anything else, meeting a foe who had no doubt.

That one stepped from the ranks of kings. His eyes glittered on either side of his helmet's nose-piece. His muscular fighting arm came down, and he pointed his short sword at the Trojan hero. "Now our hour has come, O fool of god!" Ombra bellowed.

Hector gazed at him. The doubt within him did not show on his face. "It is you, then," he said quietly.

"It is I," answered Achilles of the unfathomable rage. "Speak to your heaven, Hector. Tell it you will not return, for you shall have no grave. Your corpse will rot in this place as fodder for the dogs of Troy!"

Then savage Achilles, warlord of the barbarous Myrmidons, threw himself upon Hector with a wild cry. They fought in the midday heat, and Achilles' promise was honored—no Greeks came to his aid.

Nor did any try to restrain him after Hector had fallen. Achilles lashed the Trojan hero's body to his chariot and dragged it twelve times around the walls of Troy.

The unspeakable act—body mutilation—was seen as Achilles' revenge for his lover, Patroclus, slain by Hector. But it was not. Ombra, having used honor's promise to lure Hector from Troy, committed an act of dishonor upon his enemy's corpse. It was the mark of Ombra in the Trojan chronicles—proof, to those who read it aright, that the Dreaded One was there that day.

In the hot noon of the northern coast Ombra

now prepared a promise for Bentley Ellicott.

McGraw stood in the street in front of the charred ruins of the Stonehaven House Hotel. A crowd had gathered to watch men from the county morgue carry out Charlie Feavey's remains in a body bag.

McGraw turned away and walked down the street to the police station, mounted the steps, and opened the screen door. His head hurt like hell. Dr. Leon had stitched up his wound, and the anesthetic was wearing off.

Mike tossed his pencil on his desk and leaned back, clasping his hands behind his head. "Find Charlie, did they?"

McGraw nodded and sat down at his desk. "How's Dick?"

"Dick'll be all right," Mike answered. "Nobody in his right mind likes to kill—especially somebody you know."

McGraw stared at the morning mail on his desk. He was exhausted and depressed.

Everything should have been over—Bentley Ellicot and the Drake girl were back home, Steve Slattery was in jail, Charlie was dead, and Mike had rounded up four witnesses who swore that Willybill had been in town all evening.

But the oppression went on. McGraw still felt the pressure around him in the smoke from the burned hotel. No breeze had come to clear it out of the village.

The police chief turned on the radio beside his desk. A newscaster said that the President would speak to the nation at five in the afternoon. The strategic bombers were in the air. The hotline had gone silent. The fighting around a distant city was becoming more desperate.

McGraw turned off the radio. Something else had to happen.

Bentley sat at the kitchen table, trying not to be angry. He couldn't eat the last English muffin on his plate. He was too tight with fury. Slally was sitting across from him in a white, sleeveless blouse. Her face was pale, and she looked as if she'd been crying all morning.

Ellen sat between them, her elbows on the table and her hands clasped beneath her chin. She could feel Bentley trying to hold in his anger.

"I wonder where my dad went," he said.

"He'll be back, darling," Ellen told him. She unclasped her hands and touched his cheek. "Maybe he just didn't want to be here when we leave."

Bentley looked at the muffin on his plate. "Yeah," he said glumly. "I guess that's why he went away." He raised his head. "When are you going?"

"Sally's father will be here about three," she said.

Bentley looked across the table at Slally. "Hey," he said, "we could still have time to go down to the wharf."

Slally didn't move.

"Or maybe we could go over to Dr. Kreistein's," Bentley said.

Slally stared at him for a moment. Then she looked at her mother.

"Don't you want to say good-bye to him?" Bentley asked, bewildered.

Slally looked back at him. Very slightly, she shook her head.

"Don't you want to see *anybody* before you leave?"

"Bentley," Ellen said gently, "Bentley, darling— please don't be upset with her. I think she just wants to stay close to me."

Bentley stared at Slally. He wasn't even her interpreter anymore.

Ellen took his hand. "Please try to understand, sweetheart. She loves you just as much as ever. It's only that—"

Slally suddenly slid off her chair. Ellen was still holding Bentley's hand when they heard a choking noise coming from the stairs, where Slally was crying.

Ellen got up and went into the hall.

Bentley let himself out by the back door. He stood looking at the wall of foliage, motionless in the heat of the day. Coming home after everything he'd been through was like his daydream about coming home after he won the World Series. He smelled the thin wisps of smoke drifting up from the village. He wondered what Main Street looked like without the hotel standing on it.

Nothing can ever be the same, whispered the voice in the second air.

Bentley knew that. He knew who was saying it to him. He didn't want to hear it or know it. His rage swelled in him as the stone of Ra's power surged through him.

"*Bastard!*" he yelled furiously into the hushed air.

Willybill stood at the window of his rented room above the hardware store. The stranger's hands were shoved into the back pockets of his jeans. His bearded face was expressionless as he looked at the smoke-dimmed streets of the village and out at the islands in the sea.

Willybill knew everything that was happening on the northern coast at 2:11 that sunny summer afternoon.

He saw Richard Ellicott sitting on the grass of the ridge just below Pensionville. Richard had been there since early morning. He was trying to think of what he could say to Ellen to undo the devastation he had wrought in their lives. He couldn't think of the right words. Richard's heart was weighted with despair. When he got home, Ellen would be gone forever.

Willybill saw Mrs. Tally driving out of Stonehaven on the southern road.

He saw McGraw, Mike, and Dick Amberstam listening to the radio news in the police station.

He saw Dietrich Kreistein gesture with exasperation at Bentley.

He saw Polly Woodhouse lying on her bed in the house trailer. She was trying not to cry.

Willybill turned away from the window and sat on his bed. He leaned over and pulled on his cracked leather boots. Then he took off the rolled bandanna that bound his long hair and put on his hat.

The stranger stood up.

Inside Dietrich Kreistein's rented house the rooms were cool, though the heat pressed upon the roof and walls.

Bentley sat on the window seat in the library, glaring at the old man. Dr. Kreistein glared back at him.

This verdammte Ombra has beaten me, Dr. Kreistein said to himself as Bentley stopped shouting. *This boy is thinking only of himself and his sorrows. This is what Ombra wants—it is the same as his rage when he found the stone.*

Aloud he said, "Am I to believe that you already have this stone in your pocket?"

"No!"

"So. In spite of all this yelling about breaking the head of Prinz Ombra, you are so angry you could not locate his head in order to throw the stone at it—"

"You'd be angry, too! Helga's dead! Slally can't talk! Her mother's taking her away! I've got a *right* to be angry!"

"If you fight in this condition, Prinz Ombra will absolutely kill you!"

"I've got my magic back!"

"Please. There is no reason for such noise. I am sitting before you, not in the top of a tree."

Bentley glowered some more. If he hadn't been so enraged, he would have laughed at the idea of Dr. Kreistein sitting up in a tree.

'Why are you so proud of being angry and ashamed of your sadness, hah?" the old man said. "Being angry is a very selfish business, I assure you. You are trying to protect yourself from feelings you consider shameful."

"I'm not ashamed!" Bentley said hotly, sitting up straight on the window seat. "I've got a *right*—"

"Do not be witless!" the old man snapped back. "There is no time left for such foolishness!" He fixed Bentley with his small eyes. "*Ordinary* men make fights for such things—their rights, their pride, their wealth, this despicable nonsense they call their image! Self! Self! Self! It is not to gratify yourself that you were given your magic, your supra-will, and this stone! From Ombra you must try to win something that is *not* for yourself!" Dr. Kreistein cleared his throat. His voice softened. "To challenge what is truly evil—even if nobody else can see it—to make such a challenge and risk everything with no thoughts of our own ambitions and desires—this is the only glory offered to our lives."

"I don't want anything from him—I just want to kill him!" Bentley shouted.

Dietrich Kreistein knew he was losing. "Is there nothing, no person, for whom you would give up this self-righteous anger that is so dangerous to you?"

Bentley jumped off the window seat. He was getting even more furious because he knew the old man was right.

"The stone's *mine!*" he said. "*I* got it back all by myself! I can do anything I want with it!"

Dr. Kreistein sighed. He leaned back in his chair and put one hand on his desk. He looked at Bentley and sniffed. "There is one more story I will explain to you," he said to the trembling, dark-eyed boy. "You told it to me. It is about a man who gave up his life's greatest passion so that he could conquer Ombra." Dietrich Kreistein cleared his throat. "It is the true story of King Arthur's life. . . ."

"I don't want to talk about stories," Bentley said. His mind was filled with fantasies of revenge.

"If you go to fight when you are angry, *because you are angry*, Prinz Ombra will kill you! He has made your anger!"

Bentley didn't want to hear any more. He didn't want to surrender his dreams. They fortified him against the loss of everything that Prince Ombra had destroyed. He didn't want to argue with Dr. Kreistein any longer because the old man's words made him feel bad.

He ran.

He ran out of the library and down the narrow front hall of the house. The screen door banged behind him as he dashed across the porch and down the steps.

Dr. Kreistein sat in the sudden silence, numbed by his defeat.

Now you understand, Magician, murmured a voice from the moldy recesses of the old summer house. *You have lost him! The sun will swell to his eye, and he will see me at last before another hour is gone. Now it is almost finished. This rage of his will bring him to me. The rage will become its brother, dread, when he sees what I have become! Then Ombra's fire will ignite the world after he has left it!*

Slally opened her eyes.
Her mother was standing in the bedroom door.

"We're all packed," Ellen said. "I'm going to walk down to the end of the road to wait for Daddy. Want to come with me?"

Slally shook her head.

"All right, darling. I'll wake you up when he gets here."

Ellen closed the door. Slally heard her walking down the hall.

Slally lay on her stomach. Her head and both of her hands were deep in a large pillow. She had tried to sleep so that she could escape from her misery. But she couldn't.

She had promised to go with Bentley to the end of his journey. Now she wasn't going to be able to keep her promise because they were taking her away. She had started to cry at breakfast because she didn't want to see Dr. Kreistein or anybody else. She had wanted to spend her last time with Bentley. But she hadn't been able to tell him. He hadn't understood.

She struggled to unlock her brain, trembling as she tried to pretend that it was the time before Steve Slattery locked the boathouse door. She strained to remember how she had talked, how she had turned her thoughts into words that Bentley could understand. Her mouth was open as she worked with all her might to make a sound. But the part of her mind that sent sounds to her throat was frozen.

She sat on her bed, fighting the enchantment that Prince Ombra had laid upon her.

Bentley crouched on his sloping rock. The tide was high. The black water on three sides of the rock was moving as if an invisible hand were slowly stirring beneath it. The emptiness of the sky and the sea were full of Prince Ombra.

It seemed to Bentley that it had been a million years ago when he had stood there trying to decide whether or not to throw away the stone. He wished he'd done it. His life had been wrecked.

He tried not to think about his last argument with Dr. Kreistein. He raised his head. His hawks were cruising in the sky above him. He was safe within their circles, but he felt terrible. He kept trying to deny what the old man had told him—that it was stupid and dangerous to fight when you're mad. He already knew that he wasn't supposed to fight for himself; he knew it, but he didn't want Dr. Kreistein telling it to him. He'd already had the satisfaction of fighting for a cause outside of himself when he jumped on Joe Persis's back to protect the little kids. He'd known then that he was right. He didn't feel that he was right now.

But he couldn't control his hatred of the enemy he knew was all around him, in the water and in the air. "Bastard," he muttered at the vacant seascape.

I am the bastard child of a love lost before the world began, said the water lapping on the rock. *Your outrage is cause enough. Come from your circles and spells. Let us begin!*

Bentley tucked his arms deeper into the squat of his body and tried to make himself calm down. "I'm not ready," he said. He tried to think of a right reason to fight.

He tried to stop himself from hearing the second air. He needed more time to remember all the things Dr. Kreistein had taught him. But he still heard Lord Ombra taunting him with Helga's death, Reverend Tally's madness, and the terrible truth about his mother. Bentley put his hands over his ears, but he could still hear Ombra chanting with a craftsman's pride in Ellen's heartbreak, the mad night of Charlie Feavey, and Richard Ellicott's blasted soul.

Bentley jumped to his feet. "You're going to pay for it all!" he shrieked, shaking his fist at the sky.

Then come! I await you!

"Bastard! You big *bas—*"

He felt someone touch him from behind. Slally took his arm and pulled it down to his side and pried open the fingers he had made into a fist.

Bentley was instantly ashamed of himself because Slally had caught him standing on his rock and yelling like a lunatic. She stood before him with a gentle expression of reproach on her face.

He sat down on the rock.

Slally crouched in front of him and wrapped her arms around her legs. He was too ashamed to look at her.

One of her hands was reaching out to him. Her mouth was open; and she was trying hard to speak, tears of frustration filling her eyes. His anger dissolved into overwhelming pity.

"You're going to be okay," he said, trying to sound as if he believed it. "Listen, Slally, they can . . ."

She shook her head. Then she put her hands over her face and began to cry.

Bentley inched himself closer to her. *"Listen!*

Don't cry. You got to talk again last time, remember? Maybe after a couple of days . . ."

Without uncovering her face, she shook her head again. Her shoulders were heaving.

He didn't know what to say. He just sat there watching her. And then, suddenly, he knew the answer for them both.

He got to his feet.

One of his ospreys, sweeping through the sky, whistled a warning. Bentley looked up, squinting in the sun. Speaking without words in the second air, where all the sounds of the world remain, and beasts can understand men, he told his hawks that he knew what he was doing.

He looked out over the water to where the sky and the horizon met, where Prince Ombra straddled the world, waiting for the thousand and first battle of his lives.

"You did it to her, didn't you?" Bentley said. He didn't need to shout anymore.

All the sorrows of your life are the work of my hand. Your wrath is as righteous as the wrath of Hector when—

"Nah," Bentley said, accepting what Dr. Kreistein had tried to tell him, what his heart had always told him. "Fighting when you're mad is dumb."

Bentley pointed at Slally. "I'll fight if you fix it so that she can talk like everybody else," he said.

He felt Slally grab his leg. He knew that she was shaking her head violently. But he kept his gaze where, on the sea and in the sky, he knew the Lord of Nightmares stood.

This, said the voice in the second air, *shall be.*

Bentley leaned down and took Slally's arms from his leg. "It's okay," he whispered to her. He turned back to Ombra the Invisible. "You have to promise."

The light breeze died, and the dark water was still. Bentley was holding on to Slally's wrist. Ombra made no reply as his fourth brain brought him memories of all his noble incarnations—Goliath the challenger, angry Achilles, Modred the beautiful. As these splendid and terrible enemies, he had kept the vows that brought warriors of heaven to their battlefields.

Great is your love, Prince Ombra answered finally, *and eternal is its mystery to me. Yet honor was not denied me in the fire of Creation. Ombra, lord vanquisher of heroes, pledges this, O brother of David, Arthur the King, and Susano—the child will speak even as you fall before me. You will be remembered.*

Bentley looked down at Slally. "I know what I'm doing," he told her.

She scrambled up and grabbed his hand. Her eyes were anguished and crying protest. But Bentley's borrowed heart was saying, *Now, yes, this is the hour for which you were born, and this is the true cause of your life.*

"He says okay," Bentley said to her. "Listen, I've *got* to do it this way. If I don't, I'll fight him because I'm mad. That's dumb." He pulled his hand out of hers. "Besides," he mumbled, "you're my best friend."

He didn't know if she understood or not as she followed him back to the house. She waited on the

porch while he went up to his room. The stone of
Ra was sparkling in a corner of the toy box as if it,
too, knew that the moment had come at last.

Bentley's heart was accelerating on his way
back downstairs. He could hardly think. He was
afraid, but he was excited. He wondered what Ombra would look like, and his heart pealed ancient
songs of war.

The house was empty. It was making small summer sounds. For a moment it seemed to Bentley
that he and Slally were the only people in the
world. He went through the living room and out
onto the porch. "I've got the stone," he said to her.

The sun seemed to swell in the sky as they walked down the driveway and turned onto the dirt
road. Bentley had always known that he would
meet Prince Ombra on the cliff above the sea. As
they walked along the road toward it, the buzzing
of the cicadas grew urgent around him, and sea
gulls fled, screaming, from the sky.

Bentley took Slally's hand so that he could pretend that he was reassuring her as they went together toward the place where the Lord of Nightmares awaited them, as he had waited on a thousand other battlefields.

Willybill stopped his pickup truck at the highway and glanced up into the savage glare of the
sun. He, too, heard the berating of the cicadas in
the trees along the point. He spat through the window, shifted gears, and drove the pickup truck
across the highway. It sped through the fields and
entered the forest on the dirt road. Willybill passed Ellen without looking at her.

Bentley and Slally had come to the end of the road. They stood for a moment in front of the broken stone wall. Slally shivered, and her hand gripped Bentley's as she looked up, across the wind-blown grass of the meadow, and saw what Bentley had just seen on the top of the cliff.

"Listen," he said, swallowing hard, "maybe you'd better wait here until—"

Slally shook her head. Bentley could see how frightened she was. But it wasn't the old fear of isolation within her silence. She had lifted her gaze to the top of the cliff again, and on her face Bentley saw the awe of the witness—of the beholding squires, poets, lovers, and saints, of all the rememberers who had stood beside a thousand heroes at the place and hour of their destinies.

The shining of the sun was so powerful that all Slally could see was the silhouette of the form Prince Ombra had assumed as he waited for Bentley at the top of the meadow.

The hawks swooped down the grassy slope, whistling warnings as they came. They flew low beneath the trees where the children stood, shrilling loudly.

"Go away!" Bentley yelled at them. "Go home!"

The hawks rose into the bright air, dipped their wings in farewell, and disappeared over the eastern tree line.

Bentley let go of Slally's hand. He took the stone out of his pocket and scrambled over the wall. The coarse grasses of the meadow brushed him chest-high as he limped up the steep incline, his eyes fixed on the figure at the top. His heart was beating hard with the mortal apprehension of an eight-year-old boy and with a warrior's exultation.

As he toiled up the last fifteen feet, with Slally behind him, Bentley tried, for one last time, to think of something he dreaded so much that the specter of it could paralyze him. He steeled himself to look Ombra in the face and throw the stone with all of his strength and skill.

The wind from the sea blew his hair out of his eyes as he got to the top of the cliff. He tasted salt and breathed the iodine aroma of kelp. He shifted the stone of Ra to his right hand, his throwing hand.

He heard Slally, behind him, gasp in astonishment.

He saw Prince Ombra.

He saw himself.

Astonishment struck Bentley like a slap. He saw himself as a grown man—but not as he had imagined his adulthood in his daydreams. Looking at the figure who sat gazing out to sea was like looking at a photograph in an old album where people are sealed in lost time forever.

A tall, slender man in late middle age sat in profile on an old-fashioned wooden chair. His upper body was erect. His hands rested on a cane that stood before him. Bentley and Slally saw that he was, unmistakably, Bentley as he would be years and years in the future. The dark eyes, the nose, and the mouth were Bentley's. The swatch of brown hair that fell over one side of his forehead was streaked with gray. He was wearing a dark blue suit. A heavy gold watch chain was looped from one vest pocket to another. His black shoes were polished. A white handkerchief tucked into his breast pocket fluttered in the wind.

Slowly, his head turned, and he looked at Bentley and Slally. In his eyes there was the indelible sorrow of lost dreams. "Good afternoon," he said, smiling a slight, sad smile.

Bentley blinked, stunned by the sheer *ordinariness* of the shape Prince Ombra had taken. "Is it you?" he whispered.

The smile remained on the man's lips. But the dullness in his eyes contradicted its amiability. "No," he said. "It's you."

Bentley's heart was pounding.

"I thought you were going to be horrible," he said. "I thought you were going to try to kill me!"

"You may wish I had," his grown-up self answered.

Bentley was stiff with amazement. A current of anxiety ran through him. He could feel the profound melancholy in the man who sat before him. There was menace within him, too.

The adult Bentley Ellicott's eyes shifted to Slally. "Someday," he said, "you will understand why I don't stand up for you," he said. His voice was so controlled that it was brittle. His hands remained folded on the curved top of the cane as he looked at Slally. "I haven't forgotten," he said, his eyes narrowing. "I don't forgive." He resumed his contemplation of the sea and the bright, windy sky.

Slally looked at Bently. There was a bewildered expression on her face.

"I don't know what he's talking about," Bentley said. "I don't know what it means. I just know it's me."

He turned back to the man sitting on the

wooden chair. The cane was black and had a silver band around its handle. "Didn't you get your leg fixed?" Bentley asked.

For almost a minute the adult Bentley Ellicott neither answered nor acknowledged that he'd heard. "No," he finally said, so softly that he could hardly be heard. He looked at Bentley again. "You're—what? Ten?"

"I'm eight," Bentley said.

His grown-up self nodded. "Yes," he said. "I remember you now." He smiled again, but without kindness. "You have a very vivid imagination. Aren't you the best runner in the major leagues?"

Bentley flushed with embarrassment. "I—that's just—"

"And you're going to win the World Series all by yourself, aren't you?" his middle-aged self said. The smile was still on his face like a taunt. "Remind me—who was that man, the one who tried to bean you when you were making the last home run?"

Bentley's embarrassment was turning into humiliation. He felt especially foolish because Slally was listening. He began to get mad.

"The pitcher," the middle-aged man prompted. "The one from Arkansas."

"Cannonball Jones," Bentley muttered.

The adult raised his face into the sunlight and laughed. "That's it! 'Cannonball—*Jones!*' I'd forgotten the name I made up for him." He stopped laughing abruptly. His head came down, and he looked back out at the sea.

The wind fluttered in Bentley's ears. The hissing

of the waves as they receded from the rocks at the
foot of the cliff sounded like the warning of a serpent hidden somewhere nearby.

"I'm supposed to fight you!" Bentley blurted.
"That's what they told—"

"Don't be a fool," the middle-aged man said.
"Make-believe time is over. You were sent here to
face the facts of life. You're becoming me. Only an
ugly kernel of *you* remains in me—thank God."

"I never did anything to you!" Bentley said. He
was getting scared. But he was still angry. "I never
even saw you before!" He reminded himself forcibly that it was really Prince Ombra who was sitting in the wooden chair. But Ombra had turned
himself into Bentley's future. Years and years of
Bentley's life were in him. The Lord of Nightmares
was still himself. But he was also a middle-aged
man named Bentley Ellicott sitting on top of a
cliff.

Slowly, the phantom of the future turned his
head toward his boyhood. "You—never—did—
anything—to—me," he said, his dull eyes suddenly
full of fury. "You've haunted my life! It takes
years to root out and confront the tyrannical child
who is in us all. Most people never do. I did! You
ruined my young manhood—"

"I couldn't!" Bentley shot back angrily. "I was
you!"

The burning eyes stared into his eyes. "Yes. You
were me. I carried you, and what you did, inside
me across the years, burying the memory and the
guilt under layers of new illusions, new dreams
and absurdities." The eyes darted to Slally. "You
couldn't understand, could you?"

"She never did anything to you, either!" Bentley said.

The gusting wind blew the middle-aged man's hair in a disorderly scatter across his forehead. "Do you want to know about her?" he asked Bentley.

Bentley suddenly felt as if he were trapped in a nightmare. The dreamer knows he cannot avoid what is going to happen. But he tries desperately.

"Did Slally get to talk?" he asked.

The grownup nodded. "Yes. She talked."

"Is she okay?" Bentley asked, trying to turn the conversation to ordinary things so that the nightmare wouldn't come to its climax.

The adult Bentley Ellicott stood up and pushed his hair to one side. He turned back to the sea and the sky, leaning on the cane. "Her father died," he said as if he were speaking to the wind. "She inherited a lot of money." His eyes glittered. "She didn't need me anymore. She left me."

Bentley glanced at Slally. She was horrified. She shook her head hard.

"Not that she got to spend much of her money," the middle-aged man said. There was a look of bitter amusement on his face. "Poor Ellen. She never got over what happened between her and my father. She hated men for the rest of her life. Ellen decided that Rupert Drake had insulted her by leaving her out of his will. She hired lawyers, and they went after Slally and *her* lawyers like a war between cannibals. Those two women fought each other in court for seven—"

"Ellen wouldn't do that!" Bentley said.

The grownup turned to face him. Again, the

graying hair blew across his forehead. He looked at Bentley as if he loathed his childhood more than anything in the world.

"And if Slally left, it wasn't because she got a lot of money!" Bentley yelled. "It was because you—" He stopped in midshout as, in his mind, time that is became time that will be. He stared at his future self: The slenderness seemed gaunt; the skin pallor bespoke an illness that would never go away; beneath the wind-scattered hair, the eyes of the grown-up Bentley Ellicott were bright with cruelty. "If Slally left," Bentley whispered, "it's because *I'm* going to do something bad to her."

The grownup's smile had become a grin. "Now you get it," his metallic voice replied. "You've already done bad things to her. McGraw told Ellen and my father about how you made her break into the hotel with you. Ellen thought you were a bad influence on Slally. That's what she and my father were fighting about the night of the storm."

"About *me?*"

"You were also the reason for their last fight," his adult self went on. "Ellen loved my dad, but she decided she had to get Slally away from you after you made her run away and she was nearly killed by Charlie Feavey."

"I tried to sneak off without her!" Bentley cried. "I didn't want her to come!"

Slally grabbed Bentley's arm. He couldn't bear to look at her. The middle-aged man had already persuaded Bentley that he had stumbled through his days smashing up the lives of the people he loved, never understanding what was going on around him. That revelation made him feel so ugly and stupid that his first impulse was to deny it.

"You're a liar!"

The gaunt man beside the wooden chair glanced at Slally. "Maybe *you'd* like to tell him the truth," he said. "Speak!"

Slally's grip constricted on Bentley's arm. He felt her tremble.

The adult looked back at Bentley. "If she hadn't been your friend, Ombra would never have used Steve Slattery to silence her. If you hadn't been so scared, you would have met Ombra long before that."

Bentley's heart cried out to him to fight back, that this was the moment for which he had been born. But he didn't know how to fight back. For the first time in his life he was numbed by the anesthetic of guilt. He was torn between rage and grief over what he'd done.

"I'm not going to be like you!" he blurted.

"It's too late," his grown-up self answered. "You've already done the things that made me what I am."

Bentley yanked his arm free of Slally's hand. "You're just trying to make me feel bad!" he said. "I *wasn't* afraid to fight! I got the stone back! I didn't give up!"

The contemptuous smile was still on the grown-up's face. "You were driven on that journey by a guilt you couldn't acknowledge," he said. "I was driven by it for years and years. My mind had instantly wiped out the memory of the supreme crime—"

"I haven't done any crimes!"

"The mind can be made to forget," said the adult

Bentley Ellicott. "But the feelings won't go away. The torment of the act I had blotted out of memory never left me. *You*, the tyrannical child in me, shriveled my days with anxiety and filled my sleep with nightmares! I had to exorcise you by facing you and finding out the truth. It took years. Doctors, drugs, confessions—and then, finally, I knew what I had done."

Bentley clapped his hands over his ears so that he couldn't hear any more. But the condemning man before him spoke also in the second air. His words hit Bentley like a bolt of lightning.

"You killed Helga."

Slowly, Bentley lowered his hands. The wind sounded in his ears. The surf roared below him. Confusion was flooding his mind, breaking up his thoughts. Frantically, he tried to remember the morning Helga died.

"I was asleep," he whispered. "I was sleeping when it happened!"

"I used sleep to obliterate the knowledge of what I did at sunrise that day," his older self said. "I willed myself to forget that I woke up, scared, just before dawn. I lived for more than a half-century before I faced the fact that I had taken the stone into Helga's room, crying that I was afraid of it. She loved me, and she tried to comfort me. But I was full of cowardly panic. Helga took the stone from me and told me to watch from my bedroom window. I went back to my room and stood in the window as the sun was coming up. It was the color of gold and blood—"

"I didn't!" Bentley cried.

"I watched her go down the porch steps, barefoot, and walk across the lawn to the edge of the forest. She looked up at me in the window, smiling and showing me how she was going to take the path into the woods and throw away the stone. I saw her walk between the trees. I ran into the bathroom because, from that window, I could see her go down the path—"

"I didn't! I didn't do it!" Bentley screamed.

"I saw the bobcat in a clearing before she saw it," the middle-aged man continued, his eyes gleaming at the pale, shaking boy before him. "I saw it spring. I heard her cry out once as she went down. I saw the blood and that terrible animal clawing and slashing her. I couldn't stop watching. When the bobcat had torn apart her hand and grabbed the stone—*my* stone—I had only one thought. *Good.* The stone was gone. Nobody would ever know that *I* was the reason Helga went out there. I went back to bed. I was so horrified that I instantly blotted it all out with sleep. I made myself forget and dream my selfish dreams . . ."

Bentley was about to cry out for a third time that he hadn't done it when the images of that dreadful day broke upon him. They came in chaos —the red and gold sun, Helga and her blood—and Bentley was no longer sure of sequences. He remembered sleeping and waking, remembered being in the bathroom and looking out the window at the woods—but he couldn't remember if he'd done it that morning. He remembered Helga's dead face, and he remembered her loving him—but shock had thrown splinters of memory at him so chaotically that he no longer knew what was true about himself.

The borrowed heart of a thousand warriors pealed again, telling him that every mortal's hell is unique and like no other—and beseeching him to summon his power to strike back at the being who had crafted the torments of all lives—and was now cursing his.

Bentley choked back the third cry of denial. He heard his heart. He forced himself to look at what he would someday be. And, in the looking at the figure that stood before him, Bentley Ellicott knew, at last, what he had always feared more than anything else in the world: He had always dreaded losing his childhood and becoming a disbelieving, defeated man.

"I know what happened to you!" he cried. "When Ombra beat you, he didn't kill you! He filled you full of lies that ruined your life! Then he made you live it!"

The middle-aged man leaning on his cane frowned slightly. *"Beat* me?" he murmured. "Ombra didn't beat me. He lost! I won!"

Bentley had no words to answer. His last hope had just died within him. He was frozen by the horror of what was dawning on him. This really *was* what he would, inescapably be.

"I won," the adult Bentley Ellicott repeated. His voice was low. Bentley could barely hear it. The fierce light behind the figure was bright in his eyes. "Now. Live. Live my half-century and more. Suffer what you have made me suffer. The daydreams will wither away. Love will fail you. Finally you will want nothing. You will wish for nothing, look forward to nothing. You will wait to die and be afraid of dying . . ."

Suddenly Bentley could no longer resist what was being said to him. The great will of his thousand brothers was retreating before the panic and uncertainty of a mortal child. "Don't you remember *anything?*" he asked, forcing back his tears. "You *don't* die. You go back. Don't you even remember that part?"

"I told you—the daydreams fade!"

"It wasn't a daydream!" Bentley cried. "I didn't make it up! I remember the angel telling me—"

"It was a daydream," the specter of his future self said with such vehemence that the words spat from him. "There is no perfection! You invented the angel just as you invented Cannonball Jones!"

Bentley felt as if he were walking in a darkness of his own making. He heard the cry of his borrowed heart, but he no longer knew if it was real—or only a part of a fantasy in which he had lived his life. "I'd rather be dead than be like you!" he cried.

"Then stop your life where it is!" hissed the creature who confronted him. Sunlight glinted on the silver band as the middle-aged man raised his cane and pointed at the edge of the cliff. "Destroy the evil that is in you! Jump! This is your true destiny! Jump or you *will* become me!"

The sun was blinding Bentley. The crashing of the waves and the unbearable knowledge of what he had done resounded within him. He was terrified of falling and smashing his body on the rocks far below. But he had promised the cavern angel that he would sacrifice his mortal life if he had to in the struggle against the Dreaded One. He tried desperately to remember his birth as reality, not a dream. If he refused to jump, he would be conceding to his monstrous self that there never *had* been a cavern angel—that heaven itself, which makes life on earth endurable, was just something Bentley Ellicott had made up.

In the tumult of light and noise he looked wildly around in a last, frantic impulse to escape. He saw the blinding flash of sunlight on the sea. He saw Slally staring at him with terror and pity. He saw the wooden chair and the gray man. He saw the grassy meadow sloping down to the wall and the road. And, in that careening blur of the world, Bentley saw what a thousand other warriors of god had seen at the moment of their supreme peril and choice.

Somebody else was watching him. The cavern angel was nearby, looking at him, wordlessly demanding that Bentley decide between mortal despair and what his heart had always told him was true.

Bentley'e heart cried out with renewed power as he saw its truth confirmed in the eyes of the cavern angel—there *is* an eternal perfection, he *was* one of its countless children and its chosen warrior.

Then, in a burst of rage and joy, Bentley knew that the grownup on the cliff had told him evil's most blasphemous lie—that there is no hope. This being the supreme falsehood, everything else the contemptuous, despairing man had said to him was false, too.

He whirled around and faced the gaunt monstrosity that wasn't him and never would be.

"You're still Ombra!" he yelled. "I was born to fight you!"

"Ombra dwells in every mortal heart, O fool of god!" roared the Lord of Nightmares. "We live but to die! There is no—"

Bentley threw the stone. He threw it with all his skill, his arm looping high, his twisted leg lifting off the ground as he flung the stone of Ra as hard as he could.

Quartz and silver flashed in the sunlight as the stone hurtled across the space between Bentley and his enemy. It struck Prince Ombra on the face, spinning him backward.

A death shout split the air, louder than the pounding of the surf, mightier than the wind. It was answered by the outraged cry of Bentley's heart.

He saw the stone rattle down the bluff and plunge into a wave that was receding from the rocks, drawing its power away from the northern coast. Bentley saw Prince Ombra fall, bloodied and dying.

Then Bentley Ellicott, the thousand and first hero of the borrowed heart, saw no more.

Richard got out of his car. He had suddenly remembered what he could say to keep Ellen from leaving him. He walked across the driveway. Ellen was standing beside Rupert Drake. She looked puzzled.

"Something got into me," Richard said, ignoring the man beside her.

Ellen remembered the day she had irrationally

flared at Dr. Kreistein. "Something got into me one time, too," she said.

"I was so afraid you didn't love me anymore that I wanted to hurt you as much as I could," Richard said, telling the truth he had finally remembered to tell.

"I'll always love you," Ellen answered, remembering that he needed to be told that as much as she did. Oblivious to her ex-husband, she kissed Richard. "Where are our kids?"

Richard held her for a moment. "I don't know. But I've suddenly got the strangest feeling."

"What is it, darling?"

"It's going to be all right," Richard said, touching her face. "Something's changed. I *know* it's going to be all right."

Ellen felt it within and around her, the sudden surcease of anxiety and doubt, the benevolence in the air, the light and the breeze from the sea.

"Yes," she said. "Something's gone, something that was here for a long time."

Mike turned off the radio in the police station. He stood by McGraw's desk with a surprised expression on his face. "I'll be damned," he said.

McGraw looked at the radio. "President's speech canceled. Crisis over." He looked at his two deputies. "Sorry, gents. No war this week."

"What do you suppose happened?" Dick Amberstam asked.

"Somebody got smart," McGraw said. He twisted his big body around and looked through the screen door at Main Street. "Where in hell's that pickup truck?" he said.

"Willybill drove off five, ten minutes ago when I was coming in," Dick answered. "Why?"

McGraw was about to tell him he ought to go have himself tested for the stupids because Dick knew that the pickup had been impounded for the inquest into Charlie's death, and that Dick should have stopped Willybill. But then McGraw remembered that nobody was perfect.

He looked back through the screen door. The smoke had been cleared off by a fresh inshore wind. McGraw's heart was as bright as the sun on the water. He didn't understand what had happened to him. He was filled with a certainty he had set aside years before. He knew that he would never hate or scorn again—and the knowing made him content.

He had seen the eye of the beast. The beast was gone. Everyone it had touched, even Steve Slattery, had been helpless before the eye that had tried to blind McGraw in the stone yard.

He remembered the yellow light in Steve's eyes.

McGraw took a deep breath. "Poor bastard," he muttered.

"Who?" Mike said.

"Steve," McGraw said.

Mike raised his arms and clasped his hands behind his head. "It's a stinking life, isn't it?"

McGraw turned his head. He studied his deputy for a moment. "No," he said.

Polly sat up on the bed. She brushed her hair back from her eyes. "Who is it?" she said.

"Open the door at once," snapped Mrs. Tally's voice from outside the trailer.

"Open it yourself," Polly answered.

The door swung back, and Mrs. Tally climbed up the two cinder blocks that were Polly's front steps. She glanced around the interior of the trailer. "You're neat. I'll say that for you."

"Mrs. Tally," Polly said. "I'm not in the mood for anything heavy. Not this afternoon."

Mrs. Tally looked down at her. Suddenly all the reserve seemed to drain out of her. She sat down on the bed beside Polly. "I'm a fool," she said. "I'm a judging, condemning fool." She looked at Polly. "I ran into Mr. McGraw this morning at Dr. Leon's. He gave me a piece of his mind. I understand you were cooking Charlie Feavey's meals and trying to clean up that pigsty he lived in."

"There isn't any law against it," Polly said. She was wary.

"Of course there isn't," Mrs. Tally said, "Anybody with any brains finds out before they judge. Give me a tissue, will you?"

Polly reached for a box of tissues on her bedside table. She picked it up and started to cry. "I only went to the hotel to make you mad," she sobbed.

Mrs. Tally put her arms around the girl. "That's the most loving thing anybody's ever done for me," she said.

Polly lay her head on Mrs. Tally's shoulder. "After . . . after I stopped being mad at you, I kept going over there because I felt sorry for him. I never did anything with him!"

"Yes," Mrs. Tally said, pressing Polly close to her, "yes. I should have thought that, too. Charlie Feavey was a sad, forlorn man. Anybody with a kind heart could have seen that." She smoothed

Polly's hair. "Don't cry anymore. You have a kind heart. You have a treasure inside you, child. Now, stop that crying."

Polly got up. She pulled a tissue from the box and wiped her eyes. "I was afraid that you and Mr. Cutter were going to make me go away."

"We were," said Mrs. Tally's voice behind her. "But we're stopping such foolishness."

Polly turned around. "Maybe he still wants to."

Mrs. Tally stood up. "What Elias Cutter wants is somebody to be nice to him. We'll have him around for supper this evening."

"But—"

"Don't you worry about Elias Cutter," Mrs. Tally said. "I've had the old goat's number for years." She looked through the trailer windows at the bright afternoon. "I've just never done anything for him."

"I could make a moussaka," Polly said.

Mrs. Tally looked back at her. "We'll splurge and get a rib roast."

"But I'd *like* to—"

"A rib roast," Mrs. Tally said firmly.

Polly grinned. "Yes, Mrs. Tally."

Willybill stood at the foot of the meadow. His pickup truck was parked on the other side of the wall. He had seen everything that had happened at the top of the cliff. He stood with his hands shoved into the back pockets of his jeans, the cicadas buzzing lazily in the trees behind him. Willybill shifted a toothpick from one side of his mouth to the other. The tall grass was bending in a freshening breeze.

Willybill saw Slally standing at the upper end of the meadow. She was beckoning frantically with both hands.

The stranger took the toothpick out of his mouth and snapped it in two between his thumb and forefinger. He began to climb the slope. The grass brushed his thighs, and his hard body was bent forward as he moved upward in long, even strides. His head was down and his face was almost hidden by the brim of his hat.

The wind was so loud in his ears that he could only hear snatches of what Slally was crying to him.

He was almost out of breath when he got to the top of the cliff. The wind gusted and flipped his hat off. He grabbed it just before it flew away.

Slally was standing beside Bentley. Her hair was flying and her face was pinched with worry.

Bentley lay in the grass, one leg bent beneath the other. His arms were flung out, away from his body. His face was turned to one side. He was bleeding from a gash on his right cheekbone. His chest rose and fell in a sleeper's breathing.

Slally seized Willybill's hand and tugged at him. "We have to get him home!" she cried. Her voice was as clear as the afternoon light. "He's hurt himself, and I can't lift him!"

With the little girl pulling at his arm, Willybill raised his head. He narrowed his eyes as he looked at something that was far beyond the sun and the sky. With his free hand he held his hat against his chest as he listened.

Slally stopped tugging at him when she realized that he was hearing a sound that was not of this world.

The voices of god, which are the one voice of all the gods that have ever been worshipped, were speaking to Willybill. Heaven ordered its angel to reward its warrior, to give him what his soul yearned for more than anything else.

Willybill nodded.

Slally let go of his hand. She stood watching with the wind tossing her hair as Willybill lowered himself to one knee beside Bentley. Willybill set his hat on the grass. His jade eyes were grave as he turned Bentley's face up onto the light of the sun.

Then Willybill, the cavern angel, put his forefinger on Bentley's lips.

"Hush," he whispered. "Don't tell what you know."

Epilogue

After all these years, to this very day, Bentley still calls me Slally.

The last crusts of this winter's ice still lie in the shadowed places of the forest and on the sides of the road where the sunlight doesn't fall. The wind is cold, but in it you can taste the first, wet balminess of spring. I do believe that I will live to see another summer. We old people are full of hope.

Dietrich Kreistein's hopes were realized. He lived for eleven more years and died with dignity. Bentley didn't need him any longer, but the old man's work wasn't done. He knew, from all the mythology he'd read, that every tale has its teller. And he knew that I was supposed to be Bentley's rememberer. So the old man became my teacher.

I learned much of what he had learned about mythology during his long lifetime. Then I went beyond him. I studied at three universities and learned twelve languages, seven of them no longer spoken anywhere. I never married. I traveled the world to see all the things Dr. Kreistein had seen so that I would be able to understand fully the purpose of my life. I saw the symbols on cave walls in Spain and France. I saw legends shimmering in the glyphs and stelai on the tombs of the Nile kings. I spent many years in great libraries, reading and interpreting the tales that other rememberers had left behind them.

Then, when my mother died, I returned to Stonehaven to look after Richard. Their life together had been happy. Something that lingered after her persuaded him that she was waiting for him somewhere. So he didn't feel abandoned. We played chess together. From Richard I gathered my second treasure of knowledge. I took a doctorate in mathematics at the university in the years before he retired. I taught there after he died until my own retirement nine years ago.

McGraw is gone. Mrs. Tally and Elias Cutter have left the world. Polly married, and she's now a grandmother. Joe Persis became manager of the freezing plant on the town wharf. I saw him when I went into the village to get the mail this morning, and I asked him if any more snow was likely. "Not likely, Miz Drake, ma'am," he said. He's hopeless. He'll never stop calling me "ma'am."

Bentley is still in love with his childhood. Even though he will be seventy-five in November, there is much of the boy in him yet. Not that my brother is childish—rather, he looks out in the world with the enthusiasm of a boy. Two years ago he decided to take up ocean sailing. His wife, Adele, and I told him he was too old. He just grinned and said, "Nah." He took up ocean sailing with two other men.

His gray hair falls over one side of his forehead. He began to limp again—ever so slightly—after he turned seventy. The doctors did remarkable things to his leg in three operations when he was thirteen and fourteen. I remember visiting him in the hospital with Dr. Kreistein the night after the first operation. Bentley was lying on his bed, wide-eyed with pain. Dr. Kreistein talked to him and then said, "You will please cry for a while. It will make you feel better. Also, me." Then Bentley cried because his leg hurt.

He still, to this day, wears the tweed jackets and bow ties of his young manhood. He is a passionate baseball fan, and the World Series tickets he gives me for my birthday every year have become a family joke. But Adele and I enjoy the games, when they're near enough to get to; we are stirred up by Bentley's enthusiasm. Last year his second son, Richard, took over the insurance agency that Bentley and two of his friends established in 1998. Bentley and Adele come to Stonehaven often during the winter. We all spend the summers here in the house together. Their grandchildren are always in and out. We are what used to be called a close family.

It's hard to know exactly what Bentley remembers. Its been easier for me to deduce what he has forgotten. He remembers nothing about the time before he was born—that's obvious when dinner table conversation turns to religion and other such matters. If anybody asks him about the little scar on his right cheekbone, he tells about the day he fell and hurt himself when we were playing on the cliff. Over the years the story has expanded a bit. The current version is that he nearly fell off the cliff. His favorite story about our childhood on the northern coast is the time he ran away from home when we were both eight. He says he can't remember why he did it, but he recalls spending the night by himself out on the uplands before McGraw found him playing in Emson's stone yard. He says he was worried that he'd catch hell from my mother and Richard when he got home. But he didn't.

And as he grew into manhood, as his face and body assumed their final forms, I noticed something. It was the night before he and Adele were married. After a dinner party, Bentley and I took a walk. As we were coming up the front steps of Adele's parents' house, the porch light fell on Bentley's face in such a way as to deepen every shadow. I stopped and looked at him.

"What's the matter?" he asked.

"Do you know," I said, "you've got a cleft on your upper lip."

"So?"

"It's just that I never noticed it before."

He grinned. "Of course I have a cleft, dopey. Everybody does."

Willybill vanished from Stonehaven and nobody ever saw him again.

The seasons arrive, fade, and return in another year. Much has changed in Stonehaven and on the northern coast. And much remains the same. I cannot recall whether they ever fixed the potholes on Main Street. Perhaps the present ones are new. There is a health food store with its own garden where the Stonehaven House Hotel stood years ago. We now have five policemen. In McGraw's day we had three. McGraw, his wife, and Dick Amberstam came to my high school graduation. I went to McGraw's funeral. Bentley came back to Stonehaven for it because I said he had to.

I am an old woman, and I know where I will go next, because once Bentley Ellicott knew and he told me.

Bentley has forgotten his secret. But I have held mine for the years of my life. Now I'm supposed to tell it to you because nobody can understand the stories the rememberers leave behind them unless our secret is known. This is what it is:

The heroes are born. They live their lives, meet their destinies, and someday die as do all other mortals. But their heart returns, like the seasons, in another year. Prince Ombra comes in his terrible seasons. He lives, he fights his battles, and he returns to his storm in the vortex where his minds afflict our earthly passage even as every god ever worshipped blesses it.

But mortals must remember this terrible lord and the warriors who come forth to fight heaven's war against him.

If Prince Ombra is killed in a battle against the borrowed heart, he will be reborn at the core of the hurricane. But if men remember, in his next life Ombra will be weaker—and weaker yet again in the life after that one. If the ancient stories of heroes are told and retold, there will come, at last, a day whose dawn breaks with the radiance of perfection itself. And all men will know it, because the lord of all our nightmares will, upon that dawn, have surrendered his last life to the darkness around him.

This is why there have been a thousand and one rememberers, like me.